Caffeine Nights Publishing

Born in a Burial Gown

Mike Craven

Fiction aimed at the heart and
the head...

Mystery
Craven

Published by Caffeine Nights Publishing 2015

Published in Great Britain by
Caffeine Nights Publishing
4 Eton Close
Walderslade
Chatham
Kent
ME5 9AT

www.caffeine-nights.com

British Library Cataloguing in Publication Data.
A CIP catalogue record for this book is available from the British Library

ISBN: 978-1-910720-00-4

Cover design by
Mark (Wills) Williams

Everything else by
Default, Luck and Accident

As always, this book is dedicated to my wife, Joanne and my late mother, Susan Avison Craven. Without either, this wouldn't exist.

Also by Mike Craven

Assume Nothing, Believe Nobody, Challenge
Everything

Paperback & eBook

Acknowledgements

Like any published book, the author is just one member of a team. I'd therefore like to thank Morgen Bailey for her invaluable input early on in the process (her explanation of why I should be using the word 'began' rather than 'started' continues to haunt me...), my editor, Emma who polished the novel beyond recognition and my friend and fellow author, Graham Smith, for all his support and for convincing me to attend the marvellous Crime and Publishment event in 2014. Last but never least, I'd like to take the time to thank Darren Laws of Caffeine Nights Publishing who spotted something worth pursuing in the rough manuscript I sent him a year ago.

Mike Craven 2015

Chapter 1

It started as it always did, with a breeder. A married man with a burning need he couldn't sate at home. A married man wanting something discreet, something the boy had, and was willing to sell. He'd met him in the toilets of a club in Whitehaven. Nervous at first, the man had quickly gained his confidence and let out a stifled yell as he finished. After the money had exchanged hands, he'd made the boy a proposition. In no position to negotiate, the arrangements were made quickly.

Each transaction the boy made carried a risk, he knew that. He was in the highest risk group of what was statistically the most dangerous profession in the world but sometimes there were no more choices left to make. Some breeders paid extra to bareback, increasing the risk of disease tenfold. Others hated what they'd just done and became violent. For some, violence was part of what they wanted, what they enjoyed, as if paying for sex gave them unlimited rights over someone else. The boy's profession attracted a disproportionate amount of sadists. It wasn't just the breeders he feared. Roaming gangs of youths, eager to find someone with no social value to vent their frustrations on, were a constant threat. Even the police had been known to stick the boot in. Sometimes after enjoying the boy's companionship.

Occasionally the violence went further than a beating. Sometimes men killed to keep their secrets. He'd known four others like him who'd died before they'd reached thirty. One had been murdered, two had died from complications after being assaulted and the fourth had simply given up and hanged himself. It was a fool who thought he could beat the odds forever, and the boy was no fool. How would his time come? At the hands of a breeder or in a hospital bed, wasting away? He thought about his own mortality often.

But he wasn't thinking about it that night.

This breeder had been different. He was kind. He'd found the boy somewhere to sleep. So that night he was warm, he was safe, and had something to look forward to. Earlier, he'd played the game and won. Now he could enjoy the spoils.

That night he wasn't thinking about death.

Perhaps he should have been.

Kicked out of the family home at the age of eleven when his stepfather had made his mother choose between them, the boy had spent sporadic years in various children's homes before finally being abandoned by everyone.

A friend, and despite what had happened to him since, he still thought of him as a friend, had lured him into the trade with promises of more money than he'd ever seen before.

For the first few years, his friend had been right.

He often thought of what he called his "golden age", when the heightened value of youth meant he was in demand. He could charge what he wanted, choose whom he wanted, and always had cash in his pocket. He'd thought he was happy then. But boys in his line of work reach a sell-by date. It was a gradual decline. Previously loyal customers moved to younger, fresher products. His value decreased at the same rate as his age and before long, he was struggling to survive. Without the USP of youth, he had no choice but to drop his prices. Ten years ago a breeder would have happily paid two hundred pounds for an hour of his time. Soon he was struggling to get twenty pounds for what were becoming increasingly extreme acts.

And like countless boys before him, he tried to blot out the violence and depravity meted out to him by taking heroin. As his drug use spiralled out of control, his appearance deteriorated and his value plummeted until he was reduced to selling blowjobs in dank pub toilets for a fiver a time. Unable to afford essentials like rent or food, he became a street creature; homeless, and penniless, surviving anyway he could. In the previous year, he'd been strangled to unconsciousness twice, raped four times and beaten more times than he could count.

But two weeks ago, he'd had a break. A breeder he'd been with had offered him a place to stay during the night. Free of charge. The only cost was repaying the favour every morning. A favour for a favour. Somewhere warm and safe in exchange for something he'd done a thousand times before. The boy had accepted happily. He was still there. Sleeping safely at night, repaying the favour first thing when the breeder arrived. The boy had to leave after the act was over, forced to stay away during the day until the place was empty and he could let himself in again. A daily routine he and the breeder were happy with.

Earlier that day, he'd scored another job and surprisingly, the man paid more money than normal. He supposed he was new to the game and didn't know what was a fair price. With cash in his hand and somewhere free to stay, the boy bought the only thing he ever wanted: heroin.

He took the key the breeder had given him and let himself in.

Experience had taught him that carrying as little paraphernalia as possible was preferable to carrying dirty kit with trace residue. Residue was enough to get you locked up on a possession charge, and while brushes with the law were an occupational hazard in his line of work, he never took risks he didn't need to. A new syringe, citric powder and sterile water, all provided free by the NHS, and an empty can of Coke were all he carried. Nothing he could be arrested for. Dirty spoons, covered in heroin residue, were for beginners.

Bending the can until it was thin enough to tear in half, he used the concave base as a dish to mix the citric, water and heroin. With his only real possession, a Zippo, he heated it until the solution bubbled and darkened.

The real amber nectar.

Liquid sunshine.

Trembling with anticipation, he drew the brown solution through a cigarette filter into the syringe. Carefully setting it to one side, he removed his trousers.

A nurse had once described him as the most unsophisticated injector she'd ever seen and it had been a long time since his abscess-strewn arms and legs had offered up viable veins. He had to inject into his foot and he didn't need experts to tell him it was one of the most sensitive parts of the body. Flinching at the excruciating pain, he persevered and pushed the needle between his toes. He found a vein and pressed the plunger. The pain was replaced instantly by the rush.

This was what he did it for. The perfect moment when he was in his bubble, when nothing mattered but the high, when his ruined life made some sort of sense. That was what the nurses, outreach workers and probation officers would never understand. Why he would never, could never, quit. He didn't want to. For a brief moment in time, he could forget who he was. Why would he not want that? The initial rush was replaced by the familiar warmth and well-being that spread throughout his whole body. At peace, he settled down on the carpet to enjoy it for as long as he could. Eventually, his breathing steadied and slowed. He slept.

A noise woke him. For a second, he thought he'd overslept and panic set in. He didn't want to upset his breeder. He was supposed to be ready and waiting, with brushed teeth and combed hair. Sitting up, he realised he was wrong. It was still dark outside. He didn't have a watch but instinctively knew it could only be a couple of hours past midnight. Carefully, he peered out of the window to see what had woken him.

A dark vehicle was parked twenty yards from the building. The headlights were off but he could hear the engine was still running. The internal lights didn't come on when the driver's door opened but there was enough light coming from the nearby hospital for him to see the silhouette of a man get out and stretch. The boy moved closer to the window to get a better look. It had been the first time anyone had ever been there after dark.

The man walked away from the building, switching on a torch to navigate the darkness. For thirty yards he walked, casting his torch left and right as he searched for something. Whatever it was he was looking for, he found it. The torch stopped moving and pointed downwards instead. Apparently satisfied, he turned round and walked back towards his car. A sixth sense, developed over years of avoiding violent punters, told the boy something was wrong and his curiosity turned to apprehension. The man walked to the back of the car, looked around carefully and opened the boot. The boy shrank back into the darkness of his room. He instinctively knew nothing good would come from the man seeing him. Apparently satisfied he was alone, the man reached into the boot and dragged out something large and heavy. Despite being twenty yards away, the boy heard a sickening thud as it fell to the floor.

It could only be one thing, and as the boy gasped in recognition, his apprehension turned to abject terror.

That night, he hadn't been thinking about death.

Chapter 2

Detective Inspector Avison Fluke stared at the dripping blood without making a sound. It was crimson, almost black, in the subdued lighting, and he watched as each drop grew until it could no longer resist the pull of gravity, and fell, only for the process to start all over again.

The drips were slowing, an indication it would soon be over. Until the next time.

Fluke hadn't used his bed in nearly a year, preferring an armchair as he waited for exhaustion to give him the temporary release of sleep. He was still tired and the metronomic drip of the blood helped him achieve an almost Zen-like state. He looked at his watch and realised that he'd lost nearly an hour. He felt oddly refreshed at the thought of that. An hour was more than he'd managed at home the previous night.

His peace was interrupted when his mobile phone rang. A nurse at the other end of the cramped ward gave him a dirty look. Fluke mouthed 'sorry'.

'Bollocks,' he said, as he looked at the caller ID. Detective Superintendent Cameron Chambers. Fluke had hoped to be left alone that morning. He stared at the phone before deciding to answer it.

Chambers didn't wait to be acknowledged. 'Fluke, where are you?' He was the type of man who thought he was plain-spoken when in fact he was just rude.

'Home,' he replied, his voice raw. He'd smoked far too many cigars the previous night. Brooding and smoking. A bad combination.

'Home? What the hell are you still doing at home? It's nine o'clock, man.'

Fluke didn't answer and there was an uncomfortable pause, one he knew Chambers would fill.

'Yes, well. I need you in West Cumbria. There's a dead woman waiting there for you. I'm still on this armed robbery and will be all week, so it's your case.'

Fluke had seen the bank depot robbery update on the news the previous night and watched his boss being interviewed. There was no way Chambers was giving up the limelight. He had ambitions to be chief constable and a high-profile case like that was a wet dream for him. In his mind, he was earmarked for great things. In everyone else's, he was an isolated careerist. Everything he did irritated Fluke. They were going to come to blows before long.

'Who can I have?' Fluke asked. Most of the Force Major Incident Team were still on the robbery but he'd need help. He also knew that Chambers equated a big team with importance so would want to keep everyone he could. The bigger the case the bigger the team.

'You can have Sergeant Towler, DC Vaughn and DC Skelton. Can't let you have anyone else. The robbery's at a crucial stage. Get local help if you need more. Towler's already on scene. Get the details from him.'

Towler, that was expected. The only person people liked working less with than Towler was himself. Towler was too unpredictable, too violent. Jo Skelton, as a middle-aged mother of two, didn't conform to Chambers's vision of a young dynamic detective and Vaughn was plain weird with his whole 'I don't like to be touched' thing. With Fluke, the four of them represented FMIT's untouchables. They occasionally referred to themselves as the outcasts and preferred working independently from the main team when they could. Sometimes managing them was like herding cats but Fluke wouldn't have swapped any of them. What Chambers, that colossal moron, failed to see was that they were all brilliant detectives. Like him, they preferred to put orders through a filter of common sense first but they got the job done. They'd have been an asset to his precious robbery case if he hadn't been more concerned with how the team looked on TV than how they performed.

Fluke was distracted by someone pausing then looking in as they walked past the open-style ward. Whoever it was, he got the impression they'd recognised him. Before he could turn and look properly, they'd disappeared. Probably a gawper. Embarrassed to be caught looking. People often didn't know how to act round certain wards.

'And Fluke?' Chambers asked, interrupting Fluke's train of thought.

'Sir?'

'Don't milk it. If it's a straightforward domestic, find out who the dead woman is and arrest the husband.'

Fluke jabbed the end call button. 'Arsehole,' he said. It was strange though, what did Chambers know that he didn't? If it was straightforward, there was no way Chambers wouldn't have led on it, taking a day away from the robbery to solve a murder would, in his mind, only enhance his reputation. If he didn't want it, there was something wrong.

Fluke scrolled down his recent contacts and rang Matt Towler. He answered on the first ring.

'Ave, we've got a body, a woman. I've shut down the scene until you get here.'

'Where?' Fluke asked.

'The new hospital in the west, part of the ground they're still developing. She was under some mud in a foundation hole. The foreman found her at eight this morning.'

That almost certainly ruled out a natural death or a suicide. Dead people didn't bury themselves. A concealed corpse normally meant a homicide. Murder or manslaughter. He knew that, statistically, the street was the most dangerous place for men and the home was the most dangerous place for women. As unpleasant as he was, Chambers was right; when a woman was killed, her partner or ex-partner was usually the culprit. Most of the time for the police, it was a whydunit rather than a whodunit. Few perpetrators of domestic homicides are forensically aware. There were always breadcrumbs to follow when crimes were committed in anger, jealousy or passion. The weapons used were chosen for expediency rather than efficiency and their murders were normally solved within twenty-four hours.

'What do we know so far?' Fluke asked.

'Nothing really. Probably a relationship gone bad. Maybe premeditated,' Towler said. 'She was in a golf travel bag. It's a deposition site, not the murder site.'

'Shit!' So that was why Chambers didn't want anything to do with it. If it was premeditated, it could take time to get to the bottom of it, time away from the robbery, and more importantly, time away from the TV cameras. Anything longer than a day and he risked handing the limelight over to someone else.

By making Fluke the senior investigating officer, Chambers could sit back and poke holes in his efforts. If Fluke charged someone it would be because Chambers had delegated correctly and if he didn't, then he'd have someone to blame. He'd either take the glory or distance himself from a badly run investigation. A win-win for Chambers and a lose-lose for Fluke.

Still, Fluke much preferred working away from the main team, so the arrangement suited them both.

'She was under a foot of mud so couldn't be seen either. Even when looking directly in,' Towler said.

'So how did—?'

'And she's only been in there six hours.'

'What? How'd you know that?' Fluke asked, taking Towler's bait. He could've done without the melodramatic puzzle but he let it go.

'We have a witness. They left a note.'

Fluke impatiently pressed the assistance button above his bed until the ward nurse came over to see him. 'I need to go, nurse,' he said, standing up and sorting out his things. 'It's nearly finished anyway,' he added, pointing at the bag of blood that was clearly not empty.

'Marion,' she replied automatically. 'Do I call you 'patient'? And you're not going anywhere. I've got a bag of plasma in the fridge for you.'

Plasma? Fuck that. Plasma took longer than blood to go through.

After five minutes of argument and counter-argument, Fluke was defeated. He sat back down, grinning sheepishly at the man in the bed opposite who'd been following their exchange. As soon as the nurse left the room, Fluke stood back up. He couldn't afford to wait. The first few hours were the 'golden hours': witnesses remembered things clearly, forensic evidence was at its freshest and easiest to detect. Alibis weren't yet fully formed.

He checked that he couldn't be seen from the corridor before removing the cannula from the back of his hand, just like he'd seen doctors do countless times. He didn't have a cotton swab so he used a tissue to stem the flow of blood from the wound it left. He looked for somewhere safe to dispose of the needle. He settled with simply wrapping it in his hanky and putting it in his rucksack.

He knew he'd stepped over an unseen line in hospital etiquette and would be in trouble with Doctor Cooper later. She'd probably be on the phone before he'd even reached the car park but that was nothing compared to the trouble he'd be in if anyone at work ever found out where he'd actually been. Arriving two hours late to your own crime scene was unexplainable. Anyway, he didn't want to see Doctor Cooper. Every time he saw her, it triggered another bout of insomnia. He'd been lying to her about his side effects for over a year and the guilt was keeping him awake. He knew she only wanted what was best for him but the truth had to stay hidden. And the truth was that five months ago, he'd involved her in a crime. A crime she didn't even know about.

He hoisted his rucksack onto his shoulders, avoided the disapproving stare of the man opposite and walked out of the ward.

The more he went to hospital the more it seemed to tire him. Physically, he was getting stronger and stronger as each day passed but every time he had an appointment, he came out feeling weary. It didn't seem to matter how much he'd rested or how healthily he'd eaten, like a badly earthed battery, the hospital seemed to drain him of energy.

He put it down to being so sick of hospitals that even being in one tired him. Or perhaps Doctor Cooper had been right and he *had* needed the blood. He put it out of his mind and was out of Carlisle and on the A595 driving west in under five minutes. The thermometer in his car showed 5°C. It was biting outside. The trees were bare, their dead leaves long dispersed in the strong winter winds. Brown, rotten vegetation littered the verge. The countryside on the wane. A few evergreens were still battling the elements but everything else was waiting for spring. He turned the heater up.

His mobile rang and the caller ID displayed the ward's number. Fluke pressed the decline button. He'd deal with the fall-out later.

A layer of fog descended the further west he drove. Thick and white. It wasn't raining yet, but it was going to. He hoped proper forensic practices had been followed. He didn't want evidence being washed away before he got there. Chambers had the main SOCO team working the robbery so he knew he'd get whoever was left. It didn't matter, when it came to crime scenes, he preferred to be in total control. The crime scene managers didn't like having their autonomy removed but he didn't care. His case, his rules.

The drive would take at least another forty-five minutes, and without any details of the crime to think about, Fluke searched through the car's mp3 player for some music with a bit of pace and energy. He selected the Clash's second album, *Give 'Em Enough Rope*, and turned up the volume. FMIT were responsible for investigating the most serious crimes committed across Cumbria, and when the county was the third largest in the UK, if you didn't like driving, you were in the wrong job.

An hour after leaving Carlisle, he arrived at the rendezvous point. Towler had set it up on some hardstanding between the main building site and the smaller site where the body had obviously been discovered. It was where all the yellow earth-moving vehicles were parked, which all building sites seemed to need, their enormous tyres thick with dark mud. It was also full of police vehicles, marked and unmarked, some still with their flashing lights on. He was obviously one of the last to arrive.

Whenever possible, Fluke used rendezvous points out of sight of the crime scene to ensure everyone was fully focused on what he was saying, rather than rubbernecking at the site. Towler knew that and Fluke nodded appreciatively as he saw the site's own security fences made the scene self-contained. People were milling round, waiting to start. Most of them had white forensic suits on and from a distance it looked like a convention of Scottish sunbathers.

Fluke got out of his car and stretched. A lone seagull circled overhead, screeching like a half-skinned cat. A uniformed policeman was eating a sandwich and throwing parts of the crust to the gull. Fluke watched as it dived down to catch the last bit. With no more food, it lazily gained height then headed off in the direction of Whitehaven Harbour. Fluke could smell the sea coming off the inland breeze. It reminded him of Plymouth and his time with the Marines.

Matt Towler, a foot taller than everyone else, was speaking to a group of suited forensic staff. He saw Fluke, broke away from the group and walked over. Fluke could tell his friend was worried, and when something worried Towler, a veteran of a gulf war, Sierra Leone and three tours of Northern Ireland, he also worried. Although FMIT officers weren't officially paired up, Fluke and Towler invariably ended up working together. Barely hidden disdain of anyone below their own high standards, barrack-room sarcasm and a willingness to work twenty hours a day, seven days a week when needed meant other detectives weren't exactly falling over themselves to join them. It was something Fluke cultivated rather than tried to rectify.

'You okay, Ave?' Towler asked.

'Fine,' Fluke replied. 'Tell me about this note,' he said, as they walked towards the scene. The ground was cold and slippery and threatening to sprain his ankles. They struggled to the outer cordon and stopped.

Towler handed him a plastic evidence bag. It had a piece of paper inside.

Fluke read it.

Look in the secund whole from the door. sum1 has put a boddy in there

It was written on stationery with the same building company logo as the signs on the fences surrounding the site. He turned it over. There was nothing on the back.

The witness appeared to have used whatever had been to hand.

'Not exactly Shakespeare is it?' Towler said. 'It was by the kettle in the site office.'

The poor spelling didn't necessarily indicate age. Fluke knew the average criminal had the reading age of an eight-year-old and he already had a theory about who'd left the note. He didn't know the person but suspected he knew the type.

Fluke looked at the site office and its proximity to the crime scene, easily identifiable by the forensic tent. 'Who was first on scene?'

'Dunno. But Don Holland was managing it when I got here.'

Fluke could see Chief Inspector Holland talking to a group of uniformed officers. They'd never really got on, although neither of them really knew why. Fluke walked over.

'Chief Inspector!' he called out, as he approached.

Holland looked up, said something to the group that caused them to laugh, and sauntered over. 'What's up, Fluke? Don't tell me, you've found something to complain about already. I would say that under three minutes is a record for you but we both know I'd be lying.'

Holland laughed at his own joke. Fluke didn't join in. 'Who set up the cordons?'

'Remember who you're speaking to, Fluke,' Holland said.

'I know exactly who I'm speaking to, *Chief Inspector*,' Fluke replied. 'Who set up the cordons?'

'I did. Why? It's all correct.'

Fluke could feel himself getting angry. 'Why's the site office not in the inner cordon?'

Holland was about to respond but saw the evidence bag Fluke was carrying and realised his mistake. The office was also a crime scene and should have been cordoned off and access controlled. 'Shit.'

'I'm giving you five minutes to reset it, and in the meantime get those giggling idiots off my fucking crime scene!' Fluke shouted, pointing at the officers Holland had been holding court with. 'Don't they teach contamination control on the chief inspector's course anymore?' The raised voices had caused them all to look over. *Jesus*, he thought, *any chance of footprint evidence had all but disappeared.* Compromised crime scenes ruined cases. Defence solicitors drove tanks through them.

'Now look here, Fluke. I will not be spoken—'

'I haven't got time, Chief Inspector,' Fluke interrupted. 'Just get it fucking sorted.' For a second, he thought Holland was going to stand his ground. He stared at Fluke, nostrils flaring and lips white with anger. Eventually, he turned his back and left without saying anything. He didn't really have a choice; Fluke had him over a barrel.

'Useless wanker,' Towler said, as Holland walked off.

There was no point reliving mistakes. Fluke needed to move on. 'Who found the note?'

Towler pointed towards a grey-haired man talking to a police officer. 'The Clerk of Works, Christian Dunn, spotted it soon as he got in. Always has a brew first thing.'

Fluke asked, 'What'd he do?'

'Had a look, saw nothing, but as it was due to be filled today, he got in with a shovel and found it.'

'The body?'

'No, the golf travel bag,' Towler replied. 'He opened it, saw her face and called 999.'

Fluke knew what they were. The big bags used when transporting golf clubs abroad. They had to be big enough to fit a normal golf bag in them. The perfect way to transport a body surreptitiously. 'Let's go and have a word with him then,' he said.

Normally when Fluke spoke to members of the public who'd discovered a body they were on the verge of a breakdown. At the very least, they were in shock. If Fluke were pressed, he'd have described Christian Dunn as irritated.

He looked up as they walked over. 'Is this him? This the boss man, like?' Mr Dunn said to the officer with him. He strode towards them, indignation all over his face. He was a small man, closer to sixty than fifty, with a weathered face. Clearly someone who spent most of his time outdoors.

Fluke held out his hand but Dunn ignored it.

'You the boss man? When can I get back to work?' he asked, without preamble. He pronounced work as 'wuk'. 'It's putting me right off my schedule, this is. I've nine tons of concrete coming within the hour. I need you to move that lassie.'

His understanding of personal space was about as well-developed as his awareness of volume control. Dunn wasn't exactly shouting but Fluke could feel himself leaning back anyway. Ten minutes with him and he'd be reaching for headache pills.

'This is a murder investigation. The site's shut down, Mr Dunn,' Fluke replied.

Dunn looked at him blankly. 'My gaffer doesn't pay me to sit on me arse all day with concrete getting hard in the mixer.'

'I'm sorr—'

'What she want to throw herself down there for anyway?' Dunn interrupted. 'I know it's sad an' all that, but it's selfish. If she wants to kill herself, why can't she do it away from my building site.'

It was Fluke's turn to look blank. The idiot thought it was a suicide? She was in a bag and covered in mud.

Dunn wasn't finished. 'Look, I know you lads 'ave a job to do but my concrete's going in that hole whether you like it or not.'

Fluke didn't really know how to respond to that. Fortunately Towler did.

'Listen, you little tit, this site's gonna be closed for days. This is a murder investigation. If you go anywhere near that hole, I'll arrest you.'

Dunn stepped back in the face of Towler's aggressive outburst. 'I'm telling my gaffer about this. You'll be hearing from Mr Johnson today, don't you worry about that. It's putting me right off my schedule this is,' he muttered, avoiding meeting Towler's eye.

'Look, Mr Dunn, we'll be as fast as we can but it'll go faster if you tell me everything I need to know,' Fluke said.

'How fast?'

'Maybe an hour,' Fluke lied. He saw Towler smirk as Dunn looked at his watch.

'What do you want to know?' he said.

'Tell me about the hole and the office.'

Dunn explained that the holes were all due to be filled with concrete and rubble, part of the foundations for the new outpatient wing.

'Did anyone have a key to the site office other than you, Mr Dunn?' Fluke asked.

For the first time, Dunn looked uncomfortable rather than angry. Shifty even.

'No. Why should anyone else have a key? I'm the gaffer,' he mumbled.

'So you're the only one with access to it?'

He mumbled something again. Fluke failed to catch it.

'Speak up, please!' Towler barked.

'I'm the only one who can get in,' Dunn said, in a clearer voice.

'You sure?' Fluke asked. He stared at Dunn. He knew something about the office, he was sure of it.

Dunn broke eye contact first, said he was sure, then stumbled off.

'You want to bring him in?' Towler asked.

Fluke thought about it. 'Nah. We'll wait and see. He's not exactly going anywhere. Not when he has to "wuk".'

'Jesus, if it'd been filled in today, I doubt the body would ever have been found,' Towler said, as they watched Dunn walk off, muttering to himself.

'Not in our lifetime anyway,' Fluke agreed.

'You wanna go and have a look?'

'Yeah, I'll have a quick gander but I'm not getting in just yet,' he said. 'I want to clear the site office first. Sooner we get that done sooner it can be processed. We'll have to wait for the pathologist before we can move the body. May as well let SOCO do something.' Fluke, like a lot of older detectives, refused to call SOCO by their new name, CSI, believing it was one more unwelcome American influence. They were Scenes of Crime Officers and always would be.

As they walked towards the foundation hole, he saw Don Holland standing outside the hastily rearranged tape. He was glaring at Fluke and mouthed 'fuck you' when he caught his eye. Fluke ignored him.

'He won't forget that, Ave,' said Towler, nodding towards Holland. 'You humiliated him. He'll be after you now.'

'Yeah?' Fluke replied. 'Well, he'll have to get in the queue. I think they have T-shirts.'

'I had a quick look, just to make sure we weren't pressing the button for a fucking mannequin or something.' Towler said, changing the subject. 'There's always some fuckwit fancying themselves as Wilt.'

Fluke allowed himself a small smile. It was true. Up and down the country there'd been a spate of shop dummies being thrown down building site holes after Tom Sharpe's *Wilt* had been published. 'And?'

'It's fresh. I'm guessing less than twenty-four hours.'

'Any obvious cause of death?'

'Nope, and I didn't want to open the bag any further.'

Fluke didn't respond.

'I know we don't jump to conclusions, Ave, but it looks well planned,' he added, cautiously.

Towler was right, it was dangerous to form opinions too quickly but Fluke was getting a bad feeling. There was something about it that just sounded professional, nothing tangible, but it was there. It was a miracle the body had even been discovered.

''Course, it could just be a fucking nutter who killed his wife and didn't want to sit at home in his underpants talking to her 'til she smelt like cheese,' Towler grinned.

Fluke smiled but said nothing.

Chapter 3

After being met by Sean Rogers, the crime scene manager, Fluke donned a forensic suit and followed him down the route organised by the first officers at the scene to ensure as much evidence as possible was left undisturbed.

Fluke turned and reviewed where he was. It offered him the chance to get his bearings, a sense of scale and to assess the work that had taken place before he'd arrived. Murder investigations started with the first officer on the scene, and other than Holland neglecting to treat the office as a crime scene, everything else was satisfactory. Luckily, the building site was self-contained so there weren't going to be any egress or access problems later.

After entering the inner cordon, Fluke continued down the immediate route to the crime scene. As they got nearer, it was marked out with footboards, designed to keep any ground evidence closer to the scene intact. They'd been put in properly, which wasn't always the case. Fluke had been to one crime scene on the side of a hill when the footboards were at an angle and he'd fallen off, much to everyone's amusement.

Although it wasn't raining at the site, SOCO had erected a large forensic tent. Fluke entered and looked down into the hole. It was about six feet across, roundish, and at least ten feet deep with steep sides. Fluke could see the excavation scars the digger had made. The mud was thick clay, too dark to see the bottom.

The ladder that Dunn had used was still leaning against the side of the hole. There had been some damage to the scene, probably during his scramble back out when he realised what he'd just uncovered, but Fluke could live with that. Rarely was a crime scene undisturbed. The most difficult ones to manage were when the victim was still alive at the point of discovery. Then, all hell would break loose, as whichever service was first on the scene tried to preserve life. In their efforts to keep the victim alive, firefighters, paramedics and police officers ignored what detectives arriving later would need to investigate.

He leaned over and looked down. Rogers passed him a torch to cut through shadows as dark as freshly poured Guinness.

The black golf bag was partially buried at the bottom of the hole and the zip had been opened about eighteen inches. It was enough to reveal the head of an obviously dead woman. Her skin was grey and frostbitten and cracking. An icy sheen clung to her, the warmth of life banished. Her mouth was open and her lips were shrinking back across the teeth in an eerie grimace. Towler was right; it was no mannequin. Fluke never ceased to be surprised at how quickly the body lost its healthy pink colour once death had occurred. It was a matter of minutes.

Some of her hair had been caught in the zip, twisting her head to the side and Fluke thought his torch picked up the sparkle of a diamond earring. Even from three yards away, they looked expensive. Too expensive to leave. That ruled out a robbery. It also ruled out a domestic. They looked too easy to identify, and why leave them? They could be turned into cash. Despite what TV shows portrayed, the police didn't have legions of fences they could call on to find stolen goods. If you want to turn small items into cash it was easily done with little risk. But even a little risk seemed too much for whoever did this. Fluke felt uneasy.

It was hard to tell, but he didn't think she was a very young woman. Mid-thirties would be his guess. Like Towler, Fluke could see no obvious cause of death but he knew he was only looking at a face and an ear in a dark hole in torchlight. Things would become clearer during the post-mortem. He swung the torch round the bottom of the hole. He could see a shovel, probably the one Dunn had used to search for the body. There was nothing else. He couldn't smell any putrefaction, only wet mud. If she'd been put in the hole during the early hours of the morning then Fluke was willing to bet that she'd been killed no earlier than the day before. The pathologist would give him a time of death as well as the cause.

Fluke saw no reason to get into the hole to take a closer look. It would only add confusion to the crime scene. Patience was a discipline, and after six months in hospital, it was one he possessed in abundance. The first thing he needed to do was make sure that there were no errors made in the collection of evidence, and that meant taking the time to do it properly.

Together, he and the pathologist would decide how to recover the body without disturbing anything important. He'd seen enough.

He left the tent and handed the torch back to Rogers.

'What time's the pathologist getting here?' Fluke asked. Sometimes the body could be recovered without one, but it was a complex deposition site. He presumed someone had called for one.

'Should be within the hour, Henry Sowerby's coming up from Preston,' Rogers replied. 'I took one look and knew we'd need him at the scene. Sergeant Towler informed the coroner.'

'Good.' Fluke liked Sowerby. The pathologist was extremely professional, had a good forensic brain and was as bad tempered as they came. He'd watched him reduce senior investigating officers to quivering wrecks when he felt that good forensic practices weren't being followed. Fluke had always got on well enough with him though, and he knew the bad temper was on behalf of the victims rather than any antagonism towards the police. Once an SIO had been chewed out by Sowerby for a forensic error, they never repeated it. They learnt their lesson quickly.

Fluke would wait for him, and together they would decide how to recover the body. They would agree what evidence needed to be gathered before they moved her and what could be gathered at the mortuary. Although technically Fluke would have the final say at the crime scene, it was a brave SIO who went against the advice of the pathologist, an even braver one who went against the advice of Sowerby. Fluke much preferred to reach a consensus. He knew there were genuine reasons why SIOs sometimes had to go against a pathologist's advice, he'd done it himself on rare occasions. Sometimes the need to move quickly overrode the need to collect evidence in ideal conditions. But there was no rush here. Nothing was going to change in the next hour.

Fluke turned to Rogers. 'Who's been in the inner cordon?'

'Which one?' he asked, smiling slyly.

'The first one,' Fluke replied. He didn't return the smile. It was one thing chewing out someone for an error but Holland was still a senior officer. He might be a total dickhead but he still had to be able to command his officers. In any case, Holland was going to have to provide some officer resource to do some of the grunt work. House-to-house, crime scene security, search teams and anything else Fluke needed.

'Dunn, the responding officer, Sergeant Towler and myself. And now you. Only Dunn has set foot on the bottom. Sergeant Towler climbed down to confirm it was a body but didn't get off the ladder,' Rogers replied. 'And he used a different ladder in case Dunn ever becomes a suspect.'

Fluke nodded. There was no way Dunn was the killer. Committing a murder would have got in the way of his schedule. 'I'll go and have a look at the office now, then your lot can process it.'

'Matt,' Fluke said, turning to Towler. 'Can you ask Jo to go back to HQ and set up an incident room. The robbery team have the big one so we'll just have to make do.'

Jo Skelton was the oldest member of FMIT, a veteran of murder investigations going back twenty years, and Fluke sometimes thought she was the most valuable. She was certainly the only one he trusted to actually do the essential admin tasks; to set up databases and cross-reference intelligence without getting bored and making mistakes. She wasn't flash enough for Chambers though, which just showed what a pinhead he was.

'Will do,' Towler said, taking out his phone.

'And once she's done that, I want her checking mispers, any female between twenty and fifty. Tell her to start with Cumbria but to do a national search if she comes up blank.'

'If she's been in the ground less than a day, Ave, nobody may have noticed she's missing yet.' Towler said.

'I know. Do it anyway,' Fluke snapped. He knew Towler was right, but the only way it was going to be solved was by getting an ID. He wasn't going to wait a week until someone started missing her.

'But wouldn't it make more—'

'Look, if we don't get someone then we'll keep doing it until we do. For all we know, she's been kept in a freezer for six months and there's a family out there who reported her missing five months and twenty-nine days ago.'

Towler looked like he was going to say something but obviously thought better of it.

'Get Alan Vaughn to act as liaison between us and uniform. Go and introduce him to Don Holland and let him know we're grateful for all the help he's going to offer. He won't like it but he has no choice. His lot will probably have to do a fingertip search of the site for a weapon. Doubt we'll find one but I don't want a kid finding something after we've gone. Get West CID to do the house-to-house enquiries. That'll do for now. I'll look at the office while I'm waiting for Henry.'

Towler walked off without saying anything. Fluke watched him go. They were friends, and had been since they were kids. Fluke was godfather to Towler's daughter, but sometimes Towler's attitude to the more serious cases annoyed him. He was able to look at everything dispassionately, to stop thinking about them as soon as he left work. Fluke, on the other hand, lived and breathed every case. The bigger ones consumed him. He knew Towler's approach was by far the healthiest but it still annoyed him.

Fluke knew that Sowerby was thorough, but could be slow when it was a complex scene. He guessed it would be at least three hours before the body could be recovered and another hour to the mortuary, which would have to be the Cumberland Infirmary in Carlisle as it was the only hospital in Cumbria that could cope with forensic examinations. Fluke would accompany it, which suited him as he could go and see how much trouble he was in after his earlier stunt. The post-mortem would take about four hours so wouldn't be until the next day. With luck, he wouldn't be late for Michelle. He didn't want another row.

Chapter 4

To avoid any cross-contamination, Fluke changed into a new forensic suit to examine the office. Rogers opened the door for him and followed him in with a video camera and portable forensic kit.

Fluke had a quick look round. He hadn't noticed the type of lock but knew the door hadn't been forced. The windows were all secure and there was no reason for them to be open in winter. Either someone had a key or Dunn was lying about the note.

He didn't really know what the insides of Portakabins were supposed to look like but he imagined they were all similar to the one he was in; hardwearing carpet, heaters, a small sink, a computer, plastic chairs and the obligatory kettle. Site plans and Dunn's precious schedules adorned the wall. Nothing remarkable. There was no toilet but he'd seen a couple of portaloos outside. It wasn't a place to relax in, but a functional office for people whose primary business was conducted outdoors.

'The note was found here,' Rogers said, pointing at the kettle area.

There was a small table with ingrained coffee stains. A packet of sugar, instant coffee and an unopened bottle of full-fat milk sat alongside the cheap plastic kettle. Fluke couldn't see a fridge so assumed Dunn brought milk in every day. It hadn't been opened and Fluke guessed Dunn had checked the claims made in the note before he'd made himself a brew. He'd check the statement later.

Towler, having finished his call to Jo Skelton, walked in. There was no need for Fluke to apologise for his earlier outburst but he shrugged to indicate that he'd been in the wrong. Towler grinned. He was irrepressible. Fluke let him have a look round.

'Key?' Towler said.

'That's my guess,' Fluke replied. Criminals much preferred walking into a building rather than breaking in. Breaking in left a forensic transfer. It couldn't be helped. Footprints, fibres, hand and fingerprints. Even earprints. He'd heard recently that criminals had a new saying, 'walk in, walk out', referring to the fact that with no forensic evidence, the chances of a conviction in court were slim.

Towler said, 'According to Dunn's statement, he's still got them all, over on the keyboard by the door. He's waiting to issue them when the site goes live. I'll check with the company and find out how many sets they sent. My bet is that there'll be one missing. If it was stolen straightaway, Dunn might not have noticed.'

Fluke nodded, and Towler disappeared to make another phone call. He continued looking and soon saw what he was searching for. What he'd expected to find.

He called Rogers over and pointed to the top of the bin under the sink. The can of Coke was half-buried in the debris of everyday life on the site; crisp packets, paper towels and damp teabags. 'Photograph that can for me, please?'

He waited a minute while Rogers got the camera fired up and recorded what was needed. It was ripped in half.

Although he had rubber gloves on, Fluke took a pen out of his pocket and picked the can up through the drinking hole. Detectives all over the world had the bad habit of using pens to pick up evidence, and Fluke was no exception. He had the sneaky suspicion they all watched the same TV shows. It wasn't the bit he wanted but it would still have prints on it.

'So where's the other half,' he said to himself. He carefully removed more rubbish until he found it. It was photographed in situ before he removed it.

He turned it over and saw the brown residue on the concave base.

'Excellent,' said Rogers. 'Heroin?'

Fluke nodded. 'Better than a spoon. Disposable. Can't be arrested for carrying a can of pop.'

'You knew there'd be a can?' he asked.

'No, not a can. But I was expecting evidence of drug use. You'd be amazed at the places addicts call home.'

Rogers put both pieces in separate evidence bags and sealed them.

Fluke searched the rest of the office but found nothing obvious. SOCO would spend days going through it with a fine toothcomb and gather any trace evidence. It was time to let them get to work. Fluke thanked Rogers and joined Towler who was standing outside.

'So we have a heroin addict who has a key to this place somehow. Shoots up last night and sees something he knows he shouldn't have. He does his civic duty and leaves a note. Doesn't hang around and make our lives easier, but we can't have everything,' he said, after Fluke had brought him up to date.

'That's my take.'

'You think he was alone?' Towler asked.

'You ever seen a shooting house? They're a mess, an absolute mess. Nope, this was one person. He's probably been here every night for a week or so, prime site like this. Out the way, warm, no chance of getting his drugs taxed by some of the thugs round here. I'd bet he's been cleaning up after himself, taking his rubbish away with him, no one's any the wiser. Last night must've shaken him. He panics, forgets his routine and puts the can in the bin. If there were two halves of a can of Coke in the bin every morning, Dunn would've clicked straight away. He's the only one in here and everything in the bin should have been his.'

'No way his prints aren't everywhere then,' Towler said.

'Everywhere,' Fluke agreed. 'But these offices aren't new. They go from site to site. It'll have hundreds of prints. We'll take them all, obviously, but we'll process the can and the note first. That's how we get him. Or her.'

He was an equal opportunities police officer when it came to drug addicts.

Someone shouted for Fluke and he turned to look. It had come from the outer cordon.

'Ah,' he said. 'The pathologist's here.'

Chapter 5

Even from a distance, Henry Sowerby was a striking man. If you hadn't met him and were asked to guess what he did for a living, Fluke suspected a disproportionate amount would tick the 'mad scientist' box. Apart from Towler, he was a foot taller than everyone else and was balding in a way few men do. Rather than receding, it looked more like the dome of his head had forced its way through his hair like a mountain peak rising above the clouds. He always wore a three-piece tweed suit and carried his equipment in a battered leather case.

Appearances were deceptive though. He was an internationally renowned pathologist. It was only his love of the Lake District and its fells that kept him from taking up a teaching position at any university hospital in the world. He had the sharpest mind of anyone Fluke had met.

He was waiting at the outer cordon, a young woman with him.

His daughter? Fluke knew both of his children had grown up and flown the nest but that was all he knew.

'Detective Inspector,' he hailed, as Fluke approached. Others called out your name, some greeted you, but Sowerby hailed you. The only man Fluke had ever met who did.

'Long time, Avison. Glad to see you're back. You had us all a bit worried for a while,' he said.

They shook hands firmly, their mutual respect evident.

'So what do we have here?' Sowerby asked.

Fluke ignored the question. 'Two of you today, Henry?'

'Ah sorry, old boy, where are my manners? Avison, may I introduce Lucy Cheesebrough? Lucy's doing her PhD in forensic entomology and is seconded to our beloved north-west office for part of her field work.'

Fluke shook the hand she offered. She looked to be in her mid-twenties and appeared small next to Sowerby. She had curly hair, a serious face and wore round glasses. He guessed her pale complexion meant she probably did more labwork than fieldwork. Still, she gave him a smile, and he saw nothing to suggest she wasn't genuinely friendly.

'I want permission for her to observe me working,' Sowerby said.

'Of course,' he said. People learned by doing things so Fluke was always helpful to students when he could be. He'd never met an entomologist before, never mind a forensic one. He didn't think the victim had been dead long enough for helpful insect activity but it didn't harm to have another discipline looking.

'Pleased to meet you, Lucy,' he said. 'How many crime scenes have you been to?'

'This is my second. I went to a suicide in Blackburn two months ago,' she said.

'Not technically a crime scene, sweetheart,' Towler said, smirking.

'It was by the time I'd finished,' she replied, looking at Towler without flinching. 'I told the police in Lancashire that the body had been dead at least two days before they thought it had been. Convinced the coroner to do a post-mortem and Henry confirmed it.'

'That she did,' Sowerby said. 'Anything to add there, Sergeant?'

Towler was trying to not catch anyone's eye. 'Yeah well, good then,' he mumbled.

Go, Lucy. Fluke liked her already.

'As much fun as it is watching Sergeant Towler squirm, can you tell me what's happened here, Avison?' Sowerby asked.

'Sorry,' Fluke said, with an eye on Towler, who could behave unpredictably when he'd made a tit of himself. 'We've got a body in a bag in a hole. We think the drop was witnessed by a heroin addict. Matt spoke to the coroner after checking it was actually human.'

'Good man,' Sowerby said.

Fluke knew he wasn't joking either. He'd heard the story, they all had, about a new SIO in Cheshire who had called Sowerby out in the early hours during the Easter holidays to a corpse that turned out to be a decomposed pig. The public dressing down he'd received was legendary. Fluke met him from time-to-time at the occasional conference and he'd turned into a good SIO. But later in the bar, all anyone ever did was offer to buy him pork scratchings. One of Towler's phrases had seemed apt at the time:

'If you want sympathy, it's in the dictionary between syphilis and shit'.

'Rogers has erected a tent and put footboards down. I've had a look but not been in. Other than Matt, the responding officer and the foreman who discovered her, no one else has been near,' he said.

'Okay, let's have a chat with Rogers and see what we can come up with,' Sowerby said.

Thirty minutes later, and without any further incidents, a recovery plan was agreed.

While the SOCO team were processing the outer cordon, taking photographs and videos of the myriad of tyre and footprints, the uniformed officers from Whitehaven began their fingertip search. *Nice bit of laundry for them to do, tonight*, Fluke thought as he watched them crawling through the sticky cold mud. Not one of them was smiling, he noticed. But in a command and control structure like the police, not one of them was complaining either. Not openly anyway.

The ladder Towler had used was still there, and after Rogers had been down to video the scene, Sowerby followed Fluke into the hole which was just big enough for the three of them to stand without crowding the body. The temperature seemed to be a couple of degrees cooler at the bottom. Not as cold as a freezer but colder than a fridge, he estimated. It would have taken the body a long time to decompose. The crime scene smelled of wet cloying mud and nothing else.

'Lucy,' Sowerby called without looking up to where she was peering in. 'Keep your hands in your pockets.'

'I don't have any,' she called back down, confused. 'I've got some gloves in the car.'

Sowerby looked at Fluke and grinned. 'It's an expression, dear. Means don't touch anything until you've asked Avison. It's his crime scene, not mine,' he replied. 'Now, let's have a look at your victim,' he said to Fluke.

Sowerby placed a thermometer beside the golf bag to take the ambient temperature. He'd use it to calculate a time of death when he had the victim's temperature to compare it to. Fluke knew in the past he'd have used a complicated chart called the

Henssge Nomogram but now, like everything else it seemed, it was done electronically. He probably had an app for it.

Sowerby worked methodically taking notes and collecting samples. Fluke watched him but he and Rogers had seen it done enough times for it not to fascinate them anymore. He knew nothing that was happening would result in any immediate answers. They were samples for the lab to work on.

He busied himself with looking round the hole. It seemed deeper now that he was at the bottom. Looking up at the skyline, Fluke couldn't help feeling that he was in a grave.

In a way he was.

After calling out instructions for Rogers to take more samples: hair, mud, swabs and tapings, Sowerby stood and stared at the body.

'Tough one this, Avison. Can't do the rectal temperature. I don't want to take her out the bag here, too much evidence will be lost. Can't do the intimate swabs either. Sean can do the ones on the head but that's it. Best we can do is protect the head with a bag to avoid losing anything else. I think we have *livor mortis*, so she's probably been dead at least twelve hours. That's all I'm prepared to say at the minute on time of death. No obvious cause.'

Fluke wasn't worried. He'd rather have an accurate time of death later than an inaccurate one now.

Sowerby looked at the steep sides of the hole. Fluke could tell what he was thinking. How much evidence would be lost when they removed her?

'What to do? What to do?' Sowerby said to himself. 'It's your call at the end of the day, Avison. We can risk moving her and get everything this lady still has to tell us, or we could try and do a rudimentary examination down here and almost certainly contaminate things.'

Fluke didn't hesitate. 'I want her out, Henry. I'm not leaving her in here any longer than I have to. Give her some dignity back.'

'Let's get it done then,' Sowerby said with an appreciative look. 'You'll need to call your chums in Mountain Rescue. We'll need one of their specialist stretchers.'

The body was recovered without too much damage, although Fluke and Sowerby winced at every bump and scrape as she was manhandled onto the commandeered stretcher and pulled out of her intended grave. It was taken to the vehicle that would transport her to the mortuary. A private company provided that service in Cumbria.

'I'll get someone to sit in the van with her on the way back. I'll follow in my car,' Fluke said to Sowerby.

'I'm bringing Lucy into the PM, see what her views are on this. She tells me that if a body dies in the open it only takes ten minutes for flies to lay eggs in the mouth, nose and eyes.'

'Lovely,' Fluke said.

'So, depending on what she finds, it's possible she can give us an edge on determining where she was killed. Might help with time of death too.'

Fluke turned to look for Lucy but she was heading back to the car she and Sowerby had arrived in. 'I've never worked a case with an entomologist before. I've read the manuals and been to the briefings but I'm not sure of their value yet,' he said.

'It's a tricky one, Avison. She'll be the first to admit that, from a forensic point of view, the UK still lags behind the States and mainland Europe. The science is sound, you understand, no one's disputing that. The problem is relying on it in court. Too easy for defence teams to muddy the water with their own experts.'

'Juries here aren't yet ready to convict someone on the say so of a creepy-crawly?' Fluke asked, only half joking.

'There's a bit of that, certainly. She knows all this and accepts the limitations. She was being serious before. She overturned the police view in Lancashire about that suicide. Don't think they have anyone for it yet, but they will, now they're looking.'

'I'm not refusing any help on this one,' Fluke said.

'Excellent. Until tomorrow then. I've booked the post-mortem suite for ten o'clock.'

Chapter 6

Chambers rang as Fluke was driving back and he pulled over in the nearest lay-by. There was no point in risking a pull for using his mobile at the wheel, gone were the days where you could flash your warrant card and be on your way. Try that and you'd be up in front of professional standards on a corruption charge.

As soon as Fluke pressed 'receive', Chambers started talking. He could hear people in the background. Chambers was on a speakerphone and would be playing to an audience.

'What's happening, Fluke?' he barked.

Fluke tried to explain the situation, how he suspected that there was more to the murder than they'd originally thought. He was starting to venture an early theory that it was a professional killing when Chambers cut him off.

'When you hear hooves, think horses, Fluke, not zebras.'

Fluke winced. It was Chambers' favourite saying and a standing joke in FMIT. He could imagine the officers within earshot of him cringing with embarrassment. Fluke also knew Chambers was trying to give the impression to those around him that the murder wasn't worthy of his time, that he was too important for such basic tasks, that it was okay to delegate to one of his minions. Of course, everyone who knew him knew that he was terrified of appearing to be out of his depth. Fluke would've bet he knew the body had been professionally disposed of and it would've frightened him. There was too much that could go wrong.

'We don't know who she is yet, sir,' Fluke said as if he hadn't been interrupted. 'We've only just got her out the ground and the PM's not until tomorrow. It's possible that—'

'Okay, Fluke. Keep me updated.'

And with that, he rang off. Fluke stared at the phone for a second before throwing it on the passenger seat and starting the engine again. What Chambers would never understand with good detective work was that sometimes when you heard hooves the best thing to do was think zebras. That's how difficult cases were closed.

Fluke had never really understood where Chambers's antagonism had come from. Fluke knew Towler thought he made too much of it, that Chambers was a bit of a prick but harmless. Fluke thought it was because he was a threat to his authority. Chambers was in a job that was beyond him and knew that Fluke knew. Fluke was at least one rank lower than he should have been. He'd attended and easily passed the required courses but each time there was a chance of promotion, he either said the wrong thing or spoke his mind once too often. It didn't usually bother him; being an inspector suited him for now, it was the optimum balance between power and responsibility. Senior enough to get things done but not so senior that he was behind a desk all day.

Normally the rudeness of Chambers didn't trouble him but this time it had preyed on his mind and he was in a bad mood when he pulled up outside Michelle's house. Three other cars were already in the drive.

Shit.

He'd forgotten about her big dinner party. Something to do with a new job one of her vacuous friends had just started. That was all he needed; an evening of forced conversation, enduring their excruciatingly dull chatter.

Michelle met him at the door, and although she didn't say anything, he could tell she was annoyed he hadn't bothered to go home and get changed. He still had building site mud on his suit. She'd have something to say later, of that he was sure. She ushered him into the lounge, turning her head to avoid the offered kiss.

'Well, Avison has decided to join us at last. We can eat.'

He helped himself to a single malt whiskey, drank it without bothering with ice and poured himself another. He followed everyone into her cramped dining room. Michelle was perched beside a young man in his twenties. They were already giggling together. Michelle whispered something into his ear and he looked up at Fluke before giggling again.

Fluke wondered why he didn't care.

The only seat left was beside a middle-aged man he hadn't met before. Parts of his face were losing their fight with gravity. His jowls were uneven. Fluke offered his hand but the man either didn't see it or chose to ignore it.

Great.

He looked at the table. There was more cutlery than there was going to be courses. He reached for the red wine and settled down to ignore everyone.

An hour later his mood hadn't improved. The meal was going slowly; so far they'd only had a starter of figs and cured meats. Food he didn't understand, eaten in the company of people he didn't like. Fluke had managed to avoid speaking to anyone while at the same time drinking most of the bottle of red wine himself. He wasn't a big drinker and was feeling drunk.

As everybody else seemed to be engrossed with an anecdote someone else he didn't know was telling, Fluke thought about the case and what he needed to do next. Clearly identifying the body was going to be a priority. He hoped the prints or DNA Sowerby had taken that afternoon were helpful but he wasn't counting on it. The post-mortem would be crucial. He didn't have a cause of, manner of, or time of death yet. He wanted answers to all three the next day.

He became vaguely aware that the table had gone silent and he looked up. Everyone was looking at him.

'I'm sorry, I must've missed that,' he said apologetically.

Michelle glared at him.

The man beside him, who still hadn't introduced himself, spoke. 'I was just saying, Inspector, with all these children being abducted and killed, isn't it time we brought back hanging?'

'What children?' Fluke said blankly.

'All these children in the news? The ones being murdered.'

Fluke had no idea what he was talking about. 'I'm sorry, have I missed something? I haven't seen the news today.'

'We were talking hypothetically, Inspector,' he said, rolling his eyes.

'Who are you again?'

The man held his hand out. 'Charles. We were just talking about Ian's new job as a journalist.'

Fluke ignored his hand just as his had been ignored earlier. He put down his drink. 'I thought someone just said Ian's new job was selling advertising space with the free paper?' He could feel Michelle's stare.

'It's still journalism,' the man sitting beside Michelle said indignantly.

Ian presumably. He decided not to press the matter. 'No, I don't,' he said, turning to Charles.

'Don't what,' Charles asked.

'No, I don't think that we should bring back hanging.'

'You don't? I bet that's a first for a policeman. I'm sure if we asked the rest of them they'd agree with me,' Charles said.

Fluke emptied his glass and poured another. 'I don't give a shit,' he murmured.

'I'm sorry!'

'Has there been a recent spate of child killings I'm unaware of?' he asked.

'Of course, man. You only have to read the papers. Murderers and rapists everywhere, crime at record levels. It's been going up since National Service was abolished,' Charles said.

He was slurring and obviously a fool, and on any other day Fluke would have let it go. 'No, it isn't,' he said coldly. 'Crime's at an all-time low.'

'Nonsense, read a paper, man. Crime's rampant. Bringing back National Service would be the best thing this government could do.'

'Why?'

He clearly hadn't thought his argument through any further than the headlines. 'Discipline. Give all the scroungers a sense of discipline,' he said finally and looked at Fluke as if daring him to disagree.

Fluke stared at him. Charles tried to hold his gaze but was no match and he quickly lowered his eyes.

'Yes, well, you've obviously never served. If you had, you'd know the sense of pride you get from wearing a uniform.'

Again, Fluke would normally have let it go but he'd just come back from seeing a dead woman in a hole. His voice dropped. 'I was a Royal Marines Commando for six years. I did two tours of Northern Ireland and fought in the Gulf War. Remind me what war you fought in, *Charlie*.'

Michelle, knowing that the quieter he got the angrier he was becoming, decided to step in. 'I'm sure we can agree to disagree. Can't we, Avison?'

Fluke paused. He was breathing heavily and gripping his wine glass stem so hard his fingers were white. 'Fine,' he said eventually.

'But surely you agree that child rapists should be hung?' Ian said, clearly annoyed by Fluke's dismissal of his new job and oblivious to the mental weather change. 'In my humble opinion, if they knew they were going to be hung they would think twice.'

In Fluke's world there was no such thing as a humble opinion. The people who used the expression were never humble and for some reason thought prefacing their stupid statements with it gave it more gravitas. He noticed Ian was also slurring. Was there anyone in the room who wasn't drunk? 'Hanged.'

'Excuse me?'

'It's not hung, it's hanged. And no, I don't.'

An attractive, short-haired woman, who, to the best of Fluke's recollection, hadn't said anything all evening, decided to speak. 'Can I ask why, Inspector?' she asked softly.

Fluke couldn't sense any drunkenness or condescension in her question and calmed down slightly. 'It's simple actually. You've heard the expression "you may as well be *hanged* for a sheep as a lamb"?'

She nodded.

'It's the same principle. I don't want every sex crime turning into a murder because there's nothing to be gained by leaving a living witness.' Fluke wasn't simply disagreeing for the sake of it, although the mood he was in, he would have. No one sensible in the criminal justice system thought the right-wing approach to crime was a good idea. The people who wanted hanging brought back were either too stupid or too ignorant to understand the subtle nuances of sentencing. Fluke really didn't want every paedophile and rapist locked up for life. That was what would be risked if the sentence for murder and rape was the same. Tough on crime? The only people it would be tough on would be the victims.

She said nothing in reply, and Fluke got the feeling she'd already known the answer and she was, in her own way, showing up the fools surrounding them.

'In other words, not having capital punishment saves lives. It's as simple as that,' he added.

That seemed to kill the atmosphere, such as it was. The woman raised her glass to him and winked. Fluke noticed she was drinking water.

So, not everyone in the room is drunk.

The rest of the night passed uneventfully, with everyone, including the woman, leaving Fluke alone. By eleven o'clock, he was feeling sober again and had the beginnings of a headache. By half-past eleven it had turned into a full-blown hangover and all he wanted to do was go to bed and get ready for the post-mortem the next day. Michelle had other ideas.

'We need to talk,' she said, as soon as the last guest had left.

That was all he needed. Another row about the same thing. He didn't like her friends and they didn't like him. Sometimes he thought that Michelle only tolerated him because it had seemed glamorous to go out with someone who investigated murder for a living. A year into the relationship, though, and she'd realised that there was nothing glamorous about the job or him. He was sure he'd let her down somehow. He just didn't know how. And worst of all, he didn't care enough to find out. 'Can we do this tomorrow? I've had a bit of a day.'

She was strangely calm, far calmer than on the previous occasions they'd discussed his lack of social graces. 'No, Avison, we can't. I don't think there should be a tomorrow.'

Fluke said nothing. He knew it had been on the cards. They hadn't been getting on for a while now. Looking back, he wondered if they ever had. For her, he'd been a talking point among her friends; for him, it had been easier to say yes when she asked him out than think of a reason to say no. If he was honest, he felt relieved. 'I'll take the sofa, I'll be gone by the time you wake up.'

She looked at him. The anger was there now, bubbling under the surface, ready to erupt at the slightest provocation. Perhaps she wanted one final argument. Perhaps she was angry he'd taken it so calmly, that he hadn't wanted to fight for her. 'Will you fuck,' she snarled. 'You think I want you in this house after you humiliated Ian like that? I want you out now.'

Fluke nearly replied that Ian had humiliated himself but instead he reached for his coat and left without another word. It dawned on him that he hadn't noticed Ian leave and wondered if that was the real reason she was so keen to get him out.

'And when were you *ever* here after I woke up?' she screamed at his retreating back, before slamming the door.

Fluke had a dilemma. He'd drunk too much to drive and lived too far away for a taxi. He had no choice but to sleep in his car. He fumbled in his coat for his keys.

'I hope you're not planning to drive, Inspector?'

Fluke turned round. The woman from the dinner party was leaning against the bonnet of her car, smoking a cigarette and blowing thick plumes into the freezing night air. She was smiling.

'Just getting something out the car,' he replied.

She obviously recognised that as the lie it was. She raised her eyebrows. 'And that was Michelle shouting, "Hurry back" before she slammed the door on you, was it?'

'She's just in a bad mood is all. She gets like this sometimes,' he mumbled, embarrassed.

'What, you thought you were just going to say sorry and make up did you? Have you not met her before?' she asked.

For some reason he felt he should stick up for her. 'She's right, I was wrong. They're her friends and I'm always rude to them. She'll be all right in a couple of days.'

'She won't, Avison, you must know that. This was a make or break dinner for you tonight, and you, my grumpy friend, broke it.' She was still smiling as she talked. 'I wonder why you don't seem too bothered. Is it because, apart from you and I, everyone in there tonight was an absolute arsehole?' She held up her hand as Fluke started to protest. 'Michelle's the worst one. Anyone could see you were dead on your feet and upset about something. They deserved everything you gave them.'

'Yeah, well, what's happened has happened,' he said, as if that was any sort of explanation. 'Who are you, anyway? You don't seem Michelle's usual type of friend.'

'I'm the person giving you a lift home tonight.'

Chapter 7

Fluke was woken early by his hangover. He was drained but raring to go on the first full day of the investigation. Moving day, he called it. By the evening he hoped to have a sense of where they were going, whether they were in it for the long haul, whether he'd need more resources or whether he could release some.

He brushed his teeth, rinsed and spat. He looked down into the sink. There was even more blood than usual. Probably due to the excessive alcohol intake of the night before. The MedicAlert bracelet that Doctor Cooper had given him, and which he never wore, sat next to his toothpaste, mocking him. He checked the back of his hand and saw what he expected. It was heavily bruised where the cannula had been.

If his blood was that thin, he'd best avoid taking aspirin. He was going to have to tough out his hangover.

He started his coffee machine then quickly showered. By the time he was out, the coffee was ready and Fluke poured himself a large cup, black. He took it back into the bathroom so he could drink while he shaved.

A late night and early start meant that the face he saw in the mirror was even more haggard looking than usual. He was only forty but his dark hair was already salted with grey. He rubbed his dark stubble before smothering his face with shaving gel.

He picked up his razor, looked at it and put it back down. He couldn't risk getting a nick – it would take hours to heal. Perhaps he should have stayed for the plasma after all. He clearly needed it. He reached for his facecloth and removed the gel. He picked up his electric shaver and pushed the on button. It buzzed into life and he looked into the mirror as he ran the whirring blades over his chin.

His most striking feature stared back in the reflection. Normal to him, fascinating to others.

Fluke had heterochromia. His eyes were different colours. One was a vivid blue; the other was multi-coloured, dark green from any distance over five feet. Sometimes he could see people looking at him uneasily, aware something wasn't quite right but not able to put their finger on it. Subliminal unease, he called it.

Fluke was occasionally able to use it to good effect in interviews but most of the time he simply forgot about it. At school, an older boy, trying to impress some girls, called him 'lighthouse' once. Fluke had broken his nose and the nickname hadn't stuck although 'flat face' had for the bully.

As he shaved he thought about the surreal ride home with the mystery woman. He'd accepted the lift readily, a night on the backseat of his car hadn't appealed to him. Despite asking her, he still didn't know her name although she seemed to know all about him. They didn't discuss Michelle again or what had happened at the dinner party. Instead, they'd fallen into an easy conversation about their jobs. She was a solicitor specialising in international law and they both understood crime, albeit they approached it from different perspectives. Fluke's job was to catch criminals and hers was to get them off, except her criminals tended to be countries. Although his head had been a little fuzzy, he couldn't recall having had such a challenging and stimulating conversation for a long time.

It was only when they were about two miles from his house that he realised he hadn't given her any directions. She seemed to know roughly where he lived and only asked for help when the small road they were on turned into a succession of dirt tracks.

'Every time you see a smaller track, take it,' he'd told her.

Eventually, Fluke had been able to point her in the direction of his own road and she'd pulled up next to his house.

He'd got out of the car but before he could ask her in for a nightcap, she'd smiled enigmatically, waved once and drove off. When her car got to the end of his track, she honked the horn and drove away. He stood and stared, bemused, wondering if he'd ever see her again. He watched the retreating headlights until they disappeared, then pulled out his phone and rang Towler to arrange a lift into town to collect his car first thing.

He finished shaving and drained his coffee. Finding something to wear that didn't have mud on, he got dressed. Using his bedroom mirror, he fastened a cheap tie. Even he thought he looked unkempt. It wasn't that he dressed badly, it was just that anything he wore immediately looked scruffy. Losing so much weight so quickly hadn't helped. Towler used to call him a typical fat marine. He hadn't been, of course, he'd been on the right side of stocky. As an ex-marine, an elite force trained to march huge distances with heavy loads, he'd been extremely fit. Now his clothes hung from him like he was a child playing dress-up.

Back in his kitchen, he filled his travel mug with the rest of the coffee, remembering to turn off the machine. He'd lost count of the number of times he'd forgotten and come back to a solid, coffee-smelling mess on the bottom of another ruined jug. He went through five or six a year. He was debating whether or not he had time to sit on his porch and drink it when he heard a car pulling up.

Towler. They had a post-mortem to attend.

For the second time in two days, Fluke found himself at the Cumberland Infirmary. He decided he'd go and see Doctor Cooper after the PM; he didn't feel as though he could fob her off twice in two days. He stuck his head round the door in the ward to tell a nurse he'd be with her in a couple of hours. She promised to pass on the message.

Fluke walked down the stairs. The mortuary was in the basement of the hospital as most are. He flashed his badge at the elderly man in the office and was waved through. He'd been there enough times for all the staff to know him. Carlisle didn't have a dedicated forensic mortuary – there wasn't the demand for full-time specialist facilities like that in Cumbria – so one of the post-mortem suites had to be adapted every time the coroner requested a forensic examination. It didn't have the glass viewing rooms some did, so he would have to be in the same room as Sowerby.

The suite Sowerby was using was typical of all mortuaries. Fluke shivered. He could feel the air conditioning and hear the hum of the huge fridges that stored the cadavers. They were permanently turned on. Fluke knew bodies could be stored indefinitely at minus 20°C, and as the only hospital for forty miles, it was never short of business.

The room had an unpleasant personality all of its own. It smelled of chemicals and detergents. There were large sinks, drains and sluices, a room that had to dispose of large amounts of liquid; liquid from disassembled bodies.

White-tiled floor and white-tiled walls; easy to keep clean and sterile, easy to hose down. Laminated notices on the walls detailed actions to be taken in the event of biohazards being discovered. Fluke knew that the PM would take roughly four hours, and by the end, he'd be staring at the posters wondering if bio-emergencies had ever happened here.

It was a room where preserving the dignity of the dead took second place to uncovering their secrets. Fluke hated them.

In the middle, under huge halogen lights, was the dissection table. The body of their victim was already on it, still in the golf bag.

Towler had gone ahead and was there, gowned and with protective coverings on his feet, laughing with Lucy. Fluke didn't want to know about what. Sowerby was discussing something with the mortuary technician. Alan Vaughn was there to act as the exhibits officer, and a SOCO officer Fluke didn't recognise was preparing sample swabs and tubes. Everyone looked ready.

Fluke finished putting on his gown and foot covers, and entered the suite.

'We ready to go then?' Sowerby asked everyone as he walked towards the body.

Sowerby was one of those pathologists who said everything out loud. Instructions, comments and observations were all recorded on the built-in digital system. After some standard introductions of who was present, what the time was and which hospital they were in, he began.

'The body was recovered yesterday at a building site adjacent to the West Cumberland Hospital, in what I am told, was a foundation hole. Preliminary police enquiries suggest that the body had been in situ for no more than twelve hours. It is still in the golf bag it was recovered in. It is covered in mud, consistent with where it was found. Hopefully, whoever put her in it, inadvertently left the victim cleaner than she would have been if she'd simply been interred without it. The golf bag was too big to go into a cadaver bag. I have observed the head only. The body appears to be female. Until I have had a chance to remove the body from the bag, I would not like to estimate age or make a statement on ethnicity.'

Fluke tuned out as Sowerby directed the technician on where to photograph and what external swabs should be taken. At that point, they would only be taking samples of what was accessible: her head. They'd already taken them at the scene but were taking them again as a precaution.

Fluke's mind went into screensaver mode as the routine part of the PM continued. He thought through what the priorities were going to be in the early stages of the investigation. Clearly identifying the body was going to be key, and Fluke hoped it would be easy. With an identification, a list of people to interview could be drawn up. And with a list of people to interview, a suspect list could be drawn up. The rest was normally a slam-dunk.

Normally.

Although Fluke still couldn't rule out a domestic homicide, he knew that in reality he was looking for something different. It looked too professional to have been committed in the heat of the moment. While Fluke had been making arrangements to see Doctor Cooper after the post-mortem, Towler had received a phone call from Jo Skelton. She'd finished setting up the incident room and had got to work on the misper list. Early indications were that the victim wasn't a Cumbrian. Skelton was widening the enquiry to cover the whole of the UK but it would take time. Fluke would get a photo of the victim's head to help her as soon as he could.

The foundation hole was obviously a deposition site, and therefore the second priority was to find the murder scene.

Finding the person who wrote the note also needed to happen fast and Fluke expected a fingerprint match by the time the PM finished. It was inconceivable that a chaotic heroin addict would be unknown to the police.

After the photographs, Sowerby and the technician struggled to remove her from the golf bag. 'Some *rigor mortis* is evident,'

Sowerby said. He paused and picked up some heavy-duty shears. 'Sorry, Avison. I'm going to have to cut the bag to get her out.'

Fluke nodded. It was preferable to damaging any evidence on her body.

Five minutes later, she was laid out on the table and the golf bag was handed over to SOCO to process. As Sowerby had predicted, the bag had protected her from the mud of the building site and she was spotless. *Another break*, Fluke thought.

'Don't forget to check all the pockets that thing has,' Towler told the SOCO. 'I want to know as soon as you find anything.' The SOCO man rolled his eyes. There was an unspoken 'Well, d'uh', that luckily for him, Towler missed.

Fluke looked at her lifeless face and fought the urge to reach out and remove the long hair that had fallen over her eyes. Gravity had emptied her lips of blood. Her eyes were milky and had flattened as they lost liquid. The waxy, almost translucent, skin that Fluke had observed at the site was exaggerated under the powerful lights.

Some detectives tried to keep things as impersonal as they could to maintain objectivity. For Fluke, it was the opposite. He worked at his best when he could make a personal connection with the victim, and looking down at her, Fluke could feel anger building in the pit of his stomach.

He tossed her like garbage.

Sowerby removed her clothing, cutting everything rather than undressing her. It was the best way to preserve evidence. She'd been dressed casually but smartly; trousers and matching jacket. Her shoes were black with small heels and she was wearing stockings. They all went to the SOCO team to process.

Looking down at her naked body, stiff with *rigor* and displayed like a laboratory rat, Fluke guessed she'd be in her mid-thirties. She'd clearly been good-looking, beautiful in fact.

The technician fingerprinted her before taking a series of X-rays. A printer whirred into life in an adjoining room. Although X-rays were digitally viewed during a coroner's post-mortem, there were always hard copies made for the files.

Sowerby and the technician had to massage the body to counteract the *rigor* before they could start the external examination of her front. Fluke had always thought it looked obscene. He knew it had to be done but he decided to look away while they did it. He noticed Towler and Lucy were doing the same. It was a small gesture, but to Fluke it was important. Anything that could be done to preserve her dignity, even in death, was worthwhile. Sowerby started talking again and Fluke turned back round.

'Slight tearing of the vagina, possible recent sexual activity. Can you take a deep swab, please?' Sowerby asked the technician.

He continued with a close examination, speaking into the microphone.

He lifted up her left hand and studied it with a magnifying glass, then put it down. The nails were painted a vibrant turquoise and were beautifully manicured. He picked up the right and did the same. 'Can you get me an evidence bag, please?' Picking up a small scraping tool, he removed something from the underside of her long nails. He put it into a small plastic tube and handed it to Fluke.

Fluke held it up to the light to have a look. It was a tiny grain of something, dark brown. 'Any idea?'

'Not a clue, not for me to speculate either. That's why we have a lab.'

He went back to the body and moved the big overhead light above her head. Fluke handed the tube to the SOCO man who put it into an evidence bag. Out the corner of his eye, Fluke noticed Lucy walk over and ask to see it.

'It's difficult to be sure, but it looks like there's some slight haemorrhaging in the eyes,' Sowerby said, looking at Fluke.

'Strangled?'

'Normally I'd say that's as good a guess as anything right now but there's nothing else to support that. No marks on the neck.'

'What then?' Towler asked.

'Patience, boy. We've only just started. We won't leave here until you and Avison have something,' Sowerby said, not unkindly. Everyone in the room had the same goal.

'Looks like she may have had cosmetic surgery at some point; nose correction, poor one by the look. If they've moved bone around, I'll know more when I open her up. Nothing else of note on the anterior.'

As the body was carefully turned over, Sowerby commented, 'She's been moved after death occurred. No uniform lividity.'

Fluke knew that if a corpse lay undisturbed, *livor mortis,* where blood obeyed the laws of gravity and settled at the lowest point, set in. If someone died on their back then the blood drained from their front and settled underneath before clotting, causing a difference in colour. White on top, purple on the bottom, like cream on raspberries. If the body was moved before the process had finished then lividity was interrupted and *livor* wouldn't be uniform. The victim on the table had purple and white patches competing with each other. She had been moved in the first few hours after her death. It didn't really help; it only confirmed what they already suspected – that the building site wasn't where she'd been killed.

Fluke noticed Lucy had finished looking at whatever had been found under the victim's nails and was back observing. Earlier, he'd wondered if she'd ever attended a PM before. Now he knew.

She was obviously struggling with being in the proximity of a dead body, and he wondered whether she'd asked to see the sample just to take time out. Her eyes were red and glistening but she was yet to cry.

Wait until the bone saw buzzes into life and the top of the head comes off.

In those situations, people sometimes gave up and left. Fluke had experienced it, the embarrassed pause while the person walked out. It shouldn't be, but it was a walk of shame. She appeared determined to stay, however. She was making notes, pages of them, by the look of it. Sowerby had let her have a look at the body before he started with the external examination, and she'd stated there were no signs of insect activity. Fluke would give her a call the next day, find out how she was and what 'no insect activity' meant in her world. He suspected it meant that the victim had been either stuffed in the bag immediately or it had been too cold. It was probably both.

Sowerby glanced up, saw where Fluke was looking and gave him a slight nod of approval.

He bent back down. 'Gotcha,' he said quietly. 'Avison, come over here and have a look.'

Fluke bent over to see what he was pointing at.

'Shit,' he said. The room seemed to get colder.

The bullet hole was in the back of her skull; partially covered by hair but still visible. There was some surrounding blood on the wound which had clotted and was almost black.

'There is a hole in the occipital bone,' Sowerby said for the recorder. 'Possible GSW. Photographs, please.'

The technician moved round with his camera.

Fluke knew Sowerby would say nothing definite until he had cold, hard facts to support it but they all knew; she'd been shot.

Execution style, he thought.

A bullet hole ruled out someone covering up an accidental death. It had been a long shot anyway. FMIT officially had what Fluke had known since midday; a murder to investigate.

Fluke also knew that the bullet hole could reveal a lot more than simply the cause of death. It could reveal the manner by which it was inflicted. It was covered on the SIO course, one of those modules that was fascinating and disturbing at the same time.

Bullets entering from an angle leave an oval-shaped entrance wound. When the gun is held against the body, the wound will be round and have burn marks from the muzzle flame. Short-range shots will leave powder residue tattooed into the skin. Longer-range shots will leave no burns or powder but the hole will be smaller than the bullet calibre, due to the skin's elastic properties. When a gun is pressed against bone and fired, the bone slows the gasses down, forcing them backwards against the skin leaving a star-shaped wound.

Despite the dry blood and hair, the bullet hole was clearly star-shaped.

It was also a small hole.

This wound meant only one thing, Fluke thought. A small calibre gun pressed against the back of his victim's head and fired. Not enough power to go straight through the head or they would have seen the exit wound. The bullet would have bounced round the inside of the skull, shredding the brain. Haemorrhaging the eyes.

A professional killer's weapon.

A professional killer's technique.

No noise, no mess, no chance of survival.

After Sowerby had carefully shaved the surrounding area and measured and photographed the wound, he shouted across to the technician, 'Are those X-rays ready yet, boy?'

'Yes, sir.'

'Get them on the damned light board, man. Stop wasting time.'

The technician ignored the fact he'd been shouted at unfairly and put up the slide of the head.

There was no bullet.

'I don't understand,' Lucy said frowning and craning forward. 'It must be in there.'

'Bullets don't follow straight lines. It could be anywhere. Get the next slide up,' Sowerby said.

'Saw someone shot in the knee in Somalia, once. Bullet came out his arse. Funny as fuck,' Towler said to no one in particular.

'Sergeant Towler,' Fluke said.

'Boss?'

'Shut it.'

Towler grinned and winked at Lucy but didn't say anything more.

They found it on the third plate. In the abdomen.

'There you go, Lucy. Bullet's probably bounced off the inside of the skull, through the roof of the mouth, down the oesophagus into the stomach and into the duodenum. We'll get it later,' Sowerby said.

Despite the spree killer Derek Bird skewing their statistics, Cumbria saw very little crime involving firearms. For Sowerby, who covered Manchester and Liverpool as well as Cumbria, it was routine. 'Right, let's get back to it,' he said.

After the external examination was completed, it was time for the internal. The body was turned back over, the head raised by a body block. Sowerby was going against standard routine and starting at the head rather than the body cavity. He had a probable cause of death and would move quickly to confirm it. He knew Fluke could use the extra time the shortcut would give him.

Fluke was sure he knew what the COD and MOD would be. Cause of death would be the brain injury; manner of death would be a gunshot wound. It was more than they had that morning, although it raised more questions than it answered.

Sowerby picked up a scalpel and made an incision behind one ear, cutting across the top of the head to behind the other ear. As if the victim had been wearing a face mask, he peeled the skin away from the skull in two directions. The front was pulled down, exposing the top of the skull and the face, the other he pulled back, exposing the rear. The skull was bloody but bare.

Fluke knew that Sowerby would remove a wedge-shaped section of the skull to get access to the brain. He turned away not wanting to watch. Once was enough for anyone. He found he didn't want to stay anymore.

There was going to be some routine procedures for the next hour. He'd nip out and see if Doctor Cooper was back so he could apologise for leaving so abruptly the day before.

'Boss?' Towler called after him.

'I need to see someone,' Fluke replied, without turning.

As the Stryker saw buzzed into life, Fluke knew that the pitch would turn into a sickening shriek as it bit into bone. He sped up and was out of earshot before it happened.

Before Fluke had even left the mortuary he'd changed his mind. He wasn't going to be in a position to have more plasma until after the PM anyway. He decided to grab a brew from Costa Coffee in the main foyer rather than have a fight with his haematologist about his disappearing act the day before.

He was in the queue and just about to place his order, when his phone rang. It was Towler. Fluke had only been out of the mortuary for five minutes. 'We've found something,' Towler said.

'In the brain?'

'In the golf bag,' Towler replied.

Fluke sighed, smiled ruefully at the waiting barista and headed back towards the mortuary.

The 'something' was a small notebook.

'SOCO found it in an internal pocket of the bag. There's some other stuff, electronics mainly: a phone, a tablet and a laptop. All smashed to bits and there's no SIM in the phone. The notebook's empty but it looks like the top page has been torn off,' Towler said. 'It could have been already there, I suppose, but despite it being covered in shit, the bag looks brand new to me. If the notebook was put there by the killer then it wasn't meant to be found.'

Fluke didn't know if it was evidence or not but he wasn't taking any chances. 'Right, I want the full works. Tell the lab I'm pre-authorising all the tests they want to do. Get them there tonight. Proper chain of evidence. If there's anything, I want to know by tomorrow at the latest, today if possible. Get uniform to drive them down.'

As Towler went off to arrange a fast-track forensic examination, Fluke turned to Sowerby who was just starting with the 'Y' incision.

'Anything else, Henry?' he asked.

'Nothing really, Avison. We've taken all our external samples now: hair, pubic hair, swabs, the lot. Got prints for you as well. The brown substance under her nails looks like it may have also found its way into the turn-ups of her trousers according to your SOCO man there. The lab will tell you if they're the same. Can't say what it is.'

'Cause of death the gun shot wound then?'

'Technically the cause of death can't be officially determined until I've finished. But yes, the bullet seems to have ricocheted around the inside of the skull causing massive trauma to the brain. That'll almost certainly be the COD. I'll have the bullet with you in five minutes if you can wait.'

'Here till the bitter end, Doc,' Fluke replied.

'Don't you have an appointment with Leah Cooper?'

'What? No. Yes. How did you know?' Fluke said, all semblance of composure gone. He looked round.

'Don't worry, no one heard, Avison. No, I popped into in haematology before I came down here; the professor there is an old friend of mine. Leah asked if you were the senior investigating officer.'

'She seem angry?'

'Not especially, not with you anyway. She told me not to keep you too long, said you had a blood test to do before the day was out. Told her it would take as long as it damn well took. She nearly tore my head off,' he grinned.

If she wasn't angry about the day before he may as well go and get checked now. 'Look, this bit is going to take about two hours, am I right? I'll go and get it over with; Towler'll ring if anything urgent crops up.'

Sowerby didn't look up but waved a hand to let him know it was fine.

Fluke got to the haematology ward and asked for Leah, only to be told by the staff nurse that she'd just left.

'Okay,' he said, relieved. 'Can you leave a message and say I called in, as she asked. I'll come back later.'

'Not happening, Mr Fluke. She left clear instructions that you have to have another blood test today. Very clear instructions. I'll take the blood and run it straight away. You can go after one of the registrars has had a look at it. Unless they say you can't, obviously,' she said.

'Obviously,' he repeated, a bit too sharply.

Two minutes later, Fluke had a doctor trying to stick a cannula in the back of his hand. The first two attempts missed.

Fluke hated cannulas. Doctors always struggled to find veins, a legacy of his treatment. On the odd occasion he was having blood taken by someone who wasn't familiar with his medical history, he always ended up giving an explanation. The most common reason for poor veins was intravenous drug use and Fluke felt compelled to tell them his condition was due to chemotherapy, not heroin.

His hand would be stiff in the morning. It was getting to the point that every time he had his bloods taken, his hand froze up during the night. *Or it could just be that I'm getting old*, he thought. Today it was the turn of a small Asian doctor he'd seen around on the ward but had never spoken to, one of the multitude of junior doctors hospitals seemed to spawn.

'Sharp scratch,' she said, as she tried again.

Chapter 8

'Sharp scratch.'

Fluke vividly remembered the first time he'd heard that phrase. It was at the Patterdale Ward in the West Cumberland Hospital nearly two years ago. He'd thought then what an odd phrase it was, to describe a needle puncturing flesh as a scratch, and he still thought it now. And they all said it: doctors, nurses, phlebotomists, the lot. He assumed it was part of some blood-letting course. Or it could be the same as detectives picking up evidence with pens. Monkey see, monkey do. The first doctor to say it had no idea he'd started a global phenomenon.

At the time, the only thing on Fluke's mind had been getting out of a relationship that had run its course. Hayley, a nice woman, recently divorced and trying to rediscover her youth, but she needed someone younger. Someone who still wanted to go out Friday and Saturday nights. Fluke wasn't that man.

She'd phoned earlier asking if they could go out and Fluke had lied, saying he wasn't feeling well. He'd reheated the previous night's corned beef hash and settled down in front of the TV for the night. And in truth, he'd been feeling a bit unwell; a sore stomach that had been bothering him for some time. Not enough for painkillers, but enough for him to go and see his GP.

But she'd called his bluff and turned up anyway. She took one look and called the emergency doctor's number. Fluke would never know whether she'd been trying to make a point or she genuinely thought he looked ill. He'd been using the 'too ill' excuse more and more to get out of things.

Whatever her real motivation, he'd been given an immediate appointment. Despite living in Carlisle, the out-of-hours appointment was thirty-five miles away at the old Workington Hospital. Trapped in his own lie, he'd no choice but to play along and attend. She'd even driven him there.

Lying on a bed in a ward that wouldn't have looked out of place in a Hammer Horror film, Fluke had been expecting the standard 'I can't find anything, see your GP if it persists', medical terminology for 'fuck off and stop wasting our time'.

That wasn't what was in Fluke's immediate future, however – the doctor found something. And he hadn't had to look too hard either. His lower right abdomen was as hard as iron. When he felt it, he was amazed he hadn't noticed it himself. Looking back he remembered small things though; favouring the same side when he slept, not being hungry, heartburn.

Small things, big problems.

Admitted to hospital that same night, he was nil-by-mouth and subjected to a battery of tests. Ultra-sound, X-Ray, endoscopy, colonoscopy, bloods, urine, Fluke had the lot while the doctors stood round scratching their heads – they knew something was wrong but they didn't know what.

It wasn't solved until they rolled out the big gun. The dark mass the MRI found was obvious, even to the untrained eye. A dark mass that had insidiously wrapped itself round one of his kidneys and part of his bowel.

To Fluke's amazement, he was then discharged, booked in for a biopsy a week later and told not to worry in the meantime. At a loss what to do, he went back to work.

A week later, he was back, signing consent forms allowing a surgeon to basically do what he felt was best if a biopsy wasn't going to be enough when he opened him up. He confirmed to the anaesthesiologist he wasn't allergic to anything then went into surgery.

As with any other surgery he had no idea how long he had been under, but when Fluke woke he was told he'd undergone an eight-hour operation involving two surgical teams. With the anaesthetics starting to wear off, the pain began and it was through a cocktail of painkilling medication that Fluke learned he no longer had a right kidney, part of his bowel had been cut out and that a grapefruit-sized tumour had been removed. His wound stretched from the centre of chest to his navel and had over fifty staples holding it together. It looked like an eighteen-inch crude zip.

Two days in intensive care for pain management, two weeks on the gastro ward with a group of old men, an argument with the hospital social worker which ended with her in tears after he told her to mind her own business, and he was discharged.

While waiting for the biopsy results, during one of the daily visits from the district nurse to look after the wound, he'd begun vomiting – uncontrollable vomiting that lasted for two days – nothing stayed down, not water, not the painkillers he tried to take to manage the terrible headache the dehydration was causing. The district nurse finally had enough and called an ambulance.

That's when Doctor Leah Cooper came into his life. She introduced herself as his oncologist and that she was in charge of his treatment. A serious woman doing a serious job, she sat next to the raised bed and told him what he already knew; he had cancer. A classic case of Burkitt's Lymphoma, she'd told him. Usually confined to the jaws of children on the African continent, it was very rare in the Western world.

At least they'd heard of it, he'd thought. *Nobody wanted an illness with no name. Ah, Mr Jones, you have a bad case of Fluke's Disease.*

There was good and bad news. Because it was such an aggressive cancer, paradoxically, it was curable. The faster they grow the faster they can kill it, Doctor Cooper told him. The bad news was that the treatment was the worst there was. There was a very real chance that it would kill him. And it had to be delivered, as an inpatient, in an isolation ward.

Fluke remembered barely batting an eyelid. He wasn't stupid. He wasn't expecting her to say, 'Take two of these and go home.' Cancer was a word that struck dread into even the calmest of people, yet Fluke's reaction, she admitted much later, had surprised her.

'Okay, now what?' he'd said.

She'd explained that due to the complexity of the treatment, he'd have to be transferred to Newcastle, where the haematologist had a full support team of specialist registrars, house doctors and senior fellows. Cumbria just didn't have the resources or the need for a team that size. She'd remain his consultant but the treatment would be delivered by others. She'd attend fortnightly case meetings, be consulted on his care and, if he survived, would deliver his aftercare for the next ten years.

'So when do I go?' he'd asked, wondering how long he'd have to tie up loose ends at work.

'An hour. They're expecting you by six and you'll start your chemotherapy tonight.'

'Hang on,' he'd protested, before she cut him off.

'No arguments. The tumour we removed a fortnight ago has already grown back to the size of a tennis ball. That's why you've been vomiting. It's wrapped round your small intestine.' There was a finality to what she said next. 'We start fighting this thing now.'

A taxi drove him the hour and a half to the Royal Victoria Infirmary, known locally as the RVI, and there he'd stayed for five months.

For five months, he'd taken everything they threw at him: chemotherapy drugs that were bright green and made his hair fall out; drugs that were light sensitive and had to be kept in a bag; drugs that ruined his nerve endings through weekly intrathecal injections into the base of his spine. Some of the drugs were so complex, they needed drugs of their own to work.

Chemotherapy to kill him. Antibiotics and antifungals to keep him alive. Fluke took it all without complaint. He had a Hickman line fitted into one of the large veins in the chest as the drugs were destroying his smaller veins and for months he walked round with a plastic tube sticking out of his chest.

Each day was a learning experience on a course he hadn't signed up for.

The only way to destroy the cancer was to destroy him. The team took him as close to death as they dared then stopped and let him build up his bloods and health only to do it all over again. Three courses of treatment. Three times he was taken to the brink.

Finally, the scans showed that it had worked. His bloods were allowed to build up. Physios got to work on teaching him to walk with his nerve-damaged legs. Visitors were allowed in his room without wearing face masks. He was allowed to see his newborn nephew for the first time.

He'd been a fit man when he'd been admitted, an ex-Royal Marine, and while he was never in the same league as Towler – who was a freak of nature – the job meant he had to stay in decent shape. He left hospital a shell of a man, down to eleven stones and unable to walk without crutches and splints. He was too weak to cook but that was okay as he had no appetite.

Doctor Cooper told him it was normal. His appetite would come back. The Burkitt's wouldn't.

After nearly six months in hospital and three months of recuperation at home, putting up with well-wishers, genuine and nosey, he was ready to go back to work. Some of his strength had returned. His appetite was back. His legs were still troubling him but he kept that to himself.

One good thing had happened during his illness: Hayley decided that she didn't need the hassle of looking after anyone at her stage of life and had broken it off in his first month of treatment. Fluke didn't blame her, although others did.

He still had to see Doctor Cooper – would have to for the next ten years – every week to begin with, to get his bloods checked and his lymph nodes poked. He discussed with Occupational Health a return to work date.

In the past, someone who was off sick either ran out of sick notes and had to come back, or just decided they were fit to return and turned up.

For Fluke there were meetings with Occupational Health, with Chambers, and even the chief constable, all glad he was feeling better, all doubting he was ready. He rejected out of hand an offer of a temporary desk job.

In the end, it had taken a letter from Leah stating that he was fit to return to operational duties. Straight into the job he had nine months before: Detective Inspector, Force Major Incident Team.

Chapter 9

Fluke sat in the dayroom on the haematology ward, lost in his thoughts, while he waited for his blood test results. It obviously wasn't the right time of day for outpatients; he was the only one in there. He picked up a discarded travel magazine and flicked through it, staring at the beaches, at the five-star hotels and stunning views. It all looked so nice, but Fluke couldn't help looking past the smiles and the sunshine. Most of those tropical islands were plagued with poverty and crime. *It's the lot of the policeman*, he thought, *to see the worst of everything*. He threw it back down on the seat beside him.

You sure sucked the fun out of that, Avison.

A nurse stuck her head in the room and told him Doctor Cooper wanted to speak to him. She passed him a cordless phone.

'Doctor Cooper,' he said.

'Good morning, Avison. You made it, then? Sorry I missed you, but I'm on nights.'

'No problem. I was here anyway, as you know. PM on a girl found in West Cumbria this morning. I'll need to get back actually, he can't be far from finished.'

'That's what I rang for. Your results are in and they're fine. Your platelets are still low and you refusing plasma hasn't helped. Your haemoglobin's nearer where it should be, though. Your bloods are never going to be brilliant, not after what your bone marrow went through, but for now I'm happy to let you go.'

'And yesterday?'

'Already forgotten about, under the circumstances, but don't do it again, Avison. If you absolutely have to go, call someone, for God's sake. This isn't a prison, we can't stop you leaving. Now, go and catch him.'

Fluke was already on his feet, trying to get someone's attention, pointing at his cannula. There was no way he was going to try and take it out himself again. He didn't think he'd get away with it twice.

'Cheers, Doc. Do I need another appointment?'

'I'll get something out in the post but I want to keep an eye on you for a while. It'll probably be next week.'

Fluke thanked her and put down the phone.

As he made his way back down to the mortuary, he wondered why she'd phoned him. Anyone could have told him his results.

Sowerby had finished sewing up the 'Y' cut when Fluke returned and was just calling out some last-minute remarks to the overhead microphones.

'Ah, Avison,' he called when he saw him. 'Just finishing up here.'

'What we got, Henry?' Fluke asked.

'I'll have an interim report with you by lunchtime tomorrow and the full report by the end of the week, but I can do you a verbal?'

'Please.'

'We were right, of course, the bullet to the head killed her. I traced the path. Kept quite a neat line really; entered the back of the skull at the point of the bullet hole, obviously. Went straight through the brain tissue and hit the front of the skull just about here,' he said, pointing to his own head where the nose met the forehead. 'You'll notice this part here is quite thick. The bullet bounced down, through more brain tissue, through the roof of the mouth, as we thought. Of course, it probably started to lose shape by then so the wound on the mouth is larger than the entrance wound on the skull.'

'So she swallowed it?' Fluke said.

'Oh no, she was dead instantly. It was gravity. It probably worked its way into the stomach fairly quickly. I estimate she'd have to be upright after she was shot for three seconds at least for this to happen. When it worked its way into the duodenum is anyone's guess. Could have been immediately, could have been when she was moved.'

'Can I see the bullet?'

The bullet was in an unsealed bag as Towler had assumed Fluke would want to see it before it went off to ballistics for a possible match and a point towards the weapon used to fire it. The SOCO man carefully lifted it out with evidence tongs. It was horribly misshapen but still looked small. It had blood and other body matters on it. It wouldn't be cleaned until it got to the lab.

Fluke turned to Towler. '.22?'

'That's my guess. And I'm not really guessing either unless it's something really exotic. No, this is a .22. Low power, judging by the shape of it.'

'How so, Sergeant?' asked Lucy.

'The British Army, along with most of NATO use .22 ammunition in their assault rifles only they call it 5.56mm. They're high powered and have a tapered point for accuracy. A bullet like that it wouldn't have bounced. At that range, it would've gone straight through her head with no deviation in trajectory. Would have carried on for another five hundred yards unless something hard stopped it,' Towler said. 'This is low-powered and the naughty end is rounded, designed for short-range work where accuracy isn't important. The bullet's supposed to go in and stay in.'

'Any idea what fired it?' Fluke asked.

'Nah. No way of telling yet. It'll be a small weapon, even for a handgun,' he said. 'Easy to hide, deadly at close range. Not designed for deterrence, more for self-defence. This is about having the shot no one is expecting. Has to be used up close. It would probably bounce off someone at twenty yards. Easy to keep in a handbag or pocket. Ideal for a killer.'

'How do you know all this?' Lucy asked, with a look of incredulity.

Towler was intelligent but hid it well. Even if he hadn't been, this was his area of expertise. 'Misspent youth, Lucy. Illegal in this country, of course,' he said. 'You can't get guns over here that easily, despite what the press say, and this type even less. No demand for it. The gangbangers in Manchester and London want the bling weapons, the status symbols. Why have a gun if you can't show it off? The hard-core organised crime lot want military-grade weapons. The SIGs and the H&Ks. No one wants a tiny .22, they'd be laughed at.'

'We'll get it off to the National Ballistics Intelligence Service's Manchester hub tonight,' Fluke said. 'Matt, get someone to escort it there. Get traffic to take them in one of their pursuit vehicles. I want this with them in two hours. We'll see if they've seen this gun before.' NBIS held details on all firearms and bullets recovered from crimes in the UK. If the gun had been used before, NBIS would know.

'What else we got, Henry?' he asked as Towler went off to arrange a night on the M6 for one of FMIT's DCs.

'Couple of things but nothing significant, really. There was an absence of fall injuries which is unusual. The momentum of the bullet should have sent her falling forwards rather than crumpling to the ground. I would have expected an injury, probably on the head, but there wasn't. No bruising on the arms, wrists or feet. She wasn't restrained or tied up.'

'Held as she was shot?' Fluke said.

'Possibly, can't say definitely, of course, but it fits the facts. It would explain how the bullet had time to travel down to the stomach as well.'

Fluke filed it away for the future. 'TOD?'

'I'm putting the time of death down at around thirty to forty hours ago. *Rigor mortis* was reducing. Temperature of the liver gave me a good indication. Monday was a cold night.'

Fluke knew that the body lost 1.5°C each hour after death and kept losing it until it was the same temperature as its environment. That's why Sowerby had taken the ambient temperature when he got in the hole. If it was 0°C, it would take the average human twenty-five hours to get to the same temperature.

So, she'd been killed between ten o'clock Monday night and eight o'clock Tuesday morning. Sowerby had said she was standing when she was shot. Fluke thought it unlikely she was killed too close to the foreman starting work and most people are asleep by midnight. His instincts were telling him she'd been killed Monday night and disposed of a few hours later. More evidence of the well-planned work of a professional.

'Anything else?'

'She'd had cosmetic surgery, but I was wrong. It wasn't a botched job at all. Quite the opposite.'

'The nose?' Fluke asked.

'Not just the nose. She'd had four separate corrective procedures. All on her face. And I'm loathe to call them corrective procedures.'

'Why.'

'It was Lucy who pointed it out initially. Noticed that it didn't seem to add up.' Sowerby took off his glasses, brushed some errant hair away from his eyes and taking a sheet of mortuary blue paper towel, wiped his face. 'You understand the basic premise of cosmetic surgery, of course?'

'Sucking fat out of salad dodgers and making the rich look thirty instead of sixty,' Towler said, walking back.

'Yes, well, there's a lot of that, obviously. It's their core business despite what they say. They're in the vanity trade whether they'll admit it or not. They say they are there to improve self-esteem and to help reconstruct people after accidents, but only a few actually believe their own press,' Sowerby said.

'Seems to be a bit of a waste. Especially with a girl like this. She didn't need plastic surgery,' Fluke said.

'No, she didn't. And that's the point. Lucy pointed out that the rhinoplasty, when we actually had a proper look, wasn't correcting anything, either medical or cosmetic. Can't say so in court, but I'm certain the rhinoplasty was done to make her nose look worse, not better. Certainly has more of a point than it had originally.'

Fluke knew that Sowerby couldn't comment on the relative attractiveness of someone. The defence would discredit him without breaking sweat. Between those four walls, his opinion was valid though. If he said the nose was made to look worse, then Fluke believed him.

Sowerby continued. 'This was quality work, expensive work. That's why we missed the rest on the external. You aren't supposed to see good quality work, defeats the illusion of natural youth.'

'What else was there? I can't see anything,' Fluke said, leaning forward and studying her face.

Sowerby passed him a magnifying glass.

He first pointed to her ears. 'See here, there's some very faint scarring. She's had them remodelled. I don't think they've been reduced or pinned back either which is the normal reason someone would get them done. I think they've been made to look different.'

Fluke could see where he was going; a nose job that detracted rather than enhanced her looks, and an ear job that she didn't need. As Sowerby walked him through a chin implant and brow lift that would have changed the shape of her face, the pattern was obvious.

Lying before him was a woman who had taken extreme lengths to disguise her appearance. 'Are these reversible?' he asked.

Sowerby gave it some thought. 'I'm not an expert in this, you understand. Medically speaking, I see no reason why the chin implant couldn't be removed and the brow lift reversed. They've removed cartilage and bone from the ears so no, that's irreversible. As for the rhinoplasty, I don't know. Possibly.'

That's drastic, Fluke thought. There were many reasons why a woman might try and hide who she was. Not all of them were illegal. 'Any idea when this was done, Henry?'

'At least twelve months ago. All the wounds have fully healed. Impossible to say after that. If pushed, I'll say not that long though. The scars would fade after time and they haven't. But it's not an exact science.'

'Anyway to identify the surgeon?' Fluke asked.

'Not a chance. Could be anyone and anywhere. The implants don't have serial numbers. It may not have been done in the UK,' Sowerby said.

Cosmetic surgery was one thing. There were other ways to hide your appearance. Less permanent measures. 'Was she naturally dark-haired?' he asked.

'Platinum blonde, I think Lucy called it. Light blonde to you and me. The roots were just coming through. Her pubic hair was dyed the same colour as her head.'

Towler was out of earshot thankfully. If he hadn't been, there wasn't a disciplinary policy in the world that would have stopped him making a cuffs-and-collar joke.

'Any other way she was trying to disguise herself?' Fluke said. 'A false moustache perhaps, a—'

'Contact lenses,' Sowerby said, interrupting Fluke's sarcastic flow.

'What?'

'Her eyes are blue, not green, coloured contacts. SOCO has them if you want a look, but they're fairly common.'

Extensive cosmetic surgery. Dyed hair and coloured contact lenses. An appearance altered and not for the better. Sowerby was right, a subjective view of her beauty couldn't be recorded anywhere official. Fluke was paid to make deductions based on facts, however, and there were two blindingly obvious ones. She'd been murdered and she'd been hiding from someone.

But who from?

'There's nothing common about this case, Henry,' Fluke said. He looked down at the pale body. 'Who was after you, sweetheart?'

Chapter 10

The post-mortem finished with no new information and Fluke headed back to HQ. Twenty minutes later he pulled into his designated space at Carleton Hall. He decided to go for a quick walk round the grounds to clear his head, get the smell of the mortuary off his clothes.

The sky was grey and Carleton Hall looked eerie in the pale light. A huge red sandstone building accessible only by driving underneath the A66, it was Grade II listed and had extensive grounds. It was unfit for modern policing; poor communications, not enough room and nowhere near enough parking, like a furnace in summer and a cryogenic tomb in winter.

Fluke loved it. Loved the grandeur of it, its lines, the high ceilings, the ornate carvings on the wood panels, loved the countryside it was set in. Of course, things had been added as the years had passed. The Public Protection Unit had their own extension. Armed Response and the Dogs Unit were in separate buildings a few hundred yards away. But FMIT were in the main building.

As he wandered the gravel paths, he ran through what he needed to do. He needed an ID on the witness and he expected it that day. It would be the first hard intelligence they got back. He'd never met an addict without a record.

He also needed an ID on the victim and wasn't convinced it was going to be easy. Not after what he'd just seen at the PM. For now, she was a Jane Doe.

With luck, NBIS would come back with a positive line of enquiry on the bullet they'd sent but he wasn't sure how much help it would be. Firearms were rare in Cumbria, so it would have been obtained elsewhere in the country.

He needed someone to start working the forensic evidence. There was a lot taken from the scene. There were clothes, the notepad and the phone, and he wanted someone he trusted doing it. Jo Skelton fitted the bill.

Fluke also needed the actual murder scene since he knew West Cumberland Hospital was only the deposition site. He knew it might not be in Cumbria and if it was found elsewhere, there could be a jurisdiction issue.

It would almost certainly be a dead end, but someone had to chase up the cosmetic surgery lead. On top of that, all the routine stuff that had already started – the house-to-house enquiries, the fingertip searches, the passive data requests – needed to continue.

He sighed and headed back up to the main building. With two major investigations running, FMIT was noisy; half the robbery team were still at their desks.

The three FMIT officers working the murder and a couple of SOCOs were waiting for him.

Both incident room doors were open, phones were ringing, and there was the steady babble of noise heard whenever lots of people are talking at the same time. Fluke shut their door and thankfully the sound subsided. Jo had obviously kicked out some of the robbery team to make way for them. The room smelt of takeaway food, curries and pizzas predominantly, as incident rooms always did. There wasn't a salad to be seen. Fluke's stomach reminded him that he hadn't eaten since breakfast and he picked up a spoon and an unguarded tray of curry. It was cold, greasy and delicious.

He didn't know how much Towler had told them, but he'd go through it all again from the start. He pinned up a selection of crime scene and post-mortem pictures. The mood changed instantly. That was the first time most of them had seen the victim.

'We have a white female found in a hole at the crime scene most of you were at yesterday. Matt and I have just come back from the PM and we can confirm what you'll no doubt have heard on the grapevine. She was killed by a single gunshot to the back of the head. It's likely the gun was pressed against her skull then fired, execution style. No spray and pray here.'

He paused while they digested what he'd said.

'We're working on an interim theory that it was an easily concealed, small-calibre weapon based on the entrance wound, but we'll know more tomorrow. So remember your firearms procedures when you're closing in on suspects.'

'The victim has had extensive cosmetic surgery and our working theory is that she was trying to drastically change her appearance for reasons unknown. Possibly she was hiding from someone. Our number one priority therefore is identifying her. Until we know who she is, everything else'll be a nightmare.'

'You want her picture released, boss?' Jo Skelton asked.

Fluke thought about it before saying, 'No, Jo, not until we understand who she was hiding from. We can't predict the consequences of releasing it just yet.'

'We're looking at a pro,' Towler added. 'He seems to have been unlucky with a junkie tramp seeing him dump the body, but everything else seems to have been well executed, pardon my pun.'

'Matt's right, we think it was well planned. It's possible it had been rehearsed. It's also possible she wasn't killed in Cumbria, had never been to Cumbria, that the killer doesn't live in Cumbria and has already left the country.'

He took his time to look at the team, all faces pointed his way. A daunting task that was going to consume their lives over the next few days had been laid out before them. Some looked eager and some resigned to the long slog. Others looked apprehensive.

'Now, before Matt does the tasking, I will say one thing, and if you ask me outside this room, I'll deny it. Take my warning about personal safety seriously. I'm convinced we are looking for a professional killer.'

Fluke thought Chambers was a dick but he was technically in charge of FMIT and therefore had the right to be kept up to date. He made his way up the stairs to his office. It didn't occur to him that Chambers wouldn't be there; he wasn't called the 'Eternal Flame' for nothing – he never went out. Fluke was just about to knock when his phone vibrated in his pocket, letting him know he'd a text message. He pulled it out, wondering if it was from Michelle. Although he was glad it was finally over, it had been a sad way to end it.

But the text wasn't from Michelle, it was from Alan Vaughn.

Positive ID on the fingerprint on the coke can, boss.

Fluke turned round and left. This was important, Chambers could be briefed anytime.

When Fluke got back to the incident room, Alan Vaughn passed him the results of IDENT 1, the national automated fingerprint system that all police forces are connected to.

'No doubt, it's him. The prints SOCO lifted were excellent quality. They got another nine hits for him from inside the cabin as well.'

'Darren Ackley. Who's he?'

Vaughn handed him a thin file. Fluke knew it would be thicker by the end of the day as intel was added.

'Some scrote over in Whitehaven. There's a local DC who'll meet you and Matt at the station,' Vaughn said. 'Seems she works with those involved in the sex trade.'

'He's a rent boy?' Fluke was surprised. He'd been expecting an everyday junkie. A rent boy was exotic for Cumbria.

'"Survival sex worker", she calls him.'

Fluke grunted. Sex worker, gigolo, rent boy or survival sex worker. He was his only witness to a murder. 'She know where to find him?'

'You'd fucking think so, wouldn't you. But they haven't got a clue, useless bastards,' said a voice from behind him.

'You up for a drive, Matt?' Fluke asked, without turning round.

Half an hour later they were on the road heading to Whitehaven. Normally Fluke would have asked the officer who knew Ackley to come to HQ, but as the day was probably going to be spent in West Cumbria anyway, they decided to drive out.

Towler drove so Fluke could read the Police National Computer and SLEUTH intelligence on Darren Ackley.

PNC showed a few convictions, mainly shop theft. He was twenty-five and all his convictions had come in the previous four years – when his addiction started, in all likelihood.

The other printout was more interesting. While PNC recorded arrests and convictions, SLEUTH recorded intelligence.

As someone who worked in the sex trade, the intelligence on Ackley was impressive. Any sighting of him, any time he was searched, who he was with, which cars he was in, where he was living, it was all there.

Fluke stopped reading as they passed Bassenthwaite Lake. He looked to his left and saw the Bishop's Stone, seven hundred feet up Barf Mountain. It was one of Fluke's favourite stories and was typical of why he loved Cumbria so much. The tale of how the Bishop of Derry in 1783 drunkenly bet locals in the pub he could ride his donkey to the top of the mountain was legendary. The seven-feet-high whitewashed stone marked how far he'd climbed before he fell to his death. A smaller stone at the base of the mountain marked where he was buried.

Fluke turned back to the file as they passed Bishop's Stone and headed towards Cockermouth, his old stomping ground. 'You read this, Matt?'

'Skimmed it. Why?'

'There's nothing for the last two weeks. Seems to have dropped off the grid. I reckon he's been in that site office since then.'

Towler paused. 'Yeah, I'll buy that,' he said. 'He'll be shitting himself now, though. He won't be back tonight. He's not gonna be easy to find.'

'We'll get some local help,' Fluke said.

He grunted. 'A day spent chasing a rent boy round West Cumbria,' he replied. 'It's the fucking glamour I like in this job.'

They arrived at Whitehaven an hour after they'd left Carlton Hall. The police station was in the centre of town, only a few hundred yards from where Derek Bird started the public part of his killing spree. They drove into the courtyard and parked up. DC Helen Douglass was waiting to meet them. Neither of them knew her. They both got out and introduced themselves.

'Is this related to that body you pulled from the hospital?' she said immediately. 'Because there's no way he did it, sir.'

She was in her early thirties. Short dark hair and a face that was pleasant enough, if slightly too earnest. She was dressed in jeans and a sweatshirt. She walked with a slight limp and Fluke wondered if she was recuperating from something.

Remembering her manners, she offered to take them into the station and make them a cup of tea. Fluke declined for both of them. He needed to crack on. He gestured for her to get into the back of the car then asked if she had any leads.

'I rang his probation officer before you got here, sir. She says that he's reported to her a couple of times with someone called McNab. He lives on Pinegrove. Thinks if anyone might know where he is, it'll be him.'

Towler reversed out of the yard. Fluke knew he'd worked this part of the west so would know the infamous Pinegrove Estate well.

Don Holland came to the door and smirked.

'What's that prick want?' Towler said.

'Ignore him. Come on, let's get going,' Fluke replied. Towler edged into the afternoon traffic and they headed towards Pinegrove.

Douglass started telling them about Ackley's life and how he'd ended up selling his body.

'I'm going to stop you there, Helen, if you don't mind,' Fluke said. 'I don't need his life history; I just need to find him. Where's he going to run to if he's not with McNab?'

She looked a little put out but recovered well. Fluke didn't care. Ackley was a witness in a murder case. The social workers and probation officers could have him back when he'd finished with him.

'As you know, we've not seen him for a few days. He'd normally have been arrested at least once by now for shoplifting. He doesn't even pretend to browse anymore. Just walks in and runs out. All the security guards and shopkeepers know him.'

'What do you think's happened?'

'Honestly, sir? I think he's found somewhere safe to spend the nights.'

'We think we know where he was last night and we think he'll be in hiding now. Any idea where he'd go if he were in trouble?'

'There's no way he can go without scoring. Not even for a day. Even if he was scared, he'd have to go out and get some heroin. And he can't get it on tick so he'll have to pay for it somehow.'

'You think he's worked for it?'

She paused while she thought. 'Probably,' she replied. 'He's shite at shoplifting, I know that much.'

Fluke's phone rang. It was a Penrith number.

'Boss, it's Jo. I'm just ringing to let you know that the CCTV was a bust. Copeland Council turned all their cameras off months ago, part of their efficiency savings. We'll keep going with the house-to-house but there's been zilch so far. The entrance to the site doesn't face anything so there's no reason for people to take any notice.'

'Okay. Thanks, Jo,' Fluke said, disappointed but not surprised. 'Any news on the bullet?'

'Not yet. It got there no problems but it may take a while. They're still trying to get something off the smashed mobile, so nothing on that yet either.'

'Any good news?'

'Not sure. The lab rang just before and said they had something from the note. There were prints on the cover but they all belonged to the vic. They said they can have a look for what they call 'indented writing', basically trying to see what's been written on the page that had been ripped out. It's expensive though. They use some sort of electrical bullshit to do it.'

'What's wrong with rubbing a pencil over it?' Fluke asked. 'Yeah, tell them to go ahead. It'll probably just be a shopping list or something but even that would be more than we know now about her. How you getting on with the misper list?'

'Nothing so far. I'll get onto the lab and tell them to run their test. Oh, and can you ring the bug lady? She says she needs to speak to you.'

The bug lady? Sometimes his lot were so unimaginative. Fluke was intrigued though, he hadn't expected to hear from Lucy again. One post-mortem looked like it was enough for her; the amount of notes she'd taken would surely be enough for her thesis.

'Okay, text me her number, I'll ring her when I get five minutes,' he said.

'Will do. Where are you and Matt?'

'We've drawn the short straw, Jo. We're just about to enter Pinegrove.'

Chapter 11

Fluke knew that Cumbria was a safe county. 'A safe place to live, work and visit' was the tagline used by the authorities. There were areas of outstanding natural beauty: the lakes, fells, mountains, Hadrian's Wall, even parts of the Yorkshire Dales. Picture perfect villages, castles and stately homes. A county that took William Wordsworth's breath away. A county that inspired Beatrix Potter.

But there was another side to it.

Parts of Cumbria had a lower GDP than the Czech Republic; an underclass carefully hidden from tourists, a culture of violence and fear. Estates with third-generation unemployment. Estates devastated by the decline of industry. Where dealers and loan sharks prospered. Recruiting grounds for the extreme right parties like the BNP and the EDL. Estates bereft of hope.

The notorious Pinegrove Estate was a small island, cast adrift from the town of Whitehaven. It had its own roads in and its own roads out. There was no reason to enter it unless you lived or had business there. It wasn't a shortcut to anywhere.

Like most of West Cumbria, it had a two-tier social structure: those who enjoyed the inflated wages of the Sellafield nuclear site and those who didn't. The main feature of the estate seemed to be barbed wire. The back of the pub, the rooftops of businessess, even some of the houses had it as protection. A broken ghetto, a bleak and miserable existence. The climate of fear was palpable.

Despite this, some of the streets still thrived. Functioning and legally taxed cars were parked outside houses, and gardens were well kept. People got up in the morning and went to work. They raised their families. They bought their council houses. Parts of Pinegrove had genuine community spirit. Residents on the estate tried to lead their lives, if not within the letter of the law, then at least within its spirit.

But there were a minority who had no interest in doing so.

If negativity and resentment could generate electricity then the isolated streets they lived in would have made Sellafield redundant. Those were the streets where every other house had boarded-up windows. Cars rusted. Front lawns went untended. Rubbish was piled on the street, giving the impression parts of Pinegrove had been abandoned. Efforts by Copeland Borough Council to regenerate the area were only partially successful; there were some families who had no interest in the status quo changing. Antisocial behaviour was rife, casual violence the norm. Drugs were openly sold and consumed. Feral children roamed the streets with no adult supervision. The type of estate where some left their doors open while others bolted themselves in at night in terror. Disagreements were settled with baseball bats rather than solicitors. Everyone knew everyone and strangers weren't tolerated. The worst thing you could be was a 'grass', even paedophiles were safer. Police callouts were constant. The chief had long ago directed that no police officer would patrol Pinegrove alone.

'Welcome to Pinegrove, ladies and gentlemen. The ASBO capital of Cumbria,' Towler said, as he turned into the estate. 'Drugs, violence and underage sex. We have it all.' He paused. 'Now, where the fuck am I going?'

Douglass didn't know the estate, so Towler parked up beside an off-licence and got out. There were graffiti-covered steel shutters on the windows despite it being open. Fluke had seen less-fortified police stations in Northern Ireland. He'd never been in the shop before but knew that all the overpriced goods would be locked in cages, nothing being handed over until the owner had the cash in his till.

In less than a minute, Towler was back with directions to Seaview Terrace, the last known address of McNab, and they quickly found it.

The street was quiet. Everyone with a reason to get up had already done so. The rest were still in bed.

'It'll be one of these houses here, sir,' Douglass said as they were near the middle of the wide road. 'They take the numbers off the houses to make it difficult for us and bailiffs to find them. Even those with nothing to hide do it. They'd get called a grass if they didn't.'

It was obvious that Seaview Terrace was one of the poorer streets on the estate. About a third of the houses had windows that were boarded up and were obviously derelict. A third had windows without curtains; the remaining third had curtains that were twitching. Fluke knew their presence hadn't gone unnoticed. A group of young children walked up and started looking over the car. Towler lowered his window, flashed his warrant card and said, 'Fuck off.' They backed away but didn't disappear.

'Right,' Towler said getting out. 'Let's knock on a few doors, then.'

'We'll need uniform backup before we can do anything, Sergeant. I'll call the station, get a van out,' Douglass said.

'Don't worry, Douglass,' said Fluke, smiling, as he followed Towler out of the car. 'He's his own backup.'

For a minute, he thought she was going to stay in the car but eventually she joined them on the pavement, looking nervous.

'Right, let's try here,' Towler said, walking up the first path and hammering on the door. There was no answer. He kept banging, looking round to see if anything else was stirring.

The occupants of the next house along opened their door a fraction to see where the noise was coming from. Towler was there in an instant, jumping over the neglected fence without touching it.

'You McNab?' he shouted through the door, jamming his foot in the crack to stop it closing.

Fluke, having not moved from the pavement, watched on amused. Towler was in his element. While he had finesse when needed, this was what he liked doing. Getting down and dirty. Fluke didn't hear what the person behind the door replied, but Towler didn't like it.

'Wrong answer, dickhead,' he said, forcing the door wide open and walking in.

Thirty seconds later he was back out.

'McNab's at thirty-three, boss. Lives there with some local lass, has done for a couple of months,' Towler said. 'This house here is seven, so it should be twelve doors up if the evens are on the other side.'

'Wanker,' came the shout from the door behind him.

Towler ignored it.

They left the car where it was and walked up the street, counting the houses as they went. After a short discussion about whether they'd counted correctly, they arrived at a dilapidated semi-detached. The front lawn was overrun with weeds, dog faeces and empty cans. An old sofa sat on the grass underneath the window. There was a headless child's doll on the path. Towler kicked it into the garden and they walked up to the front door together.

Towler knocked and they heard movement inside, and some whispered talking.

The door opened, and a man of about thirty stood before them, shaven-headed and topless. Heavy muscles competed for space over his squat frame. He was covered in prison tattoos. His small eyes were dull and malevolent. Coarse black hair crept to the top of his shoulders. His body language was shouting 'I'm dangerous, don't mess with me'. He was holding a can of beer and it was obvious to Fluke that he was deliberately sucking his stomach in and tensing his muscles hoping to give the impression that it was how he always looked.

Towler smiled at him, but not in a good way.

Failing to get the fearful reaction he wanted, his stance changed from intimidation to confusion. 'What the fuck do you want?' he said.

Ignoring the insult, Fluke asked, 'Are you McNab?'

Some of the tension seemed to leave his body. He gestured to his right with the can. 'Next door mate,' he said, closing the door.

'I think that's him, sir,' Douglass whispered.

Fluke nodded at Towler and gestured towards the back of the house. Fluke waited until Towler had enough time to get round the back and knocked again.

'Mr McNab, can we have a word, please?' There was no whispering but the sound of running, a door opening and then a loud crash. Someone shouted. A child's scream rose, wild and piercing, above the sound of whatever was happening at the back. The noise got louder as a woman started crying. Fluke and Douglass ran down the side alley.

Douglass looked shocked and a little worried. Fluke saw exactly what he'd expected to see.

McNab was on his knees in front of Towler, who had him in some sort of wristlock. He was clearly in a certain amount of discomfort and was keeping as still as possible to avoid more pain. Towler was exerting minimal pressure on his wrists, which were nearly at right angles.

A woman, no more than eighteen or nineteen, was yelling at Towler and tugging at his suit. He ignored her. She wore a sleeveless T-shirt, and fresh and old bruises were visible on her pale, thin arms.

Inside the house, the baby's cries grew louder and more urgent.

'Get her out of here,' Fluke told Douglass.

Douglass tried to calm the woman and persuaded her to go and see to the child. With one last look at everyone, the girl went back inside.

Fluke beckoned Douglass over. 'Go and see if she's all right. And while you're at it, search the house. See if Ackley's in there,' he whispered. She nodded and followed the girl in. Eventually, the sound of crying stopped.

With silence restored, Towler loosened his grip on McNab who stood up warily and rubbed his wrists. He looked at Towler with a mixture of hatred and fear.

He turned to Fluke, animal cunning telling him that he was in charge. 'Bastard can't do that. I've got fucking rights, you know.' He looked round to see if there were any obvious ways out. He took a look at Towler, six feet eight and built like a whippet, and decided there was no point running. 'What the fuck do you want, anyway? I've got no charges coming up and I'm clean. Not touched smack this year, ask anyone.'

Bet you've had some steroids though, haven't you, McNab? Fluke thought, but didn't say anything.

'What's your first name, McNab? And we're not the drug squad,' he said as he got out his warrant badge and identified himself.

McNab didn't say anything.

'No first name? McNab it is then. Shame, I was rather hoping we could be friends. I want to know what you can tell me about Darren Ackley,' Fluke said.

A brief glimmer of understanding flitted across his dull eyes. *Yeah, you know something.*

'No comment.'

So it was going to be like that? The copper's anthem, no comment. Fluke wondered how many times he'd heard that said by someone on the opposite side of an interview room. Thousands probably. Like detectives using pens to pick up evidence and doctors saying 'sharp scratch', it was another of those anomalies that made little sense. Criminals watched the same bad cop shows as police officers, he guessed. Everyone arrested has the right to remain silent but they don't have to say 'no comment' to assert that right. Saying nothing is enough.

'You're not under arrest, fuckface,' Towler said.

McNab stared at him but looked away when he realised that Towler wasn't even looking at him.

'My colleague is right, of course. You're not under arrest. Now stop pissing about. When did you last see Ackley?' Fluke said.

'No fucking comment.'

Fluke had seen it countless times. When the police were involved in their lives they felt powerless. Refusing to answer anything allowed them to get some control back.

'Ackley's not in trouble, McNab. You're not in trouble either, unless you lie to me. Then you'll be in big trouble. I don't want to search your house but I will. I wonder what I'll find? What do you think, Sergeant?'

Towler turned to look at McNab, his contempt obvious. 'At the very least enough steroids to put him away for six months, boss, would be my guess. Maybe something harder.'

The flash of fear that crossed McNab's face told Fluke that he was right. Steroid abuse. It explained his muscles and the bruises on the girl's arms. Steroid abuse and increased aggression were inextricably linked.

'We think Darren may have witnessed something last night that he'd rather not have. We need to know what he saw.'

Another flicker of recognition passed across his face. Bingo. He'd seen him recently.

'No comment.'

Douglass reappeared and shook her head briefly. Ackley wasn't inside.

'McNab, don't be a tit all your life. Tell me what you know,' Fluke said, raising his voice slightly. 'If you don't, you know I'm gonna have to nick you.'

Fluke thought he saw another flash of fear cross his face. So he's scared of being arrested. Why? He must have been arrested countless times judging by the tattoos and the way he was talking to them. Hostility towards the police is a learned behaviour. Upstanding citizens were normally polite and as helpful as they could be. McNab was hiding something, that much was obvious.

As he stood and thought for a minute on how he could get the information without arresting him, Towler took matters into his own hands.

'You know something, boss, I don't think he's cool enough to be called McNab. I met a McNab once when I was in the Paras. He was doing a talk on resisting interrogation. Something he'd learned when he was caught by the Iraqis during Desert Storm.'

'Andy McNab,' McNab grunted. 'Bravo Two Zero. They made him eat his own shit.'

'Check out the military historian here,' Towler said. 'Yes, that's right McNab. Andy McNab. And I think he's a cool bloke. A credit to his country. I don't think you should have the same name as such a cool bloke. What do you think, McNab?'

McNab glared at him but said nothing.

'I think you need a different name. From now on you're called McKnob.'

There was an immediate reaction. Anger replaced the fear in his eyes. His breathing changed, became shallower, as adrenalin flooded his body. Towler was taller but McNab easily had a three-stone advantage, three stones of steroid-induced muscle, brawn and aggression. It would make no difference.

Towler would wind up a difficult suspect to such an extent that he'd provoke a primal physical reaction which gave him every reason to meet it with his own.

At that point, the girl came back out. She was holding the baby.

'Ah, just in time. Can we get a cup of tea here, please, love? McKnob here is very thirsty. He's been telling us all sorts of things haven't you, McKnob?' Towler said.

The woman looked at McNab then at Towler, decided she didn't want anything to do with what was going on and disappeared back into the house.

'You think we'll get biscuits with our tea, McKnob?'

Again McNab said nothing. Being humiliated in front of the girl had turned his face and neck bright red. Fluke could tell he was only one remark away from losing it. And that would be bad for him. He could sense Douglass fidgeting beside him, wanting him to stop the deliberate provocation but Fluke didn't have time to explain what was happening.

Towler then delivered it. 'How'd your missus get those bruises, McKnob?'

The 'quick and dirty signal' scientists call it. A survival trait where the thalamus allows the body to react without speaking to the brain first. In dangerous situations, it can save several seconds. If you know what to look for, there is a subtle change the split second before someone switches from flight to fight. With McNab, it wasn't that subtle. With a bellow, he charged and swung a giant hairy fist at Towler with a force that would probably have killed him. If he'd been where McNab thought he was.

He wasn't.

Chapter 12

Fluke was no stranger to violence. He'd been a Royal Marines Commando for six years and a police officer for eighteen so had witnessed his fair share. From pub brawls to full-blown riots, from the fully mechanised war in 1990 to women pulling each other's hair out in Carlisle city centre, he'd seen good fighters, brave fighters, psychotic fighters and any number of others.

And he'd seen Towler, and Towler was in a category all on his own.

He wasn't a martial arts expert and he wasn't the biggest dog in the pack. It was a combination of absolute confidence, controlled aggression and an utter lack of fear that made him so formidable.

During the part of Parachute Regiment basic training known as P-Company, all recruits are required to undertake a particularly brutal test called 'milling'. Two recruits of equal size are paired against each other, and for the longest minute of their lives are forced to go head-to-head in a version of boxing not seen anywhere else. Having a solid defence is frowned upon. Fancy footwork is frowned upon. Boxing skills are irrelevant and not scored. The object of the test is to demonstrate that the recruit can stand up to violence, that they won't let their head go down. That they can take a pounding and still come back for more. That they are in control of their aggression. That in battle, when they are pinned down by effective enemy fire, they will have the character to get up and fight.

The spirit of Wireless Ridge and Goose Green.

During one of the rare times their leave's coincided, Fluke had met up with Towler and a mate he'd brought up from Aldershot who he'd been going through P-Company with. After several beers and a couple of hours of Marines versus Paras piss-taking, and when Towler was in the toilet, his friend had told Fluke about their experience of milling.

Already having a reputation as a hard man, the recruit Towler was paired with was terrified. Correctly guessing that the instructors were not looking to see him simply bullying and humiliating his opponent, he opted for a different approach.

For virtually the whole minute, Towler kept his arms by his side and his gloves down. He looked straight at his opponent and allowed him to rain blow after blow on his head. His nose broke immediately. A cut above his eye restricted his vision. Still he kept his arms down and allowed himself to be beaten. With the sixty seconds almost up and the point clearly made, with a lightning quick jab which seemed to come from nowhere, he laid his fellow recruit out cold.

When he was finished telling his story, they sat in silence. Fluke didn't doubt it was true. It had that paradoxical mix of violence and compassion that made Towler who he was.

A fight wasn't the best way to describe what happened next. A fight implies two people engaged in violence with a shared aim of hurting each other.

McNab never got to lay a finger on Towler, but in trying to had run into the wall, punched it twice and hurt his neck with a missed headbutt. Fluke thought his right hand was broken and there was a nasty cut on his forehead. He was drenched in sweat and that, combined with the blood from the cut, was affecting his vision. Every time he lunged or swung something at Towler, he missed.

Fluke watched dispassionately, moving out of the way occasionally, as Towler allowed McNab to beat himself into submission. Using some fairly basic defensive moves, Towler used McNab's own strength and lack of control to make him hurt himself.

Eventually McNab ran out of steam and he stood with his hands on his hips, gasping for breath and looking with hatred at Towler, who hadn't broken sweat and was watching him with an amused look. Fluke thought that he might have had enough. Until Towler taunted him again.

Putting on a terrible Michael Caine accent, he called out, 'You're a big man, but you're out of shape, McKnob.'

Fluke groaned to himself. 'Stop pissing about, Matt, and finish this, will you,' he called out.

At the point of exhaustion, McNab charged one last time. Towler sidestepped again but, as if putting an animal out of its misery, his right arm darted out like a striking viper as McNab passed him. It firmly connected with his solar plexus and he collapsed to the ground, gasping. He moved onto his side and vomited noisily. He wasn't crying but he wasn't far off.

Towler and Fluke casually discussed the previous two minutes while McNab writhed on the ground, panting. Douglass looked shocked and Fluke didn't blame her. She asked if they needed a van to come and get McNab. She assumed they'd be arresting him. Fluke didn't think it would be necessary and said so.

It took a full five minutes for McNab to get his breath back, which was followed by five minutes of threats of violence and legal action and tears.

'Just in case you were wondering, McNab, this isn't going well,' Fluke said. 'You know I can arrest you now? Take you in for assaulting a police officer,' Fluke said. 'Trying to anyway,' he added. He heard Towler snort with laughter.

McNab looked at them both, sullen, defiant, planning a revenge he wasn't capable of. There was vomit on his chin, the side of his face and matted into his chest hair. He said nothing and carried on muttering under his breath, Fluke may have heard the words 'filthy bastards' but chose to ignore them.

As he looked at them, McNab shivered. Adrenaline extracting its payment in all likelihood. Nothing was free. It dawned on Fluke that they were maybe looking at it from the wrong angle.

McNab was scared. Not scared for Ackley. Fluke doubted he'd give two shits if something happened to him. He was scared for himself. He wasn't protecting Ackley for any altruistic reasons. But Fluke needed to know what he knew. Time to do to him psychologically what Towler had done to him physically.

'Look, McNab. If Ackley really is your mate then you need to speak to us. He's in trouble. Not legal trouble. Proper trouble.' Fluke said. 'Tell us where he is and we'll leave. Don't and you're gonna have to come with us.'

McNab stopped sobbing and looked up, his eyes red, his nose running heavily. Staring at Fluke, he tried to regain some control. Not fearing him as much as Towler. His efforts to regain some dignity were ruined however when a snot bubble coming out of his nose burst.

'We know he saw something, something that scared him.'

Like a punctured tyre, he deflated in front of them.

He's terrified, Fluke thought.

'Not out here,' McNab said, looking round.

He led them back into the house and they took seats in what Fluke supposed was the lounge. The sofa in the front garden looked cleaner but Fluke was wearing a machine-washable suit. Before they started, Fluke asked Douglass to go and stay with the woman and make sure she was okay. He wanted to keep it as restricted as possible.

'Ackers came by yesterday morning,' McNab said, lighting a cigarette and picking up an empty beer can to use as an ashtray.

'What time?' Fluke asked.

'Dunno, but it was still fucking dark. I was in me bed. Kept bangin' on the door. Ignored it to start with, thought it must've been a smackhead looking for some gear and I don't do that anymore.'

Pinegrove was a short walk from the deposition site so it fit in with what they knew so far. 'So what did you do?' Fluke asked.

'I got fuckin' sick of it, didn't I. I've been good lately, haven't really been up to much. Doing weights and that. Hoping to get on the doors in town. Good money and it's cash in hand.' He stopped and looked up, aware that he'd admitted to benefit and tax fraud.

'Go on, we're not bothered about that. What happened next?'

'I sent Siobhan down, didn't I? She was gonna be up anyway feeding the larle 'un.'

'You're a modern man, McKnob,' Towler said.

Fluke winced. Sometimes Towler's off button malfunctioned. He had McNab talking now. He could do without them going at it again. He flashed Towler a warning look.

McNab continued, 'No, it made sense for her to get the door. She's got a fuckin' mouth on her anyway. You heard her before. She's lived on the estate all her life and knows how these things go. If I'd went down and it'd been a couple of dirty smackheads I'd have fuckin' killed 'em and I'd have got lifted.'

'But it was Darren?'

'Who? Oh aye, it was Ackers. Darren. Funny that, I'd forgotten what his proper name was. I know he sells 'is arse an' that, but he's a good lad really. We were in the same children's home when we was little. He came in crying his eyes out. Said he'd seen a big fucker dumping a body up at where the new hospital's gonna be. Said he'd left a note but wished he hadn't. He's been staying there a few days. Siobhan won't have him in the house with the larle 'un because of the needles. She thinks he's got AIDS or Hep B so won't even make him a brew in case we catch something off the cup.'

'What else did he see?'

'Dunno, didn't fuckin' ask him. Told him I didn't want to know anymore. Sounded proper scary, it did. Didn't want any fuckin' part of it. Ackers was fuckin' brickin' himself like. He wanted to get out of Whitehaven.'

'And you helped him?'

'Did I fuck. What could I do? Don't have a car and he wanted a hundred fuckin' quid to get to Newcastle. I don't have that kind of money and even if I did, I wouldn't let him have it. I know he's a mate n'all but he's a smackhead. He'd have just fucked off with it. I'd not see him for six months and then he'd deny ever fuckin' lending it. I gave him a fiver from Siobhan's purse. Just to get him to fuck off. I didn't want anyone finding him here.'

'So where is he now?' Fluke asked.

McNab burst out laughing, a low guttural sound. He looked at Towler. 'You may be hard mate, but you're a thick cunt.'

Fluke looked at him, tendrils of apprehension creeping over him. He was laughing at them. What did he know that they didn't?

'You fuckin' stupid bastards,' he said, some of his earlier bravado returning. 'He's with you lot.'

Fluke's confused expression caused McNab to burst out laughing all over again.

McNab continued. 'He's at Whitehaven nick.'

Fluke was furious. Furious at Douglass, who'd only just come on shift and hadn't read her emails, and furious with himself for not believing Holland would retaliate by deliberately interfering in a murder investigation. His smirk made sense now. He knew why they were there and he knew who he had in his cells. And he knew that at some point, Fluke would know.

McNab had told them he'd been arrested for shoplifting that morning. He'd walked into Tesco, picked up a DVD player, and according to the arresting officer, simply waited outside until the police arrived.

Towler phoned the station immediately but it was too late. 'They've already taken him to court, boss. Magistrates remanded him. He's in the back of a G4S van, on his way to Durham. No way of stopping it.' He slammed his fist on the steering wheel. 'No one thought to fucking check why we were here? What did you think we doing, buying fucking ice creams?' Towler shouted down the phone. 'For fuck's sake, we look a right pair of bell ends.'

Fluke felt the same but let him rant. He knew he'd calm down soon enough. Douglass was sitting quietly in the back, chastened. It wasn't her fault anymore than it was Towler's. Fluke blamed himself. If he hadn't humiliated Holland at the crime scene Ackley would be in their custody. He asked Douglass what she thought the shoplifting meant.

She looked up, surprised to be asked. 'I can't say for certain obviously, but all the regulars at court know what the remand threshold is at any one time in case they need to get off the streets. It sounds like he deliberately passed it. I don't why he'd do that though, sir. He's never done it before.'

Fluke understood what she meant. Ackley had deliberately stolen something of a value too high for the court to bail him. Although the value changed from bench to bench, word got around quick enough. He'd wanted to be remanded into custody. It was a ploy the homeless and addicts who wanted to get clean sometimes used. Something else Michelle's friends would never be able to understand; for some people, prison was the best they could hope for in their lives. Auntie Betty's B&B. Nice, warm and safe, all the food you can eat and free healthcare. For some people, prison was a sanctuary.

Douglass didn't know why he'd deliberately got himself locked up, but Fluke did. It wasn't because he wanted to get clean; it was because he was terrified.

The custody sergeant at Whitehaven obviously wasn't prepared to take any more grief from Towler and was giving as much back. Towler rang off and threw his phone down in disgust. 'Prick.'

They dropped Douglass back at Whitehaven, and Towler drove out the station car park without saying goodbye. Fluke gave her a weak smile as they drove past her.

At least they knew where Ackley was.

As Towler got back on the phone to organise a prison visit, Fluke remembered he hadn't phoned Lucy, the bug lady. There was no time; he wanted to go back to the crime scene, to make sure it was still secure and that SOCO had everything they needed. Towler drove through Hensingham and parked in the same place Fluke had the day before.

The crime scene was still being processed by the SOCO teams. Fluke knew that the reality of forensic work was methodical, painstaking and laborious. It took days rather than hours, popular TV shows giving a false picture of what the actual job entailed.

He could see that there were journalists and a TV crew there. Word was out.

A shrine of flowers and soft toys had built up. There were candles as well but the wind had blown them all out. A crowd of onlookers had gathered and some were being interviewed by the press.

Fluke turned and surveyed his surroundings after he signed into the outer cordon. It was as he thought: the old hospital was the only building that overlooked any of the site. A combination of trees and the screens the building company had erected interrupted the view from everywhere else. It couldn't be seen from the road. He didn't really know what to make of that information. He was working on an early theory that the killer wasn't from Cumbria. Professional killing wasn't a trade Cumbrians normally moved into. So how did he know about the place? Other than being unlucky enough to have actually been observed disposing of the body, it was perfect. He took one last look at the old hospital. It was still operational, the new one wasn't due to open until later in the year, but even to his untrained eye it looked as though it had had its day. It was grubby and it was old-fashioned. Not old-fashioned in the grand architectural style of the Royal Victoria Infirmary in Newcastle, it was more the prefabricated type favoured in the seventies. It didn't look nice then, and it looked worse now. But had their killer been there? Had he stood in that old dilapidated building and seen what he must have thought was the ideal deposition site?

He walked up to the uniformed sergeant who eyed him warily. Word had obviously got out about how he'd taken Holland to task.

'Sergeant. Can you move those ghouls back another fifty yards? I don't want a suspect placing themselves here on purpose so they can claim that's why their forensics were found.'

The sergeant walked off to arrange it.

Fluke took one last look at the crime scene. There was nothing more he could do here. He turned his phone on to check his emails while he had a signal. There was only one that mattered. The NBIS report on the bullet was back.

Chapter 13

An hour later, Fluke was back at FMIT reading the report from the National Ballistics Intelligence Service. As he read it, Alan Vaughn gave him the facts.

'Matt can probably give you more info on it, boss, but there's good and bad news. The good news is that ballistics were able to make a positive ID. It's a .22 LR.'

Fluke nodded, it was the calibre Towler had thought it had been. 'LR?'

'Stands for long rifle apparently. Not really sure why as it was almost certainly fired from a handgun,' Vaughn said. 'Matt, you got five minutes?' he called out. Towler walked over. '.22 LR?'

'.22 long. Fuck,' Towler replied. 'Just about the most common bullet on the planet. In the States you buy them by weight rather than number, they're that cheap. Used as a practice bullet. Not too bad for vermin from a rifle, shit from a handgun. Range is terrible,' he said. 'Ideal for our man, though. No way is that coming out the other side of the head. It's rimfire as well: quiet.'

'Rimfire?' Vaughn asked.

Distracted as he read the report, Towler replied, 'Means the firing pin strikes the side of the bullet rather than the back. Makes it less accurate, I forget why.'

While Towler familiarised himself with the report, Fluke asked Vaughn what the bad news was.

'They've run it through their database and it's clean. Nothing at all on their system. Didn't take them long either, by the sound of things. The bloke I spoke to said there were hardly any incidents using this ammunition in the UK. No more than five in the last five years. It was the first one he'd come across.'

'Shit,' Fluke said. 'Anything good coming out of this?'

'Not really. He said if we wanted to, he could give us a list of names of gangs and individuals who may deal in this sort of thing, but it was going to be sixteen pages long and none of them are Cumbrian.'

'If he's as professional as we think he is, he's not going to be a gangbanger,' Towler said. 'He's going to use someone we don't know. No way he leaves a link back to him that way.'

'Agreed but check it anyway,' Fluke said. There was no way he was leaving anything to chance. 'You're right though, we won't catch him through the bullet. He's left us no forensics. Even though he can't have expected us to find the body, I doubt he'd have left the bullet if he knew it was traceable.'

'I'll get the list, boss, see if there's anything that sticks out,' Vaughn said.

'Any idea what type of weapon we're looking at, Matt?' Fluke asked.

'No way to tell, boss. Any number of .22s fire it. Any number of rifles fire it.'

'Best guess.'

'I'd start with revolvers, that's what I'd use. Never jam and no brass to pick up. There's some nice reliable ones being made now. Some nice small ones too. Even if we narrow the search to that though, we'll still be looking at hundreds. The rifling on the bullet may help to narrow it down a bit but not much.'

'Dead end,' Fluke said.

'Yes and no, boss. It tells us a bit more about him. If you want to kill someone quietly then this is the ammo to use. A small gun, a subsonic load in the .22 LR and it'll make more of a pop than a bang.'

'You think he put the gun to her head to make sure he hit her?'

Towler thought about it for a second. 'Nah,' he said. 'It'll penetrate the skull at twenty feet but only just, but you could be reasonably sure of hitting her at ten. There'd be no need to get up that close. Why risk the forensic transfer?' he said thoughtfully. He paused, looking at the report. 'Unless... unless he was using her head as a silencer.'

There was silence as they all thought about what that meant.

'That's disturbing,' said Vaughn eventually.

Fluke nodded in agreement.

'The skull's full of liquid, you see? You press a small gun against the head and you wouldn't hear anything. Not even if you were in the next room. The prick knew what he was doing,' Towler continued. 'Good skills,' he added, without any trace of admiration. He was simply stating the facts as he saw them.

Fluke had already come to the same conclusion. 'What else we got, Alan?'

'Second thing's a bit weird, boss. That test you ordered on the notebook came back with some writing.' He looked down at his notes. 'They used something called an electrostatic detection device. Apparently it can find writing several layers below the top sheet, years later. Found only one thing, clear as day. They've made the assumption it was one layer above the top sheet as there was no other writing, although they can't rule out someone has just rested another bit of paper on the notebook to write.'

'Name and address of the killer, the victim and where the gun is hidden?' Fluke said.

'How'd you know, boss?' then added quickly, 'Just kidding,' when he saw Fluke look up. 'No, it's numbers. Weird ones, as well. Jo and I have started running them and so far, we've come up with the square root of fuck all.'

'You got a copy?' Fluke asked.

Vaughn handed him a bit of paper. Towler bent over his shoulder to look.

2.3 8.7 92

What the hell?

'Nothing on the phone?' he asked.

'Nope. The lab's sent it off to another lab, though. Hoping to try some sort of ghost system retrieval, whatever the fuck that means.'

'Means they're looking for two systems running side-by-side,' said a small man who had entered the room, grinning. A cheer went up as everyone saw who it was.

Jiao-long Zhang had joined FMIT on secondment from the Beijing Municipal Public Security Bureau nearly a year before, on a UK/China exchange programme. Why he ended up in Cumbria had initially been a mystery, until Fluke learned of his childhood obsession with Beatrix Potter and how he'd begged the programme manager in the Met to be attached to Cumbria. Most of his spare time was spent in the heart of the Lake District exploring the landscape that was her inspiration. He knew more about Peter Rabbit and Jemima Puddle-Duck than anyone else in the building, including Jo Skelton, and she had young children. The rest of his spare time was spent mucking about with Towler and they could often be seen leaning against each other as they staggered from pub to pub at weekends, one nearly seven feet tall, the other barely over five. The odd couple, Vaughn called them, but only when they were out of earshot.

Normally, Longy, as he quickly became known, would have been expected to do time in an area CID team before joining FMIT. However, he had computer skills no one else in FMIT came close to. Even the High-Tech Unit deferred to him. Finding hidden information, easy. Recovering information from damaged machines, no problem. Smartphones weren't safe; he could unlock them and within minutes, retrieve every text and email ever sent. Every photo you had ever taken.

In the past, Fluke had had him hacking into suspects' social media accounts, breaking passwords and retrieving information that had been hidden or deleted. He was also the best person on the team for tracking suspects across Carlisle's myriad of CCTV cameras. He knew where they all were. The councils as well as privately owned.

Chambers, who was against the whole idea of Chinese secondments, never used him, so Jiao-long usually worked with the outcasts. Fluke found him to be one of the nicest men he'd ever met. Nothing was too much trouble, his manners were impeccable and he did everything with a huge smile on his face.

He'd just come back from a trip to China and he looked exhausted. Fluke knew that he'd insist on diving straight into the investigation however, and didn't insult him by asking him to go home to get over his jet lag first. 'You okay to do some work, Longy?'

'I've only been up twenty-four hours, boss, so yeah, I'm up for helping you out,' he said.

'I need you to run these numbers through every database you know of. I need to know what they are by the time we start again in the morning,' Fluke said.

'No probs, boss,' he replied absentmindedly, already absorbed in what Fluke had handed him.

'Don't worry, Longy, jet lag's all in the mind,' Vaughn said, grinning.

'And I need someone to make sure he doesn't fall asleep and get him something to eat around midnight. Thanks for volunteering, Alan,' Fluke said.

Vaughn's face fell as everyone else laughed.

Fluke went back to his office, wanting to sit quietly and reflect for an hour before he went home, to let his mind go over what they had up to then. Although he knew more than he than did that morning, there was still little to go on. All he had really were questions. Who was she? Where was she killed? *Why* was she killed? Why had she changed her appearance? Were the mystery numbers important, or were they a red herring?

He also couldn't shake the feeling that there was something there he hadn't picked up on yet, something obvious. He knew there was no point forcing it though. When flashes of inspiration came, they were never head on; they always slipped in from the side, normally when his mind was engaged with other things.

He turned on his computer and checked his emails. There were the usual ones he received as a senior manager, along with a few from HR and the policy unit. One from Professional Standards reminding staff that any gifts had to be declared. The usual nonsense.

There was also one from Chambers demanding Fluke come and brief him on the murder. Fluke wrote a quick response summarising where they were, which was basically nowhere. He knew fobbing Chambers off with an email wouldn't last forever, and at some stage he'd have to go and see him, but he wasn't ready yet. Chambers had never had an original thought in his life and didn't trust those who did. Going to him with a half-arsed theory about a professional killer was too risky. He'd either ridicule it and replace him with one of his lackeys, or worse, he'd take it seriously and want to manage it himself. Either way, the killer would never be caught.

He turned off the computer, opened the file he'd made up on the murder and started to reread the statement from Christian Dunn. He was interrupted by a knock on the door and Fran Miles, FMIT's administrator, stuck her head inside.

'You and Matt are booked on the ten a.m. slot tomorrow at Durham, boss.'

'Thanks, Fran.' Fluke yawned. Another early start and he was already tired. No wonder his blood was playing up. There was nothing more for him to do so he picked up his coat, packed a file to read and headed home.

Chapter 14

Fluke had left hospital craving solitude. Before his illness, he'd lived on a nice new-build estate in west Carlisle. After he was discharged, he'd found it claustrophobic. There was too much noise, too many children shrieking, too many dogs barking. Where he'd once enjoyed neighbours coming round for a beer or a coffee, he found himself refusing to answer the door.

Doctor Cooper told him he was suffering from post-traumatic stress disorder but Fluke dismissed it. He'd fought in wars, been shot at in Northern Ireland. If he was going to get PTSD, it would have been then. But she persisted with her diagnosis and carried out something she called 'watchful waiting'. Basically, she was waiting to see if he was going to become suicidal. Fluke didn't, but he found his tolerance of idiots had become ever lower. And it hadn't been very high before. Chambers especially wound him up.

After a massive argument with him over something trivial, Fluke had driven home and sat up all night, nurturing a beautiful anger. For the first time, he considered whether Doctor Cooper could be right. He didn't feel as though he had the energy to carry on. He needed a change. He needed a place away from the masses. He could cope with the human debris his job threw up during the day if he could get away from it all at night.

He decided he either had to make a change or wallow in self-pity forever. Luckily, a solution presented itself in the form of an insurance cheque. A critical illness insurance cheque to be precise. Enough to pay off his mortgage.

Fluke had sold up and headed for the middle of nowhere; the fells above Ullswater. Despite clearing nearly three hundred thousand, prime real estate was still out of his reach. He needed something cheap and that meant something no one else wanted. He bought an acre of woodland high up on the side of a hill that the Forestry Commission had for sale. The holiday home company that owned the adjoining land had been holding out for a lower price and Fluke had nipped in and stolen it from under their noses.

It was on a sharp incline, had too many large rocks to make logging profitable and was barely accessible. Fluke was sceptical. Until he saw the view. Although some pine trees partially obscured it, he could see down virtually the entire length of Ullswater. With selective pruning, he'd have a vista that rivalled any in the world.

He applied for planning permission for a holiday home. He spent the rest of his money on a luxury log home which he imported from Finland. Made in the Scandinavian style, it was designed internally around a large open living space. Two bedrooms and a bathroom were off to one side but that was it. But it was the external features Fluke bought it for. A covered terrace encompassed the front and one side of the house and had nearly the same floor space as the inside.

The civil engineer from Carlisle he'd initially contacted had told him he was a fool and had wasted his money on the land but the firm who supplied the house also provided the expertise to site it. Engineers from Finland. For them it was a minor project. They were used to working in denser woods and on steeper inclines. They felled a dozen trees and moved some boulders. After two days, they had an area they were satisfied with. They didn't need to be told to site the house facing Ullswater. When they were finished, they even cleared the trees that blocked his view. All but one which Fluke insisted on keeping where it was.

It was here that he lived most of his life. He ate outdoors, he read outdoors and, during the summer months, he slept on his hammock. He loved his monastic existence and rarely missed company. His neighbours were creatures of the night. Foxes prowled, owls hunted and the occasional deer came to nibble at the tender shoots of young trees.

He spent most weekends and long summer evenings making improvements to the surrounding area. The road, previously a mud track for logging vehicles, had to be improved and the backbreaking work gave Fluke a sense of achievement he'd not felt since he'd left hospital. He made a carport from an old sail to keep pine needles and the worst of the weather off his car. Fluke's hands became gnarled and heavily calloused from chopping wood for the fire pit and wood-burning stove. He wasn't yet a third of the way through the trees that the Finns had cut down. When he'd burnt them, he'd earmarked a couple of pines that, if removed, would open up the view further and let in more light. Not too much, though. He didn't want to advertise his presence. Once the cabin had been sited and the trees cleared, he'd taken a trip on one of the Ullswater Steamers, the old passenger vessels that cruised the lake, to see if his home could be seen from the water. It could, but only if you had binoculars and knew it was there. The engineers from Finland knew what they were doing.

His wood ran all the way down to the shore so technically he had a lakeside property and one of the jobs he'd planned for the coming summer was to put a series of steps down the treacherous slope. He was toying with the idea of getting a small boat. A couple of nice pubs had their own jetties that were a twelve-mile drive but only a ten-minute boat ride.

After leaving hospital, Fluke had endured an emotional rollercoaster that nearly finished him off but after his first few weeks in his new home, his troubles disappeared like cigar smoke on a breezy day.

Fluke approached the mud track that led to his home. The sign on his American-style postbox was showing he had mail. He slowed, opened his window and retrieved it. A minute later, he'd parked under his self-made canvas carport at the back of the house and had walked round to the front. As he did every night, he paused for five minutes to take in the view.

The fell on the opposite side of Ullswater was lit up in the moonlight, the bare splintered bones of shattered rock almost gleaming. He could see the network of dry stone walls that seemed to have grown directly from the land. It was a beautiful night. Fluke strongly believed that where he lived was as much a feeling as a physical location. He couldn't explain it any more than he could explain why certain pieces of music evoked such strong emotional responses.

Despite it being winter he decided to have his supper outside. He put some logs on the fire pit and lit it before going inside to put on some food and get a cigar. He browned off some lamb, chopped onions, added spices in measures he knew by heart and let the curry simmer. He'd leave it until the meat was tender; about two hours.

He opened his mail while he was inside and there was some light. Nothing of note until the last one. His stomach sank as he recognised the postmark. He sighed as he opened it. It was another letter from the council. The tone had long before stopped being pleasant.

When he bought the wood, the planning permission Fluke applied for had only been for a holiday home. It couldn't be used as his main domicile, but he guessed that as no one knew it was there, no one would know if he lived there permanently. His guess was wrong. The county council knew. Fluke suspected it was the holiday home company owners who'd told them. Six months before, he'd returned home and found a letter in the postbox. They wanted to discuss two things. The log cabin wasn't of the type on the original planning permission and it appeared to be his only home. They needed evidence he was living somewhere else in winter. It was all in an apologetic tone making it clear that the fault was all theirs and if he could provide what they needed, they would stop bothering him. Fluke wasn't surprised to get a letter from the holiday company two days later, offering to buy his land. He ignored them both.

Six weeks later, a second letter from the council arrived. Bureaucracy wasn't quick, but it was thorough. The tone was no less apologetic but, right at the bottom, it mentioned court. And they'd continued to come with depressing regularity, each more threatening than the last. However, the latest was the first letter that actually had a court hearing scheduled. He would file it with the rest.

He walked outside and pushed the letter deep into the fire pit, waited until it was burning, withdrew it and lit his cigar. He watched as the rest of the letter curled and blackened in the flames. The path he was on with the council only had one way of ending. He'd be made homeless with his savings decimated. He'd own a stunning bit of land that was next to useless. He doubted he'd even get permission for a caravan now.

He smiled. It was strange but he worried about it less than he worried about lying to Doctor Cooper.

He settled in one of his numerous outdoor seats and blew smoke out towards the lake. The mingling smell of the cigar smoke and curried lamb coming through the open door was pleasant and comforting. He relaxed, the tension of the previous twenty-four hours gradually leaving his body.

As the curry cooked and his cigar shortened, he thought about the investigation, picking up where he'd left off. Best-case scenario was that when he interviewed Ackley the next day, he would get a workable description of the killer, but he had some doubts about how useful he was going to be. A doped-up smackhead, scared stiff. Not the most reliable witness. Still, it was all he had at that moment.

He thought about the seemingly random numbers again. He had Jiao-long feeding them into every database he legally could, and some he couldn't. Fluke was confident he'd have an answer by the morning. He hoped so. All they'd done so far was increase their ignorance. He resisted the temptation to ring Jiao-long now. If there was anything significant, he'd be contacted. During murder investigations, his phone was never turned off.

As the curry continued to simmer, Fluke finished his cigar and watched the bats that lived in the wood ducking and diving as they chased their insect prey.

Insects.

He'd forgotten to ring Lucy.

Helping her with her thesis might mean he was owed an entomological favour in the future, and he had nothing to do while his curry cooked anyway. He retrieved the text with her number and called.

But she didn't want a favour, far from it. She wanted to do Fluke a favour.

'Coffee,' she said when pleasantries had been swapped and Fluke had asked her what he could do for her.

At first, he thought he was being asked out by a woman fifteen years his junior.

He was wrong.

'I was in the post-mortem as you know, Mr Fluke.'

'You don't work for me, Lucy. You can call me Avison.'

'Yes, well. Anyway, during the post-mortem, you may have noticed that I was interested in the brown substance Henry found under her nails, as well as the stuff SOCO recovered from her trouser turn-ups?'

Fluke confirmed he had.

'I'd thought it might have been blowfly puparium,' she said. She paused, seeming to know Fluke was going to ask the obvious.

'Remind me what they are, Lucy. It's been a while since I got my doctorate in flies.'

She laughed. 'Sorry. The blowfly is the first insect on a corpse. It's also the one that colonises the body in the greatest numbers and for that reason, it's been studied the most.'

Fluke paid attention. Henry had told him, that as well as helping with the time of death, insects could also help with where the victim was killed.

She continued, 'And it goes through four stages in its life cycle. An adult lays eggs and those eggs hatch into maggots, which go on to feed on the flesh of the corpse. We can measure that part of the life cycle accurately.'

'There weren't any maggots on the body.'

'No, there weren't but there was that brown substance. The next stage of the maggot is to turn into a pupa. This is the cool bit when the maggot turns into a blowfly.'

Fluke resisted the temptation to tell her it was actually the disgusting bit.

'And the shell it forms during this transformation is called a puparium. You'll have seen them, they're dark brown and barrel-shaped, they're actually made of the dead skin of the maggot, it sort of hardens around itself,' she continued.

'And they're brown?'

'Exactly. Now, no way does your crime scene guy fail to identify a fully formed puparium and no way does one fit under someone's fingernail. They're about five or six mils big and easily recognisable. However, when the adult fly has broken out of the puparium, it leaves it in pieces, and sometimes they get broken up further. That's what I thought the substance under her nails could have been.'

'So it *was* insect activity? I'd have bet a month's wages it had been too cold that night.'

'No, no you misunderstand, Avison. It wasn't bits of puparium at all. She hadn't been dead long enough for that kind of activity. And if she had, there'd have been much more it.'

'Oh. So what was it?'

'Coffee.'

'Coffee,' Fluke repeated.

'Coffee,' she confirmed. 'Ground-up coffee. I had a look at it under a microscope. Henry was kind enough to arrange for me to have supervised access to your lab. There's no doubt.'

Fluke thought for a moment. 'So our vic liked coffee. That's something else I know about her, I suppose. Doesn't help much, though? Doubt the brand could be identified and even if it could, I don't see where it would take us.'

'I've more. Have a little faith,' she laughed.

Sometimes it was the most inane thing that opened a case. Sometimes you needed that little bit of luck. The police officer who stops a killer for having a brake light out. The man arrested for drink driving, whose DNA matches a rape twenty years earlier. Was Lucy going to be his luck on the case?

'I can't tell you what the brand was because it wasn't commercial. These were fresh beans, freshly ground.'

'So?' Fluke asked impatiently. If there was a point he wanted to hear it.

'I'm a coffee lover, Avison. I'm a coffee snob if I'm being honest, although to be fair I'm not a snob about anything else. But I do like my coffee and I know a lot about it.'

'So you *can* identify the bean then?'

'Nope, of course not, no one could.'

'That's what I thought,' Fluke said, lying.

'What I can tell you is that the substance found under her nails and in the turn-ups of her trousers wasn't pre-ground. The beans weren't even ground in a shop. She ground them herself.'

'How can you possibly know that?'

Fluke got up and walked into the house. He wanted to take notes. He wrote down "coffee beans" and circled it.

'Because the grinder she used was worn. Most coffee enthusiasts use the new electric grinders that give a uniform grind, although I personally think the friction heats the beans too much.'

'Or?'

'Or they have a manual burr-mill grinder.'

'Burr-mill?'

'Looks like a small sausage maker. About eight inches. That's what I use. I have an old one my dad gave me.'

'And that's what she had, you reckon?'

'I do. What a manual grinder, especially an old one, will do is give an uneven grind. The gears wear down and the burrs rotate slightly unevenly. You don't want an uneven grind. Uniform grinds make a purer cup of coffee, the water is in contact with each grain for the same amount of time. So the only reason you would keep a grinder that didn't work properly is—'

'Because it's personal to you,' Fluke finished.

'Exactly. I don't care how uneven my grinds get, I'll never get rid of my dad's burr-mill. I love it too much. And only coffee lovers would get sentimental about a grinder.'

There was a weird kind of logic to that. It was eccentric but entirely plausible. If they ever found where she lived, Fluke would give short odds on there being exactly what Lucy described in her house. 'Okay, still not seeing how this helps. There must be thousands of real coffee drinkers in Cumbria.'

'Tens of thousands probably, but the vast majority get their beans pre-ground at the supermarket. Why wouldn't they? It's decent enough these days and most of it's fair trade. You can also get whole beans at the supermarket now, to grind at home as and when you need them, but there's far less choice.'

'Where'd you get yours, Lucy? From the supermarket?'

'No, I don't. I have my favourite bean and I like to grind it up as I need it. The oils in the bean are at their freshest then. They start to dry as soon as they've been ground. Keeping ground coffee in the fridge helps but it's always best to freshly grind them.'

Fluke knew where she was going. 'And a fiver says you can't get your favourite bean at a supermarket?'

'Nope.'

'Another fiver says you have to go to a specialist coffee shop.'

Chapter 15

Fluke was back at Carleton Hall by seven in the morning, still wiping the sleep from his eyes. The other early bird was Jo Skelton. Jiao-long was nowhere to be seen but a message on his desk said the computer search of the numbers had turned up nothing. He'd gone home but would be back in later. Fluke joined Skelton in the incident room. He summarised the previous night's call from Lucy and the possibility that their victim may have been buying coffee from a specialist shop.

Fluke left to check his emails. After he'd finished, he came back into the interview room to find Skelton with her face buried in the Yellow Pages. Intrigued, he walked over.

She looked up as Fluke approached. 'Was the bug lady sure it was specialist coffee, boss?' she asked.

'As sure as she could be, I suppose. Says she might have been a regular customer. Every other week at least, Lucy reckons,' he said. 'There can't be many of these shops, surely.'

'There's loads of them. I've trawled through Yellow Pages and cross-referenced what I found with a search on the Internet.'

'How many?' Fluke was hoping the list would be manageable.

In fact there were nearly eighty specialist tea and coffee shops in Cumbria and eighty wasn't manageable. Not without bringing in more staff and he wasn't prepared to go to Chambers with something that flimsy.

He needed to narrow the list down somehow.

Working on the assumption that a snob would avoid the international coffee chains, he removed them from the list. That left a smaller, but still unwieldy list of thirty that primarily sold what he imagined was gourmet coffee.

'We need to triage the shops,' Skelton said.

Fluke had been thinking the same thing but didn't know how to go about it. He'd been considering looking at the ones nearest the murder scene first then expanding outwards but decided that wasn't scientific enough. 'Go on,' he said.

'We'll have to search the Whitehaven area obviously, that's where the body was found.'

'Agreed.'

'Common sense would suggest that we would then widen the search in an expanding radius around the body. Do all of Copeland, Allerdale, South Lakes next, then Barrow Eden and Carlisle last.'

'Yep.'

'But the killer's a pro. You said it yourself. So if he transported the body to the deposition site, it's possible that the actual murder site was where she was living.'

'Possible,' Fluke agreed.

'I'm going to take a guess at something now. The killer knew about the deposition site in advance. Means he has either been there before or had been talking to someone who had.'

'Yep, I was thinking that yesterday. You can't see it from the road,' he said. 'It doesn't help with locations though.'

'Doesn't matter. All we're trying to do is triage the search rather than rule anything out.'

She was right. It didn't matter what order they searched, they were just trying to guess where was most likely. 'What you thinking then, Jo?'

'I'd do South Lakes and Barrow last. Neither are in West Cumberland Hospital's catchment area.'

'Nor is Carlisle,' Fluke said.

'Agreed, but if you were planning a murder and were looking for a deposition site, what would you look for, other than the quality of the site itself?'

Fluke thought about where she was going. He tried to think his way through the question. *I've killed someone. The murder site's not in the same place as the deposition site. I have less control over the murder site presumably as the victim has to be present so I'm bound by her movements to a certain extent, but I can choose where I dump the body. I need to transport the body from the murder site to the deposition site.* 'A safe route,' he said finally.

'Exactly. He needs a relatively trouble-free drive from A to B. It's possible he knows our back roads and if he uses them, he'll never get stopped by us. But he knows driving them in the dark isn't easy, there's blind corner after blind corner. They're narrow, only wide enough for one car in places so you have to use passing spaces. You have to crawl past each other.'

'And someone may remember you,' Fluke said. He thought about it for a while. She had something. 'He'd also want a decent escape route if it all went wrong.'

'I hadn't thought of that, but you're right.'

'So we rule out the back roads. Now what?' he asked.

'The next thing I considered was where point A could be. Where she lived. Matt says the bullet used would have been quiet and that he may have used her head to quieten the shot further.'

'Correct.'

'And that you think she was hiding from someone. Only reason for the type of cosmetic surgery she had.'

Fluke nodded.

'If she were hiding in Cumbria, she has two options really: she either hides in some obscure village or hamlet and keeps her head down. We're a rural county, it's possible to disappear,' she said.

'Risky though with these small places. They all talk to each other. Pretty soon the whole village knows someone new has moved in.'

'That's what I think as well. I'm ruling it out for now. The other option is that she moves into one of the big towns. Tries to blend in.'

'She hides in plain sight,' Fluke said. 'Uses people to hide in. Somewhere big enough so she doesn't stand out. Carlisle or Barrow basically.'

'Carlisle, sir. Not Barrow. The road from Barrow to the deposition site is terrible. You ever been over Corney Fell in the dark? It's a nightmare; tiny, narrow, up and down, and because it has common grazing rights, no one can put up a fence which means there's sheep on the roads as well. Even the locals avoid it at night. He'd have to take a massive detour to use semi-decent roads. Too much exposure.'

Fluke knew she was right. During the day, it was a lovely drive but better suited to fell walkers than drivers. It took about half an hour, and even on a good day, it was exhausting. It wasn't the route to take if you were transporting a body.

'So I think we focus on the shops around Whitehaven and Carlisle first,' Skelton said.

Fluke decided it was worth a gamble. When you hear hooves, sometimes you had to ignore the horses and think zebras.

'Okay, Jo, you've convinced me. We'll run with it. I'll need you to arrange it though. I'm going to be away until mid-afternoon with our witness. Can you take the morning briefing? Focus on the coffee lead. Send a photo of the vic to all area CID teams but make sure it's an E-fit. I don't want cops turning up at posh little bistros with a picture of a dead woman.'

'Requested it last night, boss,' she said.

Fluke thanked her and smiled to himself. That was what Chambers would never understand about Jo Skelton. She may not look the part but she was better than any detective working the robbery. She'd had ten minutes to think about the Lucy's theory while he'd checked his emails and she'd developed a plan to triage the coffee shops. All his team had initiative. Admittedly sometimes it backfired, Towler had used initiative once when he'd given everyone a long weekend after they'd charged the farmer who had drowned his wife in slurry. Fluke had come in to FMIT on the Monday to find the office empty. But by and large, all you had to do was point them in the general direction of a criminal and they'd do the rest.

'One more thing, Jo,' Fluke said. 'Can you make sure we keep trying to figure out what the numbers mean. Get a hard copy for everyone and hand them out at the briefing. If it's a code, I want people thinking about it. Let's get some lateral thinking going.'

'Clever stuff,' Towler said, after Fluke had explained the direction Jo was taking the coffee lead. 'May turn up fuck all, but least we're being proactive, for a change. All we've done so far is chase fucking shadows.'

Fluke nodded. He felt the same. The previous night, he'd found Lucy's theory interesting. After speaking to Skelton, he'd upgraded the theory to promising. He lapsed into silence and reread the preliminary post-mortem report. Something had been bothering him but he'd drawn a blank. Something Skelton had said that morning had made him revisit it, and he'd been thinking about it since they'd turned onto the A66. As the main road connecting the west to the east, they'd travelled it often. The wind buffeted the car and Towler had to grasp the steering wheel with both hands. Although widely regarded as one of the most beautiful roads to drive in the UK, it held few fascinations that day. Not even the wild and empty Pennines.

Towler was talking about something his daughter had said to his mother the previous night but he wasn't really listening. Towler doted on his daughter and wasn't afraid of showing it, and if anyone took the piss, they only did it once.

'You remember the PM, Matt?' Fluke interrupted. 'There was something Sowerby said that I thought was a bit odd.'

Towler briefly took his eyes off the road. 'What?'

'The bit about there being no fall injuries,' he replied. 'You're a professional killer, right? You have a gun that will kill at... what distance?' Fluke asked.

Towler thought for a few seconds. 'Like I said yesterday, ten feet to be safe. You shouldn't miss the head from that distance. Not if you know what you're doing.'

'So why kill her with a contact shot.'

'Told you, contact shot with a subsonic bullet. The skull and all the liquid in it act as a silencer. Quiet, very quiet.'

'So why not just use a silencer. He has the contacts to get the gun, yes? So why not get a silencer at the same time. Do it from a distance of what, say six or seven feet? Still kills her but there's no chance of any evidence transferring from her to him. Why stand right next to her?'

There was only one obvious answer. 'He had to catch her. Wherever he was, he didn't want her falling to the floor. Why though?'

'That's been bothering me as well. Didn't even know it had been, but Jo got me thinking about the victim differently. About how she'd hid. About the two options. Now, if she's hiding in a remote cottage then so what? He walks up to her and shoots her. No one is going to hear that, and even if they do, guns are common in the country. More importantly, no one would hear her fall. No dramas.'

'Makes sense. No point getting close to your victim unless you have to,' Towler said.

'Exactly. I think he killed her up close as he had to catch her. I think that if she'd fallen, someone might've heard. I think she lived in a flat.'

They discussed the case for the rest of the journey, everything they knew and everything they didn't. Fluke struggled to remember a case with so little to go on after forty-eight hours. Numbers in a notebook and a worthless bullet were the only bits of hard evidence he had to work with. The rest was conjecture and that was dangerous. It was worrying. An unknown victim, an unknown killer and no motive. Chambers wasn't going to stand for that for too much longer.

'Probably ex-military,' Towler said, as they passed the army ranges at Warcop. They'd spent time there when they were serving. Fluke had burnt his nose sunbathing with mortar troop one hot summer.

'It could just as easily have been a paintballer,' he said.

Towler snorted. 'Bollocks.'

Towler pulled into the Old Elvet area of Durham, and parked as near to the prison as he could.

As they walked up the hill, past the barrister's chambers towards the entrance gate, Fluke said, 'And Matt, don't wind up the prison officers this time.'

Durham prison was deceiving. It looked old. It was old. An ancient cathedral of human misery. But until a couple of years before, it had been part of the high-security estate so it had state-of-the-art gate facilities. They had their fingerprints taken at the gate with a biometric scanner, and a photo ID was printed off for them before they moved to the search area. They sat in the metal chair that detected anything concealed inside the lower body and moved on to the queue to be physically searched.

As they waited, Fluke glanced at the imposing Prison Service signs on the wall. White writing on a blue background, they clearly listed prohibited items, along with the penalties for smuggling them in. Mobile phones, keys, money and cigarettes. None of it could be taken in. They'd been on enough prison visits to know what they could and couldn't bring in, and after

Towler had left the car keys in a locker, they went through to security.

Fluke made Towler go through first. The previous time, he'd gone second so Fluke hadn't been able to stop the commotion that followed. Towler objected to the treatment of police officers by prison staff. He always had. He objected to being fingerprinted. He objected to queuing with solicitors and prisoner's families. He objected to having a chair check his anus for drugs and mobile phones.

But most of all, he objected to being searched.

It was a clash of egos, and prison officers seemed to be able to sense when they had a police officer who was going to cause trouble. With the law on their side, it was entertainment in an otherwise dull task. He'd been refused entry on at least two occasions: once for refusing to hand over a mobile for safekeeping as it contained evidence he wanted to show a prisoner and another time for refusing to take off his belt. This time, he went through with no problems and Fluke breathed a sigh of relief.

They were directed up the stairs and through a couple of security doors. If the prison had still been a Cat A, they would have been escorted everywhere but as a Cat B, they were simply given directions; up a set of stairs to the official visitors' suite where they identified themselves and were let in. Suite was a grandiose term for what was essentially a series of dirty square boxes on each side of a wide room. Eight to a side. The rooms had clear Perspex on three sides to ensure the prison officers could see into every room. It had an entrance at either end. To Fluke it looked like a small, dirty call centre. The type of call centre that might sell pornography or erection pills instead of insurance.

Each room was painted a drab green and had a table and four fixed chairs and nothing else. They were stark. The smell of disinfectant was invasive. It was the sort used when cleaning had to be quick but thorough. An institutional smell. More signs on the wall listed the suite rules. Fluke knew that the entrance at the far end was the prisoners' and presumably led back into the main prison complex. There was a desk on their right, with prison staff looking busy. Fluke and Towler said who they were there to see and were allocated room six. They entered and waited. Ackley's name was called out.

'Jesus, look at the state of this,' Towler said as Ackley exited the prisoners' entrance.

Chapter 16

The sallow, skeletal figure standing in the door looked like the picture in his file, but only if he'd been dead a week. The word 'gaunt' popped into Fluke's head. He clearly hadn't showered or washed recently, and a sour stench quickly permeated the room. Neither Fluke nor Towler commented on it. Long, lank hair framed a pallid face. White gunk formed at the corners of a mouth surrounded by spots. His teeth were badly decayed. A sheen of cold sweat glistened on his forehead. So that was what a lifetime on the game looked like. Fluke wasn't up on the rates for rent boys but guessed that Ackley was working the cheaper end of the market.

Despite being a remand prisoner, and therefore entitled to wear his own clothes, he was in standard prison-issue clothing of tracksuit bottoms and a green sweatshirt. The prison had probably decided the clothes he'd arrived in were a health hazard and removed them. He stood at the door, looking at them, vigorously scratching his arm.

'Come in, Darren,' Towler said.

As he sat down, he started to shake. Fluke initially thought he was scared. He was, but that wasn't the reason for the shakes.

He buried his head in his hands. 'I'm clucking like a cunt, man.'

Fluke looked at him blankly. He knew most Cumbrian phrases but that was a new one.

Towler interpreted for him. 'He means he's withdrawing, boss.'

Fluke said nothing. Towler would lead on the interview.

'Bastards won't put me in the hospital,' he mumbled.

'Darren, look at me.'

Ackley looked up. His bloodshot eyes were vacant.

'Do you know why we're here?'

Ackley shook his head. 'Nah, man. Leave us alone.'

'Where were you Monday night, Darren?'

There was no surprise on his face. He'd obviously been expecting that.

'Fuck off man, I'm badly.'

Badly, Fluke thought. Of all the Cumbrian sayings, he hated that one the most. No wonder people called them Dumbrians.

'I don't give a shit,' Towler said. He waited until it was clear Ackley wasn't going to say anything.

'Look, Darren, we know what happened. You saw a man dump a body. You left a note and now you wish you hadn't.'

Ackley doubled up in pain. A stomach cramp, no doubt. Fluke wasn't sure how long they'd be able to carry on. He didn't look well at all. If he were in police custody there'd be no way the doctor would allow them to interview him.

Towler continued, 'Do you know what an Osman Warning is, Darren?'

Ackley shook his head.

'It's where the police have a duty to warn someone that they're in danger. When you're released, I will personally serve the Osman Warning on you. And then I'll walk off and not give two shits about what happens to you.'

Ackley sniffed and wiped his nose on his sleeve. He said nothing.

Towler stared at him. Ackley held his gaze for as long as he could but soon put his head back in his hands and rocked back and forth.

'Look, I'll lay it out for you. We have someone who dumped a body. They seem to know what they're doing, so we think it was someone who's done this type of thing before. But this time, he's seen. And he'll know by now, there's cops all over the building site. How long before he starts looking for the witness? How long before he finds out it was Darren Ackley who saw him?'

It was clear that it wasn't the first time Ackley had thought about that. He looked terrified.

It's funny, Fluke thought, *how sometimes those with so little to live for cling onto life so fiercely.*

'I think you got yourself remanded so you'd be safe. And I understand that. If I were in your position, I might have done the same.'

Ackley looked at them both. His eyes screwed up and he wept.

Towler pressed his advantage. 'But how safe are you in here, really? We both know people can be got to in prison. There's people in here with nothing to lose, they're never getting out. They'll do pretty much anything for a pack of cigarettes or some drugs. You know this, Darren.'

Ackley sniffed up some snot that had been making an escape, and wiped his eyes with his sleeve. 'So what do you want me to do?'

'The only thing you can do, Darren,' Towler said. 'Help us catch this prick.'

Towler picked up his pen and opened his notebook, a signal that he was ready to work and that he expected Ackley to do the same.

Ackley told them everything. They prodded and poked, and were eventually satisfied that they knew everything he did. It wasn't much and most of it they'd already guessed. By the end, they were no closer to moving the case forward. The only thing that happened was they softened towards Ackley. He was a tragic figure.

He told them how he'd met a man in a Whitehaven club and they'd had sex in the toilets. Afterwards, he'd offered Ackley a place to sleep. The office on the building site of the new hospital. It was warm, it was safe and no one knew about it. He'd jumped at the chance. He'd been sleeping in there for two weeks by his reckoning, but he had a casual attitude to time, so it was only a guess.

'This good Samaritan, did it for free, did he?' Towler asked.

That got a reaction.

'Did he, fuck. He was there at seven o'clock every fuckin' morning wanting sucked off. Fuckin' old cunt never even paid me after the first time. Just came in, got his cock out and stuck it in me mouth. Soon as he shot his load, I had to fuck off. I wasn't allowed back till it was dark again.'

'And that was every day?' Towler asked.

'Near enough. There was one day, must've been a Sunday 'cos he brought some food with him, that he came in the afternoon. I was supposed to be grateful.'

'And you weren't?'

'Was I fuck. The dirty bastard didn't give a shit about me. Soon as I finished, he went and got a blow-up mattress from his car and he fucked us on it the rest of the day. He got fifty quid's worth of sex and I got some scabby chicken and minging cabbage.'

'This man, what did he look like?' Fluke asked, the first time he'd spoken since Ackley had arrived. He thought he knew the answer but wanted to hear it first-hand.

'Old bastard. Shorter than you. He was from Whitehaven, I'd seen him hanging round the club a few times. Shittin' himself most of the time. Typical fucking breeder. Wants cock but won't leave his wife to get it.'

Christian Dunn. The site foreman who'd called the police. No wonder he looked shifty. Seemed he was using his office as his personal shagging nest. Nothing wrong with that, each to their own. But he'd lied to Fluke about not knowing who'd left the note and for that, he was going to be arrested. He couldn't do anything about the way Dunn had treated Ackley, but Fluke would make sure he never lied to the police again.

Ackley's concept of time caused them problems. He told them what he saw: a car had woken him, he'd watched as a man walked onto the site with a torch before returning to get something from the boot. But he had no idea what time it had been, only that it was still dark. Towler pressed him for more details but it was clear that fear was the only thing he was remembering.

'How'd you know it was a body he got out the boot?' Fluke asked. 'We know you didn't go down and check.'

'I just knew. What else could it have been, man? Middle o' the fuckin' night, he turns up with a shovel and torch. What did you think he was fuckin' doing, planting a tree? Nah, man, it was a body. Anyway, it sounded like one when he grabbed it from the car and it hit the deck.'

'Then what,' said Towler, ignoring the tree remark.

'The fucker picked it up, didn't he? Carried it t' hole, threw it in, shovelled shite on top for ten minutes then got back in his car and fucked off.'

'Where were you?'

Ackley looked at Towler like he was an idiot. 'I was in the office, like. Haven't you been fucking listening?'

Fluke hid a smile.

'I meant, were you hiding the whole time or did you get a proper look, dickhead? In other words, are you guessing what he did or did you see it?' Towler growled. 'And if you speak to me like that again in front of my boss, I'll snap your fucking thumbs.'

Ackley looked at Towler and then to Fluke for some help. He didn't get it. 'No, I seen it all. I stuck me head back up after a while and when I did, he was carrying the bag in a fireman's lift. Still had the torch on, that's how come I could see. Fucking shitting mesel' the whole time, mind.'

'What did he look like?'

'Big fucker. Maybe not tall as you, but not far off. Had a suit on, I think. It was pitchers, like, so I cud only see an outline.'

'Car?'

'Dunno. Not mad for cars, never 'ad one. Me mate Macca's the one for cars. He'd tell ya what it was from the outline, nee bother like.'

'Macca?'

'Me mate. Davey McNab. I went t' him to get a loan like. Was gonna fuck off to Newcastle for a bit till it calmed down. He could only spot us a fiver, like. Not enough for a bus and not enough for a bag o' smack. Fucking cuntstruck he is. Scared shitless of that woman he's with. She said no t' lending us the cash, like. I could hear 'er.'

'So you went to Tesco?'

'Aye, it was the only thing I could think of. Knew I could get mesel' locked up if I took summat big enough. Had to wait by the door or the fat cunt of a guard wouldn't 'ave caught us.'

'Why'd you not come to us? Or to your probation officer, for that matter?'

'Them cunts. What the point? They do nowt for ya. "Piss into this, Ackley, do this, Ackley, stop having unprotected sex, Ackley, stop taking drugs, Ackley." Fucking knobs the lot of them. I tell you, probation can go fu—'

'The car?' Towler said, cutting him off.

'I dunno. It was a fuckin' car. Had a boot rather than a hatchback, I suppose. Biggish. Looked like a dark colour.'

Towler realised that all was he was going to get. 'Why'd you leave the note?'

His demeanour changed. Fluke could have sworn there was colour rising onto his pale cheeks. He doubled up again. He seemed to be shaking again. Fluke thought that the stomach cramps might cause him to vomit. But he was wrong, he wasn't cramping up. He was crying again.

Ackley looked up. His eyes were red and wet. There were tears on his cheeks. 'I'm a piece of shit,' he said, sobbing. 'I mean look at the clip of us. Nee family, nee friends apart from Macca, and he's a cock most o' the time. Been on the streets over ten years. When I was larle, I was getting two hundred quid a go. Now I'm lucky to get a fiver. Who's gonna give a shit when I die? Fucking no one, that's who. Who's gonna call the police when someone puts me in a hole in the ground?'

'It just seemed like the right thing to do?' Towler said, far gentler.

Ackley nodded.

After that, there didn't seem to be anything else left to discuss. As they left the interview room, Fluke turned and looked at Ackley, waiting there for a prison officer to collect him. Shivering in his own private hell.

Fluke didn't think he'd seen anything so sad in his life.

***

Chapter 17

When Fluke got back to their car and retrieved his phone, there were missed calls and a text. Both from Skelton.

He called back and she answered on the first ring. 'Jo, what's up?'

'We've got a hit on the E-fit, boss.'

Fluke could hear excitement in her voice. 'Christ, that was quick. I've only been gone four hours,' he said.

'I sent it off to Whitehaven and Carlisle first thing. Carlisle CID got it just in time to get it onto the territorial policing team shift change briefing. I thought, if we got it out early enough and followed up with detectives later, we would cover a lot more ground. See if there was anything immediate.'

'And there was.'

'Yes, sir. John Watt & Son. She was there a week ago.'

'You're joking? In Carlisle?' His pulse quickened.

'You know it, sir?'

Fluke couldn't believe it. Other than Bruccianis, where he bought his Cuban cigars, Watts – as it known locally – was probably his favourite shop in Carlisle. He bought coffee from there if he was ever passing and knew the owners well. Although they would have to confirm it with a proper photograph of the victim, it was a stunning breakthrough. 'Know it, I used to shop there.'

He felt a buzz of excitement, the first he'd felt since finding the body. It tingled in his veins and kick-started his brain. Skelton was from Ulverston and Fluke knew something she probably didn't. 'Watts is on Bank Street,' he told her. 'That place is crawling with CCTV. If it's her, we have a place to start. Get Longy back in. I'll need him to work the cameras. We may even be able to track her to her house.'

Poor Jiao-long. Only back twelve hours and he's stuck with another major task. Couldn't be helped, though. He was their best chance of finding her among the city's cameras.

They arrived back at the incident room to find it full. Everyone was waiting for Fluke, waiting to be tasked. They knew the investigation had taken a turn and would speed up. Before they'd been casting their net wide, now there was some focus. If they could find her house, they could start piecing her life together.

Find out how the victim lived and you'll find out how they died.

A mantra drummed into him by an instructor on his SIO course.

Fluke went straight into tasking. 'Longy, if we confirm she was at Watts, I want you on the CCTV. Go and base yourself wherever you need to be; probably at the council's control room initially. How many people will you need?'

He'd obviously been thinking about that as he answered immediately. 'Just me to start with, boss. If I find her and she disappears, I may need help tracking down other sources of film.'

'Okay. Hopefully we'll get a description of what she was wearing last time she was there as well,' Fluke said.

Jiao-long left to make the arrangements. Fluke knew he'd go straight to the council and, despite their objections, take over their suite. He knew his way round their machines better than they did.

Fluke remembered something. 'Longy,' he shouted to get him back. 'She may live in a flat.'

He briefly explained to everyone the theory on why she was shot at point-blank range. There was no dissent, which Fluke took as a good sign.

With Jiao-long gone, he continued with the rest of the tasks. As he did, Skelton handed something out to everyone. When he got his, Fluke saw it was a business card printed with the numbers found with the body. The logo on the back told him they were from a local printer. She must have paid for them herself. He was impressed. Carrying it about in your wallet or purse meant it was always to hand.

'Right, Matt and I will go to Watts. See what we can get from them.'

He stood, ready to leave. Everyone did the same, eager to get going. A break in the case was better than a double shot of espresso for getting the energy levels up. 'Jo's also just handed out some cards with those numbers on. Longy came back with zilch which means the answer's not on the Internet. I want you thinking about this every spare minute you get. Spread them around. They must mean something to someone,' he told them all.

He made a show of putting his in his wallet and noticed most of them did the same. He had a sudden thought and called Alan Vaughn back. 'Go to the university. See if there's a cryptographer in the maths department who might be able to help with them.'

'Does Cumbria University even have a maths department?' Vaughn asked.

'Alan, go to the university and find out if they have a maths department,' Fluke said, to laughter. 'If they don't, go across to Newcastle University. I know they do.'

'Will do, boss.'

With Jiao-long coming up blank, he knew that Vaughn was his best bet. He was as dogged as they came and would keep going until he had something. As strange as he was, Fluke liked Vaughn. By rights, he should have been a detective sergeant but refused promotions so he could stay with FMIT. That alone made him a star as far as he was concerned, but Vaughn was also a superb detective. He was a fiercely private individual, unmarried and still lived with his parents, retired vets, in a big house outside Kendal. For reasons Fluke had never been able to get to the bottom of, Vaughn seemed to dislike all forms of physical contact; handshakes, hugs, even pats on the back were avoided. He always wore long sleeves, even in the height of summer, just in case someone else's bare arm brushed his.

As well as a being a solid detective, he was also an excellent profiler with an uncanny knack for looking at crime scenes and knowing whether motivations were driven by anger, revenge or sex. He was rarely wrong. Alan Vaughn just thought about things a little differently to everyone else.

Just another oddbod in a team of oddbods. Fluke admired them all.

'What about the cosmetic surgery lead, boss?' Skelton asked. 'Do you want me to follow that up?'

'No, I'll do it straight after I've been to Watts,' he said. 'No point everyone going into Carlisle. You stay here, keep

HOLMES up to date and coordinate the intel as it comes in. I want to know everything in real time.'

With the major tasks allocated, Fluke walked back to his office to check his emails.

There was nothing on the system that needed his urgent attention. He leaned back in his chair and stared out of the window. The weather was changing. The light was poorer than it had been that morning. Rain was on its way. Fluke didn't mind. His office view encompassed fields and sheep. He liked the rain. It gave the landscape a mystical quality.

Without realising he had, he'd removed the card Skelton had given him from his wallet. He'd been shuffling it between his fingers like a Vegas dealer. He stopped and studied it.

2.3 – 8.7 – 92

It wasn't on the Internet. Fluke knew if it had been, Jiao-long would have found it. Or if it was on and he hadn't found it, then it wasn't meant to be found. He was good, but there were some closed systems he couldn't access.

Instinctively, Fluke thought it would be something normal rather than something exotic. Something obvious. Something that made you cry out, 'of course'.

2.3 – 8.7 – 92

The key to it all? Or just random numbers that were going to cost the taxpayer thousands of pounds in police hours as they tried to track them down?

Fluke stared at them again. Were they familiar? He thought they might be, but had no idea why. He thought the most likely explanation was a password to something online and if it was, they may never find out. He took one last look, but they stubbornly refused to reveal their secrets. A noise outside, getting louder, told him that Towler was on his way.

Time to go and get some coffee.

John Watt & Son had been selling coffee in one form or other in Carlisle for over one hundred and fifty years. Starting off as general grocers in 1865, they traded for nearly 130 years until the challenge of out-of-town supermarkets forced them to change to tea and coffee specialists. They were more recently known for stocking coffees and teas that were simply not available anywhere else in the county. They had a small café in the shop and Fluke often stayed for a piece of cake and a chat with the owner if he had time.

The journey from HQ took less than half an hour. Towler double-parked on Bank Street, walked over to a traffic warden, who was just starting the street, and explained who they were. The man didn't seem to want to get into an argument and Towler was soon back.

'Sorted,' he said.

It was a strange street. There were half a dozen high street banks, half a dozen charity shops and a pet shop. In Fluke's experience charity shops and banks never normally rubbed shoulders together. It was a contradiction. The poor and the organisations that made them poor.

And right in the middle was Watts.

Fluke and Towler entered.

The smell hit Fluke immediately. The scent of exotic coffee beans, acrid espressos and cinnamon lattes mingling to create a heady bouquet that made his mouth water.

The bank of jarred beans behind the counter told you everything you needed to know about Watts. Over a hundred varieties, enough to tempt the fussiest connoisseur. Beans from Brazil, Vietnam, Peru and Ethiopia. A United Nations of coffee growers. The day's special offer was from Costa Rica. The big glass jar sat on the top of the rich mahogany counter next to the till and a selection of fresh cakes under a glass cloche.

The huge grinder whirred as another customer had their beans freshly prepared, ready to be taken home and enjoyed later. Fluke hadn't bought a bag of Watts coffee since he'd moved and he vowed to stock up before he left.

Fluke didn't recognize the woman serving behind the counter.

'Hello, Avison. We were wondering if it'd be you who'd turn up,' said a cheerful voice from his left.

Fluke turned to see where the voice came from. A middle-aged woman was in the café section, serving a group of office workers. They were all wearing the same name badge; civil servants by the look of things. They looked glad to be out of their office. He knew she'd worked here for years but wasn't the owner. She seemed to know every customer by name and was never so busy she couldn't stop and chat.

'Hello, Barbara. How are you? Was it uniform you spoke to earlier?' Fluke asked.

'I'll come over,' she said. 'We can go in the back.'

After they'd settled in the small office, she answered. 'Yes, it was me initially. I've seen the poor girl a few times but it was Kath who saw her last.'

'I'll need to speak to Kath as well,' Fluke said.

'She's gone home, Avison,' she said. 'She was a bit upset.'

'I'm sorry, Barbara, I really am. But we'll need to speak to her today, it's very important.'

'I made sure she wrote everything down though,' Barbara added triumphantly, pointing at a piece of paper.

Fluke felt a surge of excitement. *Excellent.*

She'd need to be interviewed later but all he wanted was something to get Jiao-long started.

'Right, we'll get onto that in a minute.' From his conference folder, Fluke produced a photo of the victim's face taken at the post-mortem, and put it upside down on the table. 'Barbara, I want to show you a picture and it's quite upsetting. But I'd like you to look at it nonetheless.'

She smiled. 'I was a nurse for twenty years, Avison. If you need to show me a picture of a dead body, go right ahead.'

A sense of relief flooded through him. Getting someone to actually look at the photo had never been a given. He turned over the picture. A glossy photo of the victim's face, ghostly white under the post-mortem lights, stared up at them both. 'This woman shops here?' he said.

Barbara took a pair of reading glasses from her cardigan pocket and picked up the photo. She didn't appear fazed as she stared at it. 'Well, not anymore she doesn't judging by this, but yes, she did. Nice girl, quiet,' she replied.

Fluke was prepared to accept that as a positive sighting. He had a place for Jiao-long to start. 'We don't yet know who she is. Is there anything you can help us with? How long has she shopped with you?'

'Not long, a couple of months, maybe. But she was in every week.'

'Can you remember anything about her?'

'Not really, she didn't stick out. Always paid cash. Always bought a three-bean blend. One hundred fifty grams of South American Mountain for flavour, One-fifty of Sumatran for strength and two hundred grams of Costa Rican for depth. Always the same, even when we had specials on. Always the same amount, a five-hundred-gram bag. Never had the beans ground in-store. I assume she had her own grinder. Most of our regulars do.'

Score one for Lucy, Fluke thought. She hadn't got a thing wrong yet. 'You wouldn't happen to know when she was here last, would you?'

'Last Thursday, ten past twelve.'

Fluke looked at her open-mouthed, wondering if she was winding him up.

She laughed at his expression. 'We checked the till roll. Kath served her. The reason we know is because she only served two people that morning. The rest of the time she was doing the tables. More fun you see, you get to talk with the locals. She hates the till. But if we're jammed, she'll help out. She remembers her because she's never made her blend before. It's all written down here.'

Fluke read Kath's statement. It was written on Watts's stationery. Attached was a photocopy of the receipt as well as a description of what the victim had been wearing. 'This is excellent, Barbara,' Fluke said. 'She seems to have a real eye for detail.'

'Yes, well. Kath's a bit of a clotheshorse. If it had been me on the till you wouldn't have got this much detail. I wouldn't know my Prada from my Primark.'

'You've no idea how helpful this is going to be,' Fluke said, gratefully. He passed the statement over to Towler. 'Seems Kath remembered what she was wearing as well,' Fluke said.

'She didn't speak to her?' Towler asked.

'No, no one ever did. She always seemed to come when it was busy, around lunchtime. People rushing in and out.'

Fluke and Towler exchanged glances. Another way of making sure she wasn't noticed. Another indicator she'd been hiding from someone.

'Matt, can you give Longy a bell and let him know what she was wearing, along with the date and time,' Fluke asked. Towler left to make the call. 'That'll save us hours of work, Barbara.'

While he waited for Towler to come back, he looked at the photo again. A pretty woman, no more than a girl really. A life snuffed out for reasons he hadn't even started to unravel yet. Towler returned.

'All done. He's gonna give us a live update.'

Fluke turned to Barbara. 'Thanks again for all this. You won't believe how much help you've been.'

'My pleasure, Avison. Now can I get you something while you're here?'

Fluke looked round at the huge amount of coffee they stocked. Millions of beans, waiting to be ground, waiting for their oils to be released and for hot water to be added. A custom the same the world over. A custom older than Carlisle.

'I'll tell you what, Barbara. Make me up a bag of her blend can you?'

'Of course. I'll grind it right up for you.'

'Don't, I'll take a grinder as well.'

Find out how the victim lived and you'll find out how they died.

Chapter 18

Agreeing to meet first thing, Towler parked up at the hospital. They were in Fluke's car. Towler lived in Carlisle so would walk home.

Fluke walked through the huge revolving doors into the open-plan foyer. The clack of keyboards, the squeal of wheelchairs and the low voices of staff, patients and visitors combined into a cacophony of sensory confusion.

As he headed towards Oncology, Fluke was reminded how much it looked like an airport departure lounge. It was huge. It had opened to criticism that it took up too much valuable space and when it transpired that ward corridors were so narrow that two beds couldn't pass, the criticism appeared justified.

'Is she in?' he asked the nurse on the reception.

'I'll call her, Mr Fluke. Take a seat,' she replied.

Fluke elected to stand. While he was waiting, he took the business card out of his wallet and stared at it. Willing the numbers to change, to make sense. He even tried squinting his eyes, tried to look through it as though it were a magic eye picture. Nothing. But the nagging feeling persisted. They looked familiar.

'And to what do I owe this pleasure?' Doctor Cooper asked, entering the reception area.

She looked tired but then she always did. Fluke's job carried a huge responsibility, but in between the major cases, he at least had some respite. A chance to recharge the mental batteries. Consultants didn't have that luxury.

'I need your help,' he said.

'Okay,' she said cautiously. 'Am I going to like this?'

'It's nothing bad, I promise you. I just want your advice on this case. Maybe a name I can call.'

'We'd better go to my office.'

'Thanks, Doctor Cooper.'

'Look, this is ridiculous, Avison. Will you please call me Leah. We've known each other long enough now.'

'Okay,' he said carefully. Fluke was one of those people who would happily call a nurse by their first name but would insist on the deferential approach when conversing with doctors. He didn't know why that was. He certainly didn't do it for any other profession.

He followed her into her office and took a seat.

'Okay. What's it about?' she asked.

'This is going to be a bit left field, but what do you know about cosmetic surgery?'

She looked nonplussed and stared at him for a few seconds. 'Nothing, of course. I'm not a surgeon. I'm certainly not a cosmetic surgeon. There aren't any clinics in Cumbria.'

'That much I already know. I just want the basics. Where someone would go to get some surgery done? How long it takes? Would it be possible to get multiple procedures done at once? How long to heal, that sort of thing?'

'Is this something to do with that woman they found on Tuesday?'

He paused before deciding she deserved to have some background. 'Yes,' he said. 'At the PM on Tuesday afternoon, Henry found extensive cosmetic surgery. Bit of an enigma. Very high quality but it made no sense. Medically speaking.'

'Oh. Go on, why?' she said, her medical curiosity obviously piqued.

'She didn't need it for one thing.' Fluke held his hand up, knowing she was going to launch into something about how men had no right to decide what women did to their bodies. 'No, all the changes she made detracted from her looks rather than enhanced them.'

She folded her arms. 'Says you.'

Fluke didn't have the time or the inclination to get into an argument. 'Says me, says Henry and says Lucy.' He was going to add Towler's name to the list but decided against it. Although he had a young daughter, Towler knew even less about women than he did. He'd once been dumped for toilet texting.

'Who's Lucy?' she said unexpectedly.

'The bug lady,' he said, without thinking.

She said nothing. Continued to stare at him with her arms folded and her lips pursed.

'An entomologist. A PhD student working with Henry for a few weeks. She's been a big help, actually.'

'You have a theory about the cosmetic surgery?' she said, changing direction.

'She was altering the way she looked for a reason. We think she was hiding.'

Leah leaned forward. 'Were there any other supporting factors?'

'Yes.'

'What?'

'Her hair was dyed. Platinum blonde to brown.'

'Anything else?'

'Coloured contacts.'

She leaned back in her chair and appeared to be thinking. She flicked some hair from her eyes, stood up and retrieved a book from the bookcase beside her desk. She flicked through it, looking for something. She sighed and closed it. 'Look I'm not an expert on this but I know the laws on cosmetic surgery are constantly changing. It used to be an entirely unregulated business. There were more regulations governing toothbrush manufacture than there were on liposuction, believe it or not. All changing now, of course. Breast implants saw to that.'

'The ones that exploded?' he asked without thinking.

She smiled. 'At one point, there was more money being made repairing exploding tits than there was fitting them. Did she have hers done?'

'Nope, strictly above the collar. Nose, ears, chin and brow.'

'And the rest is easy to hide with clothes,' she said straightaway.

'Exactly.'

They discussed what procedures she'd been through and Leah eventually agreed that Fluke's theory was possible. Probable even.

'I take it you'd like to speak to the doctor who did the surgery?' she said.

'If possible.'

'Not a chance. There's hundreds of surgeons who do this sort of thing in the UK. You can add three noughts to whatever number we have if you include Europe and the States. Breast implants have serial numbers now but with the procedures she's had, there'll be nothing to check.'

Fluke knew she was right, and had known it before he'd left HQ. Still, another potential lead had been crossed off. Even negative intelligence was still intelligence. Detectives were taught to use an acronym: TIE. Trace, interview, eliminate. It was meant for suspects and witnesses but worked just as well for potential lines of enquiry.

'Look, I know someone in London who may be able to help. I'll call him tonight, see if he can get you a number to ring,' she said. 'You can at least hear from someone who knows what they're talking about.'

'Thanks, Leah. Anything at all will be more than we have on her so far.'

She returned the book to the shelf and sat back down. 'How are you, Avison?'

'Can't complain,' he replied, his mind already on the next task.

'Avison. How are you really? You look exhausted. How are you sleeping?'

Fluke shrugged. He wasn't comfortable talking about things like that.

'Look, it's common to feel like you did, it would be extraordinary if you hadn't. You weren't expected to live, remember? No one gave you a chance when they saw the size of the tumour. Whether you'll admit it or not, you had PTSD. That's why you were so angry with everyone. The world didn't change when you were in hospital, Avison. You did. At first, I thought moving out of Carlisle to live on your own in the middle of nowhere was a mistake but I have to admit, you knew more about how to heal yourself than I did.'

Fluke looked at her. He didn't realise she'd been paying that close attention. He rubbed his hands over his eyes, tried to remove some of the grittiness that came on with fatigue. The truth was he was no longer reliving his illness anymore. For a few months, he'd suffered badly from distressing flashbacks. He'd dreaded sleep, waking up sweating and trembling after he finally succumbed. If it hadn't been for his thin blood, he'd have used alcohol as a numbing agent. 'I'm doing better, Leah. Much better.'

It was no longer the reaction to his illness that kept him awake. It was what he'd done to her. A secret he couldn't share although he knew if he was ever to enjoy a restful night again, at some point in the future he'd have to tell her.

She leaned back in her chair and seemed to appraise him. 'Good then. Now we just need to stabilise your bloods and we'll be fine. How was dinner the other night?' she asked.

He paused. 'I'm sorry,' he said eventually. He had no idea what she was talking about.

'Dinner at Michelle's. I gather it didn't go all that well?' She laughed at his expression. 'Sorry, bit naughty of me. It's just that you met one of my friends. She says she gave you a lift home.'

For once Fluke was lost for words. The mystery woman was her friend? It seemed unlikely that Michelle and Leah ran in the same social circles. Leah seemed intelligent and reasonable. Michelle's friends were right-wing bigots. Leah must have been reading his mind.

'Don't worry, she doesn't normally run with that sort of crowd. She knew someone called Charles and he'd invited her. She was going to say no, but I convinced her to go.'

'I thought you said she was your friend,' he replied before he could stop himself. Michelle didn't deserve that. Well, maybe she did, but he liked to think he was above pettiness. 'Sorry,' he added.

He couldn't get her to elaborate on who her friend was. Fluke would've liked to thank her for the lift. He wasn't sure he'd given a good account of himself at the dinner party.

'Wheels within wheels, Avison. Wheels within wheels,' was all she'd say.

The drive home took just under an hour. It had started raining, only lightly, but enough to bring the visibility right down. He was bone tired when he made it through his front door and just wanted to go to sleep. When he'd lived in Carlisle, he'd have reached for the takeaway menus he kept in a kitchen drawer. Out here, he was on his own. He was debating whether he should reheat some of the previous night's curry, or cook an omelette, when the phone rang. He looked at the clock on the oven, briefly thought about ignoring it before deciding he couldn't.

'Boss, it's Al Vaughn. We've been trying to get hold of you for an hour.'

Shit.

He'd turned his phone off at the hospital and had forgotten to turn it back on. He hadn't even checked in with Towler on how things were going.

'What's up, Al? I'm only just in and I'm knackered. Gonna have some food and get some kip.'

'We've got him, boss.'

'Got who?'

'The man who killed our vic. Long story and we haven't actually got him, but we're nearly there. We know which family he's from.'

'I'm on my way,' he said, hanging up and reaching for his coat, all thoughts of food forgotten.

As soon as he was off the dirt track and onto a safer road, he phoned Towler for an update.

'That E-fit Jo circulated was doing the rounds at Carlisle CID and one of the DCs recognised her. She'd reported being raped last week.'

'In Carlisle?' Fluke asked.

'Yep. Looks like she was roofied or something. Says she went out for a drink, woke up the next day with no memory of the evening. Thought she'd been raped and the doc confirmed there were date rape drugs in her system. There was also some skin under her nails and a couple of foreign pubes. Got DNA from all of it, results came back this morning. Their case was a few days before ours obviously, and there was no reason for anyone to link them.'

He went on to explain that the DNA was an interfamilial, rather than a direct match. The rapist wasn't on the National DNA Database, NDNAD, but a blood relative was. Ten years before, that wouldn't have been possible but with more and more people on the database and technology retrieval methods improving, hits like that were increasingly common.

'Where'd she get examined?'

'Preston SARC.'

Good, Fluke thought. The Sexual Assault Referral Centre at Preston was the best in the north-west. 'Name and address?'

'Name's Samantha Farrar, but there's a Kay Edwards, the DC who accompanied her, who wants to speak to you about that. And she wouldn't give an address.'

'Why not?' Fluke asked. Victims of crime didn't have to give their addresses but it was unusual.

'Dunno. Scared of reprisals, possibly? Edwards is at HQ waiting for you.'

'Good.' Fluke always preferred to question witnesses himself wherever possible. He felt at his best when the information was coming to him raw. Reports and witness statements sometimes lacked things like non-verbals or what their emotional state was. How upset or angry they were. Whether they could remember a smell or a sound. Murders had been solved on such things. 'Tell me about the DNA hit. Who is he?'

'Nathaniel Diamond? Nothing to tell really. Just a fucking thug. Twenty-nine years old. From a big family that seems to think they run Carlisle. Live mainly in Meadowby. They bring in some heroin and cocaine. Run a few women, massage parlours that type of thing. Bit of rural crime. We think they do loan-sharking and payday loans as well. He's been arrested just the once. A Section 18 GBH. Never went anywhere. Victim refused to press charges.'

Fluke had vaguely heard of the Diamond family. They'd never come to the attention of FMIT, so his knowledge was sketchy. He'd never heard of Nathaniel but Grievous Bodily Harm was a nasty assault. The Section 18 signified there'd been intent. It carried a maximum sentence of life. The next charge up was attempted murder.

'They big?' he asked.

'Hard to say, boss. There's intel suggesting they're bigger than they let on. They certainly don't flash the cash, so the National Crime Agency have never got involved. But there was a snout last year who said all the crime families around here have to pay them to operate. Take a percentage of everything they do. They can't use anything but Diamond drugs apparently. The drugs team mounted an operation but got nowhere.'

'If it's interfamilial DNA, it's not him we're looking for. Who's in the mix? Who's the likely suspects?' Fluke asked.

'Nathaniel's the younger of two brothers. Wayne's the elder, doesn't have a record. Never even been arrested.'

'So it's him we're looking for?'

'That'd be my guess.'

'Anyone else?'

'There's the dad. Probably the brains in the family. He lives in a big detached house in Stanwix. Bit of a show place, apparently. Never been arrested either.'

'Wider family?' Fluke asked. He knew interfamilial DNA was far reaching, it pointed at more than just the immediate family. It was its advantage and disadvantage. Uncles, aunts, cousins, illegitimate children, they would all need to be tracked down and eliminated.

'Fucking mess, boss. You know what these lot are like. They're everywhere. Some are related, some aren't. They all fuck each other, so the children's heritage is anyone's guess. Most of them are related through incest or rape.'

'Me mam's me sister and me dad's me cousin,' Fluke said.

'That type of thing, yeah.'

'How many do we have on the database? I'm assuming they're being ruled out as we speak? I don't want to bring in twenty people who we know aren't in the frame.'

'Looks like about half of them have been arrested. The brighter ones tend to not go near the drugs at all. They have an army of mules and dealers working for them. Intel suggests that most of the wider family are enforcers and foot soldiers. They think Kenneth Diamond is the main man. Nathaniel is probably his number two.'

'You got a theory on the murder?' Fluke asked, knowing he would. He had his own, but liked others to voice theirs first.

'On paper it looks straightforward. Our victim finds herself with the unwanted attentions of a Diamond. Most of the local girls would just put up with it for the night, shut their eyes and wait for them to finish. "Pull my nightie back down when you're finished" type of thing. Better than saying no and having the family after you. But she doesn't know the family so he goes to plan B. Being in the drug trade, he has access to Rohypnol. Slips it in her drink. Takes her back to his cave. Rapes her. Dumps her somewhere. Thinks he's golden. How am I doing?'

'Same as me so far.'

'But she wakes up and knows what's happened. Reports it. There's DNA evidence and traces of the Rohypnol still in her blood. The rapist finds out and panics. They track her down and kill her. Might have been the rapist, might have been a team effort. But one of them bastards did it.'

Fluke agreed entirely. He'd keep his mind open until they had more but he couldn't really see any other explanation at present. 'Works for me. I think she came back home to hide from someone. Can't see any other reason for the cosmetic surgery. Might have been here a few weeks, might have been a year. But she was hiding. And then she runs into a Diamond and she has a whole new set of problems.'

'You want a hard arrest?'

Fluke considered it. Towler's hard arrests were something to witness. Professional Standards had investigated him three times over them but they were all above board. Sort of. All three of them had involved child sex offenders, all the victims the same age as Towler's daughter. Fluke thought they'd got off lightly. 'No, but I want it coordinated. We'll do it by the rules, but we go in early and fast. Take them all in before they can warn each other,' he said.

'We won't get them all. We don't know who they all are. They're like a virus. Spread all over the fucking city. Best we can do is get as many as we can, take their DNA and then sweat them for the rest if our man's not in the first trawl. Longy's got some new genogram software he wants to try out. He'll plot out their family tree as we go along. Make sure we don't miss anyone.'

'Shit, Longy. How's he getting on? I've forgotten about him. My phone was switched off after I'd been to the hospital,' Fluke said.

'He's still got her. Says he wants to speak to you. Thinks she's surveillance-aware. Illogical routes, doubling back, the works. Her face isn't on camera, not really. Only long shots, where she has no control. She's on foot though, which is making it easier.'

'But he's still following her?'

136

'Yeah. He's had to change systems a few times and commandeer a couple of private ones. Thought he'd lost her down by the station but one of the takeaways on the Crescent had an outward-facing camera. They'd had some bother with racists and were scared of getting their windows put through. Anyway, it picked her up heading towards the viaduct.'

'Tell him this is a no-go-home situation. Anything he wants. All overtime. I need an address,' Fluke said.

Towler rang off just as Fluke pulled into HQ. Dark skies, light rain turning heavy. A cold wind grumbling its way down from the fells. Fluke was hungry and he was tired.

He'd never felt more alive.

Chapter 19

Fluke visited Jiao-long and caught up with the passive data investigation. To be fair, Jiao-long hadn't seemed to notice the hours he'd put in. He was another one who would keep going until the job was done. Fluke's apology for not checking in on him was wasted. He confirmed what Towler had told him. The victim seemed to be surveillance-aware and he'd nearly lost her a couple of times but the city simply had too many cameras and Jiao-long knew them all. It annoyed him that he had to ask to commandeer private CCTV sometimes but his winning personality normally got him through the door.

Jiao-long made him laugh sometimes. The only real culture clash they'd had since he arrived was over the rights of the public. He couldn't get his head round the fact that people weren't legally obliged to help the police. He couldn't get his head round criminals getting free legal, and more importantly, *independent* advice. He couldn't believe the UK police had so few rights. Fluke got the impression that in China, being a policeman was a little different. He also got the impression most of FMIT envied Jiao-long.

DC Kay Edwards from Carlisle CID was waiting for Fluke in his office. A woman whose age he wouldn't be able to get within ten years of. One of those women whose hair had turned grey before she wanted it to but she still managed to look youthful. Probably never occurred to her to dye it. Good for her. Coppers, male and female, who were too bothered about their looks got on his nerves. It was an outside job predominantly. Save the make-up and the highlights for your nights off.

She stood up as he entered and reached for his offered hand with a smile that showed confidence but not cockiness. Her handshake was warm, dry and firm. He liked her immediately.

'DC Edwards. May I call you Kay?'

'Of course, sir.'

'You've heard what we have so far?'

'Yes, sir.'

'It looks like you're one of the last people to have seen her alive. What can you tell me I don't already know? Half an hour ago I didn't know her name. Now I have a name and a suspect,' he said.

Edwards took out a notebook but spoke without referring to it. Good, if you couldn't be bothered to memorise facts before a briefing then you weren't a proper cop as far as he was concerned.

'On paper it seemed fairly straightforward, sir. She says she went out for a quiet drink last Thursday. Wasn't meeting anyone but was sick of being on her own. She can't remember anything at all about the night. Doesn't even remember leaving home.'

'Did she say home or flat?' Fluke asked. *Little details*, he thought. Good detectives had an eye for them. Little details solved crimes. For the first time, she looked through her notes.

'Flat, sir. She said, and I quote, "I had no recollection of leaving my flat." Is that important?'

'It may be,' Fluke said. 'Go on.'

'Next thing she knew, she was waking up in her bed with no idea how she got there. Said her vagina was sore. Knew straightway she'd been raped. Walked into Durranhill first thing Friday and reported it. I was on duty. Just going off actually, but I've been trained to work with victims of sexual assaults.'

Durranhill was Carlisle Area's headquarters. It was on an industrial estate and some of the firms might have cameras that would help Jiao-long. He made a mental note to let him know.

'Had she been assaulted?' he asked. 'Apart from sexually,' he added quickly.

'Didn't look like it. Me and a colleague took her straight to the SARC in Preston.'

Sexual assault referral centres were fairly new concepts and all Cumbrians went to Preston. They were basically one stop shops where victims could access everything they might need but where a forensic chain of custody was in operation at all times for any subsequent prosecution. Doctors, nurses, counsellors all worked from the SARC and it was open twenty-four hours a day.

'And she was examined there?'

'Yes, sir. The doctor confirmed she'd had sex recently, there was slight tearing in the vagina and the swab for semen was positive. There were foreign hairs recovered from her pubic hair and she had skin under her nails. It's possible she'd scratched her attacker. Something to look out for anyway.'

She looked at him for affirmation. Fluke nodded for her to continue.

'The doctor took bloods and they came back this afternoon. Same time as the DNA hit, as it happens.'

'Why take blood? Is that routine?'

'It is, sir. They have to test for STDs and HIV. It's a victim's number one fear after a rape. That, and pregnancy. With date rapes being so common, and her saying she had no recollection, they screened her for all the common drugs. Came back positive for flunitrazepam.'

'Rohypnol?'

'Rohypnol's a trade name for flunitrazepam, sir. They aren't the only manufacturer.'

'I didn't know that,' Fluke said. Most officers, himself included, used Rohypnol as a generic name the same way people used Hoover to describe vacuum cleaners and Sellotape to describe sticky tape, regardless of who made it.

'Anyway, it's not the best drug to use for date rape. Stays in the system for three days so it's not used that often anymore. GHB or zolpidem have the same effects as flunitrazepam but stay in the body for just a few hours. Gone by the time the victim wakes up, usually. Makes drug-facilitated rape much harder to prove.'

He grimaced. Even rapists were evolving. What type of world was it? No wonder Towler's sex offenders always seemed to resist arrest. 'Okay, so we got lucky. We were due something. What else?'

'Obviously, she was terrified. Very upset as you can imagine. Said she came to Cumbria because of the low crime rate. Was the first time she'd been out and this happened. Wouldn't give me her address and didn't have to. Rape victims are entitled to anonymity, as you know. Said she'd report to the station as much as we wanted her to. I didn't want to push it.'

'You check on PNC or DVLA?'

'Wasn't really supposed to, sir. I'd been asked by the victim to not take down her address.'

'That's not what I asked,' Fluke said.

She paused and Fluke knew that he'd find out what kind of cop she was. Whether she was curious enough to go beyond her statutory responsibilities. There was no such thing as a detective who was too nosey.

She looked directly at him, gauging what she should tell him. Whether she could trust him. She came to some sort of decision. 'Nothing, sir. Nothing that fitted anyway. Plenty of Samantha Farrars. Plenty of Sam and Sammy Farrars too. But they're either too young to be on DVLA or they were too old. Checked for a credit rating but she didn't have one. Checked every database I have access to. Even checked Facebook, Twitter and a dozen other social media sites. Nothing. Either she gave me the wrong name or she lives off the grid.'

Fluke said nothing. Living off the grid was virtually impossible in the UK. The only real way of doing it was to have more than one identity.

'Can I speak freely, sir?

'You're in my part of the building now. Everyone's allowed an opinion here.'

'Something didn't quite add up, sir. She was upset, yes. And I'd never put this on paper, but she didn't seem upset enough. I've been to maybe a dozen of these and every reaction's different obviously so maybe it was just her way of dealing with it.'

'But?'

'But there was just something about her, sir. Intangible almost. She was given a leaflet when she arrived explaining what would happen but I didn't see her read it, and I was with her the whole time. I dunno, there was just something not quite right. Like when you're watching a film and the sound's slightly out of sync.'

Curious.

It may, of course, be nothing, but he'd learnt to trust people's instincts. Fluke was impressed with Edwards. Good insight and only once had she needed to check her notebook. Time to bring her inside.

'We'll keep that in mind, Kay. As you're going to find out, nothing about this case is straightforward. The first thing you should know is that what she gave you was almost certainly a false name.'

She looked at him. Expecting more, knowing she'd passed some sort of test but not sure how.

'The second thing you should know is that she's had extensive cosmetic surgery, all done to drastically change her appearance. Blonde hair dyed brown, coloured contacts. The CCTV that one of my detectives has her on shows she's surveillance-aware. We have a working theory that she was in hiding, and chose here. It's also possible she was originally from Carlisle.' He explained what they knew and what they thought they knew.

'We know who she's hiding from?'

'Not a clue,' Fluke said. 'But if you're in hiding, you don't give your real name, no matter what's happened.'

'Then why give it at all then?'

'Too odd. Raises suspicion. Address, understandable not giving that out, but your name? No, better just to give a false one and hope no one checks. Anything else you can think of?'

She looked at her notes. She shook her head. 'Not really, sir. Some of her answers did seem a bit evasive but I wasn't interrogating her, you understand. I talked to her on the way down in the ambulance. We're supposed to. Theory is that the more you can get them to talk the less they will dwell on what's happened. We're part of the healing process, according to the course instructor. Don't know if it's true or not but I've never seen any reason not to try. I asked where was she from, what she did, how long she'd been here, that type of thing. Looking back, all I got were superficial answers. No depth to any of them.'

'You think she was telling the truth about the rape?'

'Again, not sure. I think she was raped, definitely. Hard to come to any other conclusion really.'

'Did she ever report back to get an update on the investigation?' Fluke asked.

'No, sir. I asked her to come in on Monday but I never saw her again. But then again she may have been murdered soon after.'

'Times don't work,' Fluke said. We have a TOD we're happy with, and there's four days between the rape and the murder. There was no evidence to suggest she'd been abducted. We think this was a hit. In and out, same night. But I think you're right, there was something she wasn't telling you.'

'If you say she was in hiding then why did she even go out at all?'

The same thought had occurred to Fluke. He was in no doubt that Samantha – Fluke would think of her by her first name, it helped remind him the crime involved humans and was more than just an intellectual exercise – had been scared of someone. Surveillance aware, extensive cosmetic surgery, false name, no address. She was doing everything right to stay hidden.

And then she goes out.

In a public place. Not to meet someone. Just out, on her own.

Said she was lonely. Fluke doubted it. Women that scared didn't get lonely.

'That, Kay, is a detective's question.' He thought quickly. He'd have to take over the rape investigation and absorb it into the murder. No point in having the two running parallel. The original team would stay on the rape line of enquiry but he'd need liaison between both. He needed someone working from FMIT who knew the rape.

'I'm going to bring you across to my team for the rest of this investigation, Kay. I'll clear it with your super. Go back over the night she came in. Speak to the ambulance driver that took her down to Preston. Go to Preston and speak to everyone who saw her there. It's a murder investigation now, so don't worry too much about hurting anyone's feelings. Get as much footage as you can. I want to see if she is as aware of cameras when she's suffering from trauma. See how controlled she was. I need to know more. Before you go though, read the murder summary. Sergeant Towler will give you a copy.'

Find out how the victim lived and you'll find out how they died.

After Edwards left, Fluke looked for something to eat. When night ops were being planned, there was always plenty of it lying around and he found it in the incident room. Towler was there, in his element. An extension of a military operation, it was something he excelled at. Yelling and organising. Classic sergeant tasks. Military or police, the role never changed. Every officer reporting was given a number and a briefing pack and was told where to be and at what time. As Towler was doing all the briefings himself, they were all at different times. Some officers

143

were therefore able to disappear again for a few hours. Most didn't, however. The chance of closing off a rape and a murder in one noisy dawn raid was like a caffeine shot.

There was a contingent of armed response officers standing in a group on their own, dressed in black combats and peaked baseball caps. They would draw their weapons from the armoury later. As a firearm had been used in the murder, each arrest team would have armed response securing the premises.

The air smelt of fried food and curry. A few years before, it would have been thick with cigarette smoke as well. Things moved on, often for the better, but he didn't think making people stand outside freezing their bollocks off every time they fancied a ciggy was one of them.

Phones were ringing and keyboards were clicking. The closer an investigation got to being solved, the faster people typed. The faster they answered the phone. The louder they got.

He wandered over to see Towler to make sure they were both in the group that was taking down Nathaniel Diamond. On paper, he was the most violent, the most likely to resist and Fluke wanted to make sure he was taken down quickly and efficiently. Although not a suspect for the rape, if a Diamond had indeed killed Samantha, then Nathaniel would know who. He may have even authorised it. At the point of arrest, emotions ran high and unguarded comments sometimes slipped out before the suspect had a chance to lawyer up. If they did, Fluke wanted to be there.

Towler looked up from what he was doing and saw Fluke.

'Be with you in two, boss. Just sorting through this crap. Got one man reported sick this evening so one of the teams is gonna be light.'

'How many we got going out?' Fluke asked.

'About eighty in total, not including half of every TPT on standby to provide urgent uniformed assistance if we need crowd control. They'll be in reserve, dotted around the city in vans.'

Territorial Policing Teams were the bobbies on the beat, but could be drafted in to support operations when extra resources were required. Fluke knew they would have a better knowledge of the city than FMIT did. If things went wrong, their help would be crucial.

'Longy's not going out, is he? I need him working on her address.'

'No, and you know what he's like. Kicked up a right stink, wanted to be in on it. Told him you needed him where he was but he wouldn't have it. Says he's going to speak to you about it. Told him good luck and, in the meantime, shut up and stop acting like a fucking marine.'

Fluke smiled, refusing to take the bait. The rivalry between the Royal Marines and the Parachute Regiment was infamous. The Royal Latrines and the Parasite Regiment were the nicknames they bestowed upon each other. In reality, they were both elite units, and there was nothing to choose between them so Fluke always took Towler's piss-taking in the manner it was given – lightly. He'd never intended to be a career marine, saw it as a job, something he had to get out of his system before he settled down and did something normal.

Towler, on the other hand, had been serious about being a Para. He'd served most of his time with 1 Para and had been part of Operation Barras, when the Parachute Regiment and SAS had fought the West Side Boys in Sierra Leone before rescuing the five Irish Rangers being held hostage.

For Towler, SAS selection seemed inevitable. Fluke had assumed he'd do the full twenty-two years, finishing on a decent special-forces pension before going into the lucrative close protection business. For a couple of years' work, ex-SAS troopers were earning seven-figure sums. Fluke had thought it entirely possible he'd never see his friend again until they were old men.

And then Abigail came along and changed everything. One cold night, the rain lashing down almost sideways, the way Cumbrian rain did sometimes, Fluke's doorbell rang. Towler was standing outside, soaked. He wasn't alone. Far from it. Towler was holding a baby. His baby.

'I need a job,' were the first words he said.

To this day, Fluke had never found out where Abigail, Abi, came from. Only that her mother wasn't around anymore and Towler had needed to come back up north so his family could help raise her. He'd asked Towler once, but he'd replied, 'I'll tell you after I've told her.' Fluke had never asked again.

He'd given up a career he loved for someone he loved more, and had never regretted it.

He'd joined the police less than a month later and passed everything he was asked to. The fitness came easily enough. The restraint classes were more difficult. The police taught mainly defensive techniques. The Paras taught exclusively aggressive techniques. By the end, his instructors passed him as they didn't know what else to do. He could do everything they asked but what he knew was better. He applied himself with a dedication that had surprised even Fluke, and was soon on the beat as a probationary officer. Posted to the isolated village of Cleator Moor, a terrifying proposition for all but the reckless or the hard of understanding, Towler reduced antisocial behaviour by fifty per cent within a month, almost single-handedly.

He passed his detective's exam and was immediately posted to Fluke's team at both their requests. Towler was one of nature's sergeants and it came as no surprise to anyone when he passed his exam a year later and was immediately promoted.

But Fluke knew Towler sometimes missed the Paras, knew that the action was tame compared to what he'd been used to. He had a skill set he wasn't using, and although he didn't regret making the sacrifices he'd made, Fluke knew he was sometimes frustrated by the constraints the law imposed upon him. Therefore Fluke never took the piss out of the Paras. It wouldn't have been right. He also wasn't entirely convinced that Towler wouldn't hit him if he did.

Here he was in his element; some organisation to do, some action to come later.

Fluke went back to his office to email Chambers and the assistant chief a summary of the progress made that day. For the first time, he was able to say the investigation was actually moving forwards. By doing it that late, he could also guarantee they wouldn't receive it until the next day when it would be too late to interfere.

Chapter 20

Four hours later, Fluke felt as though electricity was coursing through his veins, he was so full of adrenalin. He could tell he wasn't the only one feeling like that in his group. The action was always where the boss went, where the key arrests were made. He was in the back of a van, along with four uniformed officers, three armed response and Towler. Nervous energy and weapons were never a good combination but the armed guys looked calm enough.

The smell of gun oil in an enclosed space brought back vivid memories of the Saracens they'd used in Northern Ireland. Fluke remembered sitting in the back with seven other heavily armed marines as they drove down the Falls Road in Belfast. He'd felt invincible back then. How times change. Not being able to rely on your body changed your perspective somewhat.

They'd driven from HQ up the M6 to the staging area, a procession of vans and unmarked cars. No lights, no sirens. It was a covert operation. It was four a.m. and Carlisle was quiet so the journey was quick. The staging area was in an empty car park on the Durranhill industrial estate, close enough to Carlisle Area HQ that the modern glass building could be seen. There was still the occasional light on as police officers working nights went about their business. It was a big operation but that didn't mean policing the city stopped.

Each call sign knew exactly where they were going and the route they would take. Some were doubled up in vehicles if their targets lived close together. Towler had decided that quarter to five was late enough to ensure they were all at home tucked up, but early enough that the few with jobs weren't up and about.

With ten minutes to go, the vans moved into their forward areas, where they would disembark. The van Fluke was in crept along the deserted streets of Meadowby as quietly as the combustion engine's throaty growl would allow. Although he couldn't see clearly from the back, he assumed they'd arrived when the van stopped and the driver cut the engine. Fluke felt a cold bead of sweat work its way down the back of his neck and under his shirt. He shivered.

There was no rush as they disembarked. They all knew stealth was more important than speed. Fluke was last out. He didn't know this part of Carlisle so was relying on others to find the correct address.

It was still dark. More of a dirty grey than black. It wouldn't be light for another three hours. After the regeneration of the infamous Raffles, Meadowby had become the most run-down estate in Carlisle. Like Pinegrove, efforts had been made to improve it and like Pinegrove, there were still streets where the residents just didn't care. Yet it was a different kind of estate to Pinegrove; more urban, more suffocating. At least in West Cumbria everyone was only two minutes away from fields and open spaces.

All the housing officers and community policing in the world weren't going to get them to tidy their gardens. Or paint their doors. Or fix broken windows. Some people don't want to be helped. Some people don't want others to help anyone else either. One thug could turn a whole street bad. There were few cars. Sensible residents parked in a different area.

Repairing street lamps was a never-ending job for the council in Meadowby, but there were enough working for Fluke's team to make their way to the target address. The house was two streets away and they walked in silence, passing houses that the owners had clearly given up on. Knee-high grass and rubbish piled high in front gardens were a clear giveaway. Fluke had always wondered why those crime families, cash-rich from the drug trade and other endeavours, insisted on living in areas they could afford to move out of. What you're comfortable with, he supposed.

They got to the house one minute before the go order was scheduled. A large blue Mercedes was in the drive. It was less than two years old and was spotless.

The house was on a better street than the two they'd passed through. Cheap cars were in the rest of the drives. All legal by the looks of things. It indicated it was a street that believed in working, in escaping the benefit lifestyle. Or maybe a street with a Diamond in kept itself tidy. A dog barked in the distance and

Fluke wondered if one of the other teams had been compromised. Doubtful, though, not at that time. There was a reason they did raids at those times. Humans naturally tire about five a.m., the spirit at its lowest ebb. Dogs, not so much.

'Everyone in position? Leaders report in with a click,' Towler said over the channel they were using for that op, a specific one that wouldn't be used by officers on other jobs.

A succession of clicks, that must have meant something to Towler, could be heard over the radio. No voices. At that point, he and Fluke would be the only ones breaking radio silence.

'We're set, boss. Okay to go?'

'Go,' Fluke said.

'Right, on me. Thirty seconds to go. In position, everyone.'

The officer selected for the actual door breach was a short stocky man Fluke had never seen before. Although he was small, he was carrying the metal battering ram like it was made of balsa wood. It was painted red but was chipped in places. Clearly not the first time it had been used. He was allowed space to quietly move to the front. He got into a position he was happy with, raised the battering ram and waited, staring fixedly at the point he was aiming for. The armed officers took positions behind him. They would be running forward as soon as the ram was in motion. They bunched up close. Their knees pressed into the back of the knees of the person in front of them. Fluke knew there were two reasons for that. It meant they could get into position in enclosed spaces. What was more important, though, was that as soon as the go order was given there was no hesitation. The forward momentum of the person behind, meant the person in front was going into that house whether he liked it or not.

Special forces breach techniques used by civilian law enforcement.

Other than the lone dog barking, there was no sound. Towler wouldn't count down the thirty seconds, only the last five. Fluke could sense a slight increase in his team's rate of breath. A team confident in what they were doing. Confident that they had enough to overcome whatever was on the other side of the door. Confident that they would soon be back at Durranhill catching up with friends from other teams, swapping stories. But there was always going to be an element of nervousness when going through a door. The fear of the unknown.

Towler caught Fluke's eye and winked. He was chewing gum.

Fluke wasn't so calm. He could taste copper and a vein on the back of his neck was pulsating. His mouth filled with saliva. Signs of stress and adrenaline. It was the first breach he'd been on since returning to work. He wasn't really strong enough, he knew that, but no way was he missing it. He needed to be there. Not just to show Chambers he was fit for duty, but also for a woman called Samantha. Someone who'd been discarded like garbage.

Time seemed to stop. Fluke counted down from thirty in his head and got to zero. He looked at his watch. He was ten seconds out.

Towler's voice came loud and clear over the airwaves as he started the countdown. 'Five.'

Fluke breathed in sharply and held his breath.

'Four.'

He heard soft clicks as the armed officers moved their safety catches to fire.

'Three.'

Another bead of cold sweat formed on the back of his neck.

'Two.'

The officer with the ram tensed.

'One. GO, GO, GO!' Towler screamed down the radio.

The secret to any breach is speed, aggression, surprise, the unofficial motto of the SAS. Carried out correctly, the suspect has no chance. Before he realises what's happening, he is face down with three police officers sitting on top of him.

The breach officer hit the door six inches above the handle. It was no match for the cold steel battering ram. Instead of opening it, the whole door flew off its hinges and landed in the hall. Before it had landed, the armed officers were through.

The noise was incredible. A combination of nerves, the release of tension and legitimate tactics to disorientate the criminal meant that every officer was shouting as loud as they could.

'Armed police! Armed police! Armed police!'

Fluke waited outside with Towler as the house was secured. There was more noise as the shouts of armed police were joined by the shouts of frightened occupants. The noise reached a crescendo then abruptly stopped. He looked down at the ruined door and noticed it still had a takeaway flyer through the letterbox. An Indian Fluke had occasionally used when he'd lived in Carlisle. For some reason, sharing a takeaway with Nathaniel Diamond bothered him. He briefly considered confiscating it.

'House secure,' came the shout from upstairs. Fluke entered.

He had a quick look around the rest of the hall. He was surprised, and then embarrassed that he was surprised. The house was spotless. He'd fully expected filth. What he found was cleaner than his own home and far more tasteful. It seemed his surprise was shared by the rest of the team. Noisy and aggressive on entry, they'd quietened and he could hear some of them picking things up that had been knocked over as rooms had been stormed into.

Fluke could hear screaming upstairs along with some muffled swearing. An armed officer walked down the stairs and approached Fluke.

'He's upstairs.'

'Who's the woman?'

The reply wasn't immediately forthcoming. The sergeant looked uncomfortable. *What now?* Fluke thought.

'You probably need to see this, sir,' was all he'd say before he made his way back up the stairs.

Fluke followed him. Another armed officer passed him on the way down. He couldn't be sure, but was there a hint of a smirk?

Like the hall, the stairs were tastefully decorated. No flying geese in this house. Prints and maps of old Carlisle were on the wall. A huge black and white photo of local landmark, Dixon's Chimney, was on the wall where the stairs turned left. Fluke had never seen that available commercially and wondered if it had been specially commissioned or whether someone in the house had taken it.

He could hear muffled cursing as he followed the sergeant into the bedroom. He stared at the scene in front of him. Nathaniel Diamond was face down on the bed. PlastiCuffs securely bound his wrists and leg straps meant he couldn't kick out. Fluke brought his attention to the woman, the screamer, also held securely with cuffs. He stared at her, not immediately registering what he was seeing for a second. When it did, the smirk from the armed officer he'd passed in the hall made some sort of crude sense.

Whatever he'd been expecting, it hadn't been that.

Chapter 21

The woman being held securely by uniformed officers wasn't a woman. She was a man. A very pretty, blond man, but a man all the same. He was naked. So was Diamond.

Fluke's immediate thought was that he had just met another rent boy. Two in one case would be a record for him, the previous high score being zero. It was his first thought but he quickly dismissed it as he studied the rest of the room. There were photos spread around the bedroom, and the blond and Nathaniel Diamond were in all of them. It was clear that they were in some sort of relationship, and seemed to be happy, judging by their expressions. It was also obvious that they'd been a couple for a long time. They'd aged together in the photos which were all taken in different locations: Las Vegas. New York. Another one looked like Paris. Another was shot on safari somewhere, probably Africa, although it may have been Australia. There was one taken at an outside cafe in a European city Fluke didn't recognise. Florence or Venice, possibly.

Fluke looked around the rest of the room. There were two condom wrappers in the bin, different brands. One for each of them?

Fluke needed to make a decision. It wasn't what he'd been expecting. Nathaniel Diamond looked like a thug in the one photo they had of him and in truth, he looked like a thug trussed up on the floor. Shaved to the bone, not smooth and shiny but rough like emery cloth. He obviously tried to keep on top of it with a razor but the hair kept winning. He had the obligatory black tribal tattoos, all over his arms and back. He was heavily muscled but not in the steroid-induced way McNab had been. They were like the muscles Towler had. Built for stamina and speed. He looked dangerous. He was watching Fluke calmly, the early anger had been replaced by curiosity.

Gay men living together in Meadowby wasn't unheard of but the estate wasn't exactly known for embracing diversity. People who were different didn't go unnoticed for long. The fact that Nathaniel and his boyfriend were in an openly gay relationship, unmolested, was testament to the reputation of his family. The fear and respect his family commanded was the only reason the animals on the estate would have left them alone. For anyone else, it wouldn't be a tenable way to live.

There was no intel on file that he was gay and Fluke wondered why that was. There was always some little scrote who'd pass on information like that to try and curry favour with the police or to get charges reduced. Either it was a very recent thing, which evidence suggested it wasn't, or the family had more influence over the criminal class than anyone had imagined. As Fluke stared into Diamond's cold intelligent eyes, he had no problem believing it was the latter.

Nothing was going to get sorted there. 'Take them to Durranhill.' he said. 'If they resist, arrest them. If they refuse, arrest them. I'm going downstairs to check in with the other teams.'

There weren't enough cells at Durranhill, so some of the Diamond family were being transported to outlying stations. A team of detectives was interviewing them, and SOCO were taking DNA samples and sending them off to the lab.

It was going to be a close-run thing. Fluke had the power to hold them without a charge for twenty-four hours only, so the DNA results would start coming in from the lab at about the same time he'd have to start releasing them. It was possible, probable even, that when they matched the DNA found on Samantha to one of the Diamonds, they would have their killer. However, there wasn't a superintendent in Cumbria who would authorise continued detention beyond the twenty-four hours if all Fluke had was 'It could be any one of them, sir.'

Fluke needed something more. Enough to charge someone or, at the very least, convince a senior officer to extend their time in custody to thirty-six hours. By then, all the DNA results would be back and he'd either have a slam-dunk rape with a conspiracy to murder charge on at least one of them or have no reason to hold any of them.

Of all the Diamonds arrested that night, Fluke decided Nathaniel Diamond was most likely to slip up. When he explained the reason for his arrest – that he wasn't a suspect in the rape and was, in effect, helping the police with their enquiries, Fluke hoped he'd get cocky and make a mistake. He was hoping to do mentally to Nathaniel what Towler did to McNab. Nathaniel was in the frame for the murder but he didn't know that yet.

Along with Nathaniel, Fluke had wanted his brother, Wayne, and his father, Kenneth. The three said to be in control of the family business. Wayne had been picked up without incident, but the father seemed to have disappeared. The team raiding his house said it didn't look like he'd been there since the weekend, judging by the mail that had built up. However, they'd collected a toothbrush and a comb and were confident they had enough for the lab to get his DNA profile to rule him in or out. Everyone else named on the target sheet was in custody. A good night's work.

It was unusual for anyone above sergeant to conduct interviews but Fluke always liked to do the big ones himself. He also preferred to interview with Towler, who had the knack of unnerving suspects without actually saying anything.

But first, he needed something to eat and a coffee. They headed for the canteen.

'How we gonna play it, boss?' Towler asked, through a mouthful of bacon sandwich.

Fluke shrugged, his own mouth also full. It was an interesting question. If their dad was the brains of the outfit, there was no doubt that Nathaniel was the enforcer. Everything about him screamed it. The very fact he flaunted his homosexuality on the Meadowby estate was proof enough of the fear he installed in people. He was probably bright enough to not be the triggerman but he'd know who had been. Even if they'd brought in someone from outside the family to do the actual hit, it was inconceivable he wasn't involved in the decision.

'Dunno know yet. We'll play it by ear to start with. See how chatty he is. Is he lawyered up yet?'

'Yep, they all are, the waiting room looks like a right wankers' convention.'

Fluke laughed but found the woman who'd driven him home the other night had popped into his mind. She'd said she was a solicitor and suddenly Towler's comment didn't seem quite so funny. The smile dropped from his face. 'Right let's do this. I'll lead.'

Nathaniel Diamond was wearing a white paper boiler suit. He'd been allowed half an hour with his solicitor. When Fluke entered the interview room, they were hunched over, talking together quietly. Actually, the solicitor was doing all the talking, Fluke noticed. Diamond wasn't saying anything.

Fluke often wondered how much information he could get by bugging privileged conversations. How many lives could he save from being ruined? Would a spared victim care if the intelligence came from the fruit of the poisoned tree? He doubted it.

Fluke believed in the law. Rather, he believed in the spirit of the law. But when he had to, he was prepared to work in the grey area that existed between the letter of the law and justice. He was proud that he'd never extracted a confession by force or planted evidence. He'd never taken money for looking the other way. He wasn't a dirty cop. If the occasional suspect got hurt while resisting arrest, that was something he could live with. If a paedophile banged his head getting into the police car, then he didn't care. He expected officers who worked with him to be sensible, not saints. Fluke's conscience was clear.

But that didn't mean he didn't have tricks up his sleeve.

Fluke sat without saying anything and spent a minute setting out various photos and documents from the file he'd been carrying. Diamond's solicitor was casually trying to read them upside down. At that point, Diamond would have no idea why he was there. It could potentially be any one of their criminal enterprises. He'd be concerned but not overly worried. Fluke assumed there were safeguards against the main players being found with anything too incriminating. He glanced up at Diamond and found him looking back with an amused expression. He was ignoring the documents Fluke was laying out.

Diamond was an interesting-looking man. Although he was of average height, a certain aura of power emanated from him. It was clear his solicitor was scared of him. From a distance, Diamond looked exactly like he did in the various photos the police had of him. He kept his ginger hair short, shaved it every day, Fluke guessed. He had heavy stubble but no one had had time to shave that morning. He knew some heavy gold rings and a thick gold chain had been taken from him as part of the booking-in process. The custody sergeant had told him that they were not the usual cheap rubbish habitually favoured by criminals. They were the real deal. Thousands of pounds' worth, he estimated. Not a bad way of carrying currency around with you if you needed cash in an emergency.

Nathaniel Diamond looked exactly like he was supposed to. A thug. A bouncer with attitude. A violent man in a violent business.

However, although he was undoubtedly all those things, Fluke suspected there was more to him than that.

It was the eyes that gave it away. The photos didn't do them justice. They had intelligence behind them. They were looking at Fluke shrewdly. Without panic. Fluke couldn't detect concern. He couldn't even detect curiosity.

Although there'd been a press release on the murder, there hadn't been one on the rape. The details of the murder released to the *News and Star* did not include a photo and Fluke wanted to gauge his reaction when Diamond saw it for the first time. It would be the key moment in the interview. Diamond had been there enough times to keep quiet but human reactions aren't so easily controlled.

Fluke sometimes used an unorthodox and unapproved method when interviewing suspects.

Some years before, after attending a multi-agency public protection meeting in Liverpool, Fluke had been having a coffee with a forensic psychologist and had idly asked him what he was working on, more for something to say than anything else – the type of thing said when two people who don't know each other are thrown together.

The psychologist had told him that he'd been commissioned to develop a two-minute interview for airlines which had flights leaving the UK for the States. They wanted to have staff talking to passengers while they waited to check in. And they wanted it to appear casual. They were trying to spot signs of deception before they progressed to the formal security checks.

He explained they'd been encouraged with the early results of a technique they'd been piloting. The theory was that the member of staff would ask a series of questions so normal it would appear the interviewer was simply killing time. Questions designed to put the passenger at ease. But they didn't want rehearsed answers. They wanted honest answers. And the best way to get honest answers was to ask questions so mundane there would be no reason to lie.

'But terrorists plan for this, don't they? They have legends that they memorise, they know which schools they went too, they know where they were last night and what they watched on television. They certainly rehearse the "did you pack your own bag" question,' Fluke had asked. He'd never worked counter-terrorism but had a rough understanding of it.

'Can I ask you something, Mr Fluke? Which was the last supermarket you shopped at?' the psychologist had asked.

Fluke paused, confused. 'Sainsbury's,' he said finally.

The psychologist looked at him. 'This is the type of thing we ask. We ask mundane questions, yes. But some of the questions we ask are that random they can't possibly be predicted and therefore rehearsed.'

He'd gone on to explain that the human brain wants to tell the truth and, in the absence of a reason to lie, will normally tell the truth. The passenger's facial micro-expressions, essentially very brief expressions, when they answered those questions contained what he called truthful indicators. If those micro-expressions were different when answering questions that could be rehearsed it indicated possible deception, and a far more rigorous security check followed. The two-minute lie detector, the psychologist called it. Passengers don't even realise they've had it.

Fluke had adapted and refined it to the point where he believed he could tell when someone was lying to him almost every time. It was virtually infallible. He couldn't remember the psychologist's name and had never seen him again to thank him.

After the usual formalities were covered: who was present, an explanation of how the digital recording worked, and what happened to copies afterwards, they began. Towler stayed silent. Silent but staring, Fluke knew without having to look. It was unnerving for the suspect. Usually.

Fluke had checked. Diamond had been arrested and interviewed eight times. To date he'd never been charged. He'd read the interview transcripts and he always went no comment. Not the McNab no comment, Diamond never actually said anything. Eight times, from the point of arrest until he walked out with no charge, he'd never said a single word. Nothing that could be misconstrued or misheard.

'Who was that you were with earlier, Nathaniel?'

For a moment, Fluke thought the interview was going to go the way of all the others. He'd planned for it, which was why he'd a whole range of photos with him. They were going to be his questions.

'Mathew.'

Fluke looked up from his notes, surprised. He honestly hadn't expected Diamond to answer that. He decided to push it a bit further.

'And who's Mathew, Nathaniel?'

'He's my boyfriend.' There was no trace of shame in his voice or any trace of defiance. He'd simply stated it as the truth.

'How long have you been together?'

'Look, Inspector. I really don't see what my client's personal life has to do with this,' Diamond's solicitor said.

Fluke didn't answer him. He noted that Diamond was looking at him carefully.

'Eight years.'

The solicitor put his hand on Diamond's arm to stop him adding anything. He leant in to whisper something but before he could, Diamond spoke. 'Get your hands off me.'

He delivered it quietly and without turning his head. The solicitor snatched his hand back as if he'd been burnt. He reddened but said nothing. He heard Towler snort. Fluke's peripheral vision caught the solicitor's florid face turn redder; embarrassed that he was being spoken to like that but too scared to protest. Fluke almost felt sorry for him. Almost. He chose to represent the family; he made a living from human misery just as surely as they did. Guilty by association. The solicitor reached into his suit and took out a silk handkerchief. He wiped the back of his neck and looked ahead, trying to avoid catching anyone's eye.

'What does Mathew do, Nathaniel?' Fluke said, looking at the solicitor as he said it, as if daring him to say anything. Everyone knew who got the last lick of the lolly in that room.

'He's a photographer. He's good. He did the photos in our house.'

Fluke nodded. 'Yeah, I saw them.'

Diamond's expressions had all been neutral but he was sure he was telling the truth. Fluke had watched his micro-expressions carefully and thought he'd recognize any changes that might indicate deception. He wanted to ask one more though. One that would ordinarily illicit an expression of anger, but if answered would be truthful.

'Where do you buy your condoms, Nathaniel?'

The solicitor couldn't help himself and exploded out of his chair. 'That's it, Inspector! This is outrageous. My client has been here two hours and so far no one has even told him—'

'Shut the fuck up, fat man. You work for me. Speak when I tell you to speak.' Delivered in the same flat tone. Diamond turned to face him. The solicitor sat back down and seemed to shrivel.

'I don't know why you called me if you're not...' He petered out under Diamond's withering gaze.

'Sorry about that, Inspector,' Diamond said. 'The Co-op on London Road.'

'What's that?' Fluke said, nonplussed.

'Our condoms. The ones we used last night were bought from the Co-op on London Road. We don't always get them from there, obviously, but I assume you only want me to go back so far.'

Fluke had always felt that the real skill in interviewing was knowing when a plan wasn't working. Diamond was far too calm, as calm as anyone Fluke had ever interviewed. His answers were all delivered as the truth, and he seemed to be hiding nothing. Fluke had been planning to ask him about drugs next, to see what he looked like when he was being deceptive but also to keep the real reason for his arrest hidden a bit longer. But he wasn't convinced that Diamond wouldn't see straight through that. He was getting the impression that Nathaniel Diamond was far more intelligent than anyone had realised. Fluke had been on the back foot since the interview started and that hadn't happened for a long time.

He was still considering what to do next when Diamond took the matter into his own hands.

'You have heterochromia, I see, Inspector.'

All doubt about Diamond's intelligence left him instantly. Not even Leah Cooper had known the correct term for his different-coloured irises. She'd had to look it up and even then it took her three goes to pronounce to correctly. Towler called them his "fucking weird eyes" and that was about as polite as anyone got. Fluke couldn't even spell his own condition, it was that rare.

A full minute passed before he answered. 'Yes, I do,' he said. He could feel Towler stirring. The big man was also getting uneasy.

Fluke didn't know what to ask next and quickly evaluated where they were. He considered stopping the interview to regroup. By revealing his intelligence, Diamond had thrown him. It hadn't been accidental either. He couldn't have made it any clearer if he'd come in with an IQ certificate. Diamond was letting him know how intelligent he was for a reason, and as he'd successfully hidden it for so long, it was for something significant. There was something going on here that Fluke wasn't yet aware of.

Fluke decided there was nothing to be gained by playing games anymore. Nathaniel Diamond may be the most intelligent criminal he'd ever sat opposite, he might even be a genius but there was one thing outside his control: micro-expressions don't lie.

It was time to see if he was involved in Samantha's murder.

It was time for the photo.

Fluke took it from the folder and placed it facedown on the table. He stared at Diamond. They knew what was coming. They knew the whole interview had been about this moment.

'Have you seen this woman before, Nathaniel?' Fluke said as he flipped over the photo. It was an 8" x 10" colour glossy of her head on the mortuary table. Diamond glanced down at it then back up at Fluke.

Fluke stared at him and saw what he'd been hoping for. Recognition.

A tiny change in his expression. It had only been there for a fraction of a second, but that was long enough for Fluke.

Diamond had seen her before.

Fluke smiled to himself. They were getting somewhere. The Diamond family were involved somehow.

'Why would I have seen her before?' he replied, calmly.

Even liars don't like to lie. Before answering questions of any consequence the liar will at first try to avoid answering it at all. Replying with a question was a classic reaction.

With no warning, Towler shouted. 'Answer the fucking question, dickhead!' Diamond ignored him. His solicitor nearly fell off his chair. Fluke didn't move a muscle. He'd been expecting it. He'd planned it.

'No, I haven't seen her before.'

There was no emotion in his answer but Diamond was no longer holding his gaze. He was looking slightly above his eye line. His micro-expressions were different. The difference between his truthful and deceptive indicators were bigger than Fluke would have expected in someone so intelligent, but as the psychologist had told him, people have very little control over them.

He was lying.

Fluke felt that it was the first time he'd actually gained anything from the interview. He was ahead and didn't want Diamond to have an opportunity to claw back the advantage. Time to change the rules. Fluke had always believed that it was best to do what the criminal wasn't expecting.

Fluke stood up and put everything back in his file.

'Thank you, Mr Diamond. You've been very helpful.'

'He can go?' the solicitor asked, surprised. It was only the fourth thing he'd said.

Diamond was watching Fluke, the same small smile he'd had at the start of the interview was back. 'Of course I can't, you fat idiot. I'm a suspect in a murder investigation.'

'You should listen to your client. I'm keeping hold of him for a while longer,' Fluke said.

'I won't be paying for your services today, Mr Potting,' Diamond said. 'I don't think you've been of any help. Would you agree?'

That got the solicitor's attention. 'My legal advice is only as good as the person listeni—'

Diamond interrupted him. 'I asked if you agreed, fat man?'

For a moment, Fluke thought the solicitor was going to stand his ground.

But his face deflated in defeat. 'Yes, of course,' he said, quietly. Diamond was looking at Fluke throughout the whole interaction.

Towler and Fluke left the room.

Fluke had new things to consider. Diamond was highly intelligent. Even his solicitor was scared of him. He was used to command, that much was obvious. Serious command. When he spoke, he expected to be listened to. It had been like a game of 'Simon Says' with the solicitor. He also knew that Nathaniel Diamond was somehow involved with Samantha. Whether he was involved in her death was something he wasn't ready to speculate on.

He rubbed his eyes.

He needed some rest. He needed to regroup.

***

Chapter 22

They drove back to HQ, and Fluke slept on the couch in his office for a couple of hours. He woke, still feeling tired and with a headache. He checked his emails. There was the usual rubbish from HR, as well as some information on current live investigations: a street robbery in Ulverston, a social worker had been found with indecent images of children on his computer, and someone had been impersonating a police officer in various parts of the county. Nothing for FMIT to get involved in. He yawned and looked back at his couch.

Instead of going back to sleep, he got up and looked for Towler. He found him sleeping in a hard plastic chair in the incident room. Towler had the soldier's knack of being able to fall asleep anywhere, and under any circumstances. The room was busy and noisy as Jo Skelton coordinated the updating of HOLMES 2 with the morning's raids and the subsequent interviews taking place around the county. People were shouting for things: links to computer files, passwords, codes, but Towler slept through it all. Fluke envied him. He and sleep had an uneasy relationship. Towler and sleep were best friends.

Fluke shook him gently by the shoulder and he woke instantly, immediately alert. Fluke was reminded just how close Towler had become to being one of the top soldiers in the world. Fluke asked him to go and get the core team together for a quick update.

Jo Skelton, Alan Vaughn and Towler crowded round the table in Fluke's office.

'So, what do we know?' he asked, starting them off.

'Nathaniel Diamond was involved,' Towler said.

'Nope,' Fluke said.

Fluke remembered once discussing with a probation officer about whether the rehabilitation of criminals was really possible. The PO had told him part of his job was equipping offenders with reasoning and consequential thinking skills. Skills most people already had. The programme facilitators would start with a scenario, before asking the group certain questions. They would then ask whether each answer was a fact, guess or opinion. Fluke had never thought about things that way before but knew several detectives who could have benefitted from separating facts from guesses.

'We know he's seen her before. I'm happy enough after the interview to call that a fact. That he was involved is a guess. What else do we know?' he said.

Skelton got up and drew a table with three rows on his whiteboard. She entered what they'd discussed up to then.

'Who raped her?' Fluke asked. 'Do we wait for the DNA results to come in or do we keep looking and interviewing?'

Vaughn was first to speak. 'Most of the family are in custody. We've questioned and released those who aren't blood-related and taken DNA from the rest. We've identified three family members we didn't know about and there were four who weren't in. There's something to be said for hanging on until the results come in.'

'There is,' agreed Fluke. 'But we aren't after a rapist, we're after a killer, so we need to keep investigating. We also have the problem of how many blood relatives there are that we don't know about. Plus there could be any number of illegitimate children that we have no way of identifying. Theories, anyone?'

Fluke liked to hear others thinking out loud. It helped him poke holes in his own ideas. Sometimes, he'd hear things that made him revise. Sometimes he'd hear things so stupid it made him think common sense should be reclassified as a superpower.

Towler gave his version of what happened, and it was remarkably close to what Fluke was thinking.

'I think one of the Diamonds raped the victim, boss. Used roofies, and thought he'd got clean away. Word gets out that she's reported it. The Diamonds don't like that and want her silenced. They don't know if they're being watched though, the drugs squad must be parked outside their houses every night. So they bring in outside help from Manchester or Liverpool, probably Liverpool given their links with the drugs trade. Then they sit back and work on their alibis.'

'Anyone got anything to add to that?' Fluke asked.

There was silence. Intelligent minds went to work on pulling the theory apart. No one could, it fit the known facts.

'No one? Okay, let me add something then. The family is big. After that interview with Nathaniel, I think they're bigger and better than we thought. They're not on a par with the gangs from the north-east, Manchester or Liverpool, but they're big for Carlisle. They're probably the biggest crime family in Cumbria, truth be told. And I would be very surprised if young Nathaniel isn't their number one. It's been a long time since I interviewed someone that bright. Other than some slight surprise when I showed him the photo, he was in total control for the whole interview. His brief's terrified of him.'

Fluke looked at them all in turn. Towler and Vaughn were looking into space, concentrating. Skelton was nodding. Psychology 101. Men nod their heads to show they agree, women nod their heads to show they're listening. He clearly hadn't convinced them of anything yet.

He continued. 'Even so, hiring a professional to kill someone is a big move, and it's not cheap. So, either the rapist is important to the family – a close relative, someone they care enough about to spend money on protecting – or, it's about protecting someone who's a key figure in the business. Their supplier in Liverpool protecting their investment, and sending someone up to fix their problem.'

There were nods from round the table.

'I'm thinking it's someone who isn't expendable. Someone who the suppliers thought was worth protecting as well,' Vaughn said. 'I doubt they'd send a cleaner just because Uncle Bob's in trouble again. Not unless Uncle Bob makes the trains run on time.'

'There's still Nathaniel's dad,' Skelton said.

Shit. Kenneth Diamond. Fluke had forgotten about him. 'Sorry, Jo, you're right. He potentially fits who we're looking for. Nobody really knows what his role in the family business is. Where do we think he is again?'

'Nobody knows. We don't think he's been home for a few days though, judging by the build up of mail. Looks like he lives on his own,' she said.

There was a short discussion about whether the UK Border Agency should be informed, but they agreed it was probably pointless. If he'd fled, he'd have already left the country. Jo Skelton said she'd inform them anyway. Fluke decided he'd only get seriously interested in Kenneth Diamond if the DNA they'd taken from his toothbrush or comb matched the semen taken from Samantha. It didn't mean they couldn't start looking for him, though. He put Towler on it.

'In the meantime, let's get back into those interview rooms. See who else we have, and see who's important to the family. Speak to someone you haven't spoken to yet. See if we can find something else out, and let's get working on that family tree. I want to know who else is out there with Diamond blood running through their veins. I'll have another run at Nathaniel. Anyone got any questions?'

They were all staring at him. No nods that time. Something was different, something had changed.

Towler looked uncomfortable. 'Boss, your nose is bleeding.'

Fluke had refused to go to hospital, and after a few minutes with his head tilted back and toilet paper stuck up his nostrils, the blood flow had at least slowed. Towler had, without appearing too urgent, cleared the room.

'You look fucking awful,' he said, as he closed the door. 'All this shit can't be good for you.'

'I'm fine,' Fluke had replied.

'You're fucking grey. The victim has a better complexion than you.'

Fluke said nothing. He busied himself getting clean. He opened a drawer and took out the new shirt he always kept for emergencies. It was still in the wrapper. He threw the old shirt in the bin then examined his tie and decided it was salvageable. 'See, good as new.' It didn't put Towler off.

'And these appointments you're having at the hospital. They're nearly every week now.'

Fluke's stomach lurched. He didn't think anyone knew about them. His appointments were always first thing or last thing. He hadn't wanted HR or Occ Health finding out. Or worse, Chambers. 'How'd you find out?' Fluke asked.

'I didn't. But you've just confirmed it,' Towler replied, holding his hand out to stop Fluke's protests. 'Look, I'm not an idiot. You're always knackered, you've got eyes like a racing dog's bollocks and now you're having fucking nosebleeds. That's the fourth one this month. Something's gotta give, boss.'

'I'm fine,' he repeated.

'Whatever,' Towler said. 'Keep going like this and I'll go and see that doc of yours myself. See what the fuck she was playing at letting you come back to work.'

Although the concern was genuine, Fluke knew it was an empty threat. 'Who else knows?' he asked. The last thing he wanted was Chambers putting him on involuntary sick leave.

Towler looked as though he was going to press his previous point but decided to let it go. 'No one. But anyone can follow breadcrumbs this big.'

'Look, after all this is over, I'll take a holiday, get some proper rest,' Fluke said. 'Honestly,' he added when he saw Towler's expression.

'Until then, take it fucking easy,' he ordered.

Fluke knew Towler was right. He wasn't concerned about the nosebleeds, they were inconvenient but not debilitating. They were a symptom. What they were a symptom of, Chambers could never find out.

'Fair enough. Don't want you worrying,' he said, grinning. 'I don't know why I let you talk to me like this, I really don't,' Fluke said.

They were interrupted by a knock on the door. Jiao-long stuck his head in.

'Found it, boss.' A massive grin split his face.

'Found what?' Fluke said, still on the back foot.

'Her house. It was a flat actually. You were right.'

Fluke stood up so quickly that he spilt his drink all over his new shirt. He ignored it – a coffee stain he could live with.

Chapter 23

Fluke got in Jiao-long's car and they drove up the M6 to Carlisle City Centre. On the way, Jiao-long briefed him on how he'd tracked down Samantha.

He'd followed her on CCTV from a variety of sources across the city. She was sneaky but Jiao-long was sneakier. She knew where most of the cameras were. He knew where they all were.

He followed her as she walked towards the west of the city, not always taking logical routes. She'd eventually turned down a small street sandwiched between the River Caldew and the railway viaduct. Viaduct Estate Road had little on it and was most often used as a shortcut to the Royal Mail sorting office on Junction Street. She should have reappeared. She didn't. The council had no cameras facing down the road. Jiao-long still had a few tricks left however. Knowing that the buildings opposite were all student accommodation and that there'd been a spate of cycle thefts, he checked whether the university had put up cameras of their own. They had.

One of the buildings had installed a high-tech machine. During daylight, it faced outwards, covering the area where students parked their bikes. At night, when all bikes were either chained up or indoors, it pointed down, and performed a safe-entry role for the front door. The daytime angle gave an uninterrupted view across the dual carriageway and down Viaduct Estate Road. Jiao-long had watched her entering the only block of flats on the street.

He'd watched the remaining hours before the camera moved down at about seven p.m., to check she didn't leave.

Fluke asked him if there'd been sight of anyone who might be their killer.

'Nothing, boss. It only points that way during the day. There are people going in and out of the flats obviously, but no one stands out. If there's an entrance to the back then it'd be in a blind spot. I've taken a copy so we can look when we get back.'

Can't have everything, Fluke thought. Three days ago, they had nothing, so it was real progress.

Fluke was banking on her flat being the murder scene. If it wasn't, he wasn't sure where he could go next. He had no more leads. Jiao-long told him that he'd viewed the surrounding cameras twenty-four hours before and after, and had seen nothing. Either she hadn't left and had been killed in her flat, or she'd left at night and somehow evaded Jiao-long. Fluke was impressed nevertheless. He always was with Jiao-long's work. Although he knew some of it was fairly routine stuff for a man who lived and breathed computers, Jiao-long had not once complained. He'd try and give him something more interesting next time.

They assembled in the car park of the flats. There seemed to be one designated space per resident. At that time of day, most of them were empty but they'd been filled with the various police vehicles already on scene. The smell of the nearby biscuit factory was making Fluke salivate. He'd need to eat soon. He looked round and got his bearings.

To his right, on the other side of the dual carriageway, sat the most besieged castle in Britain. During its thousand years, Carlisle Castle – once described as the ugliest in Europe – had been a Norman stronghold, a royal garrison and a frontier fortress in the border wars between Scotland and England, and its red sandstone walls were soaked with blood and history. Clinging to the small hill, it looked as formidable as it had to the highland clans all those centuries before. It now housed a territorial company of the Duke of Lancaster's Regiment. Fluke sometimes walked round it if he had half an hour to kill.

Not today though. He was pressed for time. He hopefully had a crime scene to process, and he wanted another crack at Nathaniel Diamond before the custody sergeant had to release him.

He turned away from the castle and viewed the flats. He wanted it done quickly and was glad to see that the breach team was already there. The same man who had smashed Diamond's door open that morning was back with his discoloured battering ram. A two-man armed response team was also waiting. Fluke knew they wouldn't have been involved in that morning's raids, there were tight controls on how many hours an armed officer could do before there was compulsory downtime.

The flats were modern and privately owned. Fluke had been thinking on the drive up about how to identify Farrar's but decided that simple was best; knock on doors and show the photo until someone recognised her and told them where she lived. Then go in with armed response. He thought it extremely unlikely that the killer would still be there but there was no point taking unnecessary risks.

They got lucky straight away.

'Quiet girl, polite, lives in number five upstairs,' a middle-aged man had told them when they knocked on the first door. His wife peered out from behind him with fear in her eyes as she stared at the men with guns. 'What's she done?' the man asked.

Fluke, politely as possible, asked him to go back inside and they made their way upstairs and quietly gathered in the stairwell below her flat.

'I'm going to knock first,' Fluke said. 'I'm fairly certain there's no one in. But we go in hard. You two first,' he said, pointing at the two officers with the H&Ks slung over their shoulders. 'Secure the flat, but remember, this is probably a murder scene so the priority is to preserve forensic evidence. I don't want to get excited about a print, only to find out it's one of yours. Got it?'

They affirmed they had indeed got it.

The short stocky officer with the battering ram worked his way into position.

Fluke knocked twice, hard. The sound was in sharp contrast to the silence that had preceded it. They waited, holding their breath, straining to hear the slightest noise, anything that might point to the flat being occupied.

Fluke knocked again. Louder.

A door opened behind them making them jump. The two armed officers swung round, flicking their safety catches off as they did. Fluke saw their response before he could see who was behind him, so was relieved when they lowered their weapons.

'Sam's not in,' said a young man.

A nerd, as Towler would have called him, stood in the doorway of the other flat on the landing. He was wearing a faded

Captain America T-shirt and looked paler than Fluke. Myopic eyes stared at them through modern glasses. He pushed them up his nose. More through fear than anything else, Fluke suspected. He had untidy hair and was stick thin but otherwise seemed normal enough.

Fluke identified himself. 'How do you know?' he asked gently.

The man looked sheepish. 'I watch out for her.'

'What do you mean, "you watch out for her"? Do you look out for her, or do you spy on her?' Towler snorted. 'What's your name? What do you do?'

'William, sir, William Robinson. I work at DEFRA. I keep their software running. I meant I like her. I speak to her sometimes. I notice when she leaves her flat.'

A crush, Fluke thought, as he fired a warning glance across to Towler. 'When did you last see her, William?' He could hear armed response getting restless behind him. They could wait.

'Not for a few days, sir. But that's not unusual. She often doesn't leave her flat. I knocked and offered to pick something up when I went to Sainsbury's one night but she said no. Said she didn't need anything. She actually goes out less than I do. And I hardly ever go out.'

'You don't say?' said Towler.

William, obviously realising that Fluke was in charge, ignored him.

'You hear anything suspicious a couple of nights ago, William?' Fluke asked. 'It would have been late, in all likelihood.'

'No, sir, but I play online games most nights and use headphones to avoid annoying anyone. I play war games and they can get noisy.'

Towler snorted again, quickly changing it into a fake cough when Fluke glared at him. 'Sorry, ignore Sergeant Towler, William. Nobody likes him very much.'

'Yes, sir,' he said. He appeared to give Fluke's question some thought. 'I'm up until about midnight then go to bed. I sometimes see the light in the corridor change when her door opens but I can't remember when I last saw her.'

Fluke needed to keep moving forward. He'd come back to speak to William later. For now, he had to get inside her flat and see if it was the murder scene. And it wasn't lost on him that he had armed police standing round in a public area doing nothing. 'Okay, William. A police officer's going to take your statement. I need you to go back inside. We're going to have to break the door down so don't worry if you hear something loud.'

William looked up. 'You don't have to break in, sir. I have a key.'

'Excuse me?'

'I have keys to all the flats. The landlord gives me money off my rent if I take care of the building's systems. They're all computerised you see. I need access to them all to reset things sometimes, heating and electric timers. Not often, our electricity's quite good as we're close to the hospital. We're on a more secure grid.'

'Okay, thanks, William. Could you get me the key, please?'

William disappeared into his flat and returned a minute later with a box of keys. He sorted through them and handed Fluke one on a red plastic key ring, bearing the number five.

After standing down the officer with the battering ram, Fluke quietly opened the door with the key and the two armed officers, in total contrast to the earlier raids, moved in quietly. Towler followed them in. Fluke held his breath. They were back out before he needed to exhale.

'All clear, boss,' Towler said. 'Nothing obvious.'

Fluke was disappointed but not discouraged. A great deal of evidence could be missed in the first sweep. Things that couldn't be seen with the naked eye. He'd have preferred a big pool of blood but, even without one, he was convinced it was where Samantha was killed. He thanked the armed response unit and stood them down. It was now a detective's job. On the off chance a weapon was recovered, he and Towler were more than capable of making it safe before it was bagged for evidence.

He called everyone together. 'Right, I'm treating this as a crime scene. That means full forensic protocols. No exceptions. When's the CSM getting here?'

'Downstairs now, boss. Just waiting for your nod,' Jiao-long said. He looked pleased to be out of the office.

'Good. Tell him to come up. I'm going for a quick look round now. No one else is to go in. Matt, make sure we set up entry cordons. Two, please. One here at the door and an outer one

173

downstairs. Longy, get a list of residents; the rest of you, start knocking on doors. I want to know what the rest of the building knows. And someone take William's statement. By the looks of it, he's got a bit of a thing for her so may know something about her movements and habits.'

Fluke struggled into the paper overalls and covered his shoes with the protective slippers. Putting on his face mask, he entered the flat. There was a worn and sad "Welcome" mat on the inside. The walls were painted a neutral cream. He knew, from his old flat, that most building companies used cream. It showed empty rooms at their best, apparently. The landlord obviously hadn't bothered to change the colour scheme.

The first room off the hall was the kitchen, and Fluke saw the coffee grinder immediately. He laughed. It was exactly as Lucy had described; like a small sausage machine. He couldn't believe their conversation two nights ago had paid off. He owed her a great deal. He'd ring her later and tell her.

He opened the fridge to check something. He knew it would be there but wanted peace of mind anyway.

The bag of coffee from Watts sat on the top shelf. The same blend as he had in his own fridge.

He opened the bag. Shiny brown beans, waiting to be ground. He thought about them and felt a little melancholic. The care and attention of the coffee farmer; the way they'd been carefully picked, dried and sold to a trader. How that trader had sold them on and eventually, probably three or four stages later, they'd found their way to a gourmet coffee shop in Carlisle. Bought by someone who appreciated them. And now they were evidence in a murder investigation. It didn't seem fair. He put them back so they were in the right place for the videos and photographs.

The rest of the fridge was bare. No milk, she probably took her coffee black. He opened the cupboards in the kitchen. Nothing of interest. Some stock ingredients: rice, pasta, tinned tomatoes, a half-eaten packet of crisps. Nothing that couldn't be found in a million homes across the country.

Fluke wandered round the rest of the flat. It was tasteful but impersonal. The only thing that wasn't generic was the coffee grinder. No photos, no flowers, no ornaments or pictures. He'd have to check to see if the flat was rented out furnished or unfurnished. His money was on furnished, it looked like the flat-packed stuff you got from Ikea. Not bad quality but you wouldn't spend too much money on it. The TV was a flat-screen but fairly basic. No satellite dish, no DVD player.

He entered the bedroom. The bed was made up with a plain cover. There was a glass of water on the bedside cabinet. A charger for something was plugged into the wall. He opened the bedside cabinet. There were a number of books in there and an e-reader, which would possibly explain the charger. He checked. It fitted. There was another charger, the lead neatly wrapped around the plug. He'd check if it fitted the mobile they found with the body later.

He opened the wardrobe and found it half-full of expensive looking clothes.

The curtains were shut and Fluke lifted them to see what she'd have been able to see. Something out of place caught his eye. There was a small pile of coins on the window ledge. He looked across at the other window and saw there was another pile there as well. Two-pence pieces, carefully balanced on top of each other. Fluke made his way out of the bedroom and checked the rest of the windows. They all had piles of coins on them.

On a hunch, he walked back to the front door and lifted the welcome mat in the inner hallway. He thought he'd heard something as he stepped on it. He lifted it up. There was broken glass underneath. A broken light bulb unless he was mistaken. Thin and curved. Very fragile. Noisy when stepped on, especially in the confined space of a hall.

Coins on window ledges. Glass underneath the mat, covering the flat's only entrance. Crude, but extremely effective anti-intruder devices, designed to alert whoever was inside that someone was trying to get in.

All he knew about Samantha told Fluke that there would also be an external device. A device to tell her that there was already somebody inside waiting for her. She was too careful for there not to be one.

He went back out onto the landing she shared with William. Towler had cleared it to make sure the inner cordon was secured. He was on his own.

Fluke groaned involuntarily as he got down on his hands and knees. He found he was doing it more and more. He knew it wasn't just his age – he was still only forty – but that his body was just weaker now, plain and simple. He hoped that some of his strength would return in time but he knew he'd never quite be the same again. A serious illness, the inevitable march of time and a secret only he knew about. *Still*, he thought, *I'm too young to be feeling this old.*

He knew from his Northern Ireland training that security devices were invariably at ground level. They were easier to set up and harder for casual observers to see.

In the movies all you needed was a folded up piece of paper wedged into the doorframe – if the paper's on the floor, the door's been opened. But in reality, that's far too easy to spot, far too easy to replace and everybody knows the trick anyway. It was the same with a strand of hair. Fluke thought that if she had an external device, it would be far more subtle. Something that wouldn't look out of place. He cast his eyes over everything at ground level but couldn't see anything. He stood back up and checked the top of the doorframe. Again, nothing.

He stepped back, still convinced he was right. If she was being hunted, as was still reasonable to assume, he knew she'd have some way of telling if someone was already inside. She wouldn't go to all the effort of plastic surgery, false names and counter-surveillance precautions just to walk into a trap.

There were two options: either a device that he couldn't see, or the killer had removed it and taken it with him. Fluke doubted the second. Why would he bother? Removing it before she arrived was the same as triggering it, and removing it after he'd killed her served no purpose. There was a third option: that she didn't have one, but he dismissed it immediately. There was something there, he just hadn't found it yet.

Fluke stepped back to get an overview, to look round the rest of the landing, see if there was anything different about her entrance compared to everyone else's. The door was the same colour as William's and the same as those he'd passed on the way up; dark blue. Each spyhole was in the same place and the flat numbers all came from the same pack. Even the external doormats were the same; a dark brown that the landlord probably hoped wouldn't show up dirt so he wouldn't have to replace them, there to encourage people to wipe their feet before standing on his carpets, no doubt. There was a light on each landing, equidistant between the two flats.

Fluke stared at the open doorway, convinced he'd missed something. He heard someone coming up the stairs and held his hand up to stop them. He wasn't ready to share the scene yet.

Fluke knew he stood the best chance of catching the killer if he could get inside Samantha's psyche – if he could think like her.

Find out how the victim lived and you'll find out how they died.

He tried to imagine how she'd have done it. It would have to be quick to set up; she wouldn't want anything that kept her out on the landing for too long. It would need to be just as quick to check, as well as being completely reliable. It would have to work every time, to fail even once would be unthinkable. Fluke started again. But everything was made of solid stuff, designed to withstand a transient population. No room for individual expression anywhere on the outside. The only thing they could even move would be the doormats. Everything else was fixed solidly in place.

He sighed. It was time to let the SOCO unit in to process the flat.

He hadn't seen anything obvious to suggest it was the murder site but he instinctively knew it was. It had to be. Science would prove him right. It was time to add chemicals and powders and special lights to things.

As he moved away from the door, he moved the mat slightly with his foot. He paused. It was heavy-duty, designed to get mud and grit off shoes and boots but Fluke had moved it by accident, far easier than he should have been able to. The friction of his shoes had been enough to move it as he turned. Frowning, he bent down and lifted it up at the corner. It had been modified. It had been hollowed out. Scraped and cut away from all but the edges. A rough job, but effective. What was originally a heavy-duty item was significantly lighter. From the outside it looked like all the rest in the complex. With the inside removed it left a gap of at least half an inch, the half-inch she needed.

Underneath the mat were some crisps. Two of the crisps were crushed into several small pieces. This was it, this was her alarm system. Cunningly simple and incredibly clever.

It also explained why the bag of crisps hadn't been finished. Fluke was a crisp addict and knew there was no way he could open a bag and not finish it. Family size ones yes, single bags, not a chance.

'Clever, very clever,' Towler said, appearing at his side and instantly recognising what he was seeing. They stared at her ingenuity in silence.

'Who are you, Samantha?' Fluke said, eventually.

He couldn't be sure if it had been broken before they got there or whether the size twelves of armed response had crushed it. There was no way of knowing but if she'd arrived back and saw broken crisps there was no way she'd have entered that flat. She'd expect to see them unbroken, dreading the day she didn't.

'But which cleverer bastard circumnavigated it?' Towler said, verbalising exactly what Fluke was thinking.

Fluke was using the same crime scene manager, Sean Rogers, and they quickly devised an evidence recovery strategy. It was far easier when there wasn't a body, no pathologist to wait for and argue with.

Fluke needed to see blood. There wouldn't be much but with a gunshot to the head there would be some. It wasn't visible to the naked eye but it would be there. If there was no blood, it wasn't the murder site. And if it wasn't the murder site the investigation was effectively over.

They agreed which route would be taken by the SOCO team and put down stepping plates. A tech went first and videoed the flat, quickly followed by the photographer who snapped everything that Fluke and Rogers thought relevant. Next, they went in with Luminol spray. Fluke knew that when Luminol came into contact with blood, the haemoglobin oxidised and went through a chemiluminescent reaction, a reaction that would be visible in the dark.

The curtains were drawn and the blinds pulled down. With the flat in darkness, Rogers sprayed each room methodically. Fluke followed him. The reaction would only last for thirty seconds but that would be more than long enough.

There was nothing in the hall and nothing in the kitchen. Rogers sprayed the bedroom and again there was nothing. The small bathroom was the same. There was only one room left.

The living room.

As soon as Rogers sprayed the room, Fluke saw it. There wasn't much, a few flecks on the carpet, spread over a circular patch a yard in diameter, but it was enough. Flecks that glowed. Beautiful and eerie at the same time. Mesmerised, Fluke stared until the luminous blue light faded, eventually disappearing.

As the room returned to darkness, Fluke felt a lurch of excitement. Up until then, he'd been three steps off the pace in the investigation. Everything they'd achieved had been through sheer luck, it seemed.

But regardless of how they'd got here, he was standing where the killer stood and where Samantha had died. He'd taken a massive step forward.

I'm coming for you.

Fluke had his murder scene.

***

Chapter 24

Fluke left Rogers to process the flat. He and his team would go in when the forensics were secured. He went outside to ring Chambers and tell him they'd found the murder scene. Chamber's frustration at the lack of pace in the case seemed mollified with the latest news. In fact, Fluke was surprised at the way Chambers had spoken to him. Gone was the antagonism, he actually seemed happy for once. Fluke didn't like it.

After he'd finished, he wandered over to where FMIT had gathered. Alan Vaughn had been to the nearby Sainsbury's to get food for everyone. Fluke looked at the selection on offer. He'd been to the reduced section judging by the yellow stickers plastered over the price labels. A man on a budget. Fluke grabbed a duck in hoisin sauce wrap and ate it, leaning on Jiao-long's car, washing it down with a bottle of water. He refused the bag of crisps he was offered and noticed Towler did the same.

Fluke idly listened to Vaughn and Towler arguing about the reduced-price food.

'Frugal my arse,' Towler said. 'You're a fucking tight bastard, mate. That's your problem.'

Fluke smiled. Some things never changed.

He'd just finished his wrap when Rogers came back out. 'We've done a preliminary sweep, sir. Your team can go in now, but there's something you need to see.'

Fluke nodded his thanks and prepared to go back inside, but Vaughn signalled he wanted a word first.

'We've just taken William's statement, boss. I asked if he'd ever seen her put down crisps, to see if there was anything to support your theory or whether she was just a minger.'

Fluke let the remark go. Vaughn was obsessed by tidiness, probably the only one in the team who was. A 'clean freak', Towler called him. Fluke was neat, but ex-forces neat, more functionary than aesthetic. His desk was organised chaos at times but he knew where everything was. Towler was a disaster.

Anything you gave him was lost as soon as he put it down. The rest of them were somewhere in-between. 'And?' he said.

'He saw it, boss. He bloody saw it. Every time, I reckon, or near enough. I reckon he was obsessed by her. He thought she was putting her keys under the mat when she went out. Said he never checked and I believe him.'

'No chance it was him?' Fluke said, doubting it.

'Nope. We've eliminated him. He's been here since the block was built. Bit of a loner but not all loners are serial killers. Likes his games, likes his films and American TV series, but I didn't see anything that made me nervous.'

That was good enough for Fluke. Vaughn wasn't normally wrong about those things. He seemed to have a sixth sense about hidden personality disorders. 'Okay, tell him we'll need him at the station at some point but for now we focus on the flat. Make sure Jo updates HOLMES. And don't forget to put through the receipt for the food.'

'Will do,' he said, walking off.

Rogers had been waiting patiently out of earshot. Fluke beckoned him over. 'What we got, Sean?'

'I can take you through the video. It's all logged. Easy job really. You'll have noticed there was nothing there other than the blood.'

'Yep, nothing personal anyway. If it wasn't for the coffee grinder, I'd bet the flat looked the same as it did before she moved in.'

Rogers nodded. 'You seen the film *Heat*, sir? When De Niro says, "Never have anything in your life you can't walk away from." It reminded me of that. There was nothing personal. Nothing at all, not even utility bills. It's for you to decide how important that is obviously, but it stood out to me.'

Fluke had seen the film and knew what Rogers meant; there was none of the usual debris of life. 'Was there anything else?'

'There was one thing, sir.' Instead of telling him, Rogers lead the way to the evidence van. All portable items potentially of interest were bagged and tagged there. He reached in and pulled out a larger bag. He signed the seal and tore it open, then held it out for Fluke to inspect. 'Found it under the bedside cabinet. No clue what it's for.'

Fluke had no idea what Rogers was holding. It seemed to be a two-part device. One part was clearly a control unit of some kind. The other looked like a plastic heat pad, the sort used by reptile keepers to keep snakes warm; flat, flexible, about a foot squared. It had a wire leading from it which fitted into the control unit. Fluke took it from him and looked it over. He couldn't even begin to guess what it was. 'Where's Longy?' he shouted.

The cry went up and Longy was soon with Fluke, the irrepressible grin still there, despite the lack of sleep. Fluke would have to make him go home soon.

'Boss?'

'Glove up and find out what this thing is, can you, Longy? I think there's a part number there on the side of the battery pack.'

As Jiao-long took out his smartphone and looked, Fluke asked Rogers when he could expect an inventory.

'Within the hour, sir. I'll send it up to Durranhill to be typed. I'll email you as soon as it's done.'

Rogers walked off to continue the supervision of his SOCO team. They still had work to do even though the initial excitement had worn off. Cases were won or lost on how thorough SOCO were.

Fluke mentally recapped while Jiao-long searched the Internet. He believed there were at least three crime scenes, and he had two of them: the murder site and the deposition site. The third crime scene would be the car the body had been transported in.

He also still had some numbers stubbornly resisting identification and a mobile phone that the techs were trying to recover data from.

While he waited for Jiao-long, Fluke got out the card Skelton had produced for everyone and had another look at the numbers. Sometimes sneaking up on a puzzle was the best way of solving it. He stared at them but the answer remained as elusive as before. He'd noticed his team picking up their cards and staring at it when they had downtime, discussing it with their colleagues when they were having a brew. Just like Fluke was. A bit of paper that you had to take out of a file or unfold wouldn't get the same attention. Fluke reminded himself to thank Skelton. It was something he'd probably replicate in future investigations.

He turned his thoughts to Samantha. It was clear she was obsessed with secrecy. The only sensible answer was that she was hiding from someone. Someone serious. She was well resourced, that was obvious. Expensive surgery, nice clothes. Refined taste with the coffee. But he had nothing else to go on. Rogers was right, she seemed ready to leave at a moment's notice. She'd have left if the crisps were broken when she returned. She'd have regretted leaving her coffee grinder but would have left anyway. There was nothing else in the flat of note except some weird gadget.

Was it the killer she'd been hiding from? Fluke wasn't sure. Common sense said 'yes'. It had taken a professional to find her. If all the cosmetic surgery was relevant, someone was looking for her long before the Diamonds entered her life. So who killed her, the Diamonds or someone else? That was the key question and one that wouldn't be answered until the DNA results from that morning's raids were in.

Best-case scenario was that the killer was one of the Diamond's or someone connected to them. That a Diamond had sex with her was beyond doubt. Avoiding a rape charge was more than enough motivation for some men to arrange a murder.

Worst-case scenario was that the DNA hit was unconnected to the murder. Fluke might struggle and secure a rape conviction but that would be scant consolation if Samantha's killer remained undetected.

Fluke tried to rearrange his thoughts into a logical SOE, sequence of events. He dismissed the order in which things had been discovered – it had little relevance to each piece of the puzzle's importance, and was misleading. There were four to reorganise: first there was Samantha getting surgery, then there was the rape. The rape was followed by the murder and finally, there was the body deposition. Eventually, everything else would fit into that timeline somewhere. Something must have preceded the surgery, something that may have started years before.

Now he'd seen her flat and the extraordinary lengths she'd taken to protect herself, something was nagging him, a slow insidious thought and one that he couldn't share. If he did, he'd leave himself wide open to a professional standards investigation and an article on the front page of the *News and Star*.

If she was that scared why did she report the rape at all? Why risk the exposure?

Fluke had attended all the relevant training and took rape investigations very seriously. They were horrendous crimes, a personal violation that most women never fully recovered from. But report it she did. Fluke was prepared to believe that the rape had been so unacceptable to her, so abhorrent, that she'd put her personal safety at risk to see justice done, but he wasn't closing his mind to the possibility that there were other factors at play here, factors that he didn't yet know about. He wouldn't share it with anyone, not even Towler. He wasn't even comfortable thinking about it himself.

Jiao-long interrupted his train of thought with a satisfied exclamation. Fluke leaned over his shoulder to see what he'd found. There was a photo of the device on his phone. Newer, with a different coloured control unit, but essentially the same.

'What the hell is that?'

'A bed-wetting alarm, boss.'

Fluke didn't know what he'd been expecting but it certainly wasn't that. 'Does that mean what I think it means?' he said, incredulously. If he'd had ten years, he'd never had guessed.

'Yep, here, read the description on the manufacturer's site,' he said, handing his iPhone over.

There was a photo of a smiling child but the corresponding text was too small for him. He handed it back, 'Just read it out, Hawkeye.'

Jiao-long grinned, looked as though he was going to comment on Fluke's age but clearly decided it wasn't the time. 'Basically, that flat bit here,' he said, pointing at the part Fluke had thought resembled a heat pad, 'that goes under the sheets, and you lie on it. If you start to have a piss, it sends a signal to the control unit which triggers the alarm here.' He pointed at the squarish box. 'It's supposed to wake you after the first few drips.'

They walked over to the van and retrieved it from the evidence bag. They put it together and worked out the mechanics of it all. Fluke was satisfied Jiao-long was right.

'So it's exactly what it sounds like then. Why would she have one? Wouldn't this type of thing be for kids? Who pisses the bed at her age? I tell you, Longy, every bit of evidence we get in this case just makes it harder to see what's happening.'

Fluke mentally reviewed the post-mortem. There had been no medical problem in the preliminary findings that he could recollect. Of course, some of the tests weren't back, so he'd need to ring Sowerby and check to be sure. As someone who suffered from nightmares himself, he believed that Samantha had demons in her head, demons that came out at night, causing serious psychological problems.

Towler had walked up and caught the last part. 'What's next, boss?'

Fluke thought about actions that needed be undertaken. There weren't any. The chaos of the raid then the rush to the flat. Armed police, excitement and blood. It was too late to re-interview Diamond. Not legally anyway. Gone were the days when you got confessions just because the suspect wanted to sleep. Fluke also wanted to rest before he went back in with him. He'd been caught off-guard last time – it wouldn't happen again.

'Wait for the DNA results to come through, I suppose,' he said.

'What you gonna do, boss? You want me to drive you somewhere?'

He looked at his watch. It was still the middle of the afternoon, and even though they'd been up for hours, it was too early to go home. He had a couple of calls to make. 'No point going back to HQ just yet, Matt. We'll head back to Durranhill.'

The phone rang half a dozen times before a gruff impatient voice answered. 'Sowerby.'

'Henry, it's Avison Fluke. You got two minutes?' Fluke was in a temporary office at Durranhill.

There was a noise in the background. Metal on metal. Sowerby was probably in a mortuary somewhere, prepping for another post-mortem.

'As long as you don't mind being on speakerphone, Avison. I've already scrubbed up. I have Lucy with me.'

Fluke's second call was going to be to Lucy to let her know what a help she'd been with her coffee theory, so he quickly brought her up to date and thanked her. She sounded pleased but Fluke could tell she'd rather it had been entomological evidence that had led to the breakthrough.

'Anyway,' he continued, 'did you find anything in the PM, Henry, that would have made her incontinent?'

'Incontinent? Don't think so, why?'

'I've got evidence she was a bed-wetter.' Fluke explained what they'd found.

'You mean adult nocturnal enuresis, then,' he said, after a short pause.

'Do I?'

'Just the doctor in me coming out, Avison, don't worry. I'll check my notes but there was nothing I can remember. I'll have the report finished by end of play tomorrow, hopefully. It's being typed up now. I just need to proof it.'

Sowerby's voice faded in the distance. Fluke was used to it; Sowerby frequently forgot he was talking on the speakerphone and drifted off, assuming everyone could still hear him.

'He's gone to find his notes, Inspector,' Lucy explained.

'Thanks, Lucy. And thanks again for that coffee link. We wouldn't have found her without it.'

'How's the investigation going otherwise?'

'Honestly? Nowhere. Well, not nowhere, but we don't seem to be able to get a bead on this bloke. It's taken me nearly four days just to find out where the victim lives. I'm not sure I even have her real name yet. I've found a motive to kill her, I'm just not sure it's the right motive.'

'Oh, dear. Surely finding the murder scene is going to help?'

'Hopefully, but so far every time I find something, all I end up with is more questions.'

They were interrupted by the sound of shuffling papers as Sowerby came back in range of the speakerphone.

'No, nothing here, Avison. There was very little wrong with her when I got inside. Liver had a little scarring. If she drank, it was minimal. No evidence of drug use. Bladder normal. Bloods showed nothing of note. I can re-check them for levels of the ADH hormone if you'd like?'

'In English, doc.'

'The antidiuretic hormone. It's a signalling hormone that tells the kidneys to produce less urine at night. Don't ask me how it works – this is something I'm dredging from med school. I've certainly never come across it in this field before. You want me to run the tests?'

Fluke thought about it. The shotgun approach to forensic evidence gathering had its uses but he preferred the targeted approach wherever possible – asking for forensic evidence when he knew what the answers were going to be. Never ask a question you don't already know the answer to, his first DSI had told him.

What would a hormone deficiency prove one way or the other? That she wet the bed. So what? That she had a bed-wetting alarm to manage her problem. So what? And if it wasn't a medical problem, then it was the type of evidence that only made sense after the fact. It wouldn't move the investigation forward. The samples would be there if he needed tests later.

'No thanks, Henry. I was just curious. I can't see how it's relevant. I'm not wasting taxpayer's money finding out why a woman wet the bed.'

Fluke had just put down the phone when Jo Skelton stuck her head round the door. 'Early DNAs are back, boss.'

As the results were computerised, they came in by email to the investigation address that linked directly to HOLMES. Fluke could see that there were at least ten emails from the lab. As each one linked to a different suspect, they were coming in one at a time. The top one was red, and the time next to it indicated that it had only just come in. All the rest were black, telling him that they'd been read.

'Anything?' he asked.

'All negative so far, boss. Everyone we locked up this morning has been cleared, including Wayne Diamond – his was the third result in. The ones we're waiting for are the samples taken from clothes, combs and toothbrushes. They take longer as we have to send off the whole thing. They have to find the DNA before they can profile it.'

Fluke gave her a look. She laughed.

187

'Sorry, boss, teaching you to suck eggs there. But someone round here might not know,' she said. 'Anyone here not know that?' she asked the team crowded round the computer.

The chorus of boos and other sarcastic remarks told Fluke that Jo had been the only one who'd found it interesting.

'Scraping the underpants of the Diamonds. Think I prefer my job today,' Towler said, to general agreement.

Jo laughed again and pressed F9, the refresh button. Another red email appeared. As she opened it, Fluke leaned forward, as if being closer to the screen meant he'd get the result quicker.

He read it to himself as it flashed on the screen. Although there were several attachments with photos of evidence labels, scientific graphs and other indecipherable bullshit, Fluke was only interested in the second line. The name the sample was taken from and the result: a cousin who was in HMP Durham but had been out at the time of the rape. An interfamilial match but negative. Fluke leaned back, disappointed.

'How many are interfamilial?' he asked.

'Everyone bar one, boss. They're all related to the sample we have, apart from Uncle Jonna or whatever it is he calls himself. My guess is he's one of those family friends who's been called uncle from such an early age, it becomes fact. I bet if you asked any of them they wouldn't know he wasn't a blood relative.'

Fluke knew it was likely. He also knew it wasn't a class or criminal thing. Towler's daughter, Abi, called him Uncle Avison. With extended and complicated families like the Diamonds, just identifying who was who was going to provide valuable intel for years to come.

Another email came in. Another negative.

'This could take ages,' Fluke said. He decided he'd go back to his temporary office and ring Chambers to let him know where he was, in case Fluke was needed at HQ. He rang and was put through to Chambers's PA. After they exchanged some banal pleasantries about Fluke's health, she asked him to wait while Chambers finished a call. As Fluke was listening to the hold music, he got a text. It was from Towler.

Got him!

Fluke put down the phone.

'Old man Diamond,' Towler said, when Fluke got to the room the team had colonised.

Fluke was genuinely surprised. Kenneth Diamond was the only one of the family who seemed to be an upstanding citizen. He was a businessman. He had the big house in Stanwix. When compared to the rapist profile in Fluke's head, Kenneth was twenty years older than Fluke had imagined. 'Wasn't he was away at the time of the rape?'

'Dunno, boss,' Skelton said. 'He's been away for a short while now, no one seems to know where he is. He's supposed to have distanced himself from the family though. Disowned the lot of them. He did it publicly, if I remember. We only checked his house to rule him out and to see if anyone else of interest had been there.'

'Are we sure the sample's definitely from him?'

'Sure as we can be, I suppose. Until we actually take a sample from his mouth, we can never be one hundred per cent.'

'They probably wear each other's undercrackers in that family,' Towler said, unhelpfully.

'Good enough,' Fluke said, eventually. 'Until we know anything otherwise, our number one priority has to be finding him. When we have him, we'll swab him so we know for certain. Good work today, everyone.'

Chapter 25

By the time Fluke had organised teams to search for Kenneth Diamond locally and sent out a nationwide alert on him to all territorial police forces, he was exhausted. Luckily Skelton had already warned off the Border Agency. He left Towler to organise searches into Diamond's personal and business life.

As Fluke left the building, he smiled to himself. Towler had done exactly what he'd have done, he'd shouted for Jiao-long. It looked like his plan to send him home for some sleep wasn't going to be a reality for a while yet. With the investigation in full flow and a manhunt being organised, Fluke felt he should really stay but he reminded himself that the nosebleed earlier had most likely been caused by overworking. It was time to go home and get some rest. His car was still at HQ so he got a lift home with uniform, and arranged for someone to pick him up first thing.

It was still light enough to sit outside for a while and he opened a bottle of Newcastle Brown Ale, poured it into a pint glass and sat on the porch of his log cabin, staring out across the lake. Long shadows were being cast on the fell on the other side of the lake. Fluke stared across and marvelled at the heat and pressure that must have forced the enormous fell up from the earth's crust, only for great rivers of moving ice to chip away at it, eventually forging a way through. Ullswater, the permanent reminder to the glacier that cut the mountain in half.

He lit a cigar and opened up the file he'd brought with him. Years before, Fluke had discovered his brain worked best looking at things in isolation, in small batches. That way, when he came to look at the thing as a whole, he knew he had an intellectual grip on everything. So instead of taking everything home, he'd only take the things he either hadn't read or wasn't sure he fully understood yet.

That evening, he'd taken the evidence log from Farrar's flat. He also took out the card with the numbers and clipped it to the top of the file. The list was short and there was nothing that stood out. The SOCO officer had obviously started in the bathroom.

Toothbrush, electric, still charged.
Toothpaste, half-empty.
Floss.
Assorted toiletries and make-up, used.
Hand mirror.
Coins, from window ledge.
Paracetamol, bottle, 15 tablets remaining.
Toilet paper, two rolls.
Bed wetting alarm and attachments.

The list continued, going from room to room. Her clothes were listed and Fluke's first suspicions were right. They were all brands he knew to be expensive. SOCO had attempted to separate out her personal items, from items that were part of the furnished flat. Fluke knew that efforts were underway to get hold of the landlord in London for an inventory, up to then without success. They would need to know how long she'd lived there, as William had been vague. Fluke also wanted to know how she was living there without any bills being paid. He suspected she'd paid the landlord a large amount of cash to keep it in his name, but Fluke needed confirmation.

Despite the cold, Fluke felt his eyes closing so he shut the file. He wasn't in the right frame of mind and would do more harm than good if he persevered. He considered ringing one of his sisters to try and get back some normality but decided against it. He usually enjoyed hearing about his nephews' and nieces' latest adventures but he wasn't in the right frame of mind. He relit his cigar and finished it, drained his beer and went to bed.

For once, he wasn't disturbed by nightmares.

It was still dark when Fluke's alarm went off and he opened his eyes. In that halfway state – not asleep but not yet awake – he was able to remember the last thing he'd dreamt of. It had been the inventory. Something in his subconscious had been bothered by it. But as his mind cleared and he woke fully, so did any chance of remembering. It would come back; there was no point forcing it. He knew how his mind worked.

Fluke had no qualms about telling everyone they were working Saturday but felt that when he did, he should be in first. He debated whether to put on some fresh coffee but decided to have one when he got to work instead.

He got to Carleton Hall to find the incident room deserted. He put a fresh filter in the coffee machine and started it off. Towler was already in but had gone to find a newsagent in Penrith to buy some milk. As the machine hissed and gurgled, Fluke thought about what he wanted to achieve.

First, he needed to check with the custody suites that everyone apart from Nathaniel Diamond had been released. Fluke wanted another go at Nathaniel. Although he wasn't a suspect in the rape, he knew something, plus his dad was now in the frame. He'd task the first DC to arrive, to go and get an additional twelve hours from the on-call magistrate to question Nathaniel. The advantage of asking in the early hours was that the magistrate would be woken at home and less likely to say no.

While Fluke waited for the coffee machine, he opened his file from the previous night. He stared at the list, willing that night's thoughts to come back but there was nothing. Apart from the bed-wetting alarm, it was still a list of everyday items. He'd mention it at the morning briefing. He turned to the photo of the alarm. It was bothering him as well. He couldn't help feeling there was something else on the list that made sense of it. The previous day, he'd thought she was running from someone and was having nightmares because of it. Now he wasn't so sure.

There was also the question that Kay Edwards, the DC who had travelled with her to the SARC, had raised. If she was in hiding, why had she even been going out for a drink at all? Fluke had initially thought it had been a fair question but it had slipped his mind before he could seriously consider it. Put alongside his own unasked question of whether anyone that scared would report a rape, it took on greater significance. He had the feeling that Samantha still had secrets to be revealed.

Find out how the victim lived and you'll find out how they died.

Fluke enjoyed those rare moments of solitude. Surrounded by the fruits of the investigation, he liked looking at things in isolation at home but in the incident room he could look at everything as a whole. It was his wide-angled lens. The board with photos of the two crime scenes was full. The previous day, photos of the different Diamonds had been staring back at him. That night, someone had replaced them with a single photo of Kenneth. It had been cut out from a newspaper article about a new business venture he was involved in. One other photograph was on the board: the cold, lifeless face of Samantha Farrar. It was up to Fluke to find out if the link between them had been the cause of her murder.

The coffee machine had quietened down and Fluke poured himself a large mug. As he drank it, he let his mind drift from one photo to the other, taking in all the pictorial evidence.

His peace was interrupted by another of his team coming in. Jo Skelton walked through the door. Surprised to see him, she was even more surprised to find that there was already a pot of fresh coffee. 'There's no milk yet, Jo. Matt's gone for some.'

'No organisation, you two,' she said, pulling a carton from her bag.

She grabbed her 'World's Best Mum' mug and filled it. She walked over and perched on the edge of the table, next to Fluke. 'You get any kip, boss?'

'Some. You?'

'Not much, nasty one this. I let Tom sleep in. He can take the kids to football today. I may struggle to come in tomorrow, though.'

Fluke nodded. He knew Jo's husband was in a band that played at weddings so he normally worked weekends. 'No gig tonight?'

'Nope bookings are down nearly thirty per cent. People just want discos and hog roasts these days. He's enjoying the extra time with the kids, though. I've been thinking about everything we have, trying to make some links but I can't get my head round it all yet. Can't remember the last one we had that was this complicated.'

'Same here. That inventory is bugging me,' he said.

'Why?'

'Can't put my finger on it yet. There's just something that isn't quite right.'

Fluke had worked with Jo for long enough to know that she was what he called a 'plodder'. He'd mentioned that to Chambers once, and he'd asked if he wanted her replaced. Fluke had had to explain that it wasn't meant as an insult. His team worked best when there were hares *and* tortoises. He needed officers who could methodically plough through hours and hours of evidence, who wouldn't get bored doing repetitive tasks, who wouldn't miss things, who would take care to set up and maintain HOLMES. The ACPO Murder Manual stated that the office manager of an incident room should be either a Detective Sergeant or a Detective Inspector but Fluke chose Jo every time. She never complained and knew she was valued highly, fully accepting her role in the team. Police work was ninety-nine per cent perspiration and one per cent inspiration. A cliché, yes, but some clichés were clichés because they were true.

'You'll get there. How's your health, boss? You've been looking pasty the last couple of days.'

Some officers had earned the right to ask questions like that and she was one of them.

'I'm tired, Jo. Weary. Can't seem to shake it off. Normally I can leave all this behind,' he said, pointing at the evidence boards. 'Not this one though. This one's staying with me. There was nothing personal about it. Every murder I've ever worked has had anger at its core, whether it's about money, sex or jealousy. At least there's a spark of humanity. Not this one. This was cold. Someone probably rang a number or sent an email, and an emotionless sociopath came up, shot her and threw her in a hole. How do you try and make sense of that?'

She blew on her drink. 'We'll get there, boss. We always do.'

They finished their coffees in silence as the incident room filled up.

Fluke appeared to be alone in his concerns over the list. No one else had given it a second thought, but as he sometimes made links that others couldn't, he knew they would all look again. No one had any new thoughts on the numbers either. Not a dead end. Just dead. He was prepared to accept that they meant nothing, but there were too many random things in the investigation already. They were all potential leads.

The rest of the briefing was spent allocating tasks for the day, most of which were about the search for Kenneth Diamond.

That was Towler's specialty; running people to ground. If he was still in Cumbria, Towler would find him.

With Towler busy with the manhunt, Fluke took Vaughn with him to re-interview Nathaniel Diamond. He took his own car and Vaughn took the pool car. Fluke needed to be mobile. He wasn't expecting anything to break early on and if he got time he'd decided, he'd go and see Leah, and check if she'd found someone to talk to about cosmetic surgery.

Fluke and Vaughn arrived at Durranhill within minutes of each other, and an hour later, they were sitting opposite Nathaniel Diamond. The custody sergeant told Fluke that, despite nearly twenty-four hours in a police cell, Diamond still looked calm. His only reaction had been when his solicitor was served the notice granting an additional twelve hours' questioning time. Apparently, he'd looked at the camera and raised an eyebrow.

The previous day, Diamond had been in control. Fluke had detected deception when shown the picture of the victim but other than that he'd remained calm.

This time Fluke wasn't leaving until he had something he could use.

Vaughn had asked if he should bring Diamond up from the cells, and Fluke was about to tell him 'yes' until he realised it would just be a continuation of the previous day. He needed something more, some sort of leverage. It was going to be a battle of intellectual heavyweights, and Fluke needed to land the knockout blow. Instead, he turned to Vaughn, 'No, Al, I want to review yesterday's interview first.'

For an hour, Fluke pored over the footage. He watched it with the sound and then without. Vaughn, a brilliant detective in his own right, looked over his shoulder but said nothing.

Fluke watched himself reveal the photo of Samantha to Diamond. There'd definitely been recognition. He watched from the beginning again. He saw himself enter. He saw himself open his folder.

And he saw what he'd missed the first five times.

Chapter 26

Fluke stared at Nathaniel Diamond across the scuffed table and studied him. Really studied him. On the face of it, he was what he looked like. A thug. An intelligent thug yes, but a thug all the same. Yet, as Fluke looked closer things cleared. The tattoos were a little too well done. No prison ink there. Expensive black tribal sleeves on both arms. His tracksuit, before it had been removed, was also expensive, according to the young officer who had bagged it. They'd also taken an Omega watch from him and that wasn't cheap. It also wasn't garish like some of the more expensive watches could be.

After what Fluke had just witnessed in the footage, he no longer thought of Diamond as an intelligent thug. He thought of him as having a once-in-a-generation mind.

Fluke now suspected his image was completely cultivated. It suited him at that moment and, like a chameleon shedding its skin, he would swap it for another when the time was right. The more Fluke thought about it, the more he came to view Diamond as the head of a large business – an illegal business, but a business all the same. No business survived for long without a business plan and without a CEO. And the CEO had to look the part. On Wall Street, the bankers, moneymen and oil analysts wore their pinstriped suits. In Carlisle, the crime families wore tattoos, tracksuits and heavy jewellery. Occasionally, a dangerous dog was thrown in for good measure. It was still an image, however. Two extremes, but the principle was the same.

Brains wouldn't have been enough in Diamond's business, however. He would've had to spend some time establishing himself among some pretty rough competition, competition that would undoubtedly have included his own family. The fact that he was the younger brother but the head of the family, spoke volumes. Violence was just another business tool, to be used when needed but only then. As well as being highly intelligent, Nathaniel would be a genuinely frightening man to get on the wrong side of.

Fluke had met hard men all his working life. The Royal Marines recruited almost exclusively from that gene pool. Some were bullies, some weren't. A few were psychopaths, and some were the nicest people you could ever wish to meet. During his time as a police officer, Fluke had met men who were arguably harder. Men who were psychotic. Men for whom violence was a daily occurrence.

What they all had in common, however, was that there was always someone harder round the corner. Someone younger and quicker coming up through the ranks. Someone just a little bit more mental. Just a little bit more fearless.

So violence would have got Nathaniel to the top, and his brains would have kept him there, but not indefinitely. The X-factor would be ruthlessness. That would be the trait that would keep him in charge and make the Diamonds a viable option for outside investment from the drug gangs of Liverpool, the type of gangs that were hunted by the National Crime Agency rather than CID.

A ruthless man could organise a murder if his business were threatened.

The previous day Diamond had been in control.

Today, it would be Fluke's turn. At first, he'd thought he was imagining it. Part of him still didn't think what he'd seen was possible. He'd had to watch it over and over again until he was sure.

Diamond held his eye as Fluke stared at him but it wasn't a battle of wills. Just as Fluke was weighing him up, he got the sense Diamond was doing exactly the same to him.

Fluke broke the silence. 'Just how clever are you, Nathaniel?'

Diamond said nothing.

'You see, I think you're a very clever man indeed. Far more intelligent than my colleagues in Carlisle have ever given you credit for. Far more than I'd given you credit for.'

Diamond stared at Fluke. There was something going on that Fluke was still unaware of, some context to the investigation that he was yet to see. Diamond could see it, Fluke was sure of that. Would he share it, though?

Time to take a risk.

'When did you learn about the airline's interview technique, Nathaniel?'

Still nothing. But Fluke sensed there was movement behind his eyes, as if the neurones in his brain had suddenly had to change direction.

'You see very few people know about that technique, Nathaniel. It's still being piloted. It's still a university project for now. I'm the only person who uses it in Cumbria. I may be the only police officer in the country that uses it. But you knew what I was doing all along. So I have two options. You either knew about the technique or you were able to work it out as I was doing it. I think you worked it out, Nathaniel. You want to know how I know?'

Diamond raised his eyebrows slightly. He was curious. Fluke had grabbed his interest.

'It's because I fucked it up, that's why,' he said. 'You knew what I was doing. You knew I was asking control questions. You reacted to every question as I'd expected. As you had wanted to. You never lost control. Even the little burst of anger at your solicitor here was part of it.'

Diamond said nothing but Fluke knew he was right.

'I had my control questions. Now I had to ask the question. The one question that it had all been for. But I fucked it up, didn't I, Nathaniel?'

Diamond continued to stare. Just as Fluke was about to continue, he nodded slightly.

'You were playing along. You were expecting the question, weren't you? You were expecting the surprise, if you'll forgive my oxymoron. You were watching me as carefully as I was watching you. I showed you the picture of my victim. That was my surprise. But it was no surprise was it, Nathaniel?'

'No, Inspector, it wasn't.' The first words he'd said since the interview had started.

'No, Nathaniel. Because when I went through the interview footage again, I noticed that when I took my papers out at the start of the interview, I had mistakenly left the photo of the victim in view for nearly two seconds.'

Fluke took the photo back out of the file and placed it on the table in front of him.

'This one in fact. But you noticed. The footage shows you noticing. You hid your surprise well. I watched it five times before I spotted it, and I had to watch it another five times just to be sure.'

Fluke picked up the photo and studied it. It was the question that was going to break the case. Sometimes it wasn't just about asking the right question, it was about asking the right question at the right time.

'So my question, Nathaniel, is this. I have you on tape fully in control of your micro-expressions. I have you on tape letting me see what I was expecting to see on my control questions. I know you'd seen the photo before I showed it to you. I know you weren't surprised by it and that you were expecting it. You could easily have cast suspicion away from your family.' Fluke stared at him. Crunch time. 'But you didn't, Nathaniel. You feigned surprise. Subtle yes, but enough so I wouldn't miss it. You made sure I'd know your family's involved somehow. Nothing that will stand up in court but enough to keep me interested.'

Diamond was watching him carefully. There was a game being played here but only one of them knew the rules.

'I want to know why, Nathaniel? I want to know why you want me investigating your family for murder?'

The room was silent apart from the sound of something dripping. There were no taps, radiators or pipes in interview rooms so Fluke assumed it was coming from some internal plumbing in either the walls or the ceiling. He counted the drips and got to thirty before Diamond spoke.

'Are you investigating my father for rape, Mr Fluke?'

Of all the responses he'd anticipated, that wasn't in the top hundred. He had to be careful. 'Why do you say that, Nathaniel?'

'I hear things,' Diamond said.

'And what do you hear?'

'I hear you have a dead girl. I hear she was raped. I hear you think whoever raped her, killed her...' he said quietly, staring directly at Fluke. 'Or arranged to have her killed, which is the same thing really.'

Fluke thought for a moment. 'I hear that too.' If they were being open with each other, he'd play along. For now. He paused for a moment. He had the feeling Diamond was trying to tell him something, something he wanted Fluke to work out. Something he wasn't prepared to say on tape.

Fluke wondered if he wanted to snitch but immediately dismissed it. Being a snitch would end his business. None of the bigger gangs would deal with him. No, that wasn't it.

Diamond was staring at him. He wanted Fluke to get the message. Needed him to understand the subtext. Fluke stared back but it wasn't a pissing contest, just two people trying to communicate without speaking. Vaughn and the solicitor were in the room as well but Fluke knew that they were the only two that mattered.

'You're going to need to give me something, Nathaniel.' Fluke felt rather than saw Vaughn turn to look at Fluke, not understanding what was happening but knowing not to interrupt. The solicitor didn't understand either but was too scared to speak.

Fluke saw Diamond look down and think, saw him deciding what he could tell Fluke and what he couldn't. He knew that the investigation was either going to stall completely or progress fast in the next few seconds.

Diamond looked up. 'The girl. You need to look at her again.'

For the second time in five minutes, Fluke was surprised by Diamond's response. There was no bone being thrown here. No suspect was going to be thrown his way. No vehement denial of involvement. Just another riddle to add to the plethora of riddles the case was attracting.

This was different though. Diamond wanted him to go in a direction he'd wanted to go anyway. Until now, a direction he'd not dared to. To do so would have been unthinkable.

Fluke understood.

Nathaniel didn't want his family investigated. He wanted Samantha investigated.

Find out how the victim lived and you'll find out how they died.

'Why do I need to do that, Nathaniel? What do you know that I don't?'

'I can't make it easy for you, Mr Fluke. If I tell you what I know, you'll stop looking. You'll take what I give you, and the investigation will end right here, right now. And the outcome would be, shall we say, unacceptable to me. I can't have that.'

Fluke believed him. 'We've looked at her pretty hard, Nathaniel. What am I missing?'

Diamond's expression remained the same but there was an urgent tone to what he said next, 'Look harder, Mr Fluke. Look harder.'

Chapter 27

Fluke had lied to Diamond. They hadn't looked at Samantha that hard. They'd looked at her as a murder victim. They'd looked at her as a rape victim. They'd looked at her as someone on the run. But they hadn't touched the surface of *why* she'd been murdered, *why* she'd been raped and *why* she was on the run.

Diamond knew something but for some reason he couldn't tell Fluke. It would stop the investigation, he'd told him.

He needed to focus on Samantha.

He already had suspicions, unshaped and unshared.

Fluke had put two local detectives on finding out her real name but he knew that he hadn't prioritised it. If he had, he'd have led on it himself.

He drove back to FMIT instead of going to see Leah. He had a new line of enquiry.

He gathered everyone together. Luckily, the first stage of the hunt for Kenneth Diamond would be done by uniform and CID, so most of the team were there.

'Listen up!' he called out. 'I'm changing the focus of the investigation. The hunt for Kenneth Diamond goes on but our number one priority is now the girl. I want to know everything about her. Nathaniel Diamond knows something we don't. Something he can't tell us for some reason. I want to know what that is.'

Towler walked over to the whiteboard, ready to start tasking when Fluke called them out.

'We know she was hiding from someone. I am now convinced it wasn't a Diamond. So we need to know more than we do now. Where's Kay?' Fluke had kept Kay Edwards on secondment to FMIT and intended to use her.

'Here, sir,' said a voice from the back.

'I want you to go through the rape again. Take Jo through it all. Get everything down. Nothing's irrelevant. Go back to the SARC at Preston and retrace everything.'

Towler wrote down the task on the board with the initials of the two officers.

'I'll go back to the hospital and see if they have a cosmetic surgeon for me to speak to yet. I'll do that on my own, Matt. Longy, I need you to look for her online. Anything. Use the name she gave. Use her DNA, fingerprint, surgery scars, anything you can think of. And don't limit yourself to UK databases. I want Interpol tapped up. The States. See if you can speak to the FBI. Start the process to check with their border security, if she's been there she'll have been fingerprinted on arrival.'

'Boss,' he confirmed.

'Al, I want a bulletin made up. Don't fuck about with the E-fit, use the best photo we have, and a summary of both crimes. I want it sent to every force in the country. Let's see if anyone else has come across her. I also want you to start on her financial footprint. She was paying cash for the flat but she had to have a source of income. Work with Longy and find it.'

He looked up from the notes he was holding. Everyone was waiting for him to dismiss them, waiting to get on with it. Energy had been renewed. Time to let them do what they did best.

'Right, Matt is going to coordinate all this so include him in any updates. When I'm not here, he's in charge.'

Half an hour later, Fluke left HQ and was driving back to Carlisle. He felt that he was spending half his life on the M6. There was no tram or underground system in Cumbria to ease the amount of driving you had to do, and the bus service was limited. In a county that big, and with a population that small, driving was the only option. The Americans had a term for it: freeway therapy, when someone was causing trouble but not enough to be sacked, they would be based as far away from their home as possible. They were then faced with either moving or spending hours driving. Fluke knew that the amount of driving he'd done over the previous few days was largely self-imposed and, as he was using his BMW X1 rather than the pool car, he wasn't getting mileage but he didn't care. Using his own vehicle gave him flexibility. Plus, you couldn't smoke in the pool cars.

He put on a Ramones CD and turned up the volume. He needed to clear his head of all previous preconceptions about the case, and loud fast music was the best way of doing that.

He'd checked with the ward that Leah was on duty and made an appointment. Anyone could have done that but he wanted to keep busy, to keep moving. He debated telling her about his nosebleed but decided against it. He knew it was down to over-exerting himself, and she'd only tell him to slow down, or worse, sit still while he had two hours' worth of plasma. With a renewed focus to the investigation, he needed to speed up if anything.

He searched for a parking space but couldn't find one. Even the overflow car parks were full. Fluke knew that you either got there at eight o'clock or you entered the parking space lottery. He and a black Saab prowled the main car park for a while before he eventually gave up and parked in the staff section, leaving a note in the windscreen that he was a police officer on official business. It didn't give him any right to park there but it might buy him some time.

Despite his struggle to park, he was early for his appointment. Playing loud music always made him drive faster. The ward nurse asked him to take a seat in the dayroom while she informed Doctor Cooper he was there. There was only one other person in the room; a middle-aged man watching the highlights of some rugby match on the flat screen TV. The volume was on mute. He was wearing a baseball cap to hide the hair-loss. He was hooked up to a portable drip stand and had two bags of fluids feeding tubes that went under his T-shirt. A Hickman line no doubt. Fluke had had one fitted during his illness. When the chemicals going in him were so corrosive that the smaller veins were being destroyed, the only option was to fix a permanent rubber tube directly into a major vessel near the heart. Surgery to get it in and surgery to take it out. Fluke subconsciously rubbed his chest where he knew his own scar was.

A nurse came in and asked the man if he needed any pain medication.

'Aye, lass,' he replied, in a voice that had little fight left.

'One or two?' she said, removing a blister pack from her pocket.

'Two, lass. Unless I can have three?'

'Away with yer,' she replied, with good humour. 'More than my job's worth.' She popped two pills and placed them into a thimble-sized container, before handing them over.

Fluke frowned. Something had flashed across the subconscious part of his mind but he didn't know why. He had the strangest feeling that he'd just witnessed something relevant. He replayed the innocuous exchange, but there was nothing there. He looked around to see if there was anything in the room that was going to help push something to the front of his mind.

It was a typical dayroom, found the length and breadth of hospitals the world over; a television and about thirty out-of-date tattered magazines. Books and games that had been donated were in a plastic storage box. There were children's toys on the floor and Fluke felt a tinge of sadness that any child should have to visit a relative under such difficult circumstances. Posters on the institutionally painted walls displayed posters reminding staff to wash their hands. Nothing jolted his memory.

The man watching the rugby sighed as the wrong team ran in a try. It seemed nothing was going right for him.

'Doctor Cooper will see you now, Mr Fluke,' a healthcare assistant said, interrupting his efforts at retrieving whatever his memory was hiding. He noticed HCAs were virtually indistinguishable from nurses these days, no doubt a strategy developed by the Minister for Health to give the impression that ward staffing wasn't as critical as the media was portraying.

Doctor Cooper and Mr Fluke, he thought. *Very formal.*

He knew the way to Leah's office but the HCA led him there anyway.

'If you can just wait outside, Mr Fluke, she's finishing a telephone call.'

Fluke took a seat, perplexed. Normally Leah would come and grab him, and they'd have a cup of tea together. Even when he was being treated, it was never that formal. He'd been a copper long enough to be on his guard. Something was different.

It was over five minutes before Leah's office door opened and by then Fluke had taken the card out again. He didn't need it anymore; the numbers were imprinted on his mind. They continued to elude him. He'd rearranged them. Added them. Subtracted them. Ignored the decimal points. Nothing.

He was staring at them when Leah walked out. She saw him and walked back into her office without saying a word. She sat down behind her desk and stared at him. The second time someone had done that to him that day. Nathaniel Diamond had been a master of it, Fluke knew behind his eyes was pure danger. Eyes that hid a thousand dirty secrets. This was worse, far worse. Leah looked angry. Angry and sad.

Her desk was empty except for a letter. He could see it had a stamp on it, the sort admin used to show the date it had been received. He didn't want to try to read it upside down, she looked angry enough. Leah picked it up and pretended to read it.

An uneasy feeling crept up on him. She hadn't found out, surely? He knew that at some point in the future, he was going to have to tell her his secret. He'd never considered she might find out on her own. He wasn't sure there was any way she actually could. This must be about something else.

'Did you find a cosmetic sur—' he started to say.

She cut him off. 'Do you know what this is, Detective Inspector?' She was holding it at such an angle that he wasn't meant to see it.

Fluke looked back at her face and was astonished to see a tear running down her cheek. She made no attempt to wipe it off.

'No, Leah, I don't know what's on that piece of paper.'

'Are you sure? Your name's all over it.'

The feeling of unease disappeared and was replaced by dread. 'My name, how? Can I see?' he asked, weakly. Fluke thought of himself as an excellent interviewer, being able to disguise his intent and knowledge when he needed to, but even he thought he sounded guilty.

She made no sign that she was going to hand it over. More tears ran down her face. She left them.

'It's from Carleton Hall. An official request for a copy of the letter I sent your Occupational Health department confirming you were fit to return to full duties.'

Fluke slumped in his seat. This was it. It wasn't 'something else', it was his secret. His terrible secret. His complete betrayal of trust. His crime.

He knew there was nothing he could say. Nothing he could do to excuse himself. He'd known that if the secret ever became known, he'd be thrown off the force. He looked up. The tears seemed to have stopped. Their tracks had dried, and left marks on her lightly made-up face.

She spoke coldly, no emotion in her voice despite the tears and obvious distress. 'Perhaps you can help me out here? Perhaps the great Detective Inspector Fluke could explain how the letter they want a copy of, the one I'm supposed to have written and signed and sent on hospital stationery, is a letter I'd never heard about until this afternoon.'

***

Chapter 28

After his treatment, Fluke had left hospital a shell of a man. After major surgery, he hadn't been in the best physical shape to begin with and the consultant in charge of his treatment had told him there would be times he'd hate them for what they would be doing. He tried to be polite to the doctors and nurses but at times it had been hard. The chemotherapy protocol for Burkitt's was the most aggressive they did, and the effects on his body seemed more devastating than the tumour had ever been. The tumour had caused him to have an upset stomach. The treatment for the tumour left him with devastating side-effects. It caused him pain he'd never experienced before. He stopped eating and he lost too much weight. Simple things like washing and shaving became ordeals. He left hospital a different man; different physically, but also different mentally.

Buoyant to be finally out and cancer-free, he had thought it was time to get back on with his life. The police had organised Occupational Health to assess when he was going to be fit to return to work. He'd realistically thought it was going to be two months of eating well, regaining some strength and completing the course of physiotherapy organised for him.

What he hadn't realised was that some of the side-effects were irreversible. He was left with thrombocytopenia. His body wasn't producing the right amount of platelets. It was manageable and it wasn't dangerous unless he was wounded. In most jobs it wouldn't have mattered. Fluke knew that the police was one of the jobs where it would. They couldn't put him out on the street knowing a small stab wound could be fatal, that his blood was no longer able to clot, that he could bleed out before help arrived. That surgery had to be carefully planned, the right bloods had to be stocked up in advance, specialist surgeons had to come in. It was a condition that would end his police career. He'd be allowed to ride a desk but, as far as he was concerned, that amounted to the same thing.

Leah had explained it was a seldom-seen side-effect. Determined to get back to work, he decided not to tell the Occupational Health nurse. He hid it from everyone. Apart from the occasional nosebleed and bleeding gums, there were no external signs that would give it away.

Gradually, his strength came back, nowhere near the level he'd previously enjoyed, but enough so that he could give the appearance of being fit. His hair grew back and he put on weight. He was ready to go back to work.

Although he'd never been career-minded, he took the job very seriously. He wasn't the type of detective who thought crimes were simply puzzles to challenge his intellectual vanity; he cared deeply about the victims. He wasn't prepared to leave the job just yet. He had nothing else to fall back on, there was nothing else he wanted to do.

He knew he should tell Occupational Health, that not telling them wasn't fair on his colleagues, but he couldn't bring himself to do it.

When it became apparent that it was going to be a serious issue, he thought about ways round it but came up against a brick wall. He needed a doctor to declare him fit to return. Something Chambers wouldn't be able to ignore. Occupational Health only summarised medical reports and what he told them. Physically he looked fit, a bit thinner, a bit paler, but nothing too startling. They wouldn't do a blood test, they would expect his consultant to provide those.

Everything came back to Leah and he couldn't see a way round it. He considered asking her to ignore his condition but knew that she wouldn't and he had no right to ask.

He became distant and withdrawn, and for a while took it out on those around him. Increasingly, his thoughts turned to how he could circumnavigate the NHS. Nothing legal sprang to mind. He thought about, then dismissed, illegal ways he could do it. But the thoughts kept coming back. He justified it to himself by saying the force was better with him in it. A half-fit Fluke was better than any other fully fit detective. That the people of Cumbria deserved him, needed him. He told himself he was being altruistic, not selfish.

He knew he was lying to himself but he didn't care.

The semblance of a plan started to come together. He needed help. He paid ten pounds to have his medical records copied as anyone was entitled to. He sent them to a struck-off doctor he'd found online advertising his services. Two hundred pounds got him a comprehensive report detailing everything he'd been through but omitting the thrombocytopenia. It was delivered on a memory stick. Fluke had a report, full of medical terminology, that gave him a clean bill of health. But he still needed a credible way of getting it to Occupational Health. One that would get him back to work with no more questions being asked. One that would avoid the need for a genuine NHS report.

For days, Fluke struggled with the best way of doing it. Every scenario he went through failed. The police weren't irresponsible employers, they weren't going to let him come back to work without a report from his consultant, and his consultant couldn't give him one. Whoever he pretended the letter was from wouldn't stop Occupational Health demanding a full report. The request would go to Leah and her reply would go to them. Fluke would be copied into it but it would be too late.

Fluke knew that the only way round it would be to do Leah's report himself. For a month, he did nothing. He couldn't bring himself to pay the price. He decided that he wouldn't do it. He'd take his chances with the truth, hope for a restricted duties job where he could still have some input into investigations.

It was a routine blood check when the opportunity presented itself. Leah had been discussing the results with him on the ward. The curtain around his bay had been closed, as if a plastic sheet gave any real privacy. In Fluke's experience, anytime a curtain was closed, everyone else on the ward strained their ears to hear what was happening.

She'd been discussing how his platelet count had been higher than the previous few visits and that she was pleased with his progress, when the crash alarm had sounded. Every member of staff ran out of the ward. Fluke was left alone.

With his file.

He looked at it for a while. He'd suddenly become nervous. His mouth went dry and the vein in his neck pulsed. He opened it and went straight to the back where he knew the patient details stickers were kept, the stickers that went on every vial of blood, on every wristband he wore. On every letter. They had his name, address, and more importantly, a barcode.

As if on autopilot, he removed a whole page and put it in his jacket.

He spent the next couple of days preparing his letter. He went to a local printer and got some good quality copies of a blanked-out page of one of his own medical letters. He then tried various options with the text on the memory stick. Different fonts and letter sizes to try and find the ones the hospital used. He amended some of the language to fit in more with Leah's style. He spent several hours trying to forge a natural signature, although like anyone who signed their name several times a day, Leah's signature was little more than a scrawl. Eventually, he was confident he had a passable enough forgery. He had enough colour copies of the stolen letterhead to get the text in the right place by trial and error. He affixed one of the stickers and forged Leah's signature. The process of stealing the stickers to having a fully forged document had taken just three days.

He'd stared at the final version for nearly an hour in silence. He knew what he was about to do was wrong. Very wrong. It was a massive betrayal of someone who had only ever had his best interests at heart. It was a betrayal of Cumbria police who had stood by him during his ill health. And it was a crime. Fraud, making a false instrument, obtaining a pecuniary advantage by deception, misconduct in a public office; take your pick, just a few of the charges he could face if he was caught. At best, he'd be thrown out in disgrace, at worst he'd do jail time. But most of all, it was a betrayal of himself, of his own values. He'd always considered himself a moral man. A man who stood up to bullies, who gave the vulnerable a voice. A man who had dedicated his life to doing the right thing, even if sometimes the right thing wasn't always legal. If he did it, he could no longer stand on the high ground looking down.

The last stage of his plan involved getting the letter sent from the hospital so it would have NHS franking marks on it. He ran through several scenarios but settled for just looking for an opportunity.

It came the next time he was getting his blood checked.

Again, he was a given a clean bill of health. Burkitt's wasn't the type of cancer that came back. It was a kill-or-cure cancer. He had to wait at the receptionist's station on the way out while they sorted out his next appointment. As a frequent visitor to the ward, the staff knew him well and always had a chat. As she read out the next available appointments, Fluke pretended to lean over to see the computer screen. As he did, he slipped the letter into the middle of the pile of outgoing mail. He'd addressed it to the Occupational Health department.

On the way out, he rang them to tell them he was fit enough to come back, requesting an assessment and to inform them that his consultant would be sending them a letter detailing his current condition which he hoped would support his return to work.

A month later, he was back at his desk in Carleton Hall. He'd spent two weeks doing a phased return at the insistence of Occupational Health, and one week receiving a handover from the temporary DI they'd installed. Nine months after being diagnosed with Burkitt's Lymphoma, he was back on the Force Major Investigation Team.

For how long was now out of his hands.

Chapter 29

'You bastard! You utter bastard. How could you?'

Fluke was surprised by her language. He'd never heard her swear before but he wasn't surprised by her reaction. He decided to say nothing. There was nothing he could say. No point in denying it. No point trying to explain it. He was categorically in the wrong and had no choice but to ride the lightning.

'Well?' she asked.

Still he remained silent. He was at her mercy now. He was curious why a copy of the original letter was being requested by HQ but the 'why' was irrelevant to what the consequences were going to be. Leah had stopped crying. Her eyes, normally so friendly, so warm, were cold, devoid of anything but anger and disappointment. Fluke was at a loss on what to say next. Everything would appear trite and self-serving. He also knew that any attempt to explain or excuse his deception would be fatal. He decided honesty was the best approach.

'I'm sorry,' he said.

She held his gaze until his shame got the better of him. He broke eye contact.

'Sorry? You're sorry? Oh, well, that's all right then. The great important detective is sorry. Do you realise what you've done? Forget the fact that you've risked your health, forget the fact that you've probably broken the law, you've put my job at risk. Why, Avison?'

She looked at Fluke and her expression had changed slightly. She looked genuinely puzzled.

'I had to, Leah.'

'No, you didn't, you wanted to. You didn't have to at all, you selfish bastard!' she shouted, anger flaring up again.

Fluke paused. He knew she was right. Selfish was a word he'd avoided using to describe his actions when he'd been justifying them to himself. But it had been. He could lie to himself all he wanted but he'd forged the letter for one reason only: himself.

'Sorry. You're right. Of course, you're right. I wanted to go back to work. The job was all I had. I know this won't mean anything but I've been wanting to tell you for a while.'

'You're right, it doesn't mean anything. What am I supposed to do now? I know what I should do, what I'm required to do – go straight to the Trust board and tell them everything. Anything else and I'm complicit in this stupid thing.'

Fluke instinctively knew that asking her not to would be the wrong thing to do. 'Of course. You should do what you think is right,' he said, lamely.

'Oh, fuck off, you patronising arsehole. Don't speak to me like that. I thought we were friends. This is me you're speaking to. What do you think I should do? What do you want me to do? I've already lied once for you this morning. I'm not in the mood to do it twice, not if you don't care enough to act like a grown-up. I'm not the headmistress, and you're not a schoolboy, Avison. What do you want me to do?'

She'd lied for him once already? He didn't understand. Things were moving so quickly he was struggling to keep up.

Fluke rubbed his hands over his eyes. He felt tired all of a sudden. There was also a sense of relief. The strain of lying to her had been debilitating. 'I don't know, Leah. I'm not trying to be coy, I'm really not. I don't want to lose my job, of course I don't. But the last thing I want is to get you into trouble. I need you to believe that.'

She looked at him and her expression softened. 'It may be out of my hands anyway.'

Fluke looked up. She must have seen the confusion in his face.

'No, I haven't said anything to anyone. Not yet anyway. But how do you think I got this letter, Avison? What in your addled mind do you think is going on here?'

Fluke said nothing. It was a letter. Letters got posted.

'Oh, you stupid man. It was hand-delivered.' She seemed to sense his confusion. 'A police officer brought it. Someone called Fenton, Alec or Alex Fenton. He showed me a photocopy of the letter they received. He asked for the original for his files. Wanted to know if I remembered writing it.'

Fluke lurched in his seat as if he'd been shot. He immediately felt nauseous. *Alex fucking Fenton.* It was very bad. As bad as it could get. He tried to speak but couldn't. His mouth had turned to ash, his tongue was a stranger.

Leah's expression changed. Anger turned to concern. 'Avison, who is Fenton? What does he do? How did he know about this letter?'

Fluke put his head in his hands and didn't answer immediately. He was in serious trouble. Prison trouble. 'Alex Fenton is the superintendent in PSD, Leah.'

She looked none the wiser. 'What's PSD, I'm not a policeman.'

'Professional Standards Department,' he said, almost resigned to his inevitable fate. 'The cop's cops. Internal affairs.'

'I don't understand, I—'

'I'm screwed, Leah. There's no need for you to get into trouble now. No need for you to cover for me. I would never ask you to anyway. I don't even think I could bear you to risk anything for me at the minute. I don't feel worth it today.'

'That's not what I was going to say, and you can cut the martyr bullshit. I'll decide what I'll do about this, not you. And certainly not Alec Fenton.'

'Alex.'

'Piss off. No, what I was going to say was, how did he know about this letter?'

'He has access to all personnel files. He can poke his nose in where he likes. Someone of his rank speaks to who he wants when he wants. He can challenge anyone, investigate anyone.'

'I'm not on about how he physically got hold of it. I mean, how did he know to ask for the original? If it wasn't for the fact that I knew I hadn't written it, it would have fooled me. It looked genuine. Nice job actually. I'd be impressed if I didn't think you were an absolute shit for doing this.'

Fluke had no clue why Fenton had thought to request the original. He would brood on that later. His time was going to become limited soon and he didn't want to waste it thinking about his future. He needed to focus on the case. Leah, it seemed, did want to continue thinking about it.

'So, tell me. Why did he ask for it? You must have done something to raise suspicions?'

Fluke thought about it. PSD wasn't the pariah that Internal Affairs was in the States. For most officers, it was something they got moved to in routine inter-departmental shuffles. It wasn't anything to be feared. Do it well and it was a good career move. Nobody was castigated for being in PSD.

Apart from Fenton. Fenton enjoyed it. Enjoyed the infamy of being the one member of PSD that wanted to stay. Enjoyed being feared. Enjoyed being able to hold grudges and act on those grudges. He'd tried to be a CID detective but had no aptitude for it, so he hated those who did. He was an arsehole, an isolated careerist, but he played by the rules. So if he'd asked for a copy of the letter then he had something concrete on Fluke, he wouldn't be fishing. Fluke was in no doubt this was the start of something formal. It might even be the end of something that began some time ago. He had no way of knowing what Fenton knew.

He briefly ran through the things that may have given him away. He settled on an early theory, although even as he said it, he knew how paranoid it sounded. 'I've been having nosebleeds,' he said. 'Someone outside the team must've noticed and told my boss. He's been after me for a while. All he'd have had to do was fake some concern, go to PSD with some suspicions and they'd do the rest.' He put his head in his hands and sighed. *Was this how it all ended?*

Important as it was, Fluke decided it would have to wait. He needed to focus on what he'd come for. Forget Fenton, forget the shit storm brewing in PSD. 'Sorry to do this, and I promise we can talk about the letter later, but did you get a chance to find me a cosmetic surgeon to talk to?'

Leah must have sensed he was finished talking about Fenton.

'I did one better actually, and I'm sorry to kick you when you're down but it's not good news. From what you described, and from the photos you provided, I was able to email my friend in London. There's little chance of identifying the victim through her surgery.'

Fluke sighed again. He hadn't really been hoping to get anything but there was always an outside chance her surgery had been so complex, another surgeon would recognise the work. 'Did you ask if all the procedures could be done at the same time?'

'Not a chance, I'm told. I didn't think it was likely but you asked me to check. He tells me that because they were all in the same area it wouldn't be possible. The face swells too much to attempt more than one at a time. Sorry.'

Fluke said nothing. That was that then. He knew he should get back to HQ and make sure the hunt for Kenneth Diamond was progressing properly, but he didn't want to leave things like they were. Leah also said nothing. She was no longer looking at him. She was looking at the card with the numbers on. He'd put it on the table when they'd been talking.

He picked it up and put it into his breast pocket. 'Sorry.'

'What was that?' she said, the edge to her voice returning.

'What, this?' he said, pointing at his pocket. 'Nothing, just something to do with the case. Something we're trying to work out. It's become a sort of unit puzzle. That's why we all carry them about.'

'No, I mean where did you get them? Tell me you didn't steal them from me, Avison. It's one thing forging that ridiculous letter but I have a duty, an absolute duty, to protect patient confidentiality.'

The tiredness Fluke was feeling disappeared instantly. His mind, full of Fenton and lost careers, raced again, fully focused on Leah. Breaks in cases came from all sorts of places.

He took the card back out of his pocket and handed it to her. 'Leah. Listen to me very carefully. What do these numbers mean?' he asked urgently.

Fluke sensed she realised it was important but she didn't understand why.

'I'm not telling you anything, Avison, until you tell me where you got them. If you got them from my desk, I'm going to the management suite right now, I swear.'

Fluke made a decision. Sometimes case integrity had to go out of the window. 'We found them at the deposition site. They were left with the body. I didn't steal them from you, of course I didn't. I know this sounds strange coming from someone who spent three days practising your signature but you have to trust me on this. Now tell me what those numbers are. This is vital.'

Her face softened. 'They're blood count results, obviously. A full blood count, the main three. Anyone can see that. You should be able to see that. You've had enough of them, for goodness sake.'

Fluke felt numb. How had he failed to see it? These were numbers he should have instantly recognised. Leah was right. He'd been twisting the answer in his hands for nearly a week now. Looking without seeing. Up until then, he'd always thought his lateral thinking was good. He knew what the numbers were; he didn't even need Leah to explain them. The 2.3 was the white blood cell count, 8.7 was the haemoglobin and 92 was the platelet count. The numbers were low. Not as low as Fluke's had been during some stages of his treatment, but lower than a healthy person. It was the blood of someone who was ill.

Fluke handed the card over to her and leaned forward. 'Is there any way we can find out who these belong to?'

Chapter 30

Fluke and Leah arrived at West Cumberland Hospital less than an hour later and parked in the staff area at her insistence. He'd argued that it was police business, that a murder investigation was no place for a doctor but she'd insisted on accompanying him. In truth, he'd no choice in accepting her help. He'd asked her to check their medical records but blood test results didn't work like that apparently.

'Look,' Leah had said, 'although everything is computerised, the analyser machines that run the full blood counts in Cumbria's haematology departments are on stand-alone systems. There isn't a database that can be searched. The blood would have been taken by a phlebotomist, entered into the analyser and a report printed out. That report would have then be given to the department who'd asked for it and they record the results on the patient's file. Searching for blood test results can only be done manually, and unless there's some way of narrowing it down, it'll take ages. Days, even weeks – and that's only if we're able to get round patient confidentiality.'

Fluke knew the last part was a big 'if'. He couldn't see any way he could reasonably ask a magistrate for permission to go through an entire department's patient records, even for a murder investigation.

'It isn't just haematology who ask for full blood counts, Avison, you know that, don't you?' she said. 'West Cumberland must do well over a hundred FBCs a day.'

Fluke didn't respond. He knew she was right, but he had a few things in his favour now. He knew the results weren't Samantha's. Up until she'd been shot, she was physically healthy. The fact the numbers had been found with her body meant that they were probably the killer's. Assuming he wrote them down when he was in her flat, Fluke had a rough idea when. He ran through the scenario. The killer arrived at her flat, circumnavigated her security systems and waited for her. Before she'd returned, he either received or made, and Fluke's money was on received, a phone call about his blood test results. He

219

wrote them down on the nearest thing to hand, a notepad. He then tore off the top page to keep and left the notepad with the body rather than leave it in the flat, fearing exactly what had happened - the numbers being retrieved by some smartarse technician in a lab somewhere.

The second thing in Fluke's favour, and why he went straight to West Cumberland Hospital, was that he thought it unlikely that the deposition site being so close was a coincidence. Fluke was sure the killer must have seen the building site when he was at the hospital. He fully expected to be able to see the deposition site from the ward the blood test came from. The third thing, and why he'd eventually agreed to Leah coming, was that she knew all the other haematologists in the county and haematology ran the phlebotomy department in all hospitals. If they didn't order the test themselves, it certainly went through them.

'It'll be easier if I go in and have a word with Nick Weighman, West Cumbria's consultant, first,' Leah mused. 'There's no way he'd ever give you open access to his files but he might give a nod in the right direction, enough for your lot to get a search warrant or at least know if you're in the right area.'

Against his better judgement, Fluke explained the case in as much detail as he dared on the journey across to the west. She impressed him by only asking the questions she needed answers to and respected there were things he couldn't tell her. He was already in a grey area legally. Despite the investigation progressing quickly in the previous two days, he had very little on the killer yet, so he wasn't much help to her.

Before they arrived, he asked Leah something that had been nagging at him for the previous quarter of an hour. 'I'm not buying him being a Cumbrian, Leah. It makes no sense. The victim was in hiding. She'd spent a lot of time, effort and money in making herself invisible.' Leah said nothing, but he thought she could see where he was going. 'And then she just happens to move to within forty miles of a professional killer? I don't think so. I think he tracked her here,' he added.

'So how was he getting results from a Cumbrian hospital?' she finished for him.

'Exactly. Unless he got a phone call from a hospital from another part of the country. In which case we're fucked.' He glanced over at her. It had been the first time he'd sworn in her presence. 'Sorry.'

She ignored it. 'It's not necessarily a problem. There are many people in the UK who have to move around with their job. Or their lifestyle. Some of them need ongoing treatment. We aren't going to turn them away.'

'What about private patients? Do we have them here?'

'Yes, we have them here. Lots of doctors also have private contracts. Pays more and it's a much nicer way to work, if I'm honest. More time with the patient, no waiting times. You'll have seen the private patient rooms at our hospital.'

'Would a private patient be able to walk in off the street and demand a blood test?'

She considered it for a minute. 'No, I don't think so. They'd have to have a doctor somewhere leading on their care. But it would be simple enough for that doctor to ring or send a letter asking for continuation treatment for a specified timescale. Cumbria gets over fifteen million tourists a year so it's not unusual. Sometimes getting away on holiday for some fresh air is worth the inconvenience of swapping doctors for a bit.'

'So, if you can ask Doctor Weighman if he's had any new patients in the last few weeks, that should narrow it down to a manageable number. Follow that with the fact that he was probably at the hospital four or five days ago. If he won't give you a name, at least try to get him to confirm he actually has someone who fits the description. I can get a court order on that basis,' Fluke said before adding, 'Probably.'

Still discussing the best way to approach Doctor Weighman, they entered the main foyer and turned left towards the Henderson Suite where haematology was situated.

Fluke took a seat in the waiting area outside the ward while Leah went to see Doctor Weighman. Fluke picked up a magazine, more to avoid having to speak to anyone than any desire to read about a miracle diet or why a particular celebrity felt it necessary to tell the world about how some botched anal bleaching 'had ruined their life'.

He spent the time reviewing the recent development and what it meant to the investigation. He'd called Towler and updated him. He asked him to get Jo Skelton on to drafting two warrants:

one for the hospital's CCTV coverage, and another to access someone's medical records although he didn't have a name yet.

It was the first lead on the killer since Ackley had left the note that started it all, a note found a few hundred yards from where he was sitting now. It reminded him he wanted to check something.

Fluke got up and walked along the corridor looking for a window. He found a walkway with windows leading to the phlebotomy lab but it was facing the wrong way and overlooked the roof of a lower part of the hospital. Fluke could see air-conditioning units and a dead seagull, but not the building site where the body had been dumped.

He walked back to the waiting area and spoke to a nurse, flashed his badge and was briefly allowed onto the ward.

He walked through the men's ward towards the window. Half the beds were occupied and most of the men appeared to be sleeping. Fluke had spent most of his time on a similar ward in Newcastle so he knew the fatigue they would be feeling. The windows were south-facing. He could see the road leading to the village of Cleator Moor. It also afforded a perfect view of the new development. Fluke could see the yellow police tape and a lone uniformed officer, miserable in the light invasive rain, guarding the crime scene. Fluke took out his smartphone and snapped a few photos.

Fluke thanked the ward nurse and walked back out. Instead of sitting down in the waiting area, he carried on along the south side of the hospital to see which other wards had views over the crime scene. There was only the dental department that would receive patients. The rest seemed to be administrative and storage. The basement floors would be too low. He considered taking the stairs to the floors above but decided he'd wait for Leah. He took the same seat in the waiting room. An elderly couple were seated near him and they smiled at him. He smiled back but said nothing. He never knew what to say to people on a cancer ward.

Fluke retrieved his phone and opened his mail. While he waited for a decent signal, he looked at the device in his hand. It could hardly be called a phone anymore. It was a computer, a calculator, a games centre, a camera and an mp3 player. He could watch television and check his emails. He had more technology in his phone than Neil Armstrong had in Apollo 11, although with so many battery-draining functions, it might as well be a landline with the amount of time it had to spend on charge. Three bars finally appeared and Fluke composed a brief email to Towler, attached the photos he'd just taken, and sent it.

An office door, offset from the ward, opened, and Leah beckoned him over.

Fluke was introduced to Nick Weighman who wasn't at all what he'd been expecting. Closer to seventy than sixty, he had a mass of thick white hair. Not the kind of drab white hair that had once been dark hair that had lost its colour. It was hair that wanted to be white. He was a tall, thin man. On his desk was a souvenir ice axe and there were mountaineering photos on the wall with him beaming in all of them. In most of them, he didn't look much younger than he did now. Some were of him in cold-weather gear on mountain ranges Fluke knew weren't in the UK. In one photo, Weighman had an arm wrapped around a man who looked like a Nepalese Sherpa. Fluke couldn't see the mountain's profile but guessed the photo had been taken during an assault on Everest. A serious mountaineer then. No prizes for guessing why he lived here. Some of the most challenging rock climbing in the UK was to be found in the Cumbrian mountains. Fluke liked him immediately.

Leah summarised the situation and at the end, Doctor Weighman gave Fluke the bad news.

'Can't do it, I'm afraid. Patient confidentiality is absolute. There's just no way round it. No way will you get permission to go through my files either, no court will allow it. If you had a name, they would. But an entire ward's files. Nope. Sorry.'

Fluke wasn't deflated; it was what he'd been expecting. Another of the many hurdles the case was throwing up. A doctor protecting the name of a suspect came as no surprise. The other thing Fluke noticed was that Leah wasn't deflated either. In fact, she looked as though she had news, news she wanted to share.

'Do you want a coffee, Inspector?' Doctor Weighman said unexpectedly.

Fluke could have used one but wanted to get back to HQ and start working on ways to get a warrant. He was just about to decline politely when he noticed Leah staring at him and nodding. Aware that he hadn't been involved in their conversation, he said yes.

'I have some things to sort out here. I suggest you go to the fresh coffee cart in the foyer and get yourself a cup, it's rather good. Get me a doughnut while you're there will you?' he said with a slight smile. 'Oh, and if Penny is on, you may want to ask her about the tall American gentleman she seems to have quite the crush on.'

Fluke stood there stupidly. 'Excuse me?' he said.

An American?

'Come on, Avison. Let's go and get a cup of coffee,' Leah said, guiding him out the office and back through the ward before he could ask anything more.

'What the hell just happened?' he asked as they walked back out towards the foyer.

'Shush,' she said in a tone that said, don't ask questions.

'Fine,' he said. He'd let whatever was happening play out.

There was a small queue at the cart, one of the fake nostalgic wooden ones that nevertheless seemed to produce excellent coffee. Fluke and Leah stood in silence while they waited to be served. The vendor was a middle-aged woman, Women's Institute or WRVS by the looks of things, one of those women who volunteer for things. Cumbria seemed to produce armies of them for some reason. He often thought that if even half of them withdrew their services, the county's infrastructure would collapse. She was chatting to every customer as if they were friends she hadn't seen for months. When it was their turn, Fluke ordered three coffees; he assumed they had to return with the doughnut anyway.

'You wouldn't be Penny by any chance, would you?' Leah asked.

'Yes I am, my dear. What can I help you with?'

Fluke stepped in and explained what they were after. Luckily, Penny seemed to have been blessed with common sense and a desire to be helpful. She readied their coffees, put up the 'Back in five minutes' sign, and found an empty table for the three of them.

Fluke briefly told her what he could; that he was looking for a man and he may be American. He added the little he'd been able to get from Darren Ackley.

Penny immediately knew whom he meant. She described him as about forty, around six feet tall. 'Looks like he spends, or spent, a lot of time outdoors. Some time abroad as well, judging by his complexion. Weather-beaten and brown.'

'And he's definitely American?' Fluke said.

Penny looked at him like he was idiot. 'He didn't have a strong accent but I've been to the States a few times; my daughter lives in New York. We travel when Geoffrey and I are over there. I couldn't place him so asked him whereabouts he was from and he was a bit vague. Just said, 'The east coast,' if I remember.'

Fluke spent the next ten minutes getting her to tell him as much as she could. There wasn't much. It wasn't that Penny couldn't remember, it was more like there wasn't actually anything that stood out. Handsome, polite, always put his change in the charity jar, always had a black coffee. Dark hair, cut short. Unremarkable clothes. No earrings or visible tattoos.

It was clear that Penny liked him. 'There was a melancholic quality to him, Inspector. He always had a smile for me but it was like the smile painted on a clown's face. It seemed to hide a sadness. I assumed he was very ill.'

'Why was that?' he asked.

'The Henderson Suite isn't a place where babies are born, Inspector,' she said simply. 'I always make sure I give everyone a smile when they come from there, but I'm aware they're all going through terrible experiences.'

'Did he have a name, Penny?' Fluke said.

She thought for a while. 'Do you know something, I don't think he ever offered it.'

Fluke and Leah got up and they all shook hands. He asked her if it would be okay for a police artist to come and work with her, and she agreed.

Fluke had walked halfway out of the dining area when he turned and ran back to Penny. She'd just reached her cart.

'Sorry Penny, one last question. How often is the charity jar emptied?'

'Ah, excellent,' Doctor Weighman said when they handed him a cup of coffee and doughnut on their return to his office. 'Never get time to eat properly these days.' He looked down at what he had in his hand, seemed to recognise the contradiction and said, 'Oh, well, a doughnut's hardly going to kill me.'

The three of them sat in silence for a minute. The coffees weren't cool enough to drink. Fluke took the lid off his and blew gently on it. The sooner he finished the sooner he could get away. He could feel himself getting closer to their killer and every moment was precious.

Doctor Weighman stood up suddenly. 'Well, I can't wait here for this to cool. I have patients to see, managers to harass, nurses to frighten. I'll be back in about twenty minutes, Inspector.'

Fluke stood up.

'No, please stay here. Finish your coffee. It's the least I can do. I feel as though I've not been as helpful as perhaps I could.'

As he put on his white coat and opened his door to leave, he turned back round. 'Twenty minutes, Inspector,' he said. 'Leah, there's a patient I wouldn't mind your opinion on if you have the time?'

'I'd be delighted,' she replied, and together they left the office, shutting the door behind them. Before she walked out, Leah turned and gave Fluke a small smile.

Fluke stared at the door. What was that all about? He didn't have twenty minutes to wait; he wanted to be back on the road in ten. He picked up his coffee impatiently and took a small sip. Doctor Weighman was right, it was rather good. And him asking for Leah's help had clearly been staged. They'd either wanted to talk about something without him being there or needed to be away from him for some other reason.

He looked round his office and stood up to take a better look at the photos. As an ex-marine, he'd been trained in arctic warfare. Skiing, mountaineering and simply surviving temperatures down to -40°C had been core skills. By the looks of things, Nick Weighman had been to places even colder. He turned to look out of the window, curious to see if he could see the crime scene from that one as well. His eyes glanced at the doctor's desk and immediately smiled.

The desk wasn't empty.

Everything made sense. Doctor Weighman wasn't able to help. He knew Penny wasn't going to be much help either. But the murder had happened on hospital grounds. It was likely one of his patients had committed it. He knew who it was. He also knew he couldn't tell him and that Fluke would never get permission to trawl his files. What had been left on his desk was the reason why Leah couldn't be in the room either. Doctor Nick Weighman had given him twenty minutes to find Samantha's killer. He stared at the item on the desk, afraid to touch it. He reached out then withdrew his hand quickly as if he'd been burnt. Irrationally, he looked round and checked the door was still shut. He reached out again but this time didn't withdraw his hand. He picked up the item on the doctor's desk.

It was a patient's file.

Chapter 31

'Dalton Cross!' Fluke shouted into his phone over the noise of the car. He listened to Jo Skelton on the other end to make sure she'd got everything correct. 'Yes, that's the name we have now. Don't ask how I got it. I want a full search. Every database we have. Every database we can tap into. Get Longy to lead on it but I want an update in fifteen minutes. I'm coming back in now but I have to stop off in Carlisle first. And I want a SOCO team standing by for me. I may have his fingerprints.'

He finalised his immediate plans and ended the call.

Fluke had asked Leah to drive so he could concentrate on what he needed to do next.

He'd spent the full twenty minutes with the file, only stopping when Doctor Weighman knocked on his door and waited a strategic ten seconds to ensure he didn't see anything untoward. By that time, Fluke had read it cover to cover.

The man's name, or the name he was using anyway, was Dalton Cross. He had dual citizenship; American and British. American father, English mother. He'd had to go through a bureaucratic process to get treatment over in the UK but as he was technically a Brit, it was never in doubt. There were reports and documents from hospitals in different parts of the UK. Manchester, London, Norwich, Glasgow, Plymouth as well as West Cumbria. No obvious pattern with the locations or the dates. He'd been zigzagging.

Or hunting.

Ironically, Fluke also knew what he looked like, but only from the inside. MRI scans, X-rays and sonograms, they were all in the file.

Dalton Cross had leukaemia and had just finished his treatment. The last entry on the patient notes were handwritten by Doctor Weighman, detailing the blood test results from a sample taken that Monday. They were an exact match with the numbers on Fluke's card. A nurse had called Cross with his results and the time fitted the chronology Fluke had in his head. She must have called while he was in Samantha's flat, waiting.

He'd given an Allerdale address when he'd arrived in Cumbria two months before, and had been allocated to West Cumberland Hospital. A quick check revealed the address's real occupants had never heard of him.

Despite all the internal photos, Fluke still only had Penny's and Ackley's vague descriptions of what he actually looked like. Patient files didn't have pictures. Jo Skelton would arrange for an artist to do some photofitting with Penny but he wasn't holding his breath for anything useable. It seemed no one could remember what he looked like. A trained grey man.

There were other phone numbers in the file but Jiao-long told him they were all burners and were no longer in service. He seemed to have a new one every time he moved. He assumed the most recent was the one Doctor Weighman's staff called him on.

Fluke had asked Penny if he could take the charity jar if he promised to put twenty quid in when he returned it. It was half-full but Fluke was hopeful that at least one coin would produce a useable print. With a print, he could check more databases. With a positive print would come a photograph.

Without the fingerprints, he wouldn't be able to get a warrant for the file. Although he knew beyond all doubt he had his man, he couldn't reveal how he'd linked the blood test numbers to a particular file without exposing Doctor Weighman's involvement. He'd worry about that later. His number one priority was catching Cross before more people died. Having a legally sound case was a low second. He was pulled from his thoughts when his phone rang. Jo Skelton.

'That was quick, Jo. What you got?'

'Nothing on that yet, boss. Longy's still doing his stuff. But we do have news. We've found Kenneth Diamond.'

Fluke's spirits, already high, were lifted even higher. When cases broke, they broke fast. He knew Diamond wasn't the killer but he was involved somehow. Nathaniel had as good as told him. He'd do the interview himself.

'Right, Jo, listen to me carefully. Nobody interviews him before I get there. Nobody. And he doesn't get to speak to a brief until I say so. We need to do this right.'

'Won't be a problem, boss.'

A sixth sense stopped him asking why. 'He's dead, isn't he?'

Chapter 32

Fluke arrived at Kenneth Diamond's Stanwix address less than half an hour later, and parked at the side of the road. He'd dropped off Leah and promised to call in when he could. She hadn't said anything about the forged letter and he hadn't been able to read her expression.

Police and SOCO vehicles were already there in abundance. In the dimming light and glare of the emergency lights, Fluke could see most of his team milling round, waiting for him.

The crime scene was the house next door to Diamond's own. The team that had gathered his DNA had been less than thirty yards from his corpse.

Fluke took his bearings. Stanwix was a prosperous part of Carlisle and the houses on Diamond's street were all detached and large. Mock Tudor, or similar.

Towler was waiting for him at the drive entrance which had been set up as an external cordon.

'How did he die, Matt?' he asked as he signed in.

'Screaming,' was all he'd say in return.

Fluke followed him into the house. The entrance vestibule had an umbrella stand and a coat rack. He could see a kitchen at the end of a long hallway. A middle-aged man was sitting at a breakfast bar, talking to a uniformed officer. The owner of the house he presumed.

'Down there, boss,' Towler said, pointing towards a door under the main stairs. It opened onto stairs descending to a cellar.

Fluke walked down them carefully. Sean Rogers, who must have been regretting not taking his holiday that week, followed him down. He stood at the bottom of the stairs and looked into the room.

The owner was using it as a wine cellar, gym and a workshop. The room was lit by a bank of fluorescent tubes and Fluke could hear the buzz of the starter motor as one of the lights flickered. The cellar had bare brick walls but seemed dry enough. A rowing machine sat in the middle of the floor. Tools were on a large shadow board on the far wall above a workbench with a vice and a bench drill. There was a half-full wine rack.

He didn't know much about the best way to store wine but was fairly sure that clean air was a prerequisite for any cellar. If that were the case, then the owner's collection was ruined. The heavy stench of a decomposing body was oppressive and cloying. Fluke's mouth flooded with saliva, the first warning of nausea. He swallowed and continued into the room.

Towler hadn't been kidding. Diamond had not died well. He had a bullet hole in the centre of his forehead but Fluke didn't need a pathologist to tell him he'd also been brutally tortured.

'Shit,' Fluke said to himself, as he circled the body, not getting too close. The scene hadn't been processed.

Diamond was sitting on a high-backed wooden chair, probably taken from the kitchen. He was naked apart from a tea towel covering his groin. It was soaked in dark blood. A pool of blood had congealed on the floor underneath the chair.

He'd clearly been there for some time. The corpse had swelled as bacteria dissolved bodily tissue. Fluid was leaking from Diamond's orifices and the smell was worse, the nearer the body Fluke was. It seemed to get into the very mucus of his nose and he knew it would remain with him long after he left the room.

Blisters had formed on his body and some had burst. Diamond's eyes were sunken and milky grey. Despite that, they seemed to be staring directly at Fluke through the swollen eyelids.

His torso was pale, almost translucent. Fluke bent down and looked at his legs. The blood, following the laws of gravity, had settled there and turned them purple. He made a mental note; Kenneth Diamond hadn't been moved, it was where he died. In that room, tied to that chair, and by the expression on his face, screaming in absolute agony.

A lone fly buzzed around and settled on some fluid leaking from his ears. Fluke knew that the body broke down fairly quickly and estimated it had been *in situ* for the best part of a week, possibly longer. When the pathologist got there, he hoped it was Henry and that he had Lucy with him. The corpse had been here long enough for her to find insect activity.

His face was swollen but Fluke couldn't be sure whether that was due to the decomposition process or the beating he'd been subjected to. Threads of drool and blood hung from his gaping mouth. The lips had stretched and he could see that some of Diamond's teeth were missing. He looked down at the carpeted floor and saw white bloody fragments scattered around the base of the chair.

Fluke walked round the back of the body and saw he'd been secured using wire coat hangers. The swelling of his wrists had enveloped the wire against his skin but he could see it joining his hands together. He thought he saw something and bent down for a closer look. Diamond no longer had any fingernails. He looked at the floor again but couldn't see them scattered among the teeth.

'Fingernails?' he said to Rogers, who until that point hadn't said a word.

'Over there,' he replied, pointing towards the workbench.

Fluke looked up, squinted and walked over. On top of the bench was a pair of bloodied pliers. Even Chambers could have worked out what they'd been used for. Lined up in two rows of five, were Diamond's fingernails. Fluke looked back to check something and confirmed that his chair was facing the bench. Someone had been making a show of it, letting him see how many he had left to go.

The bench had two other tools on it: a hammer and long bladed knife. Both were encrusted with dark blood. There was also a plastic bottle containing a clear liquid.

It was easy to see what the hammer had been used for. Diamond no longer had knees. With tremendous force and accuracy, they'd been reduced to a pink, jelly-like mush. Fluke forced himself to look closer. He could see the indent of the ball-peen end. He looked down at what had been his feet. They'd been reduced to the same bloody pulp as his knees.

What the hell?

Fluke put on a pair of gloves and carefully lifted the tea towel covering Diamond's groin.

It wasn't there for Diamond's modesty. It had been put there to stem bleeding. His testicles had been smashed beyond all recognition.

'For fuck's sake,' he said out loud. He knew he was looking at something that would haunt him for years to come but he had no choice but to continue. Fluke had thought the blood that had pooled on the floor beneath the chair was from the groin area but he realised that there was a deep smear of blood going from his mouth, down his bare chest and onto the wooden floor. His mouth or throat had suffered major trauma.

Doubting having his teeth ripped out would have caused him to lose so much blood, Fluke took out his penlight and shone it into Diamond's slightly open mouth. He bent forward and peered inside. It was filled with blood. Fluke angled his torch down and saw what had caused such massive bleeding. He dropped the penlight in revulsion and jerked back, gasping.

His tongue had been cut out.

After taking some time to compose himself, Fluke briefly considered why. Cutting out his tongue wouldn't have stopped Diamond screaming. Screams don't work that way. They come from a much deeper part of the body.

Uneasily Fluke looked back across to the workbench and the bottle with the clear liquid. Not willing to believe it was possible, he forced himself to pick his torch back up and look into Kenneth Diamond's mouth again. This time he looked past the gaping bloody hole where the tongue used to be. He angled his penlight further down the throat and saw what he was dreading.

Diamond's throat, including his larynx, had been completely destroyed by chemical burns. Fluke leaned forward and lightly sniffed, recoiling instantly from the strong smell. It didn't take Sherlock Holmes to work out what had happened. Kenneth Diamond had been forced to drink acid.

Towler was wrong. Diamond hadn't died screaming in agony. Diamond hadn't screamed at all.

Fluke felt the lurch in his stomach again and this time knew he wouldn't be able to control it. His mouth filled with saliva and he raced up the stairs, found the kitchen and vomited noisily in the sink.

He turned on the tap, waited until the water turned icy cold, picked up a mug from the drainer and filled it. He drank it all and poured another. He still felt queasy. He looked round, but the kitchen was empty. He washed his face and composed himself.

Fluke had no doubt that it was the work of the same man who had killed Farrar, but he needed confirmation before he moved forward. He shouted for Towler, who'd stayed outside managing the cordons and making sure the pathologist could get through. He appeared within seconds and Fluke asked him for his opinion.

Towler circled the scene slowly. He didn't have the same reaction as Fluke, but he hadn't expected him to have. Fluke had witnessed some bad things in the forces but knew Towler had witnessed worse. He'd be cracking jokes about it later while the rest of them were drinking to forget it.

'Poor bastard,' he said, finally.

'Who found him?' Fluke asked.

'Mr Dawson. Came back today from two weeks' sailing holiday. Him and his wife. Came down to get some wine and walked straight into this. Least he'll have something interesting to tell the neighbours, I suppose. Probably for the first time.'

Fluke said nothing. He guessed Diamond had been snatched from his own house next door and dragged here for privacy.

He found himself staring at the corpse.

Was it a punishment for the rape or for something else? Or was it just a plain and simple information extraction? If it was the latter, Fluke doubted Diamond had the information the killer wanted. No one could stand that much pain.

In the Marines, Fluke had seen the results of sectarian beatings in Belfast on more than one occasion. They were invariably rushed, had little finesse and had no pattern to them. They tended to focus on kneecappings. Shotguns, electric drills, blow torches, they'd all been used for what became known as a signature punishment the world over. Hundreds of Catholics and hundreds of Protestants would never walk again because of the Troubles.

Diamond's ordeal had been different. It was methodical. No area had been wasted in the infliction of pain. The killer had taken his time. Diamond would've passed out and there is little point in torturing an unconscious man. Fluke was betting that he'd been tortured into unconsciousness, revived and tortured again.

It wasn't a simple punishment beating.

It was a message.

'You think it's Dalton Cross's handiwork?' Fluke said.

'Difficult to tell, the head's swollen that much, but the bullet hole's the same calibre. I'd bet me bollocks.' He paused and looked down at Diamond's groin. 'Looks like he's already bet his.'

Scratch that, Fluke thought. Towler was cracking jokes about it already.

Fluke let Towler supervise the forensic process while he went outside to think. He was starting with a headache. One of those that starts behind one eye but eventually feels as though someone is drilling their way out of the back of the head. The vomiting wouldn't have helped. He pinched the bridge of his nose to alleviate the pressure. It made no difference.

Someone arrived with a dozen cups of coffee and passed them round. Fluke took one. He didn't want it, and it wasn't going to make his headache go away, but it gave him an excuse not to talk to anyone while he drank it.

Thankfully he was spared forced conversation by the arrival of Henry Sowerby. He got out of his old Jaguar. Lucy got out the passenger side. Despite the awful scene he'd just left, Fluke smiled. Although it had been less than a week since they'd all stood on that cold building site he was glad to see them again.

'What have we got here, Avison?' Sowerby boomed, causing a uniformed officer to spill his coffee. '"I'm hearing things," I said to Lucy. "The great Avison Fluke back on the force and Cumbria has two murders in less than a week. Surely not," I said.' He left Lucy by the car and walked over.

They shook hands.

'What do we have?' Sowerby asked.

While Fluke briefed them on what he'd seen, Sean Rogers walked over, ready for the crime scene briefing. They agreed his team would go and in and record everything before anything else happened. Towler walked over as Rogers disappeared to start the video walkthrough. Fluke rubbed his temples.

'Are you okay, Inspector?' Lucy asked. She was standing slightly off from the group being briefed. She wasn't formally part of the investigation and hadn't been invited in. Fluke beckoned her over. They wouldn't be where they were without her.

'Bit of a headache, Lucy, that's all. I'll be fine.'

She reached into her handbag, pulled out a box of paracetamol and threw them. He caught them and opened the box.

Fluke pulled out one of the blister packs. And stared at it.

It was a standard paracetamol box. Two blister packs to a box. Two rows of four in each. Sixteen in total. The maximum allowed in any one box in the UK. Part of the government's suicide prevention strategy.

There were five pills left.

Neurons fired. Synapses transmitted electrical impulses. A memory stirred. Something that happened earlier at the hospital was forcing itself from the recesses of his mind. Something to do with pills. Something important.

'What's up, Inspector?' Lucy asked.

He held his hand up and said nothing. He continued staring.

Sometimes Fluke could have answers to questions maddeningly out of reach for weeks. The harder he looked the deeper they hid. The answer to what had bothered him about the inventory from Samantha's flat rushed out to greet him like an old friend.

He knew what Samantha's secret was.

He knew what Nathaniel Diamond hadn't been able to tell him.

Chapter 33

The expression 'having all your ducks in a row' sprang to mind. It was what he could do that HOLMES couldn't do. It was what he brought to the investigation. Putting seemingly random bits of information together. Making the irrelevant relevant. Fluke sometimes called it the key code. Gather all the information and eventually, there will be something that makes it all make sense.

'Lucy, why are there three tablets missing from this?'

She looked confused. 'It's not a new pack, it's just one I carry round with me.'

'No, sorry, you're not following. I mean why are there *three* missing? Why not two or four? I've never taken just one paracetamol in my life. They're nearly always taken two at a time.'

'My sister came over last night with my niece and the poor thing had a headache. She's only eight, so she just had the one,' she replied, still bemused.

'Exactly,' he said. 'A child may be given one. But have you ever taken only one?'

She thought for a while. 'No, I haven't actually.'

Fluke directed the same question at Sowerby and Towler. 'Have either of you ever only taken one paracetamol?'

They shook their heads.

'And you never take more than two because it damages your liver, right?'

'What are you getting at, old boy?' Sowerby asked.

'Something that's been bothering me for a while, Henry. Didn't even realise it was. I just knew there was something not quite right. I think I know what Nathaniel Diamond was hinting at. We've been looking at it all wrong. Farrar wasn't a rape victim and that poor bastard in there isn't a rapist.'

They were silent, waiting for him to lead them through his thought processes. If Fluke had a fault, and he was prepared to accept he had several, it was that he sometimes left out links he thought were obvious and expected others to make the leap without assistance.

'That bed-wetting alarm should have been enough of a clue but it was so random, so unexpected it threw us all. But put that together with a bottle of paracetamol with fifteen pills in it and it starts to make sense.' He looked at them all. It was clear they hadn't caught up yet. 'I'll bet everything in my pockets against everything in your pockets that those pills aren't paracetamol.'

'What do you reckon then, boss? E's?' Towler asked quizzically.

'Close, Sergeant, very close. I am betting they'll turn out to be Rohypnol.'

Nobody said anything. It wasn't the embarrassed silence that sometimes follows a stupid thing the boss says. It was the type of silence that said 'let me process that'.

'Do you not see yet?' Fluke said. 'The stupid woman was drugging herself. She was drugging herself then crying rape.'

Fluke left a Carlisle CID sergeant and Sowerby to manage the recovery of the body. It was against protocol but he and Towler needed to get back to HQ and start the new line of enquiry. He ignored the speed limit and it took him less than twenty minutes. Alan Vaughn, Jo Skelton and Kay Edwards were waiting for him.

'We're working on a new hypothesis. We think she was operating a blackmail scam,' Fluke told them. 'She targets wealthy men with no criminal record. Men with no DNA to match. Has sex with them somewhere. Goes home, takes her own Rohypnol then goes to bed. In the morning, she reports a drug-facilitated rape. Goes through the sexual assault process. Evidence is found and logged. No one doubts her, the Rohypnol is conclusive.'

No one spoke.

He continued. 'I'm guessing the next part, but I think she then approaches her victim and tells them that she's reported a rape. Presents them with the facts, that the police have their DNA, that there is an active rape investigation. That fifty grand makes her disappear. Fail to pay and she starts to remember little bits of information. Doesn't have to be much. Just the name of the bar they met would be enough to lead us to them and the DNA result would do the rest. DNA and Rohypnol would make a conviction inevitable. How many rich men would pay? Particularly if they're married.'

'Why risk the stigma of a rape conviction when you can afford not to,' Towler added.

'Exactly,' said Fluke. 'When they pay up, she simply moves to another town.'

'And if they don't?' Jiao-long asked.

Fluke thought about the likely scenario if the victim wasn't in the mood to be blackmailed. It was unlikely she'd go through with it. In his opinion, she was using false names and moving about quickly. 'There'd be nothing in it for her to go ahead with a prosecution. I think she'd probably just abandon it and move on. With no victim, there's no case.'

There was silence as they absorbed the information. There were no holes in the theory. It didn't mean it was correct, only that they hadn't yet ruled it out.

'The bed-wetting alarm is part of it, I'm assuming?' said Edwards, eventually.

Fluke had kept her on the team for now. He was finding her insight into rapes invaluable. When everything had been laid out, she acknowledged the inconsistencies she'd noticed fitted the new working theory. She was taking it personally and Fluke knew she'd be a terrier for him.

'Yep, we're thinking she'd be drowsy when she self-medicated and must've had accidents in the past. It fits anyway.'

'In other words she was sick of waking up drenched in piss?' Towler added.

'Yes, very well put, Matt.' *Crude*, Fluke thought, but essentially Towler was spot on. She'd found something to wake her if it happened. It would also mean she wouldn't be remembered by landlords when she left.

'How does she find her victims, sir?' Edwards asked.

'Good question. We're assuming that she had information provided to her. She'd need access to PNC to check her victims weren't on it. If they're not on PNC then they're not on the DNA database. The only way this works is if she has time to blackmail her victim. DNA results come through fast now. It wouldn't work if the victim *was* on the database. We'd arrest them before she could get paid. That's one of our new lines of enquiry. Who'd she get the information from? Longy's going to work with the IT department to quietly look at who's accessed PNC looking for Kenneth Diamond.'

Jo Skelton, who'd said nothing up until now, spoke. 'If we assume she approached Diamond and demanded cash, why didn't Nathaniel say that when you interviewed him? His dad was a victim in all this. It would have got him off the hook.'

'Would it?' Fluke said. 'Think about it for a second. We wanted him for rape and murder. Nathaniel saying she was falsely accusing his father of rape gives him a motive to kill her. More of a motive actually.'

She nodded. 'Murder's murder. Doesn't matter what the reasons are.'

They accepted other ideas; Fluke liked that about his team. Especially when they accepted his.

'It's a perfect scam; ingenious, really. As long as she chose her marks carefully, she could have done this indefinitely,' Towler said. His brow furrowed. 'She was still in hiding though, boss. Who from and why? And why come to Carlisle? It's slim pickings here millionaire-wise. There must be easier places for her to work than this.'

'Anyone?' Fluke asked the team, opening it up. He had his own ideas but wanted to check he hadn't strayed too far from the pack.

There was a moment's silence while they thought it through. Vaughn broke ranks first. 'She was hiding from a previous mark. Got to be. She hit someone with too much clout. Someone who had the resources to find her.'

'Yep. That's what I'm thinking,' Fluke said. 'And that person, ladies and gents, is the person who hired our killer.'

'So, she's done this before then,' Edwards said. Not a question, a statement.

'Oh yes, she's done this before. Probably several times,' Fluke said.

'How can we be sure, sir? How do we know this wasn't her first time and she got it wrong?' she asked.

'It's a fair question but I think it comes down to Matt's point earlier; why was she in Carlisle? He's right; this isn't Mayfair. Millionaires aren't bumping their Bentleys into each other round here. The surgery to disguise herself wasn't cheap so she had access to money. I think she came here to hide and was running low on funds. Was probably going to tap Diamond for twenty grand or so then move on,' he said. 'And that's the second line of enquiry. We need to know where else this has happened. Jo, work on a bulletin and get it sent out nationwide. Work with Kay and make sure every rape team and SARC in the country gets it. We want rapes where the victim disappeared.'

They both nodded.

Vaughn frowned. 'Where does Diamond's murder fit in, though? It must be related, surely?'

'Must be,' Fluke said. 'I think the killer's been tracking her for a while. But this time she makes a mistake and targets someone we can trace through his son's DNA, someone who also has the resources to search the city at street level. Kenneth Diamond might have been clean but the family isn't. They would have found her eventually. Every drug dealer in Cumbria would have been looking for her.'

'How'd Cross find her though, boss?' Towler asked.

Fluke was venturing into guesswork. Educated guesswork, but guesswork nevertheless. 'He probably did something similar to her. Monitored all intelligence databases for drug-facilitated rapes until he came across any that fit her MO. He knew he only needed to look at those where no suspects were identified immediately. As soon as he got a hit, he raced over and started doing what Longy's doing now; searching PNC to see who's been looking at names with no criminal records. That's her target.'

'So, the longer she kept working the longer she was at risk. Ironically, the more careful she was with her checks the more she was giving Cross a chance to catch up to her,' Vaughn added.

Fluke nodded. He'd come to the same conclusion. It was a game that was only ever going to end one way.

Towler finished it off for them. 'So, Cross finds out that it was Diamond she's blackmailed. Grabs him, tortures him and finds out where the drop is supposed to be. We don't have a time of death for Diamond yet but I'm betting it'll be before Farrar's. He stakes out the drop site and finds her, follows her home and the rest we know.' He paused, before adding, 'Or think we know anyway.'

'He would've had to move quickly,' Vaughn said. 'When Diamond didn't show to pay, it would've spooked her. Her tradecraft was good. I think you're right; there's no way she'd ever go through with the threat of exposure. If it didn't work the first time, she'd leave. We've all seen her flat. She could pack and be out of there in two minutes. Matt's right. The time of death will be Diamond first, no more than a day before Farrar's, I reckon.'

Fluke had a drink of his tea. A natural pause in the discussion settled over everyone. He tried to poke holes in the theory and knew the team would be doing the same. Unlike Chambers, he didn't want to work with people who'd agree with everything he said. He liked people to challenge him, to disagree and have their own ideas.

He was sure, however, the crime went down the way they'd described it. There were still things they didn't know and he didn't think the Crown Prosecution Service would be too happy. Theories work fine in an incident room. In court, with a five-hundred-pound-an-hour barrister ripping witnesses and evidence to shreds, it was a different matter.

He thought about Samantha. What had made her choose a life like that? A life where she was claiming to have been violated time and time again. A life where she knew she was ruining other lives. And then the sudden realisation that she'd got one wrong. That she'd targeted someone too powerful, too well connected. Someone who had no intention of being blackmailed. Someone who had more than one way to resolve problems. And the hunter became the hunted. Fluke imagined her panic when she realised someone had gone a step further than call her bluff. The urge to flee must have been overwhelming. But she didn't, she took the time to prepare. Either that or she had a contingency plan already in place. Cosmetic surgery, some superficial alterations and she turned into a ghost, moving from town to town, from city to city, always looking over her shoulder, never daring to settle. And eventually, she travels to the northern-most city in England. Carlisle. The end of the line. Figuratively and literally.

He thought about Nathaniel Diamond. He suspected that if he'd found Farrar first, she would've quietly disappeared. Or perhaps not. He was intelligent enough to see the whole board. Perhaps he would've thought paying her off was the cautious move. He didn't have the information Fluke had about the PM and the extensive things she'd done to change her appearance, but he may have felt that there might have been a bigger player at the table. Someone who hadn't declared their hand yet. Why risk cancelling someone's asset? Nathaniel couldn't be sure she wasn't someone's employee.

He was interrupted by Towler who stood up and stretched. 'She was born in a burial gown,' he said simply.

He didn't expand and Fluke didn't need him to. He was right. It was a term he'd heard once or twice in the Marines. It was said about someone who seemed to have a death wish, someone who volunteered to do things that most people were terrified of doing. They were the first through the door and the last one to take cover when coming under enemy fire. They appeared fearless, even reckless. Maybe they were.

People who didn't know him thought Towler was like that. The truth was the opposite. Towler had fears. He'd told Fluke one night over a couple of cigars, that he was terrified of something happening to Abi. Something he brought home with him every night. A grudge held by someone he'd put in prison. Nurturing it during the twenty-three hours a day he was in his cell. Blaming Towler for his predicament. A twisted revenge fantasy that wouldn't go away. Eating at him, keeping him awake. Towler knew he had a reputation and knew it was fully deserved. His daughter would be a far easier target.

Fluke had heard a rumour a few years back. A rumour that he'd deliberately not looked into. Towler had just joined the police and Abi was still an infant. A drunk in Cleator Moor had thrown a bottle at him while he was on nights. Towler was busy putting him into the back of the van for a night sobering up in the cells, he hadn't even intended to charge him. The rumour was, that in the morning as the drunk was being let out, he'd turned to Towler and told him he knew where he lived. A none-too-subtle threat. Towler had ignored him.

Three days later the same man had turned up at A&E with two broken legs and two broken wrists. He refused to name his attacker. Fluke had no way of knowing if the rumours of a big man seen walking on the back roads of Cleator Moor on the night of the attack were true, and he wasn't going to ask.

No, Towler had fears like everyone else.

Nathaniel Diamond had been released. Fluke left instructions for the duty officer to try and locate him. Fluke wanted to speak to him before anyone else did. He'd know about his father by now, secrets weren't easily kept in Carlisle but they had a statutory obligation to tell him anyway. With their father being a widower, he or Wayne would have to formally identify the body. Fluke was going to ask him to do it from the neck up. He couldn't stop him looking at his father's broken body but he didn't think any child should see a parent in that condition. Nathaniel had shown remarkable self-control in all his dealings with Fluke up to then but he doubted it would stretch to that. Fluke didn't want a psychotic army of vigilantes on the streets of Carlisle.

He drove back to Carlisle and the crime scene but Sowerby and Lucy had already left with the body. Fluke thought the PM would probably take place the next day. He certainly hoped so. Towler could attend on his behalf. The investigation was moving fast and he needed to be in the thick of it. He knew Jiao-long would have information on who'd accessed PNC to check the name Kenneth Diamond soon. It didn't matter what user level you had, PNC left footprints. If you logged on in your own name it was recorded. Everyone protected their passwords for exactly that reason.

He'd wait for a name before deciding how to continue. The N in PNC stood for National so there was no guarantee that it would be a Cumbrian, although Fluke suspected it would be.

The bulletin to rape teams and SARCs across the country had been sent. Fluke was hopeful it would get a response, although he didn't know how helpful it would be. There would be no suspects. No victim, no case. The investigation would have struggled on without the victim but ultimately they would have filed it as open unsolved, and moved on to other things. Fluke would have no way of telling which investigation had resulted in successful payments and which hadn't. She'd have disappeared either way.

The photofit artist was interviewing Penny the next day. There was decent software available but a good artist was always the better option. Someone who understood the way faces were structured. They would have something to send out with the name by lunchtime the following day hopefully.

Fluke left the crime scene and called in at the hospital. He needed to thank Leah for her help. He also needed to see where he stood with his forged letter. He was going to ask if she could just wait until the end of the following week before she reported it. He'd know one way or the other if there was going to be an arrest by then.

She'd gone home. Fluke wished he had such luxuries.

His phone rang. It was a Penrith number. Police HQ but not one in his contact list. He answered it as he walked back to his car. A nasal voice spoke when Fluke answered. 'Ah Fluke. It's Alex Fenton from Professional Standards. I need a few words.'

He'd been expecting the call. Fenton wasn't the type of person to let an opportunity pass. Fluke would need to be careful. Fenton outranked him but was universally despised throughout the force, which evened things up a bit. Fluke's earlier despondency had lifted. If Fenton had definitive proof the letter to Occupational Health had been forged, he would've already arrested him. The prick would have probably done it at HQ, in front of everyone. Fluke suspected all he had were suspicions. He'd need proof. Proof that could only come from Leah, and Fluke knew she hadn't confirmed anything yet. Fluke's gut feeling was that it was a call to put pressure on him. To twist the knife.

The prick thought he could outthink him. There wasn't a single person in FMIT Fenton could outthink. Or anyone in CID for that matter. But he thought he could, which gave Fluke an advantage. A skilled interviewer could get more out of Fenton than he got out of them. Fluke couldn't afford any distractions, though, so decided the direct approach was the best option for now.

'Fuck off, Fenton,' Fluke replied calmly, pressing the end call button. He'd deal with him when it was finished. He turned off his work phone and sent a group text to his team from his personal phone saying it was how he was to be contacted for the next couple of days. He sent one to Jo Skelton telling her to take Sunday off. She had young children, and a husband who'd been looking after them all day. Towler would let Fluke know if he needed time off and no one else in FMIT had kids.

He immediately got a text back from Skelton, who'd ended up with the hospital warrants job. They were ready and she was driving to the duty magistrate's house now. One for the file and one for the CCTV tapes. If they were signed, and Fluke was sceptical whether they would be, Skelton would drive up to the hospital and collect everything. She'd also be able to discuss aspects of the investigation with Doctor Weighman if he was in. Fluke suspected there'd been things he'd wanted to tell him, but couldn't. He sent a text back to her, 'Buy Doctor Weighman a doughnut if he's in', before getting back in his car and heading home.

He'd just finished boiling some pasta when his phone rang.

Half an hour before, he'd looked in his fridge for something healthy to eat. There was nothing. Fluke's kitchen was functional. No decorative bottles of olive oil on the window ledge, no fancy plates, no ornamental scales in this house. The food in his cupboard was chosen for longevity rather than taste and he only ever bought fruit and veg to see how long it took to go off.

After spending the day with Leah, he thought he'd better try to have a healthy meal. He settled on dry pasta and a ready-made sauce. He defrosted a Cumberland sausage link to add some protein. He told himself he'd need it the next day, although he knew he'd ignore the pasta and only eat the meat. He was basically having a sausage for tea.

He picked up the phone and pressed the receive button. It was Jiao-long.

'Got him, boss. Gibson Tait. He's not badged; civvy in charge of IT.'

Fluke was surprised. It could have been anyone with clearance which meant every officer and half the civilian staff. The head of IT? 'Are we sure, Longy? You can't accuse civilians of anything without their unions getting involved.' It was a constant gripe of police officers everywhere that their police staff colleagues had the protection of their union in work matters whereas the police themselves were banned from joining one.

'Yeah. No doubt. He tried to hide it. Used different machines and changed his password enough times to try and confuse it, but it's him.'

'When?'

'Three times in total. Once was a PNC check. Diamond's not on so he logged out straight away. Went to a different machine and logged back in. Checked SLEUTH, but there's hardly any intelligence on him. Lots on the rest of the family but Kenneth Diamond seems clean.'

'And the last time?' Fluke asked. He suspected he knew the answer.

'It was the day before she made the rape allegation, boss.'

So, she'd someone on the inside, someone who could check a potential mark for her, make sure the police wouldn't be able to identify him before she had a chance to get paid. Once the target was identified, Fluke assumed she'd go to work, research him and prepare. One final check of the system to make sure nothing had changed, and she'd go for it. Careful. Clever.

It got her killed.

'For Cross to find out who the target was in Cumbria though, he'd also have to find out who's been searching for names without getting results. Can we check that?'

'Already on it, boss. That'll take a while though. I'll have to write a programme to search. It probably won't be a Cumbrian. I assume he has a contact in the police somewhere. It'd be a bit of a coincidence if it was Cumbria.'

Fluke agreed it was unlikely. 'I want a name though, Longy. Whoever it was caused all this carnage, he said. 'We got an address for Tait? I may go out now.'

Tait's address was suspicious enough. Bassenthwaite Village. Picture perfect. Unspoiled. Sitting at the eastern end of Bassenthwaite Lake, it was out of the price range of the average working man unless you were lucky enough to inherit property there.

'Anything I need to know about him, Longy? I've never met him.'

'Nothing I can see, boss. He's not been here that long. He may not be in; the system has him on leave this week.'

'Bollocks,' he said. 'I may have a run across and see the bastard anyway. It's only an hour away.'

When Fluke had finished with him, he'd make sure that he was implicated in the murder of Diamond and Farrar. It happened from time to time that unauthorised searches of databases took place. Police officers had been sacked for checking out their daughter's new boyfriends or potential next-door neighbours when they moved house. They'd been stupid. Tait's unauthorised use was different. It was criminal. 'What's he look like, is there a photo?'

'No, no photo. Spoke to someone in the department. He's in a wheelchair. Some spinal injury.'

Fluke had no qualms about treating a wheelchair-bound man as harshly as an able-bodied person. One of the most dangerous sex offenders he'd ever met was in a wheelchair.

'Right, I'm setting off now. I'll ring the duty officer with an update. He'll probably deny the whole thing anyway. If I nick him, I'll send for a van,' he said.

'You sure, boss? Have you seen the weather? It's going to turn bad and they're not good roads out there.'

He looked out of his kitchen window and thought it should probably wait until the morning. Tait didn't know they were onto him as far as he knew.

He looked at the pasta congealing in the pan.

'Yep,' he said. 'I'm going.'

***

Chapter 34

It was a foul night. Cold, dark and spitting. Heavy clouds grumbled overhead in anticipation of the storm they were readying to unleash. A Cumbrian winter living up to its reputation.

After ten minutes, the light rain had turned into a monsoon, each raindrop exploding on the road ahead of him like small grenades. Fluke knew he should really turn round, the hidden dips and bends, dangerous enough in good light and fine weather, were making driving treacherous. He also knew that if the rain stayed like this there would be a fair chance the road would flood. He thought about Samantha, lying in a grave of wet mud and clay. She may have been ruining lives but no one deserved to die like that. He set his windscreen wipers to double speed, gripped the steering wheel harder and drove on.

The weather was making other road users drive slowly and Fluke impatiently sat behind an old Volvo until he saw the signs for Keswick. He drove through the town, deserted in the downpour, and took the Bassenthwaite road. Visibility was down to ten yards.

After a few miles, a flash of lightning highlighted Binsey, one of the smaller and less well-known fells, and he knew the Bassenthwaite turn off was less than half a mile ahead of him. Fluke slowed and turned right.

As he drove up the narrow, twisting lane that lead to Bassenthwaite Village, his double beam picked up a sign for a Christian retreat, a sign warning drivers to watch out for red squirrels and a bicycle with a wicker basket leaning against a wooden fence. The trees were so close and the road so narrow that they formed a canopy. During summer it would be like driving through a magical green tunnel. In winter, the entwined leafless branches gave Fluke the impression he was driving into some monstrous funnel-web spider's trap. It looked a scene from a Tim Burton film and although his heater was turned up to twenty-eight degrees, he shivered.

The trees thinned within half a mile and his BMW's bright halogen bulbs highlighted one of the most picturesque villages in Cumbria. Despite the weather, it looked like a scene from a postcard, a scene unchanged for hundreds of years. If McNab's Pinegrove represented the desperation in Cumbria, Bassenthwaite represented the charm. It was a village unspoiled by tourism. It didn't really have streets in the traditional sense; it was more a collection of whitewashed cottages that just happened to occupy the same beautiful landscape.

Sitting at the edge of Bassenthwaite Lake and nestling under the shadow of the imposing Skiddaw, Fluke couldn't think of a place he'd like to live more but he knew the property prices were always going to be out of his reach. He could save for a hundred years and never be able to afford to live there. Properties were rarely put up for sale, houses and farms passed down the generations, families unwilling to take the inflated prices they could get in favour of staying. Fluke knew he earned more than Tait and wondered how he could afford to live there.

He looked at his phone, and the directions Jiao-long had texted him. Fluke had to drive through the village for a hundred yards, and Tait's house would be on the left, on its own. It wasn't a well-lit village, most of the old Cumbrian villages weren't, but after a couple of wrong turns, Fluke eventually found it.

It was set back from the road and sat at the end of a drive that Fluke estimated was about sixty yards long. Few houses in Bassenthwaite had numbers and Tait's was no exception. Two large pillars, hewn from slate, flanked either side of the entrance, remnants of what would have been an impressive gate. On one of them, 'The Lodge' was engraved, the letters filled with whitewash to highlight them.

Fluke had planned to park at the side of the road and walk up the drive, but with the rain still hammering down, he drove up the inclined drive and parked right outside Tait's front door. He turned off the engine but left the headlights on while he surveyed his surroundings. It was a cottage in every sense. Single-storey with a whitewashed, ivy-covered front. Big wooden door and a front garden that would undoubtedly be full of flowers later in the year. There was one other car in the drive.

Fluke looked for a bell and couldn't find one, so he used the large brass door knocker. The wind made it impossible to hear if anyone was coming so he was surprised when the door opened immediately and warm light spilled out into the cold winter darkness.

He stared.

Gibson Tait wasn't what Fluke had expected.

Despite being confined to a wheelchair, Fluke could see Tait was in better shape than he was. He tried not to have preconceptions of what people should look like but when Fluke heard head of IT, he expected an older version of Samantha's neighbour William. Tait looked as if he should be hosting a survival programme on TV rather than working in an office.

He had dark hair and dark eyes and, despite the chair, probably had no problems attracting women. Or men, if that was his thing. He was wearing typical Cumbrian fare; checked shirt and strong denim trousers. He looked at Fluke with mild curiosity. There was certainly no panic. He smiled encouragingly.

Fluke introduced himself and showed his warrant card and badge. Tait invited him in. There was still nothing more than curiosity on his face.

The second thing he noticed was that being confined to a wheelchair in the cottage had its advantages. Fluke guessed the cottage was at least two hundred years old. Standing, Tait would have been taller than Fluke, and the cottage had the low ceilings and doors favoured by previous generations who had been statistically shorter in stature. He had to duck through a doorway as he followed Tait into the kitchen. It was small but surprisingly modern and Tait asked him if he wanted a coffee. Fluke was going to say it was too late, but having one would give him an excuse to stay a bit longer if he needed to.

'Yes, please, Mr Tait. Black.'

'Please call me Gibson, or Gibb, Inspector. I'll fire up the machine,' he said, as he filled up an expensive-looking pod-style maker, and slotted in an espresso. It was soon spitting it out and the room filled with the aroma of fresh coffee as the cup filled. He topped it up with hot water from the kettle and handed it to Fluke. He slotted in another pod and repeated the process.

'There's a pitcher of fresh cream in the fridge. You sure I can't tempt you?' he said, wheeling himself across the kitchen.

Fluke declined and Tait opened the fridge door, stretched up and took a small ceramic jug from the shelf. He poured a liberal amount into his mug and took an appreciative sip. He gestured to Fluke to take a seat at the small breakfast bar.

Fluke placed his steaming mug on a coaster and asked, 'Mr Tait, do you know why I'm here?' It was an informal interview but Tait could end up on the wrong end of a conspiracy to murder charge. Fluke wasn't going to use first names just yet. He might have to arrest him later.

He took another sip of his coffee before answering. 'I haven't the faintest idea, Inspector.'

Fluke couldn't quite place his accent. It was English but not Cumbrian. 'How long have you worked in Cumbria, Mr Tait?'

Again, he paused. Had another drink. Completely calm. 'I've been here just over six months. I was working in Sussex for the council before that, sorting out their waste management software on a freelance basis. Although I'm in the chair most of the time, I wanted to live somewhere with fresh air and mountains. This job came up. I applied and was appointed. Didn't hurt I was in this,' he said, pointing at the wheelchair.

Fluke paused. He knew the force had disability recruitment targets the same way they had ethnicity targets. He'd never given it a lot of thought before. 'Can I ask why you have to use it?'

'I was injured playing rugby at school when I was fourteen. An incomplete spinal cord injury. Anterior cord syndrome is the formal condition.'

Fluke looked at him, nonplussed.

'It means I have some feeling below the injury, but I'm paralysed.'

'I'm sorry,' Fluke said. Tait didn't seem bothered by his intrusive questions on a Saturday night.

'I try to keep myself as fit as I can.' There was no trace of bitterness or anger in the matter-of-fact way he said it. 'I tried out for the British wheelchair rugby team for the 2012 Paralympics but couldn't get the sponsorship. Trained every day for three years but all the money goes to wounded veterans these days,' he said. 'Quite right too,' he added.

Despite himself, Fluke was warming to Tait. He wondered if his corruption was motivated by money and whether it was to get enough together for the 2016 games in Rio. Fluke had never had a grand dream like that and didn't know what he'd do to realise one if he did.

As he picked his coffee back up, it dawned on Fluke that the previous year he'd broken the law to stay in the police. His reasons looked petty in comparison to Tait's. He was going to take responsibility for his crime after the case but, for Tait, it would be that night.

'What's this about, Inspector?'

'I'm sorry to tell you this but we've traced an unauthorised use of PNC to you. A name was checked. Twice and once on SLEUTH. That person's now dead. Murdered.'

That's got his attention, Fluke thought. Visits from FMIT late at night weren't the norm. He imagined that as soon as he identified himself as someone who wasn't in PSD, Tait had relaxed slightly.

'When?' he asked. He was watchful but didn't look worried, and that worried Fluke.

'I can't remember the exact dates. Twice, a month or so ago. The other time a few days ago. The woman you passed them to is dead.' Fluke decided enough was enough. He knew he had him, time to stop playing nice. He put down his cup. 'And you, Mr Tait, are well and truly in the shit. You decide if you sink or swim in it, and you decide right now. Tell me what I need to know and I'll do my best to keep a conspiracy charge off the table.'

Fluke thought there was surprise in Tait's expression, but the fear he'd been expecting still wasn't there. If it was, he was hiding it well.

'I'm assuming this last date wasn't when I was on leave? I've been off for nearly a week. Spine tingles I call them. The doctors call them something else. Something to do with the electric impulses. I prefer to use leave to manage my disability, rather than go on the sick.'

'The dates match,' Fluke said, hoping Jiao-long had triple-checked. That's all Fenton would need to suspend him, wrongful harassment of a disabled man.

Tait didn't answer. He drained his coffee and put another pod in the machine. 'Sorry, I won't sleep tonight now. May as well give myself some fuel. Can I tempt you?'

Fluke declined with a quick shake of his head.

'We have a problem, Inspector. I haven't accessed PNC or SLEUTH, lawfully or unlawfully. There would be no reason for me to go on either system. I manage the IT department but I do very little IT work.'

'The computer doesn't lie, Mr Tait.'

'No, it doesn't. But it doesn't tell the truth all the time either. All it can tell you is whose log-on name was used. It can't tell you who used the name.'

He was right, of course. All Jiao-long had was Tait's username and password. 'I don't know a single cop who'd hand out their password, Mr Tait. I bet you don't either. Apart from the fact it's a disciplinary matter, the system's footprints are just too good.'

Tait nodded. 'True enough. No one hands out their passwords. Even writing them down is against regs.' He paused as the machine finished, he picked up his full cup and turned and faced Fluke again. 'What do you do if you can't log on?'

It had been a while since his computer had locked him out. 'Hasn't happened for a few months now.'

'But it has happened?'

Fluke nodded.

'And what did you do?'

'I can't really remember. I'll have called IT, I suppose.' Fluke wasn't sure where Tait was going with this, but he had a feeling his lead was about to go bad.

'Exactly,' Tait said, without any hint of triumph. 'You'll have rung my department. Before I got there no doubt but what they'd have done is accessed your account and reset it.'

'I suppose,' Fluke said.

'How many people have access to police systems in Cumbria, Inspector?'

Fluke did a quick calculation. There were thirteen hundred badged officers and nearly a thousand police staff. 'Just shy of two and half thousand,' he admitted.

'Just say then, that each person needs IT help twice a year. That's five thousand calls. What's that a day? Fifteen or sixteen?

On top of everything else we have to do,' he said. 'And I think that's what I'm getting at. We can access anyone's account. We have access to everyone's details. We know everyone's passwords. We have to, if we didn't, the whole system would crash. Software develops glitches, people forget their passwords or go so long without logging on that the system resets itself. It's bread-and-butter work for my department.'

'So you're saying th—'

Tait interrupted him. 'And that's not all, Inspector. Have you heard of a master-access level?'

Fluke shook his head. He was starting to feel foolish. He was being taught a lesson in not diving in before intel had been stress-tested.

'A master-access level is something all systems have to have. All secure systems anyway. It means there's one person, normally the head of IT, who has access to every part of the system. And in Cumbria, that's me. What I'm saying is that I could've accessed any part of our systems and used anyone's name. And that's not all, I have access to the system's histories. In other words, I can delete my footprints as I go along.'

Bloody Longy! Why hadn't he told him there was more than one possible explanation?

Although to be fair, Fluke knew he'd have to accept most of the blame. Jiao-long had been up non-stop since he'd got back from China.

From what Tait had just described, he should have been the first person they ruled out. The person they came to for help. Resigned to having a mess to clean up on Monday, he said, 'If you don't mind, Mr Tait, I will have that coffee now.'

Tait grinned as he prepared another pod for him. 'No harm done. I've been called a lot worse than a murderer since I've been in the chair, as you can imagine.'

Fluke said nothing. He knew children could be cruel and sometimes adults were worse. 'I'm sorry,' he said, eventually.

'Honestly, don't worry about it. I'd rather help than put in a complaint, if you'll let me.'

It was more than Fluke deserved and he knew it. 'If not you, any ideas who?' he asked.

He looked thoughtful. After maybe twenty seconds he said, 'Someone in my department, unfortunately. The thing about the master-access level is that it has to be known to all the tech guys. It's more of a departmental password than an individual one. If something is urgent, then whoever's on duty will use it. A system reboot or a software update, that type of thing.'

'How many people are in your department?' Fluke asked. It was Cumbria, so it wouldn't be a massive number.

'No more than a dozen at any one time. They're all vetted obviously but the system's not foolproof. I can get a list to you first thing Monday if you want. Make a few calls.'

Fluke thought about the best way to do this. He had twelve potential suspects. Thirteen if you counted Tait, and Fluke supposed he couldn't rule him out just yet. 'And there's no way to tell who's looked using this master code thing?'

'Sorry.'

'So, we'll have to do it the old-fashioned way. I'm afraid my team's going to have to hit your department next week, Gibson. Everyone will need to be interviewed, and interviewed hard.'

Tait shrugged. 'Can't be helped. If one of my lot's dirty, I want to know.'

'Can I send someone round to take a statement after the weekend? Save you coming in when you're on holiday? I'm not doing it now, I've wasted enough of your time,' Fluke said. He took his mobile out of his jacket but he had no signal. 'I can probably log it now? I would need to use your landline though, there's no reception on my mobile.'

'Nor mine. We're too close to Skiddaw. I don't know of any network that gets more than one bar. I have to go all the way past the Sun Inn to get any signal at all. Price you pay to live here, I suppose. It's okay, you send someone when you can. I'm not going anywhere,' he said with an element of melancholy. The first Fluke had seen from him.

'Thanks. I'll have someone up as soon as possible, but I'll make sure it's convenient. And Gibson?'

'Yes.'

'You can call me, Avison.' Fluke stretched out his hand and the two men shook.

Fluke stayed to finish his coffee and Tait told him that he'd been able to afford to live in Bassenthwaite because the school paid out an extortionate sum after his accident. He didn't really have to work but liked to feel useful. They spoke about his passion for rugby and Fluke's own passion for cricket until his stomach growled loudly. He decided that if he didn't leave he'd miss the chef at the local pub. They shook hands again and, by way of an apology, Fluke said he'd buy him a pint when the case was finished.

The Pheasant was on the other side of the lake and as Fluke drove, he smiled. He'd been planning to arrest Tait for conspiracy to murder half an hour ago, now he was planning to meet him for a drink. He'd send Towler out to take his statement and wouldn't be surprised if he bagged himself an invite as well. Towler loved rugby nearly as much as Tait did.

The Pheasant was quiet when he got there, but the kitchen was still open. He ordered a pint of Jennings Cumberland Ale and a game pie from the specials board. He sipped his drink and waited for his food.

'Bollocks,' he mumbled to himself when it arrived. He'd forgotten to order the side salad.

The drive back was even more treacherous than the journey out, and Fluke's BMW was buffeted by strong side winds over some of the higher ground. He was intending to ring the duty officer from his car and get that evening's interview logged but he thought better of it. He needed both hands on the wheel.

The wind hadn't relented when he arrived home and some of the taller, thinner trees in his wood were bent almost sideways as the wind tested their roots. One of them was actually touching his cabin roof. Something for him to deal with next time he got a chance. Fluke carefully navigated his wet, muddy drive and eventually, found somewhere he felt was as safe as anywhere from falling branches. He parked up and ran to the front door, using his case file to shield his head from the heavy rain. He rang HQ as soon as the door was shut behind him.

There was no immediate answer and he filled the time scraping the congealed pasta into the bin. Eventually, it was answered.

Alan Vaughn had drawn the night shift again. Fluke brought him up to date.

'Seems anyone in that department could have done it. We'll take Tait's statement but I think we need to think of another way to get what we need. We can't prove who it was through the databases, according to Tait. He's gonna help us but he's not back from leave for a few days.'

'He won't come in?'

'To be honest, Al, he probably would have. He seems like a nice bloke. But he's taken leave while he has these leg tingle things and I didn't have the heart to ask him to.'

'Shit,' he said. 'What's next then, boss?'

Good question. What next? Ten hours' sleep is what he needed. He'd settle for six. 'Call everyone and tell them to take Sunday off. We'll start again Monday.' he said, 'I'm assuming there are no hits on Dalton Cross yet?' The name was unusual. If it was in the system, he was betting he would be the only one, although Fluke doubted it would be easily found. Someone that good didn't leave breadcrumbs.

'Nope, but the ballistic test on Diamond is back. As we thought, it's a match with Farrar's. Sowerby did the PM this afternoon and Matt got the bullet down to Manchester as a priority. The report should be with us early next week.'

No surprises there but it was reassuring that there weren't two murderers out there.

'Right, cheers, Al,' he said. 'I'm off to kip and suggest you try and get an hour or two later.'

Chapter 35

By the time Fluke woke on Sunday morning, he'd pressed the alarm's snooze button half a dozen times. The long hours were doing him no good and he knew his blood would extract a price at some point. He'd planned to stay in bed until noon and then go and meet Towler for Sunday lunch; a tradition they had, and one that Abi loved. She was always allowed an adult portion and whatever she ordered had better come with a Yorkshire pudding or there'd be hell to pay.

By ten o'clock, he was restless. Everyone had needed a day off, himself included, but he couldn't help feeling that the killer was being allowed twenty-four additional hours to get away. Fluke had a shower, made a drink and got out the case file. It was raining so he sat at his kitchen table and spread out the papers.

He didn't have the post-mortem report on Diamond but something was troubling him about the murder. It wasn't until he stopped comparing it with Samantha's that he knew what it was. Samantha's had been a clean kill. She'd probably not known anything about it. At best she may have heard something the split second before the bullet shredded her brains. Diamond's had been anything but clean. The troubling thing about both murders was the fact that they'd only been able to link them by accident. If there hadn't been a witness, Samantha would never have been found. Her body had been too well hidden. Diamond's hadn't been.

With the forensic report on the bullets confirming they were after the same gun, Fluke wondered why they were so different. One was professional, one was brutal. The two together made no sense. Even if Diamond's had been to extract information, it was completely over the top. It looked like a punishment beating but professional killers didn't do that sort of thing. He briefly entertained the idea they were after two killers sharing one gun but that made no sense.

Okay, pretend we didn't know about Samantha.

There'd been no attempt to hide Diamond.

Why not?

Because we were supposed to find him.

Without Samantha's murder, what conclusions would we have jumped to about Diamond?

Given his alleged links to the criminal underworld, Fluke would have probably assumed it was a drug-related murder, a warning to other Cumbrians on what to expect when the big boys are crossed. They'd have thought Diamond was finding out what it was like to swim in the big pond. No way would they have suspected a professional hit.

When he thought about the murder that way, the more he thought the crime scene had been staged. He had no doubt that Diamond had information the killer needed about Samantha's whereabouts, but to go on to mutilate the body was mindless violence. Fluke didn't think their killer was prone to mindless violence. Extreme violence, yes. But mindless? Without Samantha, they would have looked at Diamond's mutilated corpse completely differently. As a way of disguising the true motivation for the murder, it was perfect.

Towler had once told him about a serial killer who'd operated in Northern Ireland during the Troubles. His victims were killed in the same way as the sectarian murders. When a Black Watch patrol caught him red-handed shooting a young Catholic in the back of the head, something didn't quite add up. The killer was a respectable man, a dentist with a large private practice without known affiliations to any paramilitary organisation. Although it was never proven, he was suspected in the killing of a dozen young men, on both sides of the religious fence. Because of the way he dispatched his victims, no one had ever considered they were anything other than sectarian murders.

He'd been hiding in the carnage of Belfast, and Fluke wondered if their killer had been doing the same with Diamond; hiding a murder in the carnage of the drug wars.

A car pulled up and the sound of small footsteps on his front porch told him his Sunday ruminations were over. He put everything back in the file and went to greet his friend and goddaughter.

He was still feeling tired when he entered HQ on Monday morning. Most of the team were already working. He asked Alan

Vaughn when he could expect the PM report and was told later that day.

'Has Longy taken today off?' Fluke asked, to no one in particular as he looked round for him. Fluke had calmed down since Saturday night and he hoped he wasn't avoiding him because of his error with Gibson Tait. The man had been awake virtually non-stop since he got back.

'No, boss,' Vaughn replied. 'He went off somewhere. Said he'll be in later.'

Fluke allowed his team to manage themselves as much as he could. It wasn't a pissing contest. The one who worked the longest hours didn't win a prize. He expected them to be able to function when they came in. He was only strict on everyone being in when the investigation was either in the very early stages or a big break had been made, the rest of the time he expected them to manage their downtime. If they needed rest, he didn't need to be asked. Fluke would take Jiao-long to one side later and make sure the error with Tait hadn't been caused by fatigue. If it had been, it was Fluke's fault.

Jo Skelton entered the incident room, holding a document. She caught Fluke's eye and grinned. 'Got it, boss.'

Fluke knew she could only be talking about one thing, and he was genuinely surprised. He thought she'd have about as much chance of finding a one-ended stick. 'The warrants?'

'Yep, both of them. Signed, sealed and delivered. Everything we need. Dalton Cross's file and any CCTV relating to him or the investigation.'

It was exactly what Fluke had asked for, but with no evidence to back it up, he couldn't see how she'd achieved it. He thought he'd sent her on a fool's errand. 'How?' he finally managed.

'Longy,' she said simply. 'Boy's a genius. We've got the warrant but that's not the only thing.'

Frustrated with his lack of success tracking down the name of Dalton Cross, Jiao-long had decided he was working his Sunday. He'd come in and fed the name into every database he had legal access to and, when that didn't work, he went home and tried databases he didn't have legal access to. Still, he drew a blank. In desperation, he rang home and spoke to someone who knew someone who knew someone. Eventually, he was put through to someone in Chinese Intelligence.

An hour later, an email had arrived. Dalton Cross was known to them, as he was to all security services apparently.

'I'm surprised the Chinese were okay with helping a British investigation,' Fluke said. 'I know we have a Beijing boy on the team but it seems a bit too helpful.'

'Yeah, I thought that,' she replied. 'But Longy reckons there's one overriding thing that would make them share.'

Fluke thought about it. It was possible that Cross was wanted in China for something. Possible but unlikely. Contract killers tended to work in their own ethnic groups. He wouldn't be able to hide in China. He was the wrong colour, the wrong size and, in all likelihood, didn't speak the language. No, it was something different. He tried to think of it from the Chinese perspective. What would make them share something they had no reason to? What would be in it for them?

When he thought of it like that, the answer was obvious. 'It's to embarrass the US isn't it? What do they know about him?'

'He was US Army,' she answered. 'He was a United States Ranger, whatever that is.'

'Yank version of the Paras. Matt's worked with them before, I think,' Fluke replied automatically.

Towler confirmed he had, and that they were good. 'Still a bunch of fucking crap hats though,' he added, just in case anyone may have thought he was being disloyal to the maroon beret.

A ranger? He hadn't needed Towler to tell him that they were one of the world's elite forces. Tough, resourceful and fearless. Exactly what you needed for special-forces soldiers and exactly what Fluke had been dreading. Part of the file Jiao-long had printed was in Chinese but there was enough in English. It was purposefully incomplete. Some years were blank and Fluke knew that wasn't because he'd been at the beach. It was because there were things in his record that were classified. So, in all likelihood a US Ranger with spook training. Perfect. Part of Fluke, the part that cared deeply for Cumbria and its inhabitants, hoped that Cross was already out of the country. That no one else was going to get hurt.

'According to Longy's contact, he went bad a few years ago. He was caught having an affair with an officer's wife. Before he could be court-martialled, he slaughtered the entire family: the wife, the officer, even their three-year-old daughter. Set up someone else for it. He'd left no trace forensics; he was wearing bags on his feet, gloves on his hands and a hairnet and had used an unregistered weapon. He knew what he was doing. He was only discovered because the wife had set up a secret camera as she thought their maid was stealing from them. The whole thing had been caught on tape. By the time they found the cameras, he'd disappeared. His name kept cropping up in some contract killings but nothing was ever proven. The Yanks are desperate to get their hands on him as you can imagine. China only know about him as he was photographed in North Korea a few years ago.'

'Christ, no wonder they were keen to share the intel,' Fluke said. 'A Yank working for the Koreans? No way they gonna pass that up.'

'Yep, that's what Longy said.'

'And he's sure he's our man?' Fluke asked. 'He was the one that sent me out in the rain to see a man in a wheelchair on Saturday night, don't forget. He's been wrong before.' If he wasn't careful he could be at the epicentre of a diplomatic incident. He'd take Jiao-long to one side and make sure nothing was going to come back on them. He didn't want either of them subject to rendition to the States on espionage charges. He didn't want to be the new Julian Assange.

'He's sure, boss. You want to know how we got the warrants or not?'

Fluke nodded.

Skelton explained that as well as the summary of Cross's heavily redacted service history, the information emailed across also included his fingerprints. All US military personnel are fingerprinted when they join, and Cross was no exception. She and Jiao-long had spent all Sunday night with the duty SOCO team and the charity box Fluke had grabbed from the coffee stall at the hospital. There was a clear match on two of the coins.

It was exceptional work, and Fluke told her so. He'd asked if there had been a photograph on the printout, and she confirmed there was but the face had been pixelated out. More evidence of classified operations. She handed Fluke a copy of the printout.

Fluke would have liked a face to go with the name so he knew who he who was looking for, but just getting the warrants had been worth them losing a night's sleep. Because Skelton had been able to link the coin at the hospital with the name of the suspect, she'd got her warrant as soon as the court sat that morning. She'd neglected to put in the application that the name Dalton Cross had originated *from* the hospital but that was just creative paperwork as far as he was concerned.

The latest development seemed to clear the Monday morning blues. Fluke could feel his fatigue wash away. He quickly handed out a few urgent tasks. Jiao-long was to go and speak to Gibson Tait as soon as he'd been home and rested. Together, they could devise a strategy to identify who the IT leak was. He followed the adage 'if you wanted something done quickly, give it to someone who's already busy'.

Although Fluke had already read the file, he'd travel to the hospital and speak to Doctor Weighman. Having legal authorisation to do so now, he was going to be a massive source of information. He'd wanted to help before, Fluke had been acutely aware of that.

The general noise of an office gearing up gradually stopped. Fluke looked up. The Chief Constable had entered the incident room.

'DI Fluke, can I have a word?'

Chapter 36

Although Fluke was firmly of the opinion you were either a police officer or a bureaucrat, he'd always liked Travis 'Action' Jackson, Cumbria's Chief Constable.

He hadn't always been a senior manager. He'd once been a tough, no-nonsense copper. He'd been part of the unflinching thin blue line in the darkest days of football hooliganism and stood toe-to-toe with the rest of them when Millwall fans had marauded along Botchergate, smashing pubs and shops. His role had changed but the man hadn't.

The Chief took the seat opposite Fluke's.

'I gather the investigation is progressing?'

Fluke told him it was and updated him on the morning's developments.

'Good, Cameron Chamber's showed me the HOLMES summary. This has been an excellent investigation, Avison. Absolutely top-class.'

Fluke said nothing.

'I'm paying you a compliment, Avison.'

'Yes, sir. Thank you, sir.'

'You know it's going to be taken from us, don't you?'

The initial excitement Fluke had felt that morning had worn off. As soon as he found out who Cross was the investigation going higher up the food chain was inevitable. They might get some local arrests. The IT leak. Whoever supplied Cross's weapon, that type of thing. But Cross himself would be hunted by people who only seemed to have first names. People who worked in offices where the floors weren't numbered and secrets were traded like commodities.

The Chief sighed. 'Did you know Cameron closed the robbery this morning as well?'

The lucky prick. He wondered who'd actually done the real work. 'No, sir, I didn't.'

'Do you know why you weren't involved in the investigation?'

Fluke shrugged. He knew why. It was because Chambers didn't want to be upstaged by a subordinate. He wasn't about to say that though.

'It's because you're not playing well with others at the minute, Avison.'

Fluke looked up sharply.

'I'm the one who kept you off it. There was no way I was letting you near a multi-force investigation. Not with your attitude. I told Cameron to keep you in reserve and to let you manage anything that cropped up in the meantime,' the Chief continued.

Fluke said nothing.

The Chief stared at him for long enough to make him feel uncomfortable. 'Look, you two are going to have to find a way of working together. This week, FMIT has closed an armed robbery that spanned four force areas and now it looks like they've brought as much closure to these two murders as we're likely to get. You think Cameron doesn't deserve any credit for that?'

As far as Fluke was concerned, the only thing Chambers should take credit for was keeping out of his way. 'Yes, sir.'

'"Yes, sir,"' the Chief mimicked. 'Fuck off, Avison. I know you think he's a prick.'

Fluke decided the best policy would be to stare slightly above the Chief's hairline and say nothing.

The Chief appeared wise to that tactic. 'I'm telling you that Cameron is a good manager. Yes, he's a bit pompous. Yes, he likes the cameras and the sound of his voice a bit too much. But he knows how to get the best out of his officers and this week he's closed two major cases. And you, Avison, are not an easy man to manage.'

Fluke was about to protest but the Chief stopped him.

'Don't argue, Avison. You came out of hospital with a chip on your shoulder the size of Helvellyn. You should have heard the way you were speaking to people. You had some sort of PTSD, you must have. You've always had an antiauthoritarian streak but for the last few months you've been taking the piss, quite frankly. You know why you've not been in trouble?'

'No, sir.'

'Guess.' He'd stopped smiling.

As far as he knew, he had no friends in the ACPO ranks. 'You stepped in, sir?' he said after a pause.

'You're the most intelligent man in any room you're in, Avison, but sometimes you're also the stupidest. No, it wasn't me who stepped in. I wouldn't interfere in the chain of command like that. It was Cameron. He knows your worth to FMIT. He knows only you can manage that team of oddballs you seem to like working with. Time and time again, he fends off other departments. Fenton complains at least once a month about the way you speak to him. Don Holland put in a complaint last week, said you humiliated him at the deposition site.'

Fluke snorted. 'Holland. The man couldn't find his arse with both hands,' he said, before adding a 'sir' on the end.

'Yes, I know he'd messed up the cordons, and Cameron told him if he proceeded with his complaint he'd be on a capability by the end of the day, so he dropped it. But the point is every time they go to Cameron he bats it back. Tells them to get off your back and let you do what you do best.'

Again, Fluke said nothing.

'You don't believe me do you? Here have a read of this.' He thrust a report under Fluke's nose. 'Read the top section, I've highlighted the relevant part.'

It was Chambers's daily briefing to SMT. It was dated the previous Friday.

> *The double murder case is progressing faster than could reasonably be expected. DI Fluke has been doing a remarkable job and has developed lines of enquiry, that, in my opinion, will close this case. As discussed with Chief Constable Jackson, DI Fluke is being left to work this case with minimal oversight as this way achieves optimum results with this officer. He has total control of his team, sufficient resources and I have no doubt he will make an arrest within acceptable timescales.*

Fluke didn't know what to say. He felt himself flushing.

'Embarrassed? You should be. The way you speak to him sometimes,' the Chief said. 'He's a good man, essentially. I know you think he's an idiot but he's the one who convinced me to let you run that team of yours. He's the one who's making your life tolerable. Anyone else wouldn't have you as SIO. You'd be exhibits officer or something. How long do you think you'd last doing that?'

'Not long, sir,' Fluke admitted.

His tone softened. 'Look, don't worry about it. The three of us will sit down after this is all over and talk it through.'

'Thank you, sir.' Fluke got up and offered his hand. The Chief remained seating.

'I'm sorry, Avison. That wasn't why I came to see you.'

Fluke sat back down. The Chief's expression was serious. It could only mean one thing.

Fenton.

Fluke refused his federation rep so the Chief insisted Chambers sit in with him. Fenton was preening. If he'd been a cat, he'd have purred. He had a sergeant from Professional Standards with him. Someone to carry his briefcase.

'Can we get on with this please, Alex?' Chambers said.

He didn't look happy, Fluke noticed. The Chief's words were still reverberating round his head, and he was seeing Chambers in a different light. It was clear he was getting no satisfaction from this.

Fenton pressed record on the digital interview camera and spoke into the table microphone. 'DSI Alex Fenton interviewing DI Fluke on suspicion of misconduct in a public office. DI Fluke is not under arrest but this interview is being conducted under caution. You have waived your right to representation, is this correct?'

Fluke said nothing.

Fenton looked at him but couldn't hold eye contact for very long. Eventually, Chambers saved him.

'Let's just get this over with, Avison, can we? I'm sure we all have real work to do.'

Fluke nodded.

'For the record, DI Fluke has nodded,' Fenton said.

'We're on video, you idiot!' Fluke snapped.

Ignoring him, Fenton got out a file. He removed the letter Fluke had forged and put it on the table. 'Have you seen this letter before, DI Fluke?'

As Chambers craned his neck to read it, Fluke said, 'No comment.'

'You must have seen it, Fluke. It was CC'd to your address.'

'No comment.'

At that point, Chambers seemed to lose patience. 'Look, Alex, I know you have a job to do but can we have some context here. This investigation has come from nowhere as far as I'm concerned, and if you're going to interview one of my men, you're going to have to spell it out for me.'

'Certainly, sir. On Tuesday, someone from PSD happened to be at the Cumberland Infirmary visiting a relative and observed DI Fluke on the oncology ward. He appeared to be having a blood transfusion. He was about to make himself known to DI Fluke when Fluke's mobile phone rang. I believe it was a call from you, sir, and was in relation to the body found in West Cumbria. My man clearly heard DI Fluke say that he was at home. On that basis, I opened a file on DI Fluke on suspicion of lying to a superior officer. I accessed his personnel record and found the letter from Doctor Leah Cooper stating that DI Fluke was fit to return to duty. This is a copy here, sir.' He handed it over to Chambers who glanced at it.

'Yeah, I've seen it. So what?'

'I asked Occ Health for their copy, sir, and they sent it to me. It was exactly the same.'

'I'm not following you, Alex,' Chambers said.

Fluke grimaced. Wait for it, it's coming. Fenton may not be a good detective but he had a sixth sense for officers in trouble.

'The thing is, sir, this letter was unsolicited. Normally HR ask Occ Health to request medical reports. This one just turned up. I showed the letter to Doctor Cooper and in my opinion it was the first time she'd seen it.'

'I see. Avison?'

Fluke breathed out slowly. Time to come clean. It was a shame as he was sure he could've closed the case given a few more days. It didn't look like he was going to get the chance. He could try and bluff it but that wasn't going to be a winning strategy and it also risked getting Leah into trouble. 'Last year—'

He was interrupted by a loud and urgent knock on the interview room door. Towler walked in without being bidden. He bent down and whispered something into Chambers' ear.

He looked up and then across at Fluke. 'We're going to have to stop this for a couple of minutes, Alex,' Chambers said.

'But, sir,' Fenton protested. 'Fluke was just about to admit everyth—'

'I'm sorry, Alex. Please stop the tape.' He left the room with Towler.

Nearly ten minutes passed. Ten minutes of Fenton pretending to read his notes, doing everything he could to avoid looking at Fluke.

When Chambers returned, he wasn't alone.

There was a woman with him. She was carrying a brown leather satchel-type briefcase. She was also wearing a black leather jacket, black jeans and had a helmet tucked under her arm. When she turned to face Fluke, he stifled a gasp.

It was the woman Fluke had met at the dinner party. The woman who'd given him a lift home.

'Hello, I'm Bridie Harper-Tarr, Mr Fluke's solicitor,' she said to a bewildered-looking Fenton.

Not half as bewildered as I am, mate, Fluke thought.

'DI Fluke's waived his right to representation,' Fenton said weakly.

'Actually, Alex, he hasn't,' Chambers said.

Fenton protested. Fluke said nothing. He knew he had. He'd nodded and it was on video, as he'd pointed out to everyone earlier.

Chambers seemed to have been paying closer attention to the chain of events than either Fluke or Fenton. 'When DI Fluke nodded earlier it was in response to my question about us all having better things to do. He hasn't actually answered your question yet,' he said. 'Is this correct, Avison?'

Lost, Fluke decided the best thing to do was agree. 'Yes, sir.'

'He can't have a civilian solicitor without prior notice,' Fenton said.

'I'm allowing it, Alex. Miss Harper-Tarr has information that should clear all this up as it happens. Not only is she a solicitor, she's also a friend of Doctor Cooper. Miss Harper-Tarr, over to you.' Chambers said it with such assertiveness that everyone sat back down and waited.

Fluke consciously checked his mouth wasn't hanging open. He had no idea what was happening. By the look of things, neither did Fenton. Fluke was also impressed with the new assertive Chambers. He was beginning to see what the Chief had been talking about.

Bridie Harper-Tarr cleared her throat and reached into her briefcase. As she did, her sleeve rode up and Fluke could see that the lower part of her arm was heavily tattooed.

She put a document on the table, turned it the right way round, and slid it to Fenton. 'Doctor Cooper wanted you to have this, Mr Fenton. She was too busy to come herself and she said she'd rather not see you again in any case. She said you were quite aggressive when you came to her office.'

'I wasn't!' Fenton blurted out.

'Regardless. She may put in a complaint later on today. She may not. It depends what happens here, I suppose. What you have in front of you is a hospital printout of the letter Doctor Cooper sent to the police's Occupational Health department. You have the original, of course. Is this the letter you asked for?'

Fenton said nothing as he read it. He put it down and got out the original, and put them side-by-side. For a full minute, he studied them.

'Why didn't she tell me she had it?' he said. There was a whine creeping into his voice.

'Doctor Cooper doesn't work for you, Mr Fenton.'

'But she's legally obliged to assist the police in their investigations in a timely manner,' Fenton said pompously, not ready to give up just yet.

Bridie Harper-Tarr smiled at him. It was the smile a shark gives a seal that's found itself too far from the ice. 'Mr Fenton, I worked at the UN for six years. I've represented countries. Do you really want to challenge me on the law? On medical ethics?'

By the looks of things, he didn't.

Chambers clearly decided enough was enough. 'Alex? Are we good here?'

Still Fenton said nothing as he desperately tried to find a discrepancy between the two documents. Fluke held his breath, mystified.

Chambers raised his voice. 'Alex. I said, are we good here?'

Fenton conceded defeat. 'It seems fine, sir.'

Fluke doubted he'd ever heard anyone sound so miserable.

'Do you have any more questions for DI Fluke?' Chambers asked.

Fenton looked at Fluke with genuine hatred in his eyes, and he knew he'd made an enemy for life. Fenton was renowned for holding grudges over the smallest things, and this one wasn't small. He'd had Fluke dead in the water, a clear disciplinary offence, with in all likelihood, criminal charges to follow. Taking down a detective inspector would have been a massive feather in his cap and now he had nothing. Worse than nothing. He'd been made to look stupid. Stupid and impotent.

'Not at this time, sir, although I reserve the right to re-interview him if the need arises.'

Everyone in the room knew it was a last effort at saving his dignity. Even the sergeant with him winced in embarrassment.

'All right then, time for you to go and shuffle some paperwork, Alex. Let Avison here get on with his job. What do you say, Alex?'

'Yes, sir.'

Fenton got up to leave. He was trying not to catch anyone's eye. As he walked to the door, Chambers stopped him.

'Oh, and Alex, can I have a written apology to DI Fluke on my desk within the hour, please?'

For a moment, Fluke thought Fenton was going to refuse. That Chambers had pushed him that one step too far. Eventually, he nodded, gave Fluke and Bridie one last spiteful look then left.

Chambers stood up as soon as the door shut. 'That was rather fun, I thought,' he said. He offered his hand to Fluke.

Fluke stood up and shook it.

'I'm a ridiculous figure sometimes, Avison, I'm fully aware of that. But know this, I've always liked you a lot more than you think. Now, orders from the Chief. You're on leave for the rest of the week,' he said. 'No arguments. Towler's more than capable of coordinating what needs to happen now. Cross is out the country. Let someone else deal with him. You've come closer to catching him than at least three different intelligence agencies. You should be proud of what your team's achieved.'

At a loss for something to say, he mumbled a weak 'thank you'.

'Miss Harper-Tarr, it's been a genuine pleasure,' Chambers said, and with that, he left.

Fluke was left alone with Bridie. She busied herself with putting various papers back in her briefcase. When it was clear she wasn't going to say anything, he couldn't contain himself. 'What the fuck's just happened?'

She looked up from what she was doing, smiled and said, 'I think you owe me a drink, Mr Fluke.'

Chapter 37

Fluke had a few things to tie up at Carleton Hall before he could get away. Once he'd composed himself, he went to see Chambers to apologise.

'I can't promise not to wind you up in the future, Avison,' he'd said. 'I want to be Chief one day and you don't. Sometimes we're going to see things differently.'

They were never going to be friends but it seemed there was at least the early form of a truce on the table.

He'd agreed to meet Bridie at a pub they both knew in the small village of Threlkeld, just outside Keswick. She needed to go to her office first to drop off some files, and as they were travelling separately anyway, Fluke decided to just head off.

With the forged letter half resolved – he still had to see Leah – he felt as if he could relax for the first time in over a year. If it wasn't for the looming threat of eviction, he might have actually smiled.

He left his phone on in case his team needed to get hold of him but the investigation was about to go global. FMIT's part was effectively over. Towler would liaise with Interpol and make the arrangements. As soon as the intelligence community took an interest, a small rural force like Cumbria got pushed to the sidelines.

It was four o'clock when he arrived at the Fox and Pheasant, too late for lunch but he could do with a decent coffee. He walked in and found a quiet table in the lounge bar. A waitress peered out of the kitchen and saw Fluke. She walked over and he ordered an Americano, black.

While he waited for his drink, he ran through the brief conversation he'd had with Bridie back at Durranhill. He'd asked her how she had a copy of his letter when the only hard drive it was on was back in his log cabin. She'd told him to ask Towler.

He had.

Towler, it transpired, had been contacted by Leah Cooper who'd told him everything. She'd wanted to help. Towler had given Jiao-long Fluke's spare key and asked him to hack into his desktop computer. That was what he'd been doing when Skelton was telling Fluke about how they got the warrants for the hospital. It had taken Jiao-long less than two minutes to find the right file and email it to Leah. With the right text, it was a simple case of printing off an identical copy of the letter.

He'd deal with Towler and Jiao-long when he came back from leave, although in truth, he wasn't angry with them.

Fluke had asked Bridie about Michelle's dinner party. It was obvious she hadn't been there by accident.

Bridie had explained Leah had been doing some matchmaking for her oldest friend who was sick of going out with boring men, and decided Fluke could be just the right man. The mysterious detective who lived alone in a wood. She'd told Bridie that he was at the wrong end of a failing relationship and that she should engineer a way of meeting him to see what she thought. As luck would have it, a solicitor she knew from court, a lecherous man in his fifties, had been invited to the infamous dinner party. He couldn't believe his luck when Bridie had asked to go with him. Although she'd driven them there, after the party ended, she'd told him to walk home. She wanted to give Fluke a lift. She'd enjoyed his brief company and decided she wanted to see him again. She had intended to wait until the investigation was over but Leah had called and told her Fluke was in trouble. They hadn't had long to come up with a plan, and in the end, they'd called Towler for help with the letter, as she'd already explained.

Fluke had been lost for words. He couldn't remember when so many people had put themselves out for him and he wasn't sure he deserved it. Leah, Towler and Jiao-long were all risking their jobs. He didn't know enough about the law to be sure, but Bridie had probably risked being disbarred. Personally, he didn't think he was worth it.

The arrival of his coffee brought him back to the present. It was served in a huge cup, more of a bowl with a handle, with a tiny Italian biscuit. A group of farmers sitting at the bar with their pints of Jennings and bowls of soup turned to look at the decidedly un-Cumbrian drink. He grinned apologetically, pointed to his keys and mouthed he was driving. As one, they turned back to the bar and continued talking about whatever farmers talked about. Fluke picked his phone up and checked his emails. There was nothing that couldn't wait.

With nothing to do but wait, Fluke idly picked up a brochure on the table. It had the rates for rooms and some of the special offers they were running.

When he had time to kill, Fluke would sometimes pass the time people-watching, trying to work out their stories from the context clues around him. The three men at the bar talking about Herdwick sheep were clearly fell farmers. No challenge there. The lounge bar allowed dogs and a Border Collie sat at the feet of the farmer on the left. As if the dog sensed it was being watched, it got up, stretched, and wandered over to the open log fire, before slumping back down.

The only other person in the bar was a petite barmaid. She looked about sixteen but Fluke knew she was at least two years older. You had to be eighteen to serve alcohol. She was a pretty-looking girl, and was wearing the required black polo shirt with the pub logo, along with a black skirt and flat black shoes. He watched as one of the farmers ordered a whiskey "for the road".

She really was small, he thought, as she stood on tiptoes to reach the optic of the whiskey the farmer had chosen from the vast array on offer. She turned and caught him watching. Instead of looking annoyed, she smiled shyly. 'I don't why they have these things so high,' she said.

Fluke said nothing. A memory was rushing back, something that had happened recently. Something to do with the barmaid serving the farmer his whiskey. He subconsciously raised his hand, as if he were reaching for the optic as well. She stared at him and the three farmers turned to see what she was looking at. He quickly lowered it. Eventually, they all turned back round.

The farmer with the whiskey spoke. 'Pass the jug o' watter, lass.' She moved across to the end of the bar and came back with a small jug. The farmer added a splash of water and thanked her.

Another alarm went off in his head. A jug. A jug and a small girl reaching for something only just within reach. He scoured everything that had happened recently, desperately trying to make the connection. He shut his eyes to blank out all external stimuli.

The case had already thrown things at him that had been just out of his reach. The numbers on the notepad he should have recognised, and the odd number of paracetamol tablets were just two. He knew that sometimes things came to him immediately and sometimes they never came at all. Sometimes he had to simply learn to live with a nagging feeling that refused to die.

He knew this was important though. He raised his hand to reach for the imaginary whiskey again. The farmers and the barmaid stared, but he didn't care.

Why was it evoking such a strong reaction?

The two thoughts collided.

The jug and the whiskey.

The whiskey and the jug.

He hardly dared to think. If he tried to focus on it, it would disappear. He would scare it away.

Clues became questions. The case had been overrun with them. Clues and questions.

But few answers.

The jug and the whiskey

The whiskey and the jug.

The debris of the collision in his mind cleared and there it was.

An answer.

The answer to the case.

Fluke knew where Dalton Cross was.

Chapter 38

Why would a man in a wheelchair keep cream on the top shelf of the fridge?

Fluke had watched Tait struggle to reach it. It was the right height for someone standing but the wrong height for someone sitting. Why make things harder than they were?

Tait had told Fluke the cream was in a pitcher.

Who said 'pitcher'? No one in England, that was for certain. It was a jug. Always had been, always would be.

Fluke knew of one country that used the word pitcher instead of jug though. A country divided from the UK by a common language.

Instantly, Fluke knew three things.

The man calling himself Gibson Tait didn't need to use a wheelchair.

The man calling himself Gibson Tait was an American.

The man calling himself Gibson Tait was Dalton Cross.

By the time Fluke had finished processing it all, he was already in his car, gunning the accelerator and roaring out of the car park. The big BMW tyres spat gravel back at the pub windows. He'd left an upturned table and a smashed coffee cup in his wake. The farmers and barmaid had stared at him in astonishment as he'd ran out but he didn't care. He had no time. He'd sent Jiao-long out there to interview him.

'Bastard!' Fluke shouted. 'Fucking bastard!'

Tait lived ten miles away and Fluke was pushing one hundred and ten as he raced west along the A66. He braked hard as he approached the Keswick roundabout. He took the third exit and put his foot back to the floor again.

Although the road had more bends than the A66, he took one hand off the steering wheel, reached for his phone and autodialled the office. Jiao-long answered. Fluke breathed out.

'Longy, thank f—!' he started to say before he was interrupted.

'Boss, Gibson Tait's talking shit. There's no such thing as a master code or whatever it was he said—'

'Longy—'

'And another thing, boss. Why would—'

'Longy!' Fluke shouted. 'Just shut the fuck up and listen!'

As he explained everything to the young computer expert, a car coming the other way had to swerve to miss him. Fluke heard its horn sound. He ignored it.

Driving at nearly seventy miles an hour on a narrow, bending road with only one hand on the steering wheel, he left instructions for Jiao-long to get armed response out to Tait's house as soon as possible. Within a minute, Jiao-long had got back to him. Armed response were on a joint exercise with the nuclear police and were at least an hour away.

Fuck! He didn't know what to do. He could, and probably should, wait for them. That would be the sensible thing to do. Fluke knew he was no match for Cross on his own.

Still, there was no harm in just going to have a look? He'd be able to tell just by driving past whether there was anyone in.

He slammed the accelerator to the floor and watched the speedometer creep past seventy again, which on the narrow twisty road was about forty too fast.

His phone rang again. He looked at the caller-ID. It wasn't Jiao-long this time but Chambers. Fluke ignored it. He didn't need to speak to him to know what he was going to say. Back off and let armed response handle it.

The real Gibson Tait was dead, Fluke was sure about that. He'd been Samantha's contact in the police. When Cross had found out it had been him doing Samantha's checks for her he'd have gone straight to him, hoped Tait could have led him directly to Samantha. But she was far too careful and he'd had to do it the hard way; going to Diamond and forcing him to reveal where the drop was.

Once they'd served their purpose, there was nothing to gain, and everything to lose by allowing Tait and Diamond to live.

Once Samantha's body had been discovered, he probably decided he needed to stay and monitor the situation. And he knew of just the place to use as a base. A small cottage in the middle of nowhere…

Fluke instinctively slowed as he entered the village and approached the quiet lane where Tait's cottage was situated.

Cross couldn't have picked a more perfect place. The Royal Marine in Fluke appreciated the location. A long drive. No obvious cover. No chance of approaching unnoticed. Thick gravel that would make a noise whether you were driving or walking. A superb defensive position.

He crawled past and surreptitiously glanced at the cottage. There were no lights on. There was no car in the drive.

Fluke braked and paused. The cottage looked empty but that didn't mean it was. He was in a good place to wait for armed response and guide them in. He could help them. He'd been inside before. Waiting was the sensible thing to do.

Fluke hadn't been passed over for promotion so many times for doing the sensible thing every time.

He put the car into reverse and carefully navigated the narrow unlit lane. Turning a hard left, he entered Tait's drive backwards. If Cross came out now, Fluke wanted to be able to drive straight out.

Cross didn't come out, however, and Fluke reversed all the way up to the front door. He stopped but didn't turn off the engine. He put the BMW into drive and stayed there for a full minute. Watching the front door through his rear view mirror. Looking at the fully drawn curtains for a twitch. Anything to suggest there was someone at home.

The house was unlit and looked unoccupied. He picked his phone up off the passenger seat but there was no signal.

There was no point sitting there, exposed. He either had to try to get inside or leave. Neither held much attraction.

He punched the steering wheel, frustrated at his own indecisiveness.

He was scared but that didn't bother him. A dark creepy cottage in the middle of nowhere and a deadly killer nearby. It was the type of thing you were supposed to be scared of. If it were a slasher film, he'd have been silently screaming at the girls in bikinis, 'Don't go in there, you fucking bimbos!'.

Fluke got out of the car. He left the door open and the engine on.

He opened the BMW's boot and took out a heavy-duty torch. It had been in there since he'd taken delivery of the car and he'd not once used it. When he pressed the on button, nothing happened. For Fluke, torches were simply cases for carrying dead batteries. The weight was reassuring though. No match for an expert with a gun but better than nothing.

He quietly walked round the back. Fluke knew what the back garden looked like as he'd seen it through the kitchen window when he and Cross had drank coffee together. It flashed into his mind that if he ever wrote his autobiography, that chapter would be called 'Coffee with a Killer'.

Fluke peered into the kitchen. It was too dark to see properly. He knew that glass had been expensive when the cottages were built and windows were therefore smaller than those on modern houses. He also knew that, as it was lighter outside than inside, he'd be sticking out like an Alfred Hitchcock silhouette. He moved past the kitchen and further into the back garden. He looked around out of habit.

Like the rest of the village's gardens, it was immaculate. Large borders with a heavy presence of snowdrops. And, as it was Wordsworth's county, there were the green shoots of the first daffodils of the year. The rest of the spring perennials were not yet ready to risk the Cumbrian frosts. There was a small pond with a tennis ball floating to discourage ice and what looked like a solar-powered fountain. Probably turned off for the dark winter months. Natural paving stones led around the outside of the lawn, providing a natural barrier between plants and grass. A couple of fruit trees, leafless. Three or four evergreen shrubs. A wooden compost heap in the corner, full and ready to be used in early spring. The garden providing its own nourishment, year on year. In other circumstances, Fluke would have liked a proper look. He turned and surveyed the back of the cottage.

There was a small set of garden furniture on the patio. A small round table and three chairs. Cast iron, painted white. Available everywhere. The table had a glass ashtray. It had been there for a while. It was full of water, stained brown by the cigarette butts floating in it.

A place to sit and relax in the evening. Much like his own.

Fluke walked further in until he came to some patio doors. He tried looking in again but still couldn't see anything in the gloom. He tried the handle gently. It was open.

This was it. If he was going to go back and wait for armed response, it had to be now. Once he was in the cottage, he was committed. If Cross was still in there, there'd be no avoiding him. He thought about Kenneth Diamond's mutilated body. He thought about the way a beautiful young woman, criminal or not, had been discarded like a fly-tipped fridge. And he thought about Gibson Tait. A man in a wheelchair who'd been killed just for checking a name on a computer.

He opened the door and walked in.

Past the point of no return.

The lounge was empty so he walked straight through, his torch raised as if it was a police baton. He stopped at the door and listened. The cottage remained silent.

He opened the lounge door into the hall and tried to get his bearings. He could see the kitchen but already knew it was empty. There were three doors leading from the hall. All closed.

It wasn't a big building, judging by the time it had taken to walk round it. Fluke guessed there would be two bedrooms and a bathroom. He walked towards the first door and put his hand on the handle. He paused.

He imagined people who risked their lives playing Russian roulette went through something similar to what he was feeling now. Being an instrument in their own death, never knowing if their next action would be their last.

Fluke raised his torch and opened the door.

It was the master bedroom. A double bed, roughly made. A wardrobe, open but empty, and a chest of drawers with a flat-screen TV on top. The remote was on a bedside cabinet, along with a couple of books and a half-drunk glass of water. It didn't smell musty and he guessed that it was where Cross had been sleeping. The room was otherwise empty. It was similar to his own bedroom at home. Functional rather than elaborate.

A small canvas bag was lying on the bed. Fluke opened it. It had clothes in and three passports. He didn't have time to look properly. It was a job for a full forensic team. One thing was obvious though. Cross hadn't left the country yet.

So where was he?

Fluke backed out into the hall.

He opened the second door.

He'd been half right. It was a spare bedroom but Tait had been using it as a study. An Apple desktop computer, heavy-duty laserjet printer, Bose speakers and a wifi router with a flashing blue light. All expensive stuff. There were bookshelves full of IT manuals, books and DVDs. An executive chair was in front of the computer. The desk was tidy. A few pens in a cracked Steve Jobs mug and a glass paperweight with a corporate logo that Fluke didn't recognise. A souvenir from some event, no doubt. The room was otherwise empty.

One to go. The bathroom. He reached for the door handle.

He froze.

There was a noise. A very faint noise. The sound of material rustling. Very faint but he was sure he hadn't imagined it.

Cross was on the other side of the door.

Waiting.

Fluke gently gripped the door handle and held it shut. He didn't want to be surprised by Cross rushing him. He'd been quiet searching the house but there was no way Cross wouldn't know he was there.

He'd been quiet but not silent.

Going back wasn't an option. He couldn't turn his back on Cross. Going forward meant coming face-to-face with a contract killer, armed with nothing more than a heavy torch.

In films where Russian roulette had been portrayed, one thing had always bothered Fluke. There had been occasions when they'd been firing a revolver and the rules of the game had not permitted re-spinning the chamber after someone's turn. Fluke had seen one film where it had dry-fired five times. The person whose turn it had been next had known with absolute certainty that there was a bullet in the chamber. Not one-in-six odds, but one-in-one. A one hundred per cent chance of death. Yet they still pulled the trigger. He'd never understood why they did it. Until now.

He had to do something. The longer he stood there, the greater the chance that Cross would just start shooting through the flimsy wood.

He didn't want to die wondering. Fluke had been trained in room breaches and knew that going in fast and noisy was better than timidly sticking your head in. Speed, aggression, surprise. SAS.

Disorientating Cross for long enough to grab the weapon was his only hope.

He flung the door open and burst into the room screaming obscenities.

A shower curtain flapped lazily in the breeze coming from the open window.

It was a small bathroom and was tiled in white from floor to ceiling. There was a mirror above a small vanity sink. Toiletries were lined up neatly on the little shelf below. The toilet was beside the sink. Fluke peered round the door to check the bath.

The room was empty.

Fluke collapsed to the floor in relief.

After a few seconds, he reached for his phone. Still no signal.

He picked himself up and waited for his heart to stop racing. He was drenched in cold sweat.

He weakly made his way out of the cottage, using the front door which was also unlocked.

He blinked in the bright evening sun.

He walked towards his car. And stopped.

At the end of the drive, staring at him, was Dalton Cross.

Chapter 39

Cross was on foot. He'd clearly seen Fluke's car and had parked his own out of sight. He had a small handgun drawn. He was pointing it at Fluke. A two-handed grip. Steady.

He was about sixty yards away.

He walked towards Fluke.

Fluke stood still, frozen to the cold ground.

Death was on its way, he had no doubt about that. He was out of options. He was still out of range of Cross's small handgun but the distance was closing fast. He looked at what he was carrying and laughed, the sound tinged with hysteria. Never bring a torch to a gunfight.

He needed a weapon and he needed one now.

Towler's description of the bullet came into his head.

It'll penetrate the skull at twenty feet. But only just.

He was damned if he was simply going to lie down without a fight. He wasn't pulling the trigger when he knew the chamber was loaded. There would be no Russian roulette for him.

Fluke ran towards his car.

Cross fired. Fluke heard the bullet hit the stone walls of the cottage behind him, and even though he knew the bullet had already missed him, he instinctively ducked.

He kept running.

Cross fired again. Missed again.

Fluke reached the driver's side and dived through the open door.

Cross fired at the car. The bullet hit the windscreen but bounced off, a small chip appeared. The type TV adverts urge you to fix before cold weather turns it into a crack.

Cross must've come to the same conclusion as Towler. He lowered the gun and ran towards the car.

Fluke struggled to get himself into a driving position. The BMW's engine was already on.

He pressed his foot on the brake and wrenched the gearstick into drive.

Cross stopped running. He paused for a second. He raised the gun again and pointed it directly at Fluke's head.

Neither of them moved.

Now it was a bit more even. Car versus gun. Stalemate.

Someone had to make the first move. Fluke decided it would be him.

He took his foot off the brake and slammed the accelerator to the floor. Like all automatics there was a slight pause but the BMW was new and German engineering is unrivalled. The engine screamed as the turbo kicked in. The thick tyres bit into the gravel drive and the car lurched forwards, pushing Fluke back in his seat.

Cross didn't fire, but he didn't seem to be panicking either. He was clearly waiting for Fluke to get nearer. To get within his gun's effective range. He simply stood with his two-handed stance and waited.

The car narrowed the gap to forty yards, accelerating all the time.

Cross still didn't fire. Even from that distance, Fluke could see he had a wry smile on his face. *Bastard's enjoying this.*

It was a test of nerves. The longer he stayed upright, the greater chance he had of hitting Cross but there was also a far greater chance the bullet would pierce the windscreen.

Twenty yards. Fifteen. The car continued to accelerate. There was an imperceptible change in the revs as the automatic engine moved up a gear. Fluke kept his eyes fixed on Cross, his right foot pressed to the floor. The engine screamed in defiance.

Ten yards. He was in Cross's effective range.

A flash from the gun's muzzle and a hole appeared in the windscreen. Fluke felt the bullet graze his ear. A sharp burning pain, instantly smothered by adrenalin.

Fluke braced himself as Cross's face filled his vision. The smile still etched onto his face. A split-second before impact, he tried to jump out of the way.

He'd left it too late. There was a sickening thump as the car smashed into him.

He heard a scream of pain. Cross was thrown in the air like a rag doll. Crumpled. Arms and legs splayed out helplessly. The car kept moving forward and Cross's airborne body slammed into the windscreen before disappearing out of sight.

Fluke could barely see where he was going through the cobweb of cracks and the car was bouncing uncontrollably on the uneven drive. Fluke leaned back and braked hard.

Nothing happened. He was going too fast for the tyres to grip the loose gravel.

Time slowed as the car went into an uncontrollable skid.

Fluke looked up.

The stone pillars that stood either side of Tait's drive filled his vision. The car was going nearly forty miles an hour as it raced towards the one on the left. Fluke wrenched the steering wheel to the right but it was useless. It was like driving on sheet ice.

He flung his arms up in front of his face just as the car smashed into the pillar.

The BMW Fluke was driving had crumple zones designed to absorb some of the impact of a car crash. The bumper and grille collapsed.

The rest of the car was still going forty miles an hour, however. It wrapped itself around the slate pillar. The tortuous sound of metal and stone as energy was transferred was deafening. The forward momentum caused the rear of the car to lift off the ground.

Eight milliseconds after the BMW's computer detected an impact, it deployed both airbags. The driver's airbag was located in the steering wheel and the hard plastic cover exploded out and struck Fluke in the face, breaking his nose instantly.

Thirty milliseconds after impact, the airbags inflated.

As the car came to an abrupt stop, Fluke's body continued to travel forwards. He wasn't wearing a seatbelt and his chest, cushioned slightly by the deployed airbag, slammed into the steering column. Although his torso's momentum had been stopped, his head continued forward. With a thud, it was driven into the broken windscreen.

Externally, Fluke's body had been stopped by the airbag, steering column and windscreen. Internally, all his organs continued moving. Heart, lungs, liver and kidneys all moved forward until they were violently stopped by his skeletal system and other organs.

The human skull has evolved over eons. Solid bone shields have provided the brain with a double layer of protection against the trauma humans were most likely to encounter. But humans have outpaced evolution. The protection the skull has afforded the brain for thousands of years has been made obsolete by modern things like car crashes and deceleration.

The brain is suspended in a liquid called cerebrospinal fluid, a fluid that allows the brain to maintain its density without being damaged by its own weight. As Fluke's head hit the windscreen his brain moved through the fluid and struck the front of his skull before rebounding back to hit the rear.

He immediately started losing consciousness.

He bounced off the windscreen and fell back into the driver's seat. The rear wheels, still spinning, fell back to the ground.

From jumping into the car to coming to a dead stop had taken less than ten seconds.

Fluke fought to stay awake.

There was an unwelcome smell. Burning rubber and diesel. Even this close to unconsciousness, Fluke knew the car was on fire. He was going to burn to death. The BMW's ruined engine finally gave in and stopped. Fluke could hear ominous ticking as it cooled. As his brain shut down, all nonessential organs and the sweet release of darkness clouded his vision, Fluke started to have auditory hallucinations.

The sound of men shouting something he didn't understand.

'Armed police! Armed police! Armed police!'

Chapter 40

At the third attempt, and only after adding a full can of Zippo fuel, Fluke managed to light the fire pit. Flames shot up into the clear winter sky.

Abi cheered.

'What we doing, lighting a fire or summoning the Rohirrim?' Bridie asked.

'Ha, ha,' Fluke answered with a smile. Sarcasm and knowledge of *Lord of the Rings*. He put down the mesh lid, gently pulled Abi away from the flames, and sat in one of the chairs surrounding it. With his one good hand, he reached forwards and enjoyed the heat.

'How's the arm, Ave?' Towler asked.

'Better thanks. Can't say the same for the nose. Still can't breathe through it.' Apart from the broken nose and a badly sprained wrist, it was only the cuts from the broken glass that had caused him any problems. He'd needed several pints of plasma to stop the bleeding but Leah had been waiting in A&E when he arrived, and despite the protests from the trauma consultant, had overseen his immediate care. All things considered, Fluke had come out of the crash relatively unscathed.

A veteran of countless broken noses, Towler said, 'It'll get better, probably be another week though.'

A silence settled over the group. Even Abi seemed to sense it was time to be quiet.

They'd discussed the remnants of the case before they all sat down for a winter barbecue. Cross had been badly injured but had survived.

'Typical marine, can't even crash into someone properly,' Towler had said.

Fluke nodded. He felt the same way sometimes. Cross had got off lightly. Far more lightly than the real Gibson Tait. He'd been found in his own compost heap. A .22 bullet hole in the middle of his forehead.

'Looks like he's going to get away with it, though,' he said.

Bridie and Towler looked at him with a start.

'You gonna tell us what happened then?' Towler was the only one who knew Fluke had been allowed to see Cross.

A concession the Chief had secured before Cross was extradited back to the States. He'd had to make a full statement detailing the crimes committed while in the UK and the Chief had argued that Fluke was the only one who'd be able to tell if he was leaving things out.

'Not really supposed to, Matt.'

'And?'

Fluke grinned at them both. He'd already told Skelton, Jiaolong and Vaughn.

Fluke had woken in hospital with a headache that only morphine could reduce. Leah had been there within five minutes of him waking, all business-like as there was actual work to do. Towler had been second through the door. He'd told Fluke that Cross was on the floor below. Two broken legs, a cracked spine and severe concussion. Everything else had been superficial. He was expected to make a full recovery.

'Has anyone interviewed him?' Fluke had asked.

'You're fucking joking, aren't you? No one's getting into see him. It's gone political. Us country bumpkins have got no chance of getting in. The Yanks want him isolated. Reckon he's a threat to national security. Wankers.'

Bridie had arrived within the hour.

'All you have to do is say "no" if you don't want to go out, Avison. There's no need to take these extreme measures.' Despite her grin, there was genuine concern behind her eyes.

Within a week, he was discharged. Instead of going home as directed, he'd driven straight to HQ and entered the Chief's office without knocking.

'Ah, Avison. Right on time.' He was sitting at a table with Chambers and a man in a suit he didn't recognize. 'I was telling Mr Mortimer here that you wouldn't do as you were told and would be on your way here instead.'

The man in the suit stood up and offered his hand. Fluke awkwardly reached with his left. His right arm was still too sore.

'Mr Mortimer was just laying out the ground rules for your

interview with Cross.'

'Sir?' Fluke said. It wasn't going as he expected.

'You didn't think we'd let him out the country without getting something back, did you? The Home Secretary might be bending over for the Americans, but we aren't. Part of the extradition agreement is that he makes a full statement of what he did here. If he misses anything out then he stays. He thinks he can cut a deal over there so he's pretty keen to get back, as you might imagine.'

Fluke looked at Mortimer. He didn't look happy. Fluke realised he hadn't been told who he worked for. The intelligence community it was, then.

'Mr Mortimer will sit in with you. If Cross tries to tell you anything about his life before he got here, the interview will be terminated.'

'Why me, sir? Why not a spook?'

'You're the only one who'll know if he's missing something out. We can only speak to him the once. We have to get it right first time.'

In the end, it had been easy. Eager to make sure his extradition didn't fall through, Cross was keen to talk.

He was being held in a secure hospital room in the Cumberland Infirmary. Armed guards were outside the door. He was immobile but alert. One of his wrists was handcuffed to the metal bed frame.

Fluke took a seat near the bed. Mortimer took one near the rear of the room.

'Who hired you?' Fluke asked.

Cross told him. It was as Fluke suspected. A nobody thinking he was a somebody. A 'dot.com' millionaire who couldn't bear to lose. He'd been a victim of Samantha's. Instead of paying, he'd tried to kill her at the drop. She was too good for him but she knew her card was marked in the States. She'd fled back to the UK. Cross had been hired to find and terminate her.

The FBI had already arrested 'dot.com'. Some of the crimes in the case had been committed in the States. Soliciting murder. He'd never see the light of day again.

'How'd you find her?' Fluke asked. 'She'd changed her

appearance. You had no idea what she looked like.'

'No. But I knew what she did. As long as she kept on doing it I knew I'd catch up with her. It's what I do. It was time-consuming but the result was inevitable.'

'I want more details than that, you prick,' Fluke said. 'If I walk out, the deal's off. You can fucking rot here.'

'Empty threat, Mr Fluke. We both know as soon as I can walk, I'm going home.'

Fluke said nothing. Cross stared at him and realised that Fluke wasn't bluffing.

'I knew she was back in the UK. I came over and started tracking her. I monitored the police computers for drugged rapes, ones where the victim had disappeared. Every time I found one I had someone search your PNC for me. I was looking for name searches in the same town with no hits. It was laborious but eventually, I found one of her victims. He refused to speak to me, but at least I knew my methods were working. The next victim I found was in Birmingham, the one after that in Glasgow. All rich men with too much to lose.'

Fluke nodded. It was a variation on how he'd thought it had happened. He understood how Cross had tracked down old victims. He didn't yet know how he'd managed to get ahead of her though. Cross was just getting to that part.

'The next man I spoke to was a landowner in Norwich. Landed gentry, I think you call them. He was with her when she got a phone call. Before she could hide the screen he'd seen the number. He recognised it as a Cumbrian area code. 01539 apparently. Kendal. He knew the code because he has a friend up there he goes grouse shooting with.'

'So?'

'So. What if this was her researching a potential victim. She must select them somehow. She'd get most of her intel before she arrives in a city. That's how I'd do it anyway.'

'So you came to Cumbria to look for her?'

'How do you catch a ghost, Mr Fluke?'

Fluke shrugged.

'You wait for the ghost to come to you. So yes, I came to Cumbria. A calculated risk but I literally had nothing else to go on. Nothing at all. This had been the only slip up she'd made and it could've meant nothing. I monitored all drug-assisted rape allegations up here through a contact I made in your police force, hoping for a break.'

'Gibson Tait?'

'No, not Gibson Tait. He was her contact it seems. I had someone else. I don't think they even knew they were breaking the law.'

'And she did go back to work?' Fluke said, thinking of Kenneth Diamond.

'Yes, I had a break. A rape, drug-assisted, was reported. The victim couldn't remember her attacker. It fit the profile. I now just needed to identify him before she could get paid. Before she became invisible again.'

'Bit of a stretch,' Fluke said.

'I could only work with what I knew about her. I knew her methods. Knew she chose men without criminal records. She didn't want the police identifying them. It would have defeated the purpose.'

'How'd you find him?' Fluke knew how FMIT did it but it wouldn't have worked for Cross. He'd have needed to find Kenneth Diamond to find Samantha. They found Samantha first.

'I persuaded my man to search your PNC to see who'd made searches without hits. Searches for men in Cumbria who weren't on the computer.'

Fluke understood. Samantha had asked Gibson Tait to see if Kenneth Diamond was on PNC. He wasn't, but the computer recorded the search anyway. Cross had simply got someone to check who was looking at names without results. He could probably narrow it down to a couple of days before the rape was reported. Fluke knew Samantha had asked Tait for one final check to make sure nothing had changed.

Cross continued and confirmed Fluke's suspicions. 'There were eight names in the period I specified. I spoke to four of them. Pretended I was a detective from the rape team. The first three didn't know anything.'

Shit!

Fluke remembered getting an email a few days ago about a man impersonating a police officer investigating a rape. Two separate complaints if he remembered correctly. Nothing had been stolen and CID hadn't been putting too many resources into it. Fluke hadn't given it a second thought.

'The fourth man was Kenneth Diamond. As soon as I explained what I was there for I knew it was him. He tried to tell me he was being blackmailed and that he was innocent. I removed him from his property without difficulty, he thought he was being arrested. I took him to the empty house next door and into a cellar they used to store cheap wine.'

'You tortured him.'

'I got what I needed.'

'You're a psychopath.' Fluke remembered looking at Diamond's face. It was so swollen, his features so badly mutilated that it had been impossible to tell what he looked like.

'Maybe,' Cross conceded. 'But I needed information straight away and I needed to be able to rely on it, I didn't have much time. From what I understood from my client, she doesn't wait long to get paid. She approaches her victims, demands cash and expects it straight away. I needed to get to the drop before her.'

Fluke reached for the water jug and poured himself a glass.

'He told me that he was a powerful man although I've since found out that it's his youngest son who leads the organisation. He threatened me, he begged me. He told me his family were out looking, and I knew she'd disappear if those idiots got within a mile of her. I had to be sure he was telling me the truth first time. I was only going to get one chance at this.'

Fluke's jaw tightened. Nathaniel Diamond was anything but an idiot. If he ever found out who'd killed his father he didn't think there was a cave dark enough or a safe house so remote that he wouldn't find Cross.

'You smashed his elbows and knees with a hammer. You crushed his testicles. All you had to do was tell him you had a shared goal. He'd have told you all you needed to know.'

'I did and he did.' Cross was showing no remorse. He'd stopped smiling at least. He was discussing it with Fluke the way a TV repairman might explain why a diode wasn't working correctly. Calmly, using small words. 'As soon as I showed him my Ruger, he told me everything I needed.'

'So why torture him? You don't strike me as a sadist. Psychotic obviously but you seem to be in control.'

'I think you know the answer, Mr Fluke.'

'Humour me or you can humour the inside of Durham nick for the next forty years.'

Cross raised his eyebrows and rolled his eyes. 'Very well. When I found Diamond, I was improvising. He threatened me with his criminal underworld contacts so I decided to make it look exactly like that. An underworld execution. If you hadn't found Samantha, you would have no looked no further than a drugs connection. You certainly wouldn't have linked it with a rape allegation.'

'What about Tait though? You used the same gun. We were bound to link them. He's not involved in the same business as Diamond,' Fluke said.

'I'll help you there, Mr Fluke. I hadn't decided what to do with him, that's the simple truth. I considered setting him up for Diamond but couldn't make it work. I could have made him disappear for a while but someone would have started looking eventually. In the end I put him in the compost heap to hide the smell. By the time I was ready to do anything, you had found Samantha, as you call her. I decided moving him was too dangerous. I sat and waited, to see how close you were getting. And you came knocking. You've no idea how close I came to killing you. How'd you like my English, by the way? Courtesy of the CIA linguistics department.'

'That's enough, Cross,' Mortimer snapped. The first thing he'd said during the whole interview.

Cross ignored him. 'I got through your interview with my fake accent and a bit of computer nonsense. I knew it wouldn't hold, though, and that I'd have to leave.

'What did Diamond tell you?' Fluke said, deciding that he needed to move on.

'Everything.'

'Talk me through it.'

Cross ignored him again. 'You already know. She phoned him. Told him that she'd reported him for rape. Laid out all the evidence the police had and explained the only thing they didn't have was his name. Fifty thousand pounds would make the whole thing go away. Told him she'd ring with the where and when.'

'He had that kind of cash?'

'Not to hand, no, but his family did and, in the meantime, they went looking for her. He put his son in charge of finding her. I don't know what their intentions were but I suspect her passing would have been cruel and unusual compared to mine. I took his phone and when she rang it was me she spoke to, not him. I'm good at accents.'

'She told you where she wanted the money?'

'She did. I had an hour to get there and set up observation. I only had once chance. Fail, and she'd never resurface.'

'Where was the meeting?'

'The library in the mall in Carlisle. If you can call something so small a mall.'

The Lanes was Carlisle's indoor shopping centre. Not big compared to other towns and cities but it had a reasonable selection of cafes and shops. It was also home to the council-run library. A decent enough place for a cash drop. Busy but not crowded. Large windows covering the main approach. Fire exits leading out to the shopping centre but also into the delivery areas.

'You got there first?'

'Oh no. She was good. She would've already been there. That's where she would've have called from. She'd have been able to slip out quietly if she sensed trouble. If Diamond turned up with help or the police showed.'

'So how did you get in without her seeing? You didn't even know what she looked like.'

'I didn't know what she looked like but I still knew what I was looking for. I also knew what I'd have done. All I had to do was cover the exit she'd use. No way would she leave by the main exit. If there was someone waiting, that's where she'd have expected it. She'd be slipping out through the staff exit, into the delivery areas. I waited there for her.'

'And?'

'Fifteen minutes after the agreed time, she came out. She was good. Very good. I nearly lost her twice, but I was better it seemed. I've been trained to follow the best.' He paused and looked at Mortimer. 'Sorry,' he said. 'Bit too much information there, Mr Fluke. Where were we? Ah yes, she was careful but I followed her home. I watched her flat all night and all the next day.'

Fluke hadn't yet made any notes. Up to then, everything Cross said fitted with the facts.

'I waited until she went out. I got into her flat quickly enough. I avoided the crude anti-intruder alert under her doormat and the lock wasn't challenging. I waited in her living room. Two hours later, she came back. She came in carefully but the potato chip under the mat was undisturbed. She wasn't expecting anyone. She ground some coffee and filled her filter machine. She came into the living room to wait for it. I treated her with respect. She was dead before she knew I was there. One shot to the back of the head. I caught her before she fell. No noise.'

Fluke had heard nothing comparable before. He'd heard killers confess. Normally crimes committed in anger or passion. The perpetrator wanting to talk, to get it off their chest. Sometimes he'd heard confessions from murderers whose lies had talked them into such tight corners, only the truth was left. Cross was different. He could have been telling him how he'd got rid of the weeds in his lawn. It was descriptive rather than emotive. There was no pride. There was no remorse. He was just telling him what happened.

'You've seen the golf bag I'd brought with me. A marvellous invention for my trade. No more rolled up carpets for contract killers,' he said, smiling wryly at his own joke. Fluke didn't join in.

'What could be more innocent than someone taking their golf clubs to their car?

'When did you write down your blood test results?' Fluke asked.

Cross looked surprised. 'So that's how you found me? I was wondering about that. I got the phone call when I was waiting in her flat. Jotted them down, more habit than anything else. I'm cured now. Well, in remiss—'

'You took her body in Diamond's car?' Fluke interrupted. He didn't give a shit about his health.

Cross looked mildly hurt. 'No, Gibson Tait's,' he replied.

There was a natural pause in the conversation.

Cross spoke again. 'How did you find her, by the way? I've been doing this a long time and not once has a body been found that wasn't supposed to be, and not once did I have anywhere near as good a place as that.'

It wasn't quid pro quo. Cross could die wondering. 'Why does it matter? We found her,' he said.

'Professional curiosity,' Cross replied. He waited for an answer with a bemused expression. 'Can I assume by your reticence that there was a witness? It can't have been that boy who lived opposite her. He didn't see me, I know that. Even if he did, all he'd have seen was me walking out with a golf bag. He didn't know where I was going. It could only have been someone on the site. It must have been that office.'

Fluke said nothing.

'Don't worry, Mr Fluke, I won't be arranging retribution.' He waited for Fluke to speak. 'Oh, well. Sloppy work on my part but I thought the site was ironclad. No way was she being found. Not for centuries.'

He reached for his glass of water. Because of the angle of the handcuffs, he struggled to get a proper drink. He coughed. Fluke thought the restraints were a bit of overkill but knew it was pointless arguing with anyone. Cross didn't deserve any of his compassion anyway.

Fluke yawned, a big one that he couldn't stop. He hadn't realised how tired he was.

'Who was your contact in the police?'

Cross gave him a name that meant nothing to him. For the first time, he made a note. It would be someone for the team to arrest at least.

Mortimer looked at his watch and stood up. 'Time's up, Inspector. You got everything you need?'

'One more thing, Mr Mortimer.' He turned to Cross. 'Do you know who she was. What her real name was? Where she was from?'

Cross looked at Fluke. 'I have no idea. I told you she was a ghost. English is my bet. She fled to where she knew when she was in trouble. Other than that, I can't help you.'

Fluke had been expecting that. It was possible her real identity would always remain a secret. He'd always remember her as

Samantha though.

'That it?' Mortimer said.

'For now.'

Cross smirked. 'There's no for now, Mr Fluke. This is it. As soon as I can get on a plane, I'm out of this shithole. Time to get Stateside, see what type of deal they're offering.'

'Waterboarding and black sites would be my guess,' Fluke said.

'Ah, Mr Fluke. But you don't know what I know. I have things my country wants and I only want my freedom in return. And access to my money of course. They'll deal, we both know that.' He smirked. 'You never know, we may meet again one day.'

Fluke turned and walked out.

'Nice place,' Bridie said, eventually. The first thing anyone had said since Fluke had finished telling them about the interview with Cross.

Fluke looked over at her. She was hugging her knees to her chest and staring into the fire. She was wearing a black vest and her tattooed arms seemed to be alive as the flames danced in the darkness. Her skin was a creamy white. She was beautiful. More *Guns and Ammo* than *Vogue* but stunning nonetheless.

He nodded sadly. 'Yep. For how long, though, I don't know.'

She looked at him quizzically. Fluke explained the situation with his illegally built cabin. To his surprise, she laughed.

'Is that all? I thought you were going to say something serious.'

'It is serious,' he protested. 'I've got a court date.'

She burst out laughing. 'You've just singlehandedly taken out an international assassin and you're worried about the county council. You crack me up.'

'You think he has a case?' Towler asked.

She stopped laughing. 'You're serious? Are you telling me the pair of you have been worrying about this?'

Fluke nodded and saw Towler do the same.

'Listen. I think I can handle the county council's planning department.'

'Yeah, you do international law. This is local. It's different,' Fluke said.

'The only thing that's different is that they're terrified of a court case with someone who knows what they're doing. They can't afford it for one thing. I'll send them a letter first thing tomorrow saying I'm representing you, and I've instructed Mr Tinnings to act on our behalf.'

'Who?' Towler asked.

'My secret weapon. A barrister friend of mine in London who owes me a favour. Charges ten thousand pounds a day.'

'I can't afford that!' Fluke burst out.

Bridie smiled. 'We won't need him, silly. Just the name will terrify their solicitor. They won't risk losing and having to pay his fees.' She looked at them both. 'The law's not always about who's right and who's wrong. Sometimes it's about who has the most to lose. And anyway, I've only just got here. You think I'm letting them take it away? Not a chance.' She smiled at Fluke.

They fell into silence once more. Fluke felt a strange peace settle over him. *I may even get some sleep tonight*, he thought.

Abi broke the silence. 'What's a stalker?' she asked.

'Where did you hear that word, Abi?' Fluke asked.

'Daddy says that Bridie's yours.'

What could have been an uncomfortable silence was broken by Bridie roaring with laughter. Before long, Fluke had joined in. Towler, embarrassed, eventually grinned as well.

'Yes, I am, Abi. Your daddy's right,' Bridie said when she'd stopped laughing.

Fluke offered Towler a cigar and they lit up. A sense of peace settled over them all.

'This is beautiful,' Bridie said. 'I bet you get a different view every day. It's a shame about that dead tree there, if you took it down you'd have an uninterrupted view across the lake. I have a friend who's a tree surgeon. She'd take it down for you for a cup of tea. I'll give her a call if you want.'

This time it was Fluke and Towler who laughed and Bridie's turn to look confused.

'You want to tell her why we can't chop that tree down, Abi?' Towler said.

'That tree?' she said pointing. 'That's where Hooty McOwlface lives.' She giggled delightedly at Bridie's obvious astonishment.

'There's a tawny owl that lives there. He's out hunting at the minute but he'll be back later,' Fluke explained. 'He's out getting a nice fat mouse for Abi.'

'Yuk,' she shrieked.

Fluke got up to pour more wine. Towler put his hand over his glass.

'I'm driving mate.'

As they sipped their drinks and looked out across the lake and fells, it dawned on Fluke that Bridie hadn't covered her glass. He knew she didn't drink and drive. She must be planning to stay the night. Apparently Towler had also come to the same conclusion. He gave Fluke a crude wink.

Bridie looked at Fluke and raised her glass in his direction. He looked back at her and raised his own.

In the distance, an owl hooted.

Epilogue

Six weeks later.
HMP Durham.

Dalton Cross was wearing a suit. He was still on crutches but he was fit to fly. He was being moved from hospital to Durham Prison while a specially chartered flight was being arranged.

'Cross. This way, please. Grab your things. Follow me!' the prison officer barked.

He picked up a bag containing prison issue toiletries, blankets and a pillow and followed the prison officer.

'Now. You've been told that our remand wing is full? You're going to have to go onto general population with convicted prisoners for now. We're putting you on the lifer wing though, it's a bit calmer, and remember, you're still a remand prisoner so you still have remand rights. You can wear your own clothes, you're entitled to more phone calls and more visits. You can spend more money. With any luck, you'll be where you need to be by the end of the week.'

He wasn't worried. He'd been in far worse places and he'd be back in the States within the week. He hadn't been lying to Fluke. He had information he hadn't told anyone about yet. Enough for a deal. He had passports and funds tucked away in case of emergencies. If he played it right, he might even get a nice CIA pension.

The wing he was brought onto could have been lifted straight out of a scene from *Porridge*, a sitcom he'd enjoyed since coming to the UK. He knew it wasn't a new prison but it looked more like a film set than somewhere to spend the night. He shrugged. It was better than that gulag in the Ukraine he'd once had to spend a month in.

The prison officer stopped outside a cell halfway down one of the landings. He took a bunch of keys out of a leather pouch on his belt and unlocked the door. He stepped aside and waited for Cross to walk in.

'There's a button to call if you need something. This red one here. Press it for anything less than a fire and you're in the shit.

302

We're locked down for the night. You have your breakfast in the bag you've just been given. Eat it tonight and you go hungry in the morning. Don't eat it tonight and someone'll take it off you. Your choice. Doors will be unlocked at eight am. Sleep well, Cross.'

He watched as the door shut with a heavy clang. A sound only a prison door can make. A sound heard by thousands before him. A sound that made good men despair and brave men cry. Cross smiled. It was going to be easy.

He stared at the door for a second before turning to survey his cell. To his surprise he wasn't alone.

Someone was getting up from the bottom bunk. A small, shaven-headed man. He was wearing a pair of shorts and nothing else. Crude tattoos covered his body. He had the look of someone who'd spent a lifetime in institutions.

Cross nodded at him and smiled. He might be on crutches but he was still capable enough to put the idiot down if he tried anything.

The man smiled back. 'You want a brew, mate?' He had a thick Geordie accent.

With nothing else to do, he said 'yes'. While the man busied himself making the drinks with the in-cell kettle, Cross settled his meagre belongings on the top bunk and tried to put the sheets on the rubber mattress. They seemed too small and he eventually gave up.

'Here ya gan, mate,' the man said. Cross got down and reached forward for the drink he was being offered.

Before he could take it, the man hurled it at him. It struck him on the bridge of his nose. The cup smashed.

Cross screamed.

Boiling water covered his face. Some went down his throat and he instinctively swallowed. Excruciating pain exploded in every nerve ending. He tried to wipe it off but it was sticky. Sticky and burning. His hands stung as well. Even through the pain, he knew what it was.

Sugar and boiling water.

Prison napalm.

He could feel parts of his face melting and he tried to scream even louder. Nothing happened. His vocal cords had been

303

damaged. His throat swelled and he gasped for breath, clawing at his face, trying to remove the blistering mask he was wearing.

One of his eyes went dark as molten sugar fused his eyelids together.

Cross fell to the floor, still frantically tearing at his face, incapacitated.

The man stood over him, watching calmly.

Cross could see he was holding something. Even with only one eye, he recognised what it was. It was unmistakable.

The shank in the man's hand looked crude but deadly. Cross had used a variety of weapons in his life but he'd never considered how a toothbrush could be fashioned into something so sinister-looking.

He tried to reach the red panic button but the man was on him before he was halfway.

The man said nothing. He held the sharpened toothbrush so Cross could see it clearly.

'What do you want?' he rasped through his ruined vocal chords. His voice was barely above a whisper.

The man still didn't say anything.

Cross saw rather than felt the first blow. He thought he might have just been punched until he felt a warmness that could only be blood. The pain of the wound wasn't able to compete with his burning face. Half a dozen quick stabs followed. All in the same place. Not deep but deep enough.

He tried to say something, anything but the words wouldn't form. He stared at the man with his one working eye. The man looked down without expression. He showed Cross the toothbrush shank up close. Cross shrank back as it was held up to his eye. It was razor sharp and bloodied. Beyond fear, he watched as the man pushed the shank towards his throat. He pressed it against him, just hard enough to break the skin.

'I'm going to kill you now, Mr Cross,' the man said.

He gently but firmly pushed the sharpened toothbrush into Cross's neck. He could feel it going through skin and flesh before finally meeting resistance in the thin muscular wall of the great jugular vein. The man grunted with effort as he plunged the shank in. Cross felt warm liquid around the wound. His shirt was drenched in seconds. He felt weak and lightheaded.

He lost control of his bowel and his bladder.

The jugular takes blood back to the heart rather than being powered from it, so there was no arterial spray, rather the steady flow of death. The man removed the shank and watched him.

Cross had cut enough throats during his career as a contract killer to know his wound was fatal. Of all the places he thought he might die, on the filthy floor of an English prison cell drenched in his own piss hadn't even come close.

As his heart struggled to find enough blood to keep him alive, he went into the first stages of cardiac arrest. Before Dalton Cross slipped into the unconsciousness that would precede his death, the man leaned over and whispered something into his ear.

'Nathaniel Diamond says hello.'